INTRIGUE

Seek thrills. Solve crimes. Justice served.

Monster In The Marsh
Carla Cassidy

The Sheriff's To Protect
Janice Kay Johnson

MILLS & BOON

MONSTER IN THE MARSH
© 2024 by Carla Barcale
Philippine Copyright 2024
Australian Copyright 2024
New Zealand Copyright 2024

First Published 2024
First Australian Paperback Edition 2024
ISBN 978 1 867 29961 5

THE SHERIFF'S TO PROTECT
© 2024 by Janice Kay Johnson
Philippine Copyright 2024
Australian Copyright 2024
New Zealand Copyright 2024

First Published 2024
First Australian Paperback Edition 2024
ISBN 978 1 867 29961 5

MIX
Paper | Supporting
responsible forestry
FSC® C001695

Published by
Harlequin Mills & Boon
An imprint of Harlequin Enterprises (Australia) Pty Limited
(ABN 47 001 180 918), a subsidiary of HarperCollins
Publishers Australia Pty Limited
(ABN 36 009 913 517)
Level 19, 201 Elizabeth Street
SYDNEY NSW 2000 AUSTRALIA

Cover art used by arrangement with Harlequin Books S.A.. All rights reserved.

Printed and bound in Australia by McPherson's Printing Group

Monster In The Marsh

Carla Cassidy

MILLS & BOON

Carla Cassidy is an award-winning, *New York Times* bestselling author who has written over 170 books, including 150 for Harlequin. She has won the Centennial Award from Romance Writers of America. Most recently she won the 2019 Write Touch Readers' Award for her Harlequin Intrigue title *Desperate Strangers*. Carla believes the only thing better than curling up with a good book is sitting down at the computer with a good story to write.

Visit the Author Profile page
at millsandboon.com.au.

CAST OF CHARACTERS

Josephine Cadieux—Lives in the swamp and is haunted and hunted by an assailant.

Jackson Fortier—A bored businessman. Does he have what it takes to protect the woman he loves?

Lee Townsend—Had his rage over his divorce driven him into the swamp to do the unthinkable?

Sonny Landrey—Had the single man ventured into the swamp for some sexual excitement?

Police Chief Thomas Gravois—How much does he know about Josie's assault and the murders of three women from the swamp? Whom might he be protecting?

Chapter One

Jackson Fortier pulled his car into one of the back parking spaces on the side of Vincent's Gas and Grocery Store. The little store was the last establishment before the vast swamp that more than half surrounded the small town of Black Bayou, Louisiana.

There were more than a dozen cars parked there as Vincent Smith, the owner of the place, allowed people who lived in the swamp to keep their vehicles there. His sleek sports car stuck out like a sore thumb amid the old model cars and banged-up pickups.

It was just after noon and the late August sun was bright and cast down waves of heat. He got out of the car and pulled a note from his pocket. On the sheet of paper were directions to his best friend, Peyton and her husband, Beau's shanty.

He'd never been to their place in the swamp before. Peyton had offered to meet him here and lead him in, but he'd insisted he was a big boy and with directions he could get himself there.

However, as he stood and stared up the trail before him, he was sorry he hadn't taken Peyton up on her offer. Tangled vines, overhanging leaves and Spanish moss made the path disappear into semidarkness.

Where the sunlight did manage to penetrate through, it shone on pools of water on either side of the path, dark waters that were filled with gators and snakes and all sort of other mysterious creatures.

The only place Jackson was at home on a trail was when he was walking the greens on a golf course. He fingered the directions in his hand as a wave of apprehension shot through him. It wasn't too late to call Peyton and have her meet him here, but he was reluctant to do so.

Surely if Peyton could traverse these paths alone, then he could as well. He glanced down at the directions. *Go straight ahead until you reach a fork. Take the path to the left.* That's all he read. He'd look at the next part when he reached the fork.

He drew a deep breath and then began to walk slowly forward. There was a distinctive odor in the air. It was a combination of something sweetly floral coupled with greenery and earthiness and the distinctive scent of decay.

Insects buzzed and clicked all around his head, creating a cacophony of sound that was totally alien to him. A rustling came from either side of him as if small creatures were running away from his presence. At least he hoped like hell they were running away from him.

The apprehension inside him rose higher as he forged ahead, watching every single step where he placed his feet. He admitted he'd been a fool to attempt this for the first time all alone.

He could easily fall into the dark waters on either side of the path and be eaten by a gator or bitten by a venomous snake and die an agonizing death. Hell, he could get lost in the vast depths of the swamp and never be seen or heard from again.

He'd like to think the sheen of moisture that covered his skin was from the heavy humidity that hung in the air, but he suspected it was the perspiration of fear.

Hell, he could face down a shark across the table in a boardroom and beat most any man in a financial game, but walking into the swamp had him on edge like nothing he'd ever experienced before in his life.

"Suck it up, man," he said aloud to himself. He crept along at a snail's pace and dodged the low hanging branches that threatened to take his head off. He jumped and cursed as a large splash sounded far too close for comfort in the waters to his left.

He took a couple more steps, then stopped and whirled around as a rustling noise came from behind him. His heart raced and his body filled with fight-or-flight adrenaline. He saw nothing. Hopefully, it was just another little animal scurrying through the brush and not a wild boar bent on eating him.

He turned back around and took another couple of steps. The rustling came again and this time when he turned around to look, his right foot stepped off the narrow path and directly into the dark water.

A string of curses escaped him as he quickly yanked his foot up and out. Dammit, it had been stupid for him to wear his good loafers and nice black slacks. All of his clothes, including the nice shirt he had on would probably be ruined by the end of this trek.

He stopped cursing and immediately heard the sound of musical laughter coming from someplace behind him. He whirled around again and there she was…one of the most beautiful women he had ever seen in his life.

She was clad in a pair of jeans and a white sleeveless blouse that showcased her deep tan. Long dark hair spilled down her back and her dark eyes sparked with obvious humor. "First time in the swamp, Mr. Fancy Pants?"

"What gave you that idea?" he asked with a touch of humor and a bit of embarrassment.

She laughed once again and even though he knew she was laughing at him, he couldn't take offense. He probably looked like a silly fool to anyone who had been watching him bumbling his way along. But he suddenly had other things on his mind besides his own embarrassment, like who was this beautiful woman?

"My name isn't fancy pants, but it is Jackson... Jackson Fortier. And you are?"

"Josephine Cadieux, but folks around here just call me Josie," she replied. "What are you doing out here in the swamp? It's obvious you aren't a frequent visitor."

"Definitely not. I'm on my way to visit with friends. Maybe you know them, Peyton LaCroix and Beau Boudreau?"

"I not only know them, I'm friendly with them," she replied.

"I agreed to come for a visit today and insisted Peyton didn't have to meet me to lead the way in and instead she could just give me the directions." He held out the piece of paper he'd been clutching in a death grip in his hand.

"They are close neighbors of mine. Would

you like me to take you to their place?" she asked.

"That would be great," he replied with a sigh of relief. Not only would he like her to take him in, but it would also maybe give him a chance to get to know her a little better.

Her attractiveness definitely piqued his interest. And it had been a very long time since he'd been interested in any woman. He watched as she walked in front of him. "Just follow me," she said.

He couldn't help but notice the perfect roundness of her rear end, just as he had noticed the full breasts beneath her white blouse. The jeans she wore clung to her long shapely legs. Ah, there was no question that Josie Cadieux was a real stunner.

"Watch your step here," she said as the trail narrowed.

"Thanks. So, you mentioned you're a neighbor of Peyton's. Do you have a family?" he asked.

"No, it's just me," she replied. They reached the fork in the trail and she led him to the left.

"What do you do out here?" he asked. The fact that she'd said she lived alone had further intrigued him.

"I fish. That nice piece of red snapper or catfish you ate in one of your fancy restaurants in town might have been caught by me." She stopped and turned around to look at him. Her eyes held a teasing sparkle he found enchanting. "And what do you do besides wear inappropriate clothes for a visit to the swamp?"

He laughed, delighted that she had some sass to her. "I deal in real estate," he replied. It was an understatement because he dealt in all kinds of finance. It was how he'd become wealthy... and completely bored with his life.

She turned back around and continued forward. She moved with an agility and grace he admired. He followed after her, trying to step exactly where she stepped as he dodged Spanish moss and vines that threatened to consume anyone who got too close to them.

He tried to pay attention to where they were going but it was difficult to concentrate on anything but her. "So, are you single?" he asked.

"It depends on who asks me," she replied.

"What if I'm asking?"

"I'd have to think about it."

"How long would you have to think about it?" he asked.

"I'm not sure." They took a sharp fork in the trail and a shanty appeared. "That's Beau and Peyton's place." She turned and smiled. "You have arrived safely despite your fancy clothes and stumbling start."

"That's thanks to you," he replied. "You said you were neighbors of Beau and Peyton. So, where's your place?"

"Around," she replied, and there was something in her tone that let him know he'd overstepped boundaries with the question.

"So, are you usually around the same place around the same time where I met you today on other days?" He didn't want to leave here without some opportunity to see her again. He was drawn to her and wanted to get to know her better. She was so different from all the other women he had known.

It wasn't just that she was gorgeous, but it also had to do with her obvious self-reliance and the inner strength he sensed in her. He'd never thought much about the women who lived in the swamp, other than three of them who had been in the newspaper headlines recently as murder victims.

"I could possibly be around the same place again tomorrow," she replied. Once again, a flirtatious sparkle filled her eyes. "Are you sure you want to venture out here again?"

"Definitely," he replied. "Will you know tomorrow if you're single?"

She cast him a slightly mysterious smile. "We'll see tomorrow. Enjoy your visit," she said and took several steps away from him, quickly disappearing into the darkness of the swamp.

A DARK BAG stole Josie's breath away as it fell around her head to her neck and a string pulled it tight, threatening to suffocate her. Wha-what was happening? She raised her hands to get it off her, but a hard push cast her to the ground.

With a cry, she fell forward to her hands and knees. Before she could regain her footing or figure out what was happening, she was rolled over on her back.

Immediately, somebody was on top of her, grabbing her wrists and attempting to tie them together. She tried to fight back, but he managed to tie her wrists together anyway.

Shock and fear shot through her. Was this the person who had killed three women? Was she about to become the fourth victim of the Honey Island Swamp Monster?

Josie came awake and jerked up to a sitting position, her heart pounding a thousand beats a minute as sobs ripped from the very depths of her.

Looking around the bedroom with the aid of a shaft of moonlight that danced in through the nearby window, she tried to center herself. It had not only been a horrible nightmare, but it had been what had happened to her a little over ten months ago.

It took her several moments and then she managed to stop crying. She swiped the last of her tears away and then slid her legs over the side of the bed and got up. She went into the living area and lit a couple of kerosene lanterns that were on a shelf. She could have started her generator and flipped on an electric light, but it was too much trouble and, in any case, she often preferred the softer glow of the lanterns.

There was no way she was ready to go back to sleep, not with the taste of the nightmare still bitter on her tongue and thick in her chest.

She went to her front door, unlocked it and then stepped outside on the narrow porch that encircled her shanty. The sounds of the swamp surrounded her...the throaty bellow of frogs and the slap of fish in the water. Insects buzzed and clicked in a nightly chorus and there was also the rustling of night creatures as they scampered along through the nearby brush.

She'd never been afraid in the swamp. It was her home. From a young age, her parents had taught her the good plants and the bad, the things to be afraid of and the places to avoid.

No, she'd never been afraid in the swamp until that night when she'd been violated and even then, it hadn't been anyone from the swamp.

The man who had raped her had been from town. His hands had been far too soft to be anyone from the swamp. He'd smelled of expensive cologne and even though he'd only spoken a few words to her, she knew she would never ever forget the sound of his deep voice.

She'd immediately reported the assault to the chief of police, Thomas Gravois. She knew if she'd been a young woman from town, Gravois would have moved heaven and earth to solve the crime. But because she was from the swamp, next to nothing had been done about it.

That didn't mean she was just going to forget about it. One way or another, she intended to find the man and expose him. However, there was a huge obstacle standing in her way.

As a woman from the swamp, she had no invite into the inner circle of wealthy men that ran the town of Black Bayou. And she believed with all her heart that was where her personal monster hid.

She thought about the man she had led in to Peyton and Beau's place. The minute she'd seen him, she'd known who he was. Jackson Fortier was one of the most eligible single men in the small town. He was not only wickedly handsome, but he was also extremely wealthy.

Josie didn't give a damn about his money, but he could potentially be an entry into where she wanted to go. Or she could possibly never see him again.

One thing was certain, he wasn't the man who had attacked her. She'd know the sound of her attacker's voice and Jackson wasn't him.

With the nightmare finally behind her and the lullaby of the swamp soothing her, she went back inside and returned to her bed. She stared up at her dark ceiling and finally sleep claimed her once again.

She awakened just after sunrise. She dressed quickly and went out her back door where a pirogue was tied up. The small boat was what she used to check the lines that she'd baited the night before.

She added her push pole and an oar, along with her tackle box and then she got into the pirogue and used the push pole to glide slowly away from her home.

Mornings in the swamp were positively magical as far as she was concerned. The sunlight dappled the glistening water with gold tones and birds sang from the treetops. Fish jumped high, as if rested by the night and now eager to show off their prowess.

There was a peace here, a reassurance that the ecosystem was working the way it should and all was well. She glided across the water, barely making a ripple as she used her paddle only when it was necessary.

Josie didn't need to make a lot of money. She paid no rent and had no utility bills. But she did need money for the gas she put in her generator to give her a little electricity when she wanted it. Just like any other twenty-seven-year-old, she liked to occasionally buy a new outfit for herself, although she had few places to go where anyone might admire her choice of fashion.

Most of the time, her money went into a large jug she kept in the closet in her bedroom. It had grown to be a healthy savings account, although she had no idea what she was saving it for.

Many of the women she knew were saving their money so they could, somehow, someday escape the swamp. Josie had never really had a desire to leave this place that was in her heart and very soul. There had just been two times when she'd wished things might have been different, but she didn't want to think about those times now.

She reached the place where her fishing lines were located and began to pull them up. She was eager to discover what had been caught overnight.

An hour later, she was heading home, pleased with her catch of the day. When she reached her shanty, she placed the fish she'd caught into a cage she had in the water. They would stay alive until she had enough caught to take them into town and sell.

Once the fish were squared away, she started her generator and went back into the house. Her parents had worked hard to make their shanty as updated as possible.

The generator not only provided electricity for lights and small appliances, but also a heated water system for showering. The only thing they hadn't been able to have was a working refrigerator. So, every couple of days, Josie went to Vincent's and bought ice and a few items to keep in a large ice chest.

Although she did much of her cooking on top of the potbelly stove, there were mornings when it was too warm, or she just didn't want to go to the trouble to build a fire.

She now plugged in a single burner cooktop and the toaster. She then got two eggs out of her cooler along with a stick of butter.

Minutes later, she sat at the small table in the kitchen area to eat. It was at this time when she missed her parents the most. The three of them had always eaten breakfast together. They'd talked about the day to come and share happy laughter. Unfortunately, her father had passed two years ago from cancer and her mother had followed him six months later and died from a massive heart attack.

The past year and a half had been lonely for Josie, although soon after her mother's passing, she'd thought she'd met the man of her dreams. Even though he'd been a town guy, she'd been certain their love story had been written in the stars. She'd been so wrong and that experience had taught her a valuable lesson.

She washed up her dishes and then went in for a quick shower. As she stood beneath the warm spray of water, she wondered if Jackson would really show up today. She intended to be there just in case he did, but she wouldn't be surprised if he didn't come.

After showering, she changed into a pair of capri jeans and a hot pink sleeveless blouse that she knew looked good on her. It always took her a few minutes to brush through her long hair. Normally, she didn't wear makeup, but today she put on a little mascara and then spritzed on her favorite perfume.

Just beneath the waistband of her jeans, she tucked in a sheath that carried a small but wickedly sharp knife. Since her assault, she never left the house without the weapon. She would never be caught utterly defenseless again.

By then it was time for her to leave. She

grabbed her key to the front door, shoved it in a pocket and then left the shanty.

An edge of excitement raced through her as she headed back to the place where she had first seen Jackson the day before. A smile curved her lips as she remembered watching him bumble his way into the swamp.

Even though he'd been very tentative and she'd found him slightly comical, there was no question that he was a hot hunk.

His dark hair had looked thick and rich and his bright blue eyes had been unexpected yet beautiful. His facial features were strong and bold and wonderfully handsome. Even beneath his fancy lavender shirt, she could tell his shoulders were broad and his waist was slim. Oh, yeah, definitely a hunk.

If he did show up today, then it would mean he was interested in her. And if she played her cards right with him, then she might be welcomed into the wealthy inner circle and she'd potentially be able to identify her assailant.

If she didn't like Jackson, she'd pretend she did anyway. If she did like him then it would certainly make things easier for her. No matter what happened, she wouldn't lose sight of the reality that she intended only to use him for a little while to get what she wanted…what she needed, and that was justice.

She might pretend to have a romantic interest in him, but she wouldn't allow herself to catch any real feelings for him or any other man from town. That had been the lesson she'd learned after her past relationship. She'd been there, done that, and her heart would remain closed forever.

She finally reached the spot where she'd seen Jackson the day before. She was early. As she waited to see if he'd show up, a new rush of excitement filled her. She was putting herself out there as bait and all she was hoping for now was that Jackson would take the bait and run with it.

Chapter Two

Jackson had dressed more appropriately for his trek into the swamp today. He was clad in a plain light blue cotton shirt and a pair of jeans, along with an old pair of boots he used to wear to construction sites.

Would she be there today? God, he hoped so. The lovely Josie had been in his thoughts all night long. He'd asked Peyton and Beau about her. "She's an incredibly strong woman," Beau had said. "She was very close to her parents before they passed but she seems to be making her own way just fine."

"We don't know much else about her personal life," Peyton added. "She's always friendly, but she pretty much keeps to herself."

Thankfully, when he was finished visiting with Beau and Peyton, Peyton had then walked him out of the swamp and to his car. Now he was ready to go back in with hopes of meeting up with the lovely Josie again.

A sweet anticipation filled his veins as he parked his car in Vincent's parking lot. There was no question that if she didn't show up today, he'd be disappointed.

He stepped out of his car and into the noon-day heat and humidity. He looked up the mouth of the pathway and into the thick foliage and murky waters.

There were many other trails into the swamp from all over the small town. What were the odds of meeting a beautiful woman on this particular path?

Even though it was still rather daunting for him to enter into the swampy interior, he wouldn't have to go far before he would be at the place where he'd first seen Josie.

He began the trek in, feeling a bit more confident than he had the day before. He still watched every step he took in an effort to stay on the narrow path.

He hadn't gone too far in when he saw her. She stepped out from behind a tree, a smile curving her lips. His heart beat just a little faster at the sight of her.

"You came," she said.

He grinned. "And so did you." He looked around. "Is there someplace we can go to sit and talk?"

"Definitely. Just come with me." She turned

and started up the trail. He followed right behind her, wondering if she was taking him to her place. He was definitely interested to see the place she called home. He was interested in everything about her.

She turned on a path he hadn't been on before and then stopped abruptly. Ahead of her was a large downed dead tree trunk. She sat on it and then gestured for him to have a seat next to her.

Although he was surprised, he shouldn't have been. She certainly didn't know him well enough to take him to her house. "This is one of my favorite places to sit and think," she said.

He sat next to her, not so close as to intimidate her, but close enough he could smell the scent that emanated from her. It was wonderful, a combination of mysterious flowers and exotic spices that instantly called to something inside him.

She looked beautiful in the pink blouse that seemed to pull a little color into her cheeks and looked gorgeous against her shiny black hair. Her jeans showcased her slender but shapely legs.

"Do you sit and think here a lot?" he asked.

"Whenever I need to," she replied. "Where do you sit and think?" she asked curiously.

"I guess I do most of my thinking in my

home office, although I don't usually just sit and think."

"Sitting someplace beautiful and just thinking is very good for the soul," she replied.

He laughed. "Then I suspect my soul needs a little tending."

She returned his laugh with musical tones of her own. "Then you'll have to work on that."

"I will. So, tell me about a typical day in Josie Cadieux's life," he said, wanting to learn everything he could about her. One thing he immediately noticed was her eyes were not jet black as he'd initially thought they were, but rather they were a deep gray with bright silver shards. Beautiful.

"I get up early and go out on the water to check my fishing lines and see what I've caught for the day. I bring what I caught back to my house where I put them in a holding cage and then just before sunset, I do that all over again. Once I have enough fish to take to market, I load them up in my truck and go into town."

"Who do you sell them to?" he asked curiously.

"I sell some of them directly to Marie Boujoulais at the Black Bayou Café and I also sell directly to Tremont's Restaurant. Then whatever is left over I take to Mike's Grocery store."

Mike's was the grocery store in the center of

town that served everyone while Tremont's was a high-end restaurant where Jackson often ate with his friends.

"Sounds like a lot of work," he replied.

She shrugged her slender shoulders. "It's my life and I don't find it difficult at all. In fact, I think I have a wonderful life."

"What's so wonderful about it?" he asked.

"I make enough money to pay for my needs. I spend a lot of time outside in the beauty of the swamp. I can run when I feel like running or visit with friends when I feel like talking to somebody. I rarely have a worry in the world." She smiled. "Now tell me about a typical day in your life."

Her world sounded incredibly free and un-complicated. As he told her about meetings, both in person and over FaceTime, he realized how boring he sounded. He rarely took any time off and when he did, he spent that time with people who were exactly like him.

"Your world sounds very complex," she observed when he was finished.

"I just now realized it is and maybe I need to make some changes. I'm certainly not enjoying my life much right now," he admitted. The only other person he'd ever shared his general un-happiness with was his friend Peyton. He was vaguely surprised that he'd shared this so easily with Josie, a woman he barely knew but felt surprisingly comfortable with.

"Life is too short to be unhappy," she replied.

"I agree with that. Sitting here and talking to a lovely woman certainly makes me happy," he replied.

She laughed. "Jackson, are you flirting with me?"

He grinned at her. "Maybe a little bit. I won't pour on the full force of my flirting power until I know for sure that you're single." He locked his gaze with hers. "So, have you decided yet? Are you single?"

Her lovely eyes drew him in as they sparkled brightly. Sure, he wanted to get to know her and there was no question that he was physically drawn to everything about her.

"Just for you, I've decided I'm single," she finally replied.

He smiled at her once again. "Josie, are you flirting with me?"

"Maybe just a little," she replied and then broke the eye contact with him. "So, tell me, are your parents still alive?"

"They are alive and well. I try to have dinner with them at least once a week or so," he replied.

"That's nice. Unfortunately, I lost my father two years ago and my mother a year and a half ago."

"I'm sorry for your loss. Were you close to them?"

"Extremely close," she replied. "In fact, we all lived together and they were my very best friends."

He heard the sadness that had crept into her voice and he reached his hand out and covered hers. "I'm really sorry," he said softly and then quickly pulled his hand back from hers, afraid of overstepping her boundaries.

"Thanks."

"So, tell me more about you. What's your favorite color? What sign are you? What's your favorite food?" he asked in an effort to turn the direction of their conversation to something lighter.

"My favorite color is deep purple and I'm a Libra. Right now, my favorite food is fish, because that's mostly all I've ever eaten in my life."

"So, you've never had a big juicy steak?"

"Never," she replied.

"Well, that definitely needs to be remedied," he said.

"I'll bet I can guess what your favorite color is," she said with a teasing light in her eyes.

"What do you think it is?" he asked.

"Green for money. And I would also guess

that you're an Aries because they like to be number one and they're very ambitious."

He sniffed in exaggeration. "Uh, is that judgment I smell in the air?" he asked.

"No judgment," she quickly replied. "It was just an educated guess."

"I'll have you know my favorite color is blue and I'm actually a Cancer."

"A Cancer...hmm. Interesting," she replied. "I guess I still have a lot to learn about you."

He smiled. "And I want to learn a lot more about you."

"Are you flirting with me again, Mr. Fortier?"

He laughed. "Absolutely."

For the next hour or so, they talked about themselves and each other. He learned that she'd been homeschooled by her mother. Her mother must have done a good job for Jackson found Josie to be both intelligent and well-spoken.

She was quick-witted and had a wonderful sense of humor and he was positively enchanted by her. He'd never sat and talked to a woman before where he didn't feel the need to try to be clever and superficially charming.

He'd never felt like he could just let his guard down and be himself, but that's exactly what he was doing with Josie. She was wonderfully easy to talk to.

"I hope you're keeping yourself safe while you're out and about," he now said.

"I'm assuming you're talking about the Honey Island Swamp Monster." Her eyes darkened slightly.

"He's already killed three women," Jackson said.

"Don't I know it," she replied dryly. "But he's not a monster from the swamp. I believe it is a man from town who is somehow luring the women out of the swamp and to a place where he kills them and then leaves their bodies in an alleyway."

He looked at her in surprise. "I know it's a monster of the human kind, but I believe Chief Gravois thinks the killer is from the swamp."

A dry laugh escaped her. "As far as I'm concerned, Gravois does very little actual thinking for himself. And, of course, he believes the killer comes from here. He believes everything bad, everything evil, comes from the swamp. I doubt if he's even investigating the murders. After all, it's only women from the swamp who are being killed."

Bitterness was rife in her voice. She must have realized it for she laughed once again, the laughter now sounding a bit hollow and forced. "Sorry, I didn't mean to go on such a rant. But just don't get me started on Gravois."

"Don't apologize for telling me what you really think, and I agree with you that Gravois isn't much of a deep thinker. He's definitely the laziest man I've ever met," he replied. "I don't think he ever leaves his office unless he's going someplace where he's getting a free meal."

She laughed and then sobered, her gaze once again holding his. "So how much thought have you given to the murdered women?"

He thought about lying. He really wanted to put his best foot forward with her, but he suspected she'd see right through his lie. "Not much," he admitted.

She nodded, as if she'd expected his answer.

"However," he continued, "maybe it's time me and some of my buddies put some pressure on Gravois about the murders."

A slow smile curved her lips and heated his blood. Damn but she was beautiful. "I would really appreciate that," she said.

"Consider it done," he replied.

"Do you like to fish?" she asked.

"I don't know. I've never been fishing."

"Really?" She looked at him in surprise. "Would you like to go fishing with me?"

He could think of a lot of things he'd like to do with her, but fishing certainly wasn't at the top of his list. Still, he recognized that she was bidding him an entry into her life with the invitation. "Sure, I'd like that."

"I have a sweet spot to sit and throw in a couple of lines and I've got a pole with your name written on it," she replied.

He looked at her nervously. "Aren't you afraid of the alligators?"

She laughed. "Let's just say I have a very healthy respect for them. Besides, usually when I'm fishing in that particular spot, Gator Broussard is around."

"He's the man who helped save Peyton's life."

"He is. Have you ever met him?"

"No," Jackson replied.

"Gator is older than dirt and loves catching gators. He even lost three of his fingers when he was fighting with one of the beasts."

"He sounds like a real character," Jackson said.

"Oh, he is. Maybe you'll get to meet him tomorrow morning."

He looked at her in surprise. "What's happening tomorrow morning?"

Her luscious lips curved upward again. "We're going fishing." She rose to her feet. "Why don't you meet me here around six thirty in the morning?"

"Okay," he replied, wondering exactly what he was getting himself into and yet excited to have another opportunity to spend time with her. He just hoped he didn't get eaten by a gator.

AFTER SHE LEFT JACKSON, Josie decided to pay Beau and Peyton a visit. She knew Peyton was good friends with Jackson and she wanted to know a little bit more about the man before she invested any more of her time with him.

Beau Boudreau and Peyton LaCroix shared a strange love story. They had been young lovers and then Beau, a swamp rat, had been accused and sent to prison for a murder he hadn't committed. He'd spent years in jail and once he got out, he returned to Black Bayou to clear his name.

By that time, Peyton had become a criminal defense lawyer. He'd enlisted her aid and, in the process, the two had realized they'd never stopped loving each other. The real killer had been exposed and despite Peyton being a townie, she'd moved to the swamp to be with the man she loved. They now shared the best of both worlds, splitting their time between Beau's shanty in the swamp and her house in town.

It took Josie only a few minutes to reach their place. She knocked on the door and Peyton answered. "Hey, Peyton, do you mind a visitor for a few minutes?"

"Of course, we don't mind," Peyton replied.

"Come on in." She opened the door and gestured Josie to the sofa. "Beau is off in town giving a bid on a deck."

"I really just wanted to talk to you," Josie replied as she sank down on the sofa. Beau had started his own carpentry business and, from what Josie had heard, he was doing quite well.

"Can I get you something to drink?" Peyton asked.

"No, thanks, I'm good."

Peyton sat in the chair facing the sofa in the small room. "So, what's up with you these days?"

"Not much, but I just got finished having a long visit with Jackson and I just wanted to ask you a few questions about him," Josie said.

Peyton's blue eyes widened. "You…and Jackson? Oh, that's a lovely thought. I'll tell you what you need to know about him. He's a wonderful man with a soft, kind heart. He would never hurt anyone so you'd be safe with him."

That was exactly the kind of information Josie had been looking for. "So, if the two of us were alone in my shanty, I shouldn't be afraid of him."

"Definitely not. I've known Jackson since we were kids and I'm positive he would never ever hurt a woman." Peyton then laughed. "Don't get me wrong, he isn't a saint. Jackson can be sarcastic and superficial. He has a wicked sense of humor but he is also capable of making fun of himself."

Peyton leaned forward. "So, do you have plans to see him again?"

Josie grinned. "I'm taking him fishing in the morning."

Peyton's eyes opened wide in surprise and then she laughed again. "Oh, I wish I could be a fly in the air to see him in your element. I can't even believe it. It's going to be so amusing."

"We'll see if he really shows up in the morning," Josie replied.

"If he does show up, then it means he must like you a lot. I can't imagine Jackson stepping so far out of his comfort zone for just anyone."

"Thanks, Peyton." Josie got to her feet. "You answered the major questions I had about him."

Peyton stood as well. "Give him a chance, Josie, and try not to break his heart."

"That's certainly not in my plans," Josie replied.

Minutes later as she made her way back home, she replayed the conversation with Peyton in her head. The real thing she'd wanted… needed to know was if she would be safe with Jackson. While she respected Peyton's opinion, Josie wasn't about to stop wearing her knife when she was around him.

Besides, it wasn't just Jackson she had to worry about. There was a serial killer loose, and he liked young swamp women. The townspeople had deemed the killer the Honey Island Swamp Monster, which was a real legend but not here around the Black Bayou.

According to the local gossip, the three women had been stabbed in the stomach and then mauled to death by some sort of animal claws. The victims had either been killed in the swamp and their bodies carried into town, or they had been lured out of the swamp and killed in town.

Josie didn't know anything else about the murders, but she knew enough to be wary when she was out and around. Hopefully, Jackson had been telling the truth when he'd told her he and his buddies would put some pressure on Gravois to solve the crimes. Three murders were definitely three too many.

According to Peyton, Jackson would really have to be interested in her to go fishing. It was going to be curious to see if he really showed up in the morning.

At six twenty the next morning, Josie sat on the dead tree trunk to await Jackson's arrival. She had with her two fishing poles, a tackle box and a container of nice fat worms.

She'd already run her lines that morning and

gathered the fish she'd caught. Either later today or tomorrow, she needed to head into town to sell all of them.

She hadn't been sitting there long when she heard him coming. He crashed through the brush like a wild boar in a frenzy and she had to stifle a laugh as she heard a splash and then a deep string of curses.

He stepped into view and grinned at her with a shake of his head. "I can't seem to keep my right foot out of the water."

She laughed. "You'll get better in time. At least you're dressed appropriately for fishing this morning." He wore a pair of jeans that hugged his long legs and a royal blue T-shirt that stretched taut across his broad shoulders. The blue of the shirt was a perfect match for his sparkling eyes. Overall, he looked casual and very, very hot.

"I'm learning," he replied. "And you look very pretty today," he said. There was a warmth in his gaze that reinforced his words. The heat in his eyes leaped right into the pit of her stomach. It had been a very long time since a man had told her she looked pretty.

"Thanks," she replied and stood. "Are you ready to catch some fish?"

"As ready as I'll ever be," he replied.

She heard the slight trepidation in his voice.

Still, she grabbed the two poles and handed him one of them, then she grabbed her tackle box and the can of worms. "Just follow me," she said.

"How long of a walk is it to your fishing spot?" he asked as they began the trek.

"About fifteen minutes or so," she replied and turned her head to glance back at him. "Are you okay?"

He flashed her a bright grin. "Lead on, oh, beautiful wood nymph."

She laughed and turned back around. The trail darkened and narrowed as they continued forward. She had to admit, he was a good sport to be doing this and she knew the only possible reason he would put himself through this was to spend more time with her.

He was looking like a live one...the perfect man for her to use in order to catch her assailant. Hopefully, he would eventually invite her outside of the swamp and into his world. But she didn't know if he would actually do that or not. Only time would tell.

The trail widened out once again and ahead was a small clearing that led to the dark water's edge. "We have arrived," she said. He stepped up next to her and looked around.

"We just throw our line in the water and we catch fish?"

"That's what we hope for." She sat down her fishing pole and opened up the can of worms. "Do you need me to bait your hook?"

"No, I think I can manage a little worm." As he stepped closer to grab the bait, his scent wafted to her. He smelled like minty soap, shaving cream and a fresh-scented cologne. It was a combination that drew her in.

They got their hooks baited, threw out the lines and then sat side by side on the ground. "Do you come here often?" he asked.

"About two or three times a week. I get most of my fish on the lines that I run. I just come out here to sit and relax."

"I can see where this would be relaxing," he replied. "You're making me realize I need to work in more down time for myself."

"What's holding you back from doing that? Do you need to keep working so hard to make more money? From what I've heard, you're already extremely wealthy."

He laughed. "I guess the gossipers stay busy in this town."

"Honestly, Jackson, I could care less about your net worth," she said.

He held her gaze for a long moment and then nodded. "If I thought your only interest in me was because of my wealth, I wouldn't be sitting here next to you right now."

She smiled at him. "I'm glad you're here."

He returned her smile. "I can't think of any place else I'd rather be. Actually, that's a lie. I can think of lots of other places I'd rather be with you next to me."

He jumped suddenly as the tip of his pole dipped. "Oh, I… I think I've got one." He got to his feet and she did as well.

"Give it a little jerk to set the hook," she said. "Reel it in, Jackson." She laughed as he reeled as fast as he could and finally got a good-size catfish on the shore.

"I did it," he said with a boyish joy. He set down his pole, grabbed her into his arms and spun her around. "I caught my very first fish." He put her back down and took a step back from her. "I'm sorry. I got a little carried away."

"It's okay," she replied and laughed once again. "I definitely appreciate your enthusiasm." For just a moment, being held in his arms had felt wonderful. It had surprised her. She had thought she'd never want a man's arms around her again. "Uh…let's get that fish off the hook."

They sat and fished for about an hour, talking about all kinds of things. She shared stories from her childhood with him and he did the same. There was no question that they'd had different upbringings, but the common element was how much love they'd each enjoyed from their parents.

He caught another fish and she caught two and then they called it a day. She put the four fish on a hook to carry back to her place and then they headed out.

"I have to admit, I was dreading this yesterday, but this has been very nice," he said as he followed behind her on the narrow trail.

"It was nice to have your company this morning," she replied. It was true; she genuinely enjoyed him. He was funny and charming and easy to talk to. She almost felt bad that she just wanted to use him. Under different circumstances, she might have allowed herself to really like him.

However, if history had taught her anything at all, it was not to give her heart to a man from town.

Chapter Three

Jackson was definitely smitten. Josie made him feel more alive than he'd felt in a very long time. She intrigued him more than any other woman had in a very long time. He was excited about her and didn't want the day with her to end.

"What would you think about having dinner with me this evening at the café?" he asked once they'd reached the fallen tree trunk.

She looked at him in genuine surprise. "I think I would love that," she replied.

"Great. Why don't I meet you here about five thirty, then."

She smiled at him. "I'm not going to make you walk in to get me. How about I'll meet you in Vincent's parking lot at five thirty."

"That sounds perfect," he replied. "And this afternoon I intend to gather up a couple of my buddies and have a visit with Thomas Gravois. Hopefully, we'll be able to light a fire under him as far as these murders are concerned."

"Thank you, Jackson." She placed her hand on his arm, the touch immediately shooting a pleasant warmth through him. "I really appreciate it." She dropped her hand back to her side.

"Okay, then I'll just see you later this evening," he replied.

Minutes later, he was back in his car and headed to his townhouse. He was already anxious for the evening to come. He wanted to wine and dine her and maybe feed her her first bite of steak.

He hadn't been lying to her about having a visit with Gravois. He should have done it long before now. Three women brutally murdered should be on everyone's mind, no matter whether they were town women or from the swamp.

They were all women of Black Bayou and people should be up in arms about the vicious murders. He felt ashamed that it had taken Josie to really bring it to his full attention.

At one that afternoon, a knock sounded at his door. He answered and allowed in two of his friends. Brian Miller was a tall man with brown hair and green eyes. He also worked in real estate and owned properties all over the United States.

Lee Townsend had gone prematurely bald. His father had owned sugar cane fields and that was now Lee's business, making him a wealthy man.

"What's up?" Lee asked as Jackson ushered them into his living room.

"Sonny is supposed to be here, so I'll just wait for him to arrive before I tell you why I called you all here," Jackson replied.

"That man is always late," Brian said.

"Yeah, he'll probably be fifteen minutes late to his own funeral," Lee replied with a laugh.

At that moment, another knock fell on the door and Jackson ushered in Sonny Landry. Sonny's father was a retired prosecuting attorney and Sonny had made his money working in the textiles industry.

The four men had grown up together. They had come from family wealth and worked hard to obtain their own money. They'd run the streets as young kids and dated most of the women in town.

They had all gone to different colleges, but wound up back in Black Bayou where they renewed their close friendships. There were two other men they were all close to, but Jackson hadn't been able to get a hold of them for this meeting.

Brian was married and had two young children and Lee was in the middle of a contentious divorce. Sonny, like Jackson, was single and dating around.

"So, what's up?" Sonny asked as he joined the other two on the large black sofa. "Have you called us all here for an emergency drinking session?"

Jackson laughed. "I don't know. Do we need one of those?"

"I definitely do," Lee said mournfully. "This divorce is killing me. Sherri's trying to take everything I own from me."

"You've got a good lawyer," Brian said. "You'll be just fine." He turned his gaze to Jackson. "So, what's going on? Why'd you call us all here?"

"I'm hoping in the next few minutes you will all go to the police station with me where we can have a discussion about what our chief of police is doing to solve the swamp murders," Jackson said.

All three of them looked at him in surprise. "Since when do you care about what the law enforcement is doing in this town?" Lee asked.

"Since I met a beautiful woman who has opened my eyes to some important things," Jackson replied.

"A beautiful woman who lives in the swamp?" Brian asked.

Jackson nodded. "Her name is Josie and she's

not only beautiful but she's also intelligent and interesting and has a great sense of humor."

"Hmm, somebody sounds quite infatuated," Sonny said with a grin. "When did you meet this paragon of womanhood?"

"Yesterday," Jackson replied. "But she's made me really think about the fact that three women have been brutally murdered and our chief of police doesn't seem to be working very hard to solve these killings," Jackson replied. "He hasn't even publicly addressed the issue."

"Gravois doesn't work too hard at anything but politicking and baby kissing," Lee said.

"Well, I want him to work harder at solving these murders," Jackson said firmly. "Will you all go with me to the station now so we can put some pressure on Gravois?"

"Sure, I'm in," Brian said.

"I'd love to," Lee replied. "Personally, I can't stand the man."

"Count me in, too," Sonny added.

About fifteen minutes later, they all pulled up and parked in front of the building that housed the Black Bayou Police Department and they all got out of their cars.

Jackson led the way into the small reception area where Officer Ryan Staub greeted them all with a touch of surprise. "What can I do for all you gentlemen this afternoon?" he asked.

"We'd like to speak to Chief Gravois. Is he in?" Jackson asked even though he knew what the answer would be. Gravois was always in.

"Yeah, he's here. Let me just go tell him you all are here to see him," Staub said. He got up from behind the counter and disappeared down a hallway only to return a few moments later. "Last door on the right," Staub said and opened the doorway that would allow all the men into the interior of the police station.

Once again, Jackson led the way down the narrow hallway. They passed several closed doors on either side of the hall and then reached Gravois's office. Jackson knocked twice on the door and then opened it.

Gravois sat behind his desk and didn't rise as they all piled into the small office. "Well, this is a surprise. To what do I owe this unexpected visit?"

Thomas Gravois was a tall fit man. Although he was only in his mid-fifties, his dark hair was graying and there were deep lines around his blue eyes. He looked like a man who worked hard, but the gossip had always been that he was more than a little bit lazy. He had been married years ago but rumor had it his wife had left him. He lived alone in a house off Main Street.

"We're here as concerned citizens to check

on the progress of the murder investigations of the three women," Jackson said.

Gravois raised an eyebrow in obvious surprise. He then leaned back in his chair and released an audible sigh. "Unfortunately, there hasn't been much forward progress on those cases. I'll tell you what, those swamp people are tight-knit and they aren't talking to me or any of my officers."

"Are you still interrogating people to see if there were any witnesses to the crimes?" Lee asked.

"There's really no point, like I said, they are all closed off and not talking," Gravois said. "I think they're protecting one of their own."

"Surely, there was some blood evidence," Brain said. "I heard their faces were ripped off. The perp had to have been covered in tons of blood. Have you found footprints or handprints of any kind?"

"Nothing. It was like a ghost wild animal killed them and left no prints or other evidence behind," Gravois replied. "I think it's obvious somebody from the swamp is responsible."

"And why is that so obvious?" Jackson asked, his temper flaring just a bit.

"You know, most of those people are nothing more than uneducated pests," Gravois replied.

Jackson knew there was a general prejudice

amidst the townspeople against the people who lived in the swamp, but for an elected official to espouse something like that was not only shocking and unprofessional, but it also showed what an uneducated swine Gravois was.

"It wasn't anyone from the swamp who tried to kill Peyton LaCroix, it was a well-respected business man from town," Jackson said.

Jack Fontenot, a man who owned a successful construction company had not only framed his best friend, Beau Boudreau, for the murder of a young woman, but when Peyton's investigation into that crime got too hot, Fontenot had gone after Peyton. Thankfully, she'd survived the attack and Jack was in jail, awaiting trial on charges that would probably send him away for the rest of his life.

"Look, I'm doing the best I can to solve these murders. You boys know I'm shorthanded and without any real clues they've been difficult to investigate." Gravois's voice turned slightly whiny.

"Surely, you have enough in the coffers to hire another officer or two, if that's what you need to do," Brian said.

"Yeah, I seem to remember you got a huge budget passed at the beginning of the year," Lee added.

"Nobody around here has applied for a job

and I don't see anyone coming to this small town to live and work," Gravois said.

"You're full of a lot of excuses," Jackson said. "Isn't this an election year?"

Gravois's face reddened and his eyes narrowed in obvious anger. "I told you all I'm doing the very best that I can and that's all I can do."

"Maybe you should put some ads in the papers in New Orleans and some of the surrounding areas and see if you can get another officer or two to come in and help with the investigation," Sonny suggested.

"We'd just like to see more forward progress in these cases," Jackson said.

"Believe me, we all want the same thing," Gravois replied as he stood. "I appreciate you all stopping in here and letting me know your concerns." It was an obvious dismissal.

Minutes later, the four men stood next to Jackson's car. "Thanks for coming with me," Jackson said to his friends.

"No problem. Gravois is a man I'd love to kick in his lazy, prejudice ass," Brian said.

"That makes two of us," Lee replied. "I can't believe what he said about the people from the swamp."

"I'm hoping that now that he knows we're looking at him, he'll get up off his chair and do a true investigation of these murders," Jackson replied. "It's past time this killer is caught. Anyway, thanks again for all the support."

"Anytime," Lee replied and the others echoed that sentiment.

Later as Jackson drove home, he eagerly anticipated the evening to come with Josie. He was excited to see her again and to tell her about the conversation with Gravois. He was ashamed that it had taken him this long to have the talk with the police chief and he would tell her that, too.

JOSIE STOOD IN front of the floor-length mirror on the back of her closet door and pronounced herself ready to go. The Black Bayou Café was casual dining and so she wore a nice pair of jeans and a royal blue fitted long-sleeved blouse.

The jeans fit her snugly and showcased not only her slender waist but also her long legs. The blouse had a V-neck that hinted at her cleavage but didn't give too much away.

She'd pulled her hair back at the nape of her neck and secured it with a gold clasp and small gold hoop earrings hung from her ears. She'd gone heavy on the mascara and dusted her cheeks with a wisp of blush.

"This is as good as it gets," she said to the reflection in the mirror and then turned and left her bedroom.

She went into the living room and sank down on the sofa. It was a little too early for her to make her way to Vincent's parking lot to meet Jackson. She leaned back and took a couple of deep breaths to calm the nervous energy that danced inside her.

Tonight would be her very first time going to the café with a date. In all the time she had dated Gentry O'Connal, a man from town, he'd never taken her out of the swamp. Of course, she hadn't cared because she'd believed herself to be completely in love with Gentry, and she'd thought he loved her, too.

She'd been such a fool. That had been a little less than a year and a half ago and the whole experience with him had built a hard shield around her heart. But she couldn't help but be excited about Jackson.

This night was the first in her plan to catch her assailant. If she could keep Jackson interested in her, then he might invite her to something more than the café, someplace where she would meet a lot of his friends and acquaintances. Among those men, her attacker was hiding and she was determined to use Jackson to find him.

With this thought in mind, she got up from the sofa and left her shanty. As she walked slowly down the path, she drew in the scent and sounds of the surrounding swamp. This was her home and she couldn't imagine living any place else. The swamp calmed her and gave her peace.

The minute she stepped out of the marsh, she saw him waiting for her. His dark blue car was sleek and shiny and when he saw her, he immediately got out from behind the steering wheel. He wore a pair of jeans and a royal blue polo shirt that once again showed off his broad shoulders.

"Hi, beautiful," he said with a wide smile.

"Hi yourself," she replied, shocked by the wild jump in her heartbeat and the pool of warmth that filled the pit of her stomach at the sight of him.

He went around the car to the passenger side and opened the door for her. "Thank you, sir," she said and slid into the seat.

The interior smelled of leather cleaner and his pleasant fresh-scented cologne. She watched as he walked around the car to the driver side.

She was definitely attracted to him. But the fact that she found him extremely pleasing to the eyes didn't mean she was going to put her heart on the line. She reminded herself that she was on a mission and nothing more. She would absolutely not allow herself to like him too much.

He got in the car, started the engine and then

turned to look at her. "You look positively gorgeous this evening," he said.

A warmth filled her cheeks. "Thank you."

He put the car into gear and took off. "Are you hungry?"

"Starving," she admitted.

"I'm determined tonight to get you to take your first bite of a nice medium-rare steak."

She laughed. "I'm always willing to try new things. Have you ever had fish stew?"

"No, I can't say I have," he replied.

"Then maybe tomorrow night you could come to my place and I'll make you some fish stew."

He flashed her a quick glance. "Thank you, I'd really like that."

Inviting him into her personal space was a big deal. The only other men who had ever been there had been her father and then Gentry. But she was willing to invite him in if it got him to take her out around town more.

As he continued the quick drive to the café, they only had time to talk about the weather before he was parking in front of the eating establishment. There was a possibility of storms later that night but when they got out of the car, the skies were clear.

Josie had only been in the Black Bayou Café once as a diner and that had been about a year ago when she and a girlfriend from the swamp had eaten lunch here. However, when she'd been a child, she'd often hung out in the kitchen while her mother visited with Marie Boujoulais, the owner of the café. The two women had been good friends for many years.

Nothing much had changed since then. The walls were painted a cheerful yellow and two of them had hand-painted murals, one of Main Street and one of cypress trees dripping with Spanish moss.

Jackson took her by the elbow and led her to one of the booths toward the back of the place. As they passed the occupied booths and tables, most of the people greeted Jackson with a friendly nod or quick pleasantries. It was obvious he was well-liked and respected in the small town.

They reached their spot and she slid in on one side of the booth and he sat across from her. The booth had a window that looked out on Main Street. The lighting inside was fairly low and even with the big window, the space felt rather intimate.

He smiled at her, his eyes filled with a pleasant warmth. "Did I tell you that you look gorgeous this evening?"

She returned his smile. "You told me something like that."

"Well, let me say it again, you look absolutely beautiful this evening."

"My, my, Mr. Fortier, you'll turn my head with all that sweet talk."

"Aside from your physical beauty, I like you, Josie. I like your intelligence and your sense of humor. I like that you're thoughtful and make me think about how superficial my life has become."

"I like you, too, Jackson. The fact that you're questioning anything about your life shows me that you aren't superficial at all."

The conversation was interrupted by the arrival of their waitress. "Can you give us just a minute or two," Jackson asked the perky blonde who wore a name tag identifying her as Heidi.

"Sure, how about I take care of your drink orders and then I'll be back for your dinner orders," she said.

"Perfect." Jackson looked at Josie. She ordered a sweet tea and he did the same. Once Heidi left the booth, Jackson and Josie looked at the menus.

By the time their drinks were delivered, they were ready to order. She got the grilled salmon and he ordered a rib eye. "Guess what I did this afternoon," he said once Heidi had left with their orders.

God, he was hot with his blue long-lashed eyes shining so brightly. His lips looked firm yet soft and she found herself wondering what it would be like to kiss him. She had a feeling he would probably be a good kisser. She was surprised by the quick fire of sexual desire for him. It was the first time she'd felt anything like this since her attack. It felt healthy and good, making her realize she was hopefully moving beyond the trauma.

"Josie?"

"Oh, sorry," she replied, realizing she'd zoned out for a moment. Why on earth would she care how he kissed? Jeez, what was wrong with her? "So, what did you do this afternoon?"

"Me and three of my buddies went to have a chat with Gravois."

She stared at him for a long moment. He'd told her he intended to do it, but she honestly hadn't believed him. She was ridiculously pleased that he had followed through. "What did he have to say?" she asked.

"He said the investigation was going nowhere because you swamp people were tight-knit and unwilling to answer any questions. He also said he was certain the guilty party is from the swamp because of the heinous nature of the crimes."

"He's totally vile," Josie said. There were a lot more stronger words that she'd have liked to use to describe the man, but she swallowed hard against them.

"I agree. But he now knows he's got eyes on him. Hopefully, we put enough pressure on him that he'll do his damn job and really work hard to solve the murders."

She reached across the table and touched the back of his hand. "Thank you so much, Jackson." She quickly pulled her hand back, surprised by the warmth that momentarily flooded through her at the simple touch.

What was wrong with her? She hadn't even thought about a man in almost a year and yet there was no denying that Jackson was sparking something deep inside her, something slightly exciting and definitely hot. It was also something dangerous. She was definitely going to have to hang on to her emotions where he was concerned.

Their meals arrived and as they began to eat, they talked more about their families. She was surprised to learn that Jackson had a sister. Her name was Gwen and she was married and lived in Houston, Texas.

"She's five years older than me and we weren't really that close growing up," Jackson now said.

"Did you get closer when you got older?" she asked curiously.

"We were fairly close when we were in our twenties, but then she met her husband and they moved to Houston for his job. She now has three kids and we occasionally text back and forth but she leads a pretty busy life."

"Speaking of children, would you like to have any?" she asked.

"Sure, in a perfect world I'd like to be married and have a couple of kids. But so far, I've been stuck on the married part. But I'm thinking maybe my luck has changed in that department." He cast her that charming warm grin that made her heart inexplicably dance in her chest. "What about you? Do you want kids?"

"In a perfect world if I found the perfect man, then yes, I'd like to have children," she replied.

For the next few minutes, they fell silent and focused on their food. The fish was delicious and the fried potatoes and greens that had come with it were also good.

"Have you ever eaten any kind of meat?" he asked when they were halfway through the meal.

"My mother fixed pork chops for us a couple of times and I've had the occasional ham and cheese sandwich at Big Larry's, but that's it."

Big Larry's was a popular sandwich and burger joint in town.

"Then I must introduce you to steak, and this one is particularly juicy and flavorful." He cut off a piece of his and then reached across the table with the steak bite on his fork.

It felt oddly intimate for her to lean forward and take the meat off his utensil with her mouth, but that's exactly what she did. It was just as he'd described it…juicy and flavorful.

"What do you think?" he asked as he leaned back in his seat.

She finished chewing and swallowed and then replied, "It's really good."

"So, if I invited you to my place for a barbecue of steaks, then you would come and eat the steak?"

She laughed. "Yes, I would come and eat whatever you prepared for me."

"Then we'll have to plan it for one night."

Things were moving very fast with him and yet she didn't want to slow it down. The more time she spent with him, especially in public, the more opportunities she might have to meet her attacker.

More than once while they were eating, people stopped by their booth to visit with him for just a minute. She paid special attention to each male he introduced her to, but she knew by their voices that none of them so far were the man she sought.

Once they finished the meal, Jackson insisted they have dessert and coffee. She ordered a slice of chocolate cake and he got the apple crisp.

As they waited for it, she glanced out the window, but it was dark enough outside now that she couldn't see anything. She looked back at Jackson. "Even though it's relatively early, it looks like it's really gotten dark outside."

"Yeah, the weathermen forecasted clouds and rain overnight and into tomorrow," he replied.

"Then maybe you won't want to come to my place tomorrow evening for fish stew," she replied.

"Trying to back out on me, Josie?" he asked with a teasing sparkle in his eyes.

She laughed. "No, not at all. I was just thinking about you."

The twinkle left his eyes as his gaze lingered on her. "Honestly, Josie, I would walk through a hurricane to spend more time with you."

His words found a softness in her heart that she hadn't realized still existed. He was moving very quickly with her. Surely, he hadn't come to that depth of caring about her yet. Still, his words were very nice to hear.

She'd believed her ordeal with Gentry had

hardened everything inside her and the assault had taken any softness that had been left behind.

Jackson was definitely getting to her and she couldn't allow that. She refused to allow another man to ever hurt her again.

HE SAW THEM in the café window and momentarily froze in his tracks. One of his best friends and the woman he had attacked apparently having dinner together. Jesus, what was Jackson doing with her? How in the hell had the two of them hooked up?

He quickly crossed the street and headed to his car, his head screaming a wild cacophony of thoughts. Had she told Jackson about that night when a wildness and a rage had filled him? Had she told him about the assault on her that had happened months ago?

It was obvious she hadn't been able to identify him, at least by name. Otherwise, Gravois would have arrested him by now. The bag he'd pulled over her head had prevented her from seeing him…at least that's what he hoped.

But what if she had gotten a brief glance of him? What if she saw him again in a different setting? Would she be able to identify him as her attacker? What if she recognized his voice again? Damn, he should have never said anything to her on that night, but he hadn't been able to help himself.

He got into his car and grabbed the steering wheel tightly in order to halt the violent shaking of his hands. He closed his eyes and tried to remember all the details of that night.

He'd left his place filled with a rage that knew no boundaries. He'd like to think he hadn't planned what happened, but he knew in his heart that wasn't true.

Otherwise, why had he grabbed the bag from his garage? Why had he headed to the swamp to see whom he might encounter? He now knew from Jackson that her name was Josie, but he hadn't known it that night. He hadn't specifically targeted her; she was just the first female to come into his sights.

Her back had been toward him and it had been a perfect storm. He'd bagged her and then tagged her. He had his way with her and then ran, filled with a self-hatred but also empty of the enormous rage that had initially driven him away from home.

He hadn't been back to the swamp since then, although he'd been tempted on several different occasions when his anger had reached a boiling point. He'd managed that anger on those occasions by going to the Voodoo Lounge, a dive bar on the west side of town. He'd managed to drown his anger in a bottle of gin.

He glanced back toward the café. He was a hell of a businessman and had worked hard to gain his place in society. One thing was certain, there was no way in hell he was going to let a swamp slut take him down.

Chapter Four

Josie had swept the floors and dusted all the surfaces in her home. The place was completely clean and as far as she was concerned, it looked homey and inviting.

She had cans of soda, a couple of beers and bottled water on ice to go with the evening meal. The fish stew was simmering on the electric burner and she'd bought fresh-baked corn bread and coleslaw at the store that day.

She now sank down on the sofa to wait for the time to meet Jackson at their tree trunk and walk him to her shanty. She could hear the slight hum of her generator working and the air smelled of fish and tomatoes and onions, along with the other spices she'd used to make the savory stew.

He'd kissed her last night. It had been a quick sweet kiss at the end of the night that surprisingly had made her want more from him.

There had been moments during their meal

last night where she'd forgotten that she had an ulterior motive for being with him. There were moments when she'd just found herself enjoying his company as any woman might enjoy a date with a handsome charming man.

Their conversation had flowed easily and yet she'd experienced a simmering warmth in the pit of her that was both pleasant and disturbing.

Maybe he was the wrong man for her to attempt to use. So far, he seemed so nice and kind. But if she didn't use him, then how long would she have to wait for another man of his social stature to wander into the swamp?

No, Jackson was perfect and she just needed to stuff any personal feelings she had for him aside. She needed him to put her in a position to find her assailant and nothing more. Still, she couldn't help but wonder what it would be like if he pulled her into his arms and gave her a real long deep kiss.

She jumped up from the sofa and walked into the bathroom to take a last look at herself. The sleeveless red blouse cinched her waist and looked nice with her jeans. Once again, she'd clasped her long hair back at the nape of her neck. With a glance at the time, she left the bathroom, turned off the hot plate under the stew and then headed for the door. It was time to go pick up her date.

As always, when she walked through the swamp with its scents and vivid colors surrounding her, her head cleared of everything and she was at peace.

Jackson was waiting for her on the tree trunk and when he caught sight of her, a wide smile curved his lips. Damn his smile, for it created that crazy heat to swirl around deep inside her.

"Hey, handsome. What are you doing hanging out in these parts of the woods," she said in greeting.

He rose from the log. "I'm just sitting here, hoping a beautiful young woman will come along and take me with her for a delicious home-cooked meal."

"You just happen to be in luck. I have a nice stew simmering at my place and my table is set for two," she replied. She reached her hand out for his. "Come on, I'll take you there."

As she led him into the depths of the swamp to reach her shanty, they talked about the heavy cloud cover portending rain and the fact that he had eaten very little at lunch in anticipation of her fish stew.

She suspected part of his chatter was to mask his tension as she led him deeper into the wildness. She knew he hadn't been this deep into the swamp before and he would probably not be able to find her place again on his own.

They finally reached her home. They crossed the bridge that would lead up to her porch and then she dropped his hand. "Welcome to my humble abode," she said as they walked into the front door.

He stopped inside the threshold and looked around. She followed his gaze. The dark brown sofa held a couple of turquoise and yellow throw pillows. A matching brown chair sat opposite it. Against one wall was the small potbellied stove with cookware on top.

The living room flowed into the kitchen area that had just enough space for a small table and chairs. She'd used two white plates and turquoise cloth napkins for the meal.

"This is nice," he said. "Very homey, and something smells delicious."

"That would be your dinner." She walked over to the hot plate and turned it back on to warm up the stew. "Would you like a cold beer or soda while we wait for this to warm up?"

"A beer sounds good. Are you going to have one with me?"

"Sure." She plucked the two beers out of the ice chest and handed him one. "Sit down and relax." She gestured to the sofa. He sank down on one end and she sat on the other. Together they cracked open their beers.

He took a deep drink and then smiled at her. "So, how has your day been?"

"Like most of them are, fairly quiet. I did my fish run this morning and then just pretty much puttered around here until noon and then I made a run to the grocery store and came home to fix the stew. What about you?"

"I did some paperwork this morning and then had a light lunch with a couple of my friends and now I'm here with you." He took another drink and scooted closer to her. "This is definitely the best part of my day."

"You are quite a charmer, Mr. Fancy Pants," she replied.

He laughed. "I don't know about that, but I do know that it's nice to see where you live. Now when I think of you, I'll envision you snuggled among the turquoise and yellow pillows on the sofa as the frogs croak and the fish jump just outside your front door."

"So, tell me about your townhouse so I can envision you there," she said.

"I'll do one better. How about Friday night I take you there so you can see it for yourself," he said. "I'll grill you a nice steak for dinner. Would you be up for that?"

"I would definitely be up for that," she replied.

"Good." His eyes shone with a light that shot

a small shiver up her spine. It was an intimate gaze that made her feel as if he were both seducing her and probing into the very depths of her soul.

"Excuse me for a minute." She jumped up from the sofa and went to stir the stew. *Remember, you're just using him...nothing more*, a little voice reminded her. Seeing that the stew was warm, she placed the coleslaw, the corn bread and the butter on the table and then got two bowls down from the cabinet. "This is ready if you are," she said.

He picked up his beer and stood. "Does it matter which seat I take?"

"It doesn't matter at all," she replied.

As he sat, she dipped up the stew in the bowls and added them to the table. "This looks really good," he said and unfolded the napkin on his lap.

"I hope you like it. It's my mother's recipe," she replied. "We had it a lot as I was growing up, but I don't fix it very often now."

She watched as he took a spoonful of the stew and popped it into his mouth. He chewed for a moment, swallowed and then grinned at her. "Josie, this is absolutely delicious."

She expelled a small sigh of relief. "I'm so glad you like it. And help yourself to the corn bread and slaw."

"Thanks. So, tell me more about your mother. Did she enjoy cooking?"

"She did, although she cooked almost every meal on the potbellied stove while I broke down and bought an electric stovetop burner, which serves me well."

"Tell me something else about your parents."

The meal passed pleasantly with her reminiscing about her parents and then him sharing more about his own parents.

"My parents are still madly in love with each other and they are also best friends," he said. "They've been a really good role model for me on how a relationship should work."

"Same with my parents," she replied. "They were still crazy in love with each other until the day they died. I envision them right now in heaven sitting on a sofa and holding hands."

"That's a nice vision and that's the kind of relationship I'd like to have," Jackson said.

"Me, too," she agreed although she didn't really believe she'd ever find that kind of love for herself. She'd thought she'd found it with Gentry but that certainly hadn't panned out.

Before long, the meal was over and she insisted they leave the cleanup for later and instead move back to the sofa for more conversation.

It felt good to have him here with her. She had to admit that there were times when she got lonely and missed having somebody to talk to…somebody to share things with. It was especially lonely in the hours between dinnertime and bedtime.

Although she had several girlfriends who lived nearby and a couple of male friends as well, at the end of the day they weren't what she wanted. She didn't want casual friendships to fill that time. She yearned for somebody special.

There was no question that there was something exciting about sitting on the sofa with Jackson. His gaze on her was so intent and held the undeniable spark of physical attraction. It was exciting and just a little bit frightening because she felt an undeniable spark of attraction to him.

Was he the same kind of man as Gentry? Was he only after a quick roll in the hay with a swamp woman? Was he just a townie looking for something that was a bit taboo and exotic? That's what most town men who ventured into the swamp were looking for.

No, she couldn't believe that about Jackson. He'd already treated her with more respect than Gentry ever had. Gentry had never taken her anywhere in public. Jackson had taken her to the café and he'd acted proud to be seen out in public with her. That was proof in and of itself that Jackson was a different kind of man from Gentry.

They continued talking until darkness had fallen outside and it was time for her to take him to the place where he could make his way back to his car. She grabbed a flashlight from a kitchen cabinet, knowing that he would feel more comfortable with a light even though she didn't necessarily need it.

The minute they stepped out of her door, the scent of impending rain hung heavy in the air. "We should probably hurry so you don't get wet," she said.

"I'd rather get wet than hurry and accidentally fall into the deep dark waters of the swamp," he replied. "I'm convinced I'd be a tasty morsel for some alligator lurking nearby."

She laughed. "I promise I won't let you fall into the water and get eaten by a gator."

Together they took off, her leading the way and him following her closely behind. The swamp breathed heavily all around them with the sounds of night creatures awakening and day creatures nestling in for the night. A heavy breeze whistled through the treetops as tousled leaves added to the myriad sounds.

She kept the flashlight directed to the ground more for Jackson's benefit than her own. She knew these paths as well as she knew her own heartbeat but tonight there wasn't even a ray of moonlight to illuminate the paths. The sky was as dark as the swamp waters that surrounded them.

It took only a few minutes for them to reach the fallen tree trunk where they always met. "I can't tell you how much I enjoyed both the meal and the company," he said as they stopped.

"It's been a real pleasure, Jackson," she replied. Her heart picked up its pace as he took a couple of steps closer to her.

"Thank you for sharing your home with me." He took another step forward and now stood so close to her that she could feel his warm breath on her face.

"You're welcome."

"Josie, can I kiss you good-night?"

"I… I'd like that." She was surprised to realize it was true. She wanted him to kiss her again and she hoped it was more than the little peck they had shared the night before.

She leaned slightly forward and he gathered her into his arms. He took her lips with his, plying hers with an incendiary heat that she couldn't help but answer with a fire of her own.

He deepened the kiss, his tongue dancing into battle with hers as he drew her closer against him. It surprised her, the fact that she felt undeniably safe in his arms…so safe with him.

Yet at this very moment, a delicious desire flooded through her veins. She wanted him. She wanted more than his kisses and that shook her up. She'd believed after the assault that she'd never want a man again. At the very moment she considered bringing him back to her cabin to finish what they'd started, a flash of lightning rent the sky, followed by a deafening boom of thunder.

She sprung back from him, the mood shattered by the vivid show of nature. "I have to tell you, Josie, when I kiss you, I see fireworks in the sky and I feel the earth move under my feet," he said.

She laughed at his silliness. "You'd better get out of here before you feel the rain of the gods soaking your butt."

He returned her laugh. "Good night, Josie."

"'Night, Jackson."

She watched as he turned and headed down the path that would take him back to his car in Vincent's parking lot, then she pivoted to go back home.

Lightning once again slashed through the darkness with another boom of thunder afterward. The minute the thunder quieted, she heard it…the slap of footsteps close behind her.

It was possible it was Gator Brossard. The old man was known to wander about in the darkness of the swamp no matter what the time or weather. However, the person was moving far too quickly to be Gator.

She cast a quick glance over her shoulder and gasped. A man wearing a ski mask over his head was gaining on her. Who? Wh-what did he want? Whatever he wanted, it couldn't be good given his face covering. Her heart accelerated and she grabbed the knife sheath from her waistband and pulled out her knife.

She certainly didn't want to confront the man. However, if she had to, she'd use her knife to defend herself.

Instead, she picked up her pace. She ran as fast as it was possible into the very depths of the swamp. The last thing she wanted to do was lead this person to her shanty.

Branches slapped at her and Spanish moss dripped down from the trees, half-blinding her as she raced for her life. And it did feel like she was running for her life. The masked man definitely screamed to her of imminent danger.

A gasp escaped her as a light filled the area. Oh, God, the person chasing her had turned on a flashlight. Up until now, she had hoped to outrun him and disappear into the darkness. But he was gaining on her and now he could see her as she ran.

She left the path, zigzagging through the

thicket. Thank God she knew almost every inch of the swamp. Her breaths came in deep gasps as she frantically bobbed and weaved through the thicket.

Tree limbs clawed at her and roots in the ground tried to trip her up. The brush came alive with animals trying to escape her wild dash and the sound of wild boars rooting nearby added to her fear.

The lightning overhead was her enemy as it flashed a bright illumination and the thunder only added to the madness of her wild race through the marshland.

She didn't know how long she ran before she was utterly breathless. Panting, she realized she needed to stop and take a breath. She couldn't go on running as she was completely out of gas. But he was still somewhere behind her. Frantically, she looked around for a good hiding place.

Cautiously, she stepped down into the murky water near her and around a big knobby cypress tree. Grateful that it wasn't too deep and she didn't see any gators around, she crouched down and waited. Her heart still banged with frantic beats as she drank in deep gulps of air as quietly as possible.

She drew in a deep breath and held it as the light appeared flashing all around. Oh, he was definitely hunting for her. Was he the same person who had attacked her almost a year ago? Or was he the Honey Island Swamp Monster looking for his next victim? Either way, she definitely didn't want to be found.

She pulled her body tight against the tree root and slid even deeper into the water in an effort to stay hidden. The light continued to flash all around as she held her breath. Thankfully, it didn't find her. She hoped the next flash of lightning wouldn't bring her into his view.

After several long minutes, the person turned and headed away from her. She slowly expelled her breath. She waited a long time before she finally moved from her position and slowly rose from the water.

Her heart had not stopped its frenzied beat and it continued to beat that way as she slowly made her way to her shanty. She no longer heard footsteps behind her and was relatively certain she had lost him.

Still, once her home was in her sights, she remained hidden in the brush nearby as she watched it for several long minutes. She needed to make sure the person who had chased her hadn't somehow found her shanty and waited for her there.

Seeing nobody in the area, she quickly ran across the bridge and to the front door. Once inside she locked the door and then immediately ran to look all around. Thankfully, she was alone. She hurried over to the window and peered out. Nothing stirred and the frogs had resumed their croaking melodies, which indicated to her that nobody was around.

She finally sank down on her sofa and began to cry. The residual fear fell from her in deep sobs. She eventually stopped crying. Even though she was soaking wet, she didn't move from her seat as the horrifying event whirled around and around in her head.

Who had he been? There was no question that he'd had bad intentions with the ski mask hiding his face. Had he merely been looking for somebody…anybody to prey on or had he been hunting for her specifically? That thought terrified her even more.

THOUGHTS OF JOSIE filled Jackson's head from the moment he woke up the next day. He showered and went into his home office to get some paperwork done, but he found it hard to concentrate as all he could think of was her.

He wasn't sure what he'd been expecting, but he'd found her home small, but both charming and inviting. The fish stew she had prepared was delicious, but it was definitely the fire of their goodbye kiss that had stayed with him.

He wanted her. He wanted her not just because her body had fit so perfectly against his own and not just because her kiss had shot flames of desire through him, but also because he liked her. In fact, he thought he might be falling in love with her.

It sounded completely crazy after having known her for such a short period of time, but he'd spent more time with her in the past week than he'd spent with the last woman he had dated for three months.

Josie touched him on all levels. Intellectually, she challenged him and emotionally she stirred him in ways no woman had ever done before. And then there was the physical desire he felt for her and if the kiss they'd shared was any indication, she desired him, too.

It felt like she was the woman he'd been searching for in his life. He'd dated so many women in the past and had been unable to find the one who fit him so perfectly. So far, Josie was the woman who fit him perfectly.

He hated the fact that he wouldn't see her again until tomorrow night. He hated even more that she didn't own a cell phone so he could call her when they were apart. She'd told him she'd never felt the need for a phone before and had no plans to ever get one in the future.

Last night as they'd walked back to the tree trunk from her place, they'd made arrangements for him to meet her in Vincent's parking lot Friday night at six o'clock.

He didn't know how long he'd been sitting there, staring off into space with thoughts of her when his phone rang. The caller ID showed him it was Lee. "Hey, man, what's up?" he asked.

"I was wondering if you want to meet me for lunch today at Tremont's. I just got out of a court hearing and I'm totally depressed."

Jackson looked at his watch, shocked to realize it was already almost eleven o'clock. "Sure, I can meet you."

"Great. How about noon?"

"Sounds perfect, I'll be there," Jackson replied.

It was quarter to twelve when Jackson pulled up in the parking lot of Tremont's. The upscale restaurant was housed in a sleek black and gray building with the name in large silver lettering.

He got out of his car and went inside where Layla Brighton stood at the hostess stand. "Good afternoon, Mr. Fortier," she greeted him with a big smile.

"Hi, Layla, are you staying out of trouble?"

The young woman laughed. "I'm definitely trying. Are you dining alone today or meeting other people?"

"I think it's just two of us today. Lee

Townsend is meeting me and should be here shortly."

She picked up two menus. "If you'll follow me, I'll get you seated. Booth or table?"

"I always prefer a booth," he replied.

She led him to the seat located halfway toward the back. "Perfect," he said as he slid into the side facing the door.

"A waitress will be with you shortly," she said as she set the menus on the table. "And I'll bring Mr. Townsend back as soon as he arrives."

"Thanks, Layla," he replied.

He settled into the booth and looked around. He waved and nodded at several people he knew and at that moment a waitress arrived to take his drink order.

She'd just delivered his glass of sweet tea when Lee showed up. He slid in across from Jackson and ordered a scotch and soda from the waitress.

"Bad morning?" Jackson asked.

Lee shook his head with a deep frown. "The worst. Sherri has gone completely, money-hungry crazy. She's not only asking for the house to be mortgage-free and put in her name, but she's also asking for an astronomically high amount of money monthly for alimony."

"Thank God the two of you don't have kids," Jackson said.

"I don't even want to think what that would have cost me, but Sherri never wanted to have any children. Just tell me, what woman really needs nine thousand dollars a month to live? Nine thousand dollars. I mean, does mascara and hair spray really cost that much a month?"

Jackson couldn't help but laugh. "Surely, your lawyer is going to fight everything."

"He is, but I was really hoping we could do all this amicably and reasonably, but she's going for my throat. All I ever did to her was love her." He stopped as the waitress arrived with his drink and then took their food orders.

"I didn't even want the divorce," Lee continued once the waitress was gone. "It was all her idea. She's the one who decided to leave me."

"I'm sorry this is all going to be so painful for you," Jackson said.

Lee took a sip of his drink and then shook his head once again. "We were married for eight years. You think you know somebody but when the chips are down, the person you thought you knew turns into a stranger. Anyway, enough of my sob story, how are things going with you?"

"Really good."

"You still seeing that swamp woman?"

"Josie…her name is Josie and yes I am," Jackson replied. "In fact, I'm more than already a little bit crazy about her."

"Wow, that was fast."

"I know, right? But so far things are going great between us," Jackson said.

"Are you planning on bringing her to Mrs. Patty's gala next weekend?" Lee asked.

"I'd forgotten all about the gala," Jackson replied with a frown. About twice a year Patty Bardot, a wealthy older widow, opened up her home for a fancy gala. These parties were considered must-not-miss social events.

"Yes, I'll definitely bring Josie if she'll come with me," Jackson said, excited by the very thought. He didn't know if Josie would have an appropriate dress to wear to the fancy event but, if necessary, he would provide her with whatever she needed to be his date for the big gala.

"That will make a lot of people talk, you bringing a woman from the swamp," Lee replied. "And it will definitely tick off all the women in town who have been chasing you for years."

Jackson laughed. "I don't give a damn about people talking about me and I've dated most all the eligible women in town and never found a connection. The heart wants what the heart wants and right now my heart wants Josie."

"I never thought I'd see the day that you would be off the market because of a swamp woman," Lee said.

"Stop calling her that," Jackson said with an irritated tone. "The swamp is just the place where she lives. It has nothing to do with who she is. She's Josie, period."

Lee raised an eyebrow. "Oh, you definitely have it bad for her."

At that moment, their lunch was delivered. Jackson had ordered a club sandwich and Lee had ordered a burger. As they ate, their conversation lightened up. They talked about work and the storm that had moved through overnight and some of the news headlines of the day.

Finally, the conversation returned once again to Lee's divorce. "I'm just so damned angry about it all," he said. "And I don't know what to do with all this rage I have built up inside me."

"Maybe it's time you go to the gym and lift some weights or punch some bags," Jackson suggested.

"Maybe," Lee replied listlessly.

"Buddy, you've got to buck up," Jackson said. "This will all pass and you'll be just fine. A year from now you'll be living your best life."

Lee grinned at him. "That's why I wanted to have lunch with you today. I knew you would remind me that I'll be okay."

"You will be," Jackson replied firmly.

After lunch was over and the two men parted ways, Jackson returned home. He wished he would have made plans to see Josie that evening, but he hadn't.

Time seemed to move ridiculously slow over the next day, but finally it was time to meet Josie at Vincent's. When he pulled into the parking lot, she was there, looking gorgeous in a yellow dress that showed off her perfect figure. Her hair was loose...a black waterfall of richness that fell around her shoulders.

He got out of his car and she ran toward him, a smile on her lips that warmed him as if he'd swallowed the sun whole. "Hi, beautiful," he said.

"Hi, handsome," she replied.

He walked her to the passenger side of the car and opened the door. After she slid inside, he closed the door and then hurried around to the driver's door. He was excited to spend more time with her. He was looking forward to her seeing his home and excited to cook for her. He'd never felt this way before. Damn, he was definitely falling hard for her.

He got into the car and grinned at her. "You look absolutely gorgeous this evening."

"Thanks," she replied with a smile of her own.

"Are you hungry?"

"I'm definitely getting there," she replied.

"Then let's get you to my place where I've

got a couple of filets mignons just waiting to be thrown on the grill." He started the car engine and headed out of Vincent's parking lot.

"I'm looking forward to you seeing my place tonight," he said.

"I'm looking forward to it, too," she replied.

"So, what's new with you since I last saw you?" he asked.

"The last time we saw each other and parted ways at the tree trunk, I was chased through the swamp by a man wearing a ski mask," she said.

Jackson slammed on his brakes, nearly coming to a full halt in the middle of the street as he shot her a horrified glance. "Are you joking with me right now? Please tell me you're joking."

"Trust me, it's no joke," she replied somberly.

"So…so…tell me more. God, Josie, I'm just glad you're here with me right now." He stepped on the gas once again after shooting a worried look at her.

"There isn't much more to tell," she replied. "He chased me and I managed to escape him. If he would have caught me, I carry a knife at all times for my protection."

"Do you carry it at your waist?" he asked.

"I do… How did you know?" she asked curiously.

He shot her another quick glance. "When we embraced the other night, I felt it and wondered what it was. Do you have any idea who it was who chased you?"

"Not a clue."

"Do…do you think it was the Honey Island Swamp Monster killer?" He reached out and took her hand in his. He held it tight, thinking of how frightened she must have been.

"It could have been, but I don't want to talk about all that right now."

"I'm just so glad you're here and that you weren't hurt," he replied.

She gently pulled her hand away from his. "Both hands on the steering wheel, *mon cher*. You're carrying precious cargo."

"I am, indeed," he replied. His fear for her still caused his heart to beat an accelerated tempo. Somebody in a ski mask had chased her? Who? Who could it have possibly been and what had he wanted with her? It could have only been something bad. Thank God, she had escaped.

He would honor her wishes not to talk about it anymore right now, but he couldn't promise he wouldn't talk to her about it later on.

It took only a few more minutes for him to pull into his driveway. His townhouse was one of four units. He'd bought into the condo style of living for simplicity. These units were high-end and here his lawn was mowed and the exterior of the building was kept up by the association.

He'd lived here for eight years and still found it to be perfect for him.

"Come on in," he said as he opened the front door and allowed her to sweep past him. Once again, as she walked by him, he caught the scent of her, that heady fragrance that half-dizzied him.

As she walked into his living room and looked around, he followed her gaze. His black sofa was long and sleek, as was the matching side chair. The coffee and end tables were glass and silver and there was a nice built-in bar in one corner of the room.

He'd always been satisfied with his living conditions, but now as he looked around, he realized they were cold and sterile and without a hint of the person who lived here.

"Very nice," she said.

He laughed. "Don't lie. I just now realize that the place definitely needs a woman's touch. Please, have a seat." He gestured toward the sofa. "Would you like a drink?"

"If you have it, I wouldn't mind a cola with a splash of whiskey," she replied as she sank down on the sofa.

"Coming right up." He went over to the bar to prepare their drinks. He'd already made a salad and baked the potatoes so all he had to do was start up the grill on his patio and cook the steaks.

He made her drink and then one for himself and joined her on the sofa. "Now, tell me what you really think about my space."

She took a sip of her drink and then placed it on one of the coasters that were on the coffee table. "It's beautiful, but there's really nothing of you here. Didn't you tell me your favorite color was blue?"

"It is," he agreed, surprised that she'd even remembered that minute detail about him.

"Then why not bring some blue into this room?" she asked. "Maybe some pictures on the walls or some accents in blue?"

"Why don't you help me with decorating in here? I told you, it needs a woman's touch and I can't think of any other woman I'd want decorating it than you." He took a drink but kept his gaze solely focused on her.

"If you really wanted me to do something in here, I would be willing to help you. But, Jackson, don't change things in here on my account."

"I'm not, but I wouldn't mind some changes to make things a little brighter and homier. And speaking of that, why don't we take our drinks out to my patio and I'll put the steaks on." If he sat next to her on the sofa for too much longer, he'd want to pull her into his arms and forget all about dinner.

Tonight, he was really hoping that they would take their relationship to the next level and they'd make love. It began with dinner and hopefully it would end up in his bed.

Chapter Five

Dinner was absolutely delicious. The salad was crisp and refreshing and the potato was also good. The steak was cooked to perfection and she really enjoyed it all.

She and Jackson sat in his dining room to eat and, as always, their conversation flowed easily. He was interesting and funny and she really enjoyed the time she spent with him.

She kept having to remind herself that she was just using Jackson, because the truth of the matter was he was getting to her. As much as she hated to admit it, he was definitely getting into her heart.

She'd heard through the grapevine that Patricia Bardot was having one of her big galas next weekend, and she wondered if Jackson would invite her to go with him? Or was he actually like Gentry and would not want to be seen with her in such a huge public setting?

Having dinner with her at the café hadn't

been a big social outing of the two of them together, nothing like the gala where everyone
who was anyone would attend. The gala would
be the perfect place to get the opportunity to
identify her rapist. If she could just smell him
again and hear his voice, then she'd know who it
was. And she was fairly certain the man would
be at the gala.

After dinner, she insisted she help with the
kitchen cleanup and once that was done, they
got fresh drinks and returned to the sofa in the
living room.

"Dinner was absolutely delicious," she said
once they were seated. "I loved the steak. It was
so flavorful and juicy."

He grinned. "My next goal is to make you a
good juicy cheeseburger."

She laughed. "You can try all you want, but
a good piece of fish will always be my first
choice."

"Ah, but you haven't tasted my cheeseburger
yet." His eyes gleamed with the teasing light
she loved.

"And you haven't tasted my grilled fish yet,"
she replied.

"I see some cook-offs coming in our future. And speaking of the future, I don't know
if you've heard about it or not, but Mrs. Patty
Bardot is having one of her big galas next Satur-

day night, and I was wondering if you'd be my date. I'd love to show you off to all my friends."

A warmth of feminine pleasure washed over her. It had nothing to do with the fact that she'd wanted this to catch her attacker. For just a moment, it was strictly the fact that he wanted her by his side and it was a place she wanted to be.

"I'd love to go with you," she replied.

"Great. And I'd be happy to buy you a dress to wear for the evening."

She stiffened and narrowed her eyes at him. "And I find the very idea of that highly offensive."

He instantly looked at her apologetically. "I'm sorry. I didn't mean to offend you. I just… I've often bought dresses for my dates in the past."

"I would never allow a man to pay for my clothes for a date out. I buy my own clothes and I assure you I will be appropriately dressed for the gala." She continued to pin him with her gaze, irritated that he would even think she would accept such a gift from him.

"Don't be angry with me, Josie. I forgot for a moment that you aren't like the other women I've dated in the past. Even though they came from money, they were always eager for me to buy them clothes, and if they could get a piece of jewelry from me, it was even better. I'm truly sorry that I would even believe for one minute that you were like them."

He looked so miserable she couldn't maintain any further anger toward him. He couldn't help it that, in this instance, he was nothing more than a creature of habit. She found it despicable that the women in his past had obviously taken advantage of his wealth and kindness.

"I accept your apology. But just remember, Jackson, I'm with you because I want to be, not because of anything I can get from you."

A warm smile lit his features. "I really like that about you."

She laughed. "And there are many things I like about you, too."

"I hope so," he replied, suddenly serious. "Because I'm more than a little bit crazy about you, Josie."

He leaned forward and she knew he wanted to kiss her. And she wanted his kiss. Oh, how she wanted it. She bent forward into him and his mouth took hers.

It began as a sweet, tender kiss, one that swelled a simmering heat inside her. Quickly, he deepened the kiss by swirling his tongue with hers. She welcomed it, leaning even closer to him.

The kiss went on until she was half-breathless and she finally pulled away from him. His eyes were filled with a wild hunger that shot a warm delicious shiver down her back.

"Josie... I... I want you," he said, his voice sounding deeper than usual. "I want you so badly."

"And I... I want you, too." It was true, the kiss had stirred up a wealth of desire inside her. She definitely wanted him, too.

He stood and held his hand out to her. "Josie, will you come with me to my bedroom?"

She hesitated only a moment and then stood and took his hand. Her heart raced with both excitement and a touch of anxiety as he led her down the hallway.

They passed what looked like a spare bedroom with a queen bed decorated in blacks and yellows, then a bathroom decorated in the same colors.

Finally, he led her into a large bedroom with a king-size bed, a long dresser with a mirror and a small lamp illuminating the room from one of the nightstands.

The bed was covered in a navy spread that matched the curtains at the window. He immediately took her back in his arms and his mouth sought hers once again. She molded herself to him and he wrapped his arms tightly around her. The kiss deepened, but as he strengthened his grip on her, an unexpected flashback rushed through her brain.

A bag falling over her head…hands shoving her to the ground…her hands tied in front of her…and…she gasped and took a step back from Jackson. For a brief moment, she was trapped between the past and the present, caught between desire for Jackson and the horrible encounter with her assailant.

Jackson instantly dropped his arms to his sides. "Josie?" It was a tender inquiry and to her horror, she burst into tears.

"Hey, honey… Josie, what's going on? If you don't want to be with me, it's okay," he continued.

She shook her head as her tears continued to flow uncontrollably. She sank down on the edge of the bed and he sat beside her, leaving several inches between them.

"Josie, please talk to me. Tell me what's going on." His voice was soft and filled with a tenderness she hadn't realized she'd yearned for until this moment.

She cried for a few more minutes and then finally pulled herself together, although she couldn't look at him. "Almost ten months ago I was raped." The words fell from her with a new wave of tears seeping out of her eyes.

"Oh, Josie. Honey, I'm so sorry that happened

to you." His voice held both a touch of outrage and a wealth of gentleness. "Can...can I just hold you right now?"

"I... I'd like that," she replied.

He wrapped his arm around her shoulders and pulled her into him. Weakly, she leaned into his strength, his warmth, and she was surprised as always that she felt so safe and secure there.

"Do you want to talk about it?" he asked softly.

She hadn't spoken to anyone about the assault since she'd talked to Chief of Police Gravois on the night that it had happened. There had been nobody to talk to about it. But now there was Jackson, sweet and kind Jackson.

"I'd just made a fish run into town and was coming back home," she began, fighting to keep her wild emotions in check. "I had only gone a few feet into the swamp when he came up behind me. Before I even knew he was there, he pulled a black bag over my head and tightened it around my neck. I... I thought he was going to strangle me to death, but then he shoved me hard and I fell to my hands and knees. He flipped me over to my back and managed to tie my wrists together and then...then he raped me."

The words fled from her in a rush, as if the faster she spoke them the less chance they had to hurt her. But the outrage of the violation, her anger over the injustice of it all, gripped her before the actual physical and emotional pain of the attack did. That let her know she was healing. But she still wanted justice for herself and anyone else the man had assaulted. Maybe he'd done it to other women who hadn't reported it.

"Josie, I'm so very sorry that happened to you. Honey, you definitely didn't deserve it," Jackson said. They were words she hadn't realized she needed to hear until this very moment.

"This makes me so damned angry for you," he continued. "Did you report this to the police?"

She nodded. "I spoke directly to Chief Gravois the moment I managed to untie myself, pulled myself together and could get to the police station."

Jackson's arm tightened around her. "And what did he do about it?"

A small bitter laugh escaped her. "Nothing. He made a report and told me he'd check it out, but as far as I know he did nothing except tell me I should be a lot more careful walking through the swamp alone."

Jackson released a string of curse words. "I swear, we've got to do something about that man. He's not worthy of his position." He drew in a deep breath and then released it audibly.

"Do you have any idea who attacked you? Did you see anything that might have given you a clue to his identity?"

The last thing she wanted was for Jackson to somehow put it together that she was using him in the effort to identify her assailant. "I'm guessing it was one of the men from the swamp, but I don't know enough to specifically identify him."

"I can't say it enough, Josie. I'm so sorry for what you went through. Something like this should never ever happen to any woman."

"Thank you. I think one of the hardest parts was that I had nobody to talk to about it."

"Well, now you have me. Josie, anytime you feel the need to talk about it, anytime you need a reminder that you are important and this should have never happened to you, then you come directly to me," he said.

Her heart warmed with his words, with the way he was handling her with such kindness, such gentleness. A deep wave of guilt also flashed through her.

She looked up at him and offered him a half smile. "Poor Jackson, here you were expecting a night of wild romance and instead I give you all this."

"Honey, there will be many more opportunities for wild romance between us but only when you're sure you're ready." He kissed her on her forehead. "Now what do you say we go back into the living room and have another drink."

She nodded and together they got up from his bed and she went back to the sofa while he grabbed their glasses and returned to the bar. As she watched him making their drinks, a new wave of guilt swept through her. The guilt over using him was coupled with the surprising realization that she was falling for him. How had that happened and so quickly?

Still, no matter how much she cared for him, she told herself that she wasn't looking for a real relationship with him. There was no way she'd put her heart on the line to be hurt another time. She had to keep her heart carefully locked away from him.

"Have you heard of Mrs. Patty's galas before?" he asked once they each had a drink again and he was back on the sofa next to her.

"I've heard a few stories about them," she replied. "I've heard they are over-the-top with alcohol flowing and expensive tidbits being served and naked dancers on all of the tables."

He laughed. "You're definitely right in the first two descriptions, but I have yet to see anyone dancing naked on the tables. However, for the last gala Mrs. Patty flew in thousands of

different types of butterflies and had them released all at the same time."

"Now that's a woman who has way too much
money," she observed.

"You're right. She was quite wealthy on her
own and then she married Harry Bardo who
was a multimillionaire. When he died, he left
her everything. She now has more money than
she could ever spend in five lifetimes. She's
definitely the richest woman in Black Bayou."

"I hope she's donating some of that money to
charity," Josie said.

"I know one of her pet projects is a dog rescue. She has events specifically to raise money
for it. I've heard she also donates heavily for
breast cancer."

"Well, that's good to hear."

"And I'll tell you something else about the
upcoming gala." He grinned at her and his eyes
sparkled brightly. "I can't wait to walk in with
you on my arm."

"That's what makes you different from the
last man I dated," she replied.

He raised an eyebrow. "Want to tell me about
your past relationship? Or maybe you find it too
personal to talk about with me."

She laughed. "I'd say I've already talked
about some pretty personal things so one more
thing won't matter now. Besides, I'm the one

who brought it up. You might know him, Gentry O'Connal?"

Jackson frowned. "Yeah, I know him. So, you dated him?"

"I did. I don't remember why he was around the swamp in the first place, but I ran into him one evening when I was on my way to Vincent's for a few groceries. He was very nice and flirtatious and he asked me if he could meet me the next day. Anyway, we dated for almost six months but we always spent our time together at my place."

She shifted her position on the sofa and quickly took a sip of her drink, and then continued. "I finally asked him if we could go to the café to eat or someplace else besides my shanty and that's when he told me what he really thought about me. He said he enjoyed spending time with me, but I was a swamp woman and he had no interest in pursuing anything deep with me or being seen in public with me. That's when I realized I was nothing more to him than a dirty little secret and that was also the last time I saw him."

"I've never liked him and I definitely like him even less now," Jackson replied. "As far as I'm concerned, I have always found him to be an arrogant jerk." His gaze held hers. "Were you in love with him?"

She thought about it for several seconds. "I thought I was in love with him at the time, but looking back I think I was just lonely and this all happened immediately after my parents were both gone. He momentarily took the pain of their loss away and soothed some of my loneliness."

He reached out and took her hand in his. "I'll tell you this, Josie, you deserve far better than a man like Gentry. I can't imagine not wanting to take you out and show you off. I want my friends to not only see how beautiful you are, but also how bright and intelligent you are, too. When I look at you, I don't think swamp and when I think about myself, I don't think town. I think of us as two people with different backgrounds who are enjoying each other's company."

She squeezed his hand. "I don't know how I got so lucky to meet you, Jackson."

"I feel the same way about you. I had just about given up on finding a woman who would touch me on all the levels that you do," he replied.

She gently pulled her hand away from his. "I think on that note, I'd like to go home. This has definitely been an evening of crazy emotions for me and I'm exhausted."

The truth of the matter was she wanted to

stop him before he said anything else about the way he felt toward her. Although she loved hearing it, at the same time she didn't want to hear it. She had to remember what she was doing with him.

"Of course," he said and stood from the sofa.

"I'm sorry if this evening didn't work out as we thought it was going to," she said as she also got up.

"Josie, please don't apologize. I'm glad we're at a place where you felt you could trust me with everything you told me." He grabbed his keys from the end table and together they left out his front door.

Darkness had fallen and as she slid into the passenger side of the car, she realized she really was mentally and emotionally exhausted. Talking about the rape had been extremely difficult for her, but she was glad she'd shared that traumatic event with Jackson. She'd been surprised how much his kindness and words of support had touched her heart. He was getting in so deep…too deep. Somehow, she needed to slow things down with him.

When she'd seen the opportunity to use him, she'd never expected to like him so much. The best thing that could happen would be that she identified her attacker at the gala and then she would break things off with Jackson and never see him again.

That way he wouldn't have a chance to break her heart, because if she continued seeing him, she believed that eventually, just like Gentry, he would break her heart.

THEY WERE BOTH silent on the ride home. It wasn't an awkward silence, but rather a companionable one. He glanced over to her several times as he drove, wanting to assure himself that she was okay.

The thought that she'd been raped burned in his very soul. He'd love to meet the man who had assaulted her and beat his face in. When he thought of her fear...her violation in that moment, it made him so angry he couldn't see straight.

The fact that Gravois hadn't taken the crime seriously only fueled his anger to a higher level. The man was utterly useless and maybe it was time to lead some sort of a recall effort and get him out of office once and for all.

He finally pulled up in Vincent's parking lot and stopped his engine. "I'll walk you in to your place," he said.

"Don't be ridiculous," she replied with a small laugh. "You'd get lost and then I won't have a date for the gala."

"Surely, I'd find my way out in a week," he protested with a laugh of his own.

"I don't know. There are legends about townies who entered the swamp and got lost for years. They wander the wild half mad and howl at the moon at night."

"You just made that up," he accused her.

She grinned. "Busted. Still, there's no way I want you to walk me home. Seriously, Jackson, I'll be fine. I have my knife and I can find hiding places in the swamp that most people wouldn't even know about." She reached out and touched the back of his hand. "Please, don't worry about me."

"I can't help but worry about you," he replied. "It was just a few nights ago that somebody chased you through the swamp."

"But he didn't catch me. Now, it's time to say good-night." She opened the car door and got out and he did the same. They reached each other at the front of the car.

"Josie, can I give you a hug?" he asked, sensitive to what she might or might not want or need from him right now.

"I'm hoping you're going to give me a big hug and a kiss," she replied.

He pulled her into his arms and she immediately leaned into him. "Oh, God, Josie, I wish I could magically take away all your pain," he whispered into her ear. "I wish I could take away any bad memories that you have and replace them with wonderful ones."

"You're definitely helping," she replied. She looked up at him and her dark gray eyes shone silver in the moonlight. "Please, kiss me, Jackson."

She didn't have to ask him twice. He covered her mouth with his in a tender kiss that he hoped reached in and soothed all the rough edges her past had created in her. She'd been through so much and yet had survived it all with strength and dignity. He admired her so much for that.

The kiss lasted only a moment and then he released her and she stepped back from him. "Will I see you tomorrow?" he asked.

"I could meet you at the tree trunk," she replied. "Whatever time works for you."

"Why don't I bring lunch and we can have a picnic there," he suggested.

"Oh, that sounds like fun. Then we'll meet around noon?"

"Bring your appetite," he replied.

"I will. Good night, Jackson."

"'Night Josie." He watched until she disappeared from sight, swallowed up by the swamp that had created her. He hoped she made it home okay but he couldn't help but worry.

There was a murderer loose who had the

women in the swamp in his sights. Was that who had chased Josie a few nights before? Had it been the killer dubbed the Honey Island Swamp Monster?

He turned and got back into his car, his head filled with all the things Josie had shared with him tonight. She had definitely been through a lot, but he was amazed and awed by her strength and resilience.

She was exactly the kind of woman he'd always dreamed of for himself. He'd wanted a strong, independent woman who was formidable in her beliefs and convictions, a woman who would both challenge and delight him.

He'd given up on finding that woman. He'd dated a lot before Josie, but he found most of the women he dated were either after his money or simpering women who agreed with everything he said.

Josie was exactly what he wanted and he hoped she wanted him, too. He definitely wanted to help her get over her past traumas. Right now, he just hoped she got home safely and would meet him the next day for lunch.

He was far too wired up to just go home and go to bed. It wasn't that late, so he headed for Tremont's for a drink before returning home.

On a Friday night, the place was hopping. The dining room was full and half a dozen men sat at the long polished bar. He immediately spied Brian at the end of the bar with Sonny sitting next to him.

"Gentlemen," he greeted them.

"Hey, man," Brian said.

"Am I intruding?" Jackson asked.

"Hell no, grab a stool and join us," Sonny said. "We're just sitting here bitching and moaning about life."

Jackson sank down on the stool next to Sonny. "Are we bitching and moaning about anything in particular?"

"Nah, just life in general," Brian replied.

"How are Cynthia and the kids doing?" Jackson asked Brian.

"They're all good. It's the stock market that's driving me crazy right now."

"Ha, that's driving everyone crazy right now," Jackson replied. "One day it's up and the next day it's down."

Jackson ordered his drink and for the next half an hour he and his buddies talked about business, Sonny's latest dating escapades and Brian's kids.

"What would you all think about starting a recall effort on Gravois to get him out of office?" Jackson asked.

"I'd be in," Sonny said. "But do you have any

idea what is involved in trying to do something like that?"

"No, but I intend to research it to find out," Jackson replied. "He's inept and lazy, among other things. I wonder how many other people in town have lost faith in law enforcement because of him?"

"I wonder how many people have just stopped reporting crimes because they know nothing will be done about them," Sonny said.

"That's definitely a horrible thought," Jackson replied.

"I think you have to start a petition and get so many signatures on it to start," Brian said.

"So, if I get this thing started, will you both help me get the signatures that are required?" Jackson asked.

They both said they would be in to help and by that time Jackson was ready to call it a night. He said his goodbyes and then walked out of the restaurant and into the sultry night air.

The rest of the week flew by quickly. His picnic lunch with Josie was lighthearted and fun and he saw her two more days during the week, one day for more fishing and another when he took her to his parents' house for dinner.

By the end of the evening, his parents positively adored her. Jackson was at an age where his parents didn't care who he fell in love with, they just wanted him happy in love. His mother definitely wanted to see him get married as she was looking forward to having grandchildren as soon as possible.

Finally, the evening of the gala arrived. As he dressed for the night, excited energy raced through him. He couldn't wait to see Josie. He couldn't wait to spend hours at the gala with her by his side.

Mrs. Patty's galas warranted formal attire so Jackson was wearing his navy tuxedo. He had no idea what Josie was wearing. She had refused to even tell him the color of her gown. Whatever she wore, he knew she would look absolutely stunning.

Finally, it was time for him to leave to pick her up. As usual, he was meeting her in Vincent's parking lot. As he left his place, he was grateful that the weather was perfect. The skies were clear and it was a little cooler than it had been, making it a perfect night for a party. He knew from past parties that much of the gala would take place on the patio and in the vast gardens in Mrs. Patty's huge backyard.

As he drove toward Vincent's, a new burst of excitement danced inside him. He was eager for his friends to meet Josie. He knew without a doubt she would charm them all. Even Lee, who hated all women right now, would be unable to find fault with sweet, wonderful Josie.

It was important to him that his friends like her. In the future, there would be times where they would all be together both for social events or just hanging out and having beers and conversation with each other. She would fit right in with all of them.

He saw her the moment he turned into the parking lot. She was an absolute vision in a one-shoulder gown that fell in a column of coral silk to her feet.

He thought his breath might have stopped for a moment as he took in her beauty. Her hair was twisted up, but the beauty of the darkness against the color of the gown stole his breath away. She looked like a Greek goddess.

As she smiled at him, a burst of warmth shot throughout his entire body and he knew in that moment that he was definitely madly in love with her.

Chapter Six

Josie carried with her a plastic bag containing the jeans, blouse and shoes she had worn to leave the swamp. She had dressed for the gala in Vincent's ladies' room. Thankfully, Vincent always kept the restrooms pristine.

She'd been ridiculously nervous about how she looked, but as Jackson got out of his car to greet her, she knew by his smile and the heat in his eyes that she looked okay.

"Josie, you are positively stunning," he said in greeting.

"Thank you, and you look very nice, too." He looked better than nice in the navy tuxedo that fit him perfectly and brought out the bright blue of his eyes.

He opened the car door for her. "Let me get you inside quickly before another man comes along and steals you right away from me," he said.

She laughed. "You don't have to worry about

another man stealing me away from you, Jackson." She slid into the car. "I always go home with the man I come with."

"Aside from looking gorgeous, are you ready for this big gala?" he asked once he joined her in the car.

"I've had nervous butterflies darting around in my stomach for most of the afternoon," she confessed. "And right now, they are definitely flying around fast and furiously."

"Don't worry, you'll be just fine," he assured her.

"Just make me one promise."

"And what's that?" he asked curiously.

"Promise me you won't leave my side. I won't know a soul there except for you."

"That's an easy promise to make," he replied with a smile. "When you're with the prettiest woman in the place, you don't ever want to leave her side." He flashed her another smile that warmed her from head to toe, then he started the car and they took off.

She couldn't help but be super nervous. She would be spending the evening with people she didn't know, many of them who shunned anything and anyone from the swamp.

However, she would do anything possible to find the man who had raped her. There was no question in her mind that he would probably be there tonight. This night could possibly be the beginning of the end of her time with Jackson.

That thought shot an unexpected piercing pain through her heart. She already felt incredibly guilty for using him, particularly since she'd had dinner with his parents. They had been lovely and welcoming, and Josie had felt like she was there under false pretenses.

In the end, she knew there would be no love story between her and Jackson. They were from two different worlds and she would never truly trust a town man again with her heart.

She shoved these thoughts out of her head as she once again focused on what her mission was for the night. As Jackson flashed her a heated gaze, she realized despite her desire to the contrary, Jackson had managed to get into her heart. That would make her telling him goodbye all the more difficult.

She sat up straighter in her seat as they approached Mrs. Patty's home. It was a massive white two-story with six huge columns in the front. It was easily the biggest house in the town. The driveway was a circle and as vehicles pulled up, several valets in uniform helped the ladies out and then took the keys from the men and parked the cars in the side yard.

There was already a line of vehicles in front

of them. "Looks like it's going to be a full house tonight," Jackson said.

"I certainly didn't expect a valet service to park the cars," she replied.

"Mrs. Patty definitely likes to do things right," he said.

She watched as ladies in lovely gowns and men in tuxedos got out of the cars and strolled up the long walkway to the front door.

Then it was their turn. Jackson got out of the car and handed his keys to the attendant, but instead of allowing one of the uniformed men to help her out of the car, he hurried around the car and opened her door.

For just a moment, she wanted to tell him to get back in the car as quickly as possible and drive away. She couldn't do this. Her nerves pulsed through her entire body as she thought about the night to come.

"Josie?" He held out a hand to her. She mentally shook herself. She had a mission tonight. This might be the very best chance for her to catch her predator. She grasped his hand firmly and got out of the car. Once she was out, he grasped her elbow firmly. "Are you okay?" he asked.

"I'm fine...just ridiculously nervous," she admitted.

He squeezed her elbow and flashed her a

bright smile. "Don't worry, Josie, I told you that you're going to be just fine," he repeated to her. "Just be yourself."

The moment they walked through the double doors, she wasn't fine; she was completely overwhelmed. The foyer was large, with high ceilings and an ornate round table holding a colorful flower arrangement that was huge. Couples mingled all around, some with drinks in hand and others without.

Music played overhead and the sound of laughter and chatter filled the air. Jackson took her hand and led her through the foyer and into an enormous living room. There were only a few people standing and talking together in here.

Ahead, she saw where the real party was. Wide glass doors opened out to the night. "Before we do anything else, we need to pay our respects to Mrs. Patty," Jackson said as he guided her toward the open doors.

They walked outside into a piazza-like area with silver flagstones under their feet and low lights shining from several tall attractive light fixtures. The air was sweetly scented with all the flowers that lined the various pathways that wound through the lawn.

People stood around, laughing and talking

in small groups as uniformed waitstaff offered hors d'oeuvres and drinks from silver trays.

There were a lot of men there with wives or dates. How awkward would it be for her to ask if she could smell them and hear them talk? Of course, that would be ridiculous, but hopefully by the end of the night Jackson would have introduced her to most of them and at least she would be able to hear them speak. She knew that was the way she was going to definitely identify her monster.

Mrs. Patty sat in an oversize white wicker chair on one side of the festivities. Josie would guess the woman was in her mid-eighties. Her snow-white hair was pulled up into an attractive twist, exposing her elegant long neck and the sparkling blue earrings that hung from her ears.

She was a slender woman and her blue gown showcased her bright blue eyes. Although her features were all soft, an aura of steely power radiated out from her. It was obvious that she was holding court from her chair.

"Good evening, Mrs. Patty," Jackson said. "Thank you so much for inviting me to this evening's festivities."

"Jackson, you know the only reason I invite you here is because I like eye candy," she replied. "Now, introduce me to this lovely lady by your side."

"This is Josie Cadieux," he said.

"Josie." Mrs. Patty held out a hand and Josie took it with hers. "You are a beautiful woman, but are you also a smart woman?"

"I like to think I am," Josie replied.

"Then what are you doing here with Jackson?"

Josie smiled at the older woman. "I like eye candy, too."

Mrs. Patty stared at her for a moment and then laughed. She gave Josie's hand a squeeze and then released it. "Go, get yourself drinks and some food and enjoy yourselves." She shooed them away.

"She likes you," Jackson said as they moved away from the older woman.

"How do you know?" Josie asked.

"She likes people who make her laugh."

"Then I feel like I just passed a huge test," she replied.

He laughed and grabbed her hand. "You did, and now let's get a drink and then mingle."

And mingle they did. Jackson seemed to know everyone and she was introduced to tons of people within the first hour. She listened carefully to each man she met, but none of them had the particular voice she sought.

The scents that filled the air was a combination of garden flowers, booze and the various perfumes and colognes that everyone wore. It was impossible to pick out the man who wore the particular scent she remembered from that horrible night.

It was about that time when he introduced her to Andrew Bailey and his girlfriend, Belinda. "Hey, I've been looking all over for Brian and Sonny and Lee. Have you seen any of them around here tonight?"

"No, but Sonny told me they weren't going to make it tonight because the three of them were heading to Florida this morning to check out some piece of real estate that Brian is interested in buying."

"Oh, it must have been planned in a hurry because none of them mentioned anything about it to me," Jackson replied.

"I don't know about when they planned it, but I got the definite impression it was a spur-of-the-moment thing. I just had a quick phone call with Sonny this morning and he mentioned they'd be missing tonight because of the trip," Andrew replied.

"I guess I'll just catch up with them all when they get back in town," Jackson replied.

"Well, that's a bit disappointing," he said as they walked away from Andrew. "I was really hoping you'd meet my close friends tonight."

"There will be another time," she replied.

He continued to introduce Josie to more people as the evening continued. She sipped on a fruity drink and also enjoyed the food that was offered, little tidbits that popped with flavor. There were crackers with cream cheese and caviar, lobster bites on puffed pastry and dozens of other delicious items.

For the most part, she found everyone pleasant and welcoming, but there was a group of women gathered around the bar and at one point she caught tidbits of their conversation. They apparently had imbibed in more than a few drinks and were unaware of how loud they were talking.

"I just can't imagine what Jackson is doing with her," a short blonde said.

"Oh, I can certainly imagine. You know those swamp women have no morals at all," another tall brunette woman said. "Who knows what she's doing under the sheets with him, if you know what I mean."

"When I was younger, her mother used to clean for us. She was one of the laziest women we'd ever had and we had to fire her after a couple of weeks," a third woman said with a mean laugh.

Josie tightened her hands into fists as a rich anger swept through her. She knew the woman who had spoken. Her name was Allison Ingraham and Josie's mother had quit that job because the Ingraham house was a filthy big hoard.

Jackson, who was visiting with one of his friends, wasn't aware of the women talking and despite Josie's anger over the mischaracterization of her hardworking mother, she did nothing.

The last thing she wanted to do was cause a scene and to what end? She knew there were probably a lot of people here tonight who didn't believe she belonged among them, who saw her as trash. She'd seen the surprised looks and had been aware of the whispers that had occurred as they passed various people.

The real disappointment of tonight was that she felt as if she'd met nearly every man at the gala and most of the men who lived in town and none of their voices identified one of them as her attacker.

The night ended with an explosion of fireworks. As the fiery colorful show filled the sky, Jackson pulled her into his arms and gave her a tender kiss.

The feel of his lips against hers moved the explosions from the sky to the very pit of her stomach. She was definitely more than a little bit crazy about Jackson.

"I'm still disappointed that you didn't get to meet my buddies tonight," he said once they were in his car and headed back to Vincent's.

"Surely, there will be another chance for me to meet them," she replied.

"For sure. I can't wait to show you off to them." He cast her a quick glance and smile. "I was so happy and so proud to be with you tonight. Did you have a good time?"

"I had a very good time," she replied. "Everyone was very nice, the food was delicious and my date was wonderfully attentive and charming."

"That's nice to hear. From my take, my date was not only the most beautiful woman at the party, but you were also gracious and welcoming to everyone. Seriously, Josie, I was so proud to have you by my side."

"Oh, Jackson, you're making me blush."

He laughed. "I love your blushes. You were also the most intelligent woman at the gala."

"And what makes you think that?" she asked.

"Well, you were there with me, so that shows me how very intelligent you are to pick me as your date."

It was her turn to laugh. "I hate to burst your bubble, but you were my only option as a date."

"Then I guess that makes me one lucky guy," he replied.

By that time, they had arrived in Vincent's parking lot. Jackson cut the engine, she turned and grabbed her bag of clothing from the back seat and then together they got out of the car.

"Thank you, Jackson, for inviting me tonight," she said. "I really had a wonderful time."

"Whoa, I'm not going anywhere yet. Go change your clothes and I'll wait here for you." He leaned against the car and so she hurried to the restroom to change back into the clothes that were in the bag.

She exchanged the elegant gown for a T-shirt and jeans, and her pretty high heels for tennis shoes. She paused for a moment and stared at her reflection in the warped mirror over the sink.

She'd gone into all this with Jackson in order to use him to find her rapist. She'd never intended to develop any real feelings for him.

But she had, and now she didn't know what to do. She'd sworn after Gentry she would never ever date a town man again. In fact, after her rape she'd decided that she would live the rest of her life alone. She'd made an exception with Jackson because she'd been on a mission.

She needed to break things off with him… before she fell more deeply in love with him. She would never believe there was a future with him.

However, there were still some of his friends she hadn't met yet. Was it possible one of his close buddies was the guilty man? For Jackson's sake, she certainly hoped not, but she couldn't be sure until she met them.

No, she couldn't stop yet. She at least had to meet his friends. She'd give it another week or so and if she hadn't found her assailant by then, then it would be time to let Jackson go. Both for his sake and for hers.

IT WAS ON Wednesday when Jackson finally heard from his buddies and they all planned to meet for lunch at Tremont's. As he drove to the restaurant, as always Josie was on his mind.

He'd never felt this kind of love for a woman before. Josie had stirred a depth of feeling inside him he'd never had before. Each time he was with her, his love for her only deepened. Each time he was with her, he dreaded the time when he had to tell her goodbye for the day.

However, he had no real clue what she felt for him. Oh, he knew she liked him and apparently enjoyed spending time with him. When he kissed her, she responded to him with the same fire that he had, but was she really falling in love with him?

He desperately hoped so. He wanted to marry her. He was ready to start planning a real future with her. He knew already that he wanted to spend the rest of his life with her. But maybe things were moving a little too fast for her.

He wanted to tell her how he felt, but he also didn't want to scare her away if she needed more time. There was no question that his feelings for her had developed very quickly.

He shoved these thoughts out of his mind as he pulled into a parking space in front of the restaurant. When he went inside, Lee and Sonny were already seated at a table.

"Ah, the vagabonds have finally returned," he said to them as he joined them.

"We got back in town late last night," Sonny replied.

"Is Brian joining us?" Jackson asked.

"Yeah, he called a few minutes ago and said he's running a little late, but he'll definitely be here," Lee said.

"He probably had a bunch of honey-dos this morning after being gone for a couple of days," Sonny said with a laugh.

"So, how was your trip? I was surprised when I heard at the gala that you had all gone out of town," Jackson said.

"It was kind of a last-minute thing. A hotel that Brian had his eye on went up for sale and he wanted to get down to Florida, check it out and make an offer," Lee explained.

"And here's the man of the hour now," Sonny said as Brian approached their table.

He took the last seat at the table. "Hey, guys. Sorry I'm late."

"No problem," Jackson said. "They were just starting to fill me in on your trip. So, did you buy it?"

"Nah, once I got a closer look at the property, I realized it was going to cost a ton to renovate it and the owners weren't willing to budge at all on their price point, which was too damned high to start with. So, in the end I walked away from it."

"So, what took you all so long to come home?" Jackson asked.

"I twisted their arms into staying and enjoying a little mini-vacation. Our hotel was right on the water so we did some surfing and other water sports before coming back," Lee said.

"We also drank more than a little bit and hung out in the awesome bar right there in the hotel," Sonny added.

"But for God's sake, don't tell Cynthia any of that. As far as she is concerned, this trip was strictly business," Brian said.

"Well, you all missed a great gala," Jackson said.

"Needless to say, I wasn't going to go anyway," Lee said mournfully. "It's no fun to go places like that solo."

"But I knew you would be going with your new squeeze and that's why I didn't invite you on our little trip," Brian explained.

"My *new squeeze* was definitely the most beautiful woman at the party," Jackson replied. "She was charming and gracious and we both had a wonderful time."

"You sound like a man in love," Brian said.

"I am," Jackson admitted.

"I can't believe it took a swamp woman to get you out of the dating market," Lee said.

"I wish you all would stop referring to her that way," Jackson said in frustration. "Her name is Josie, not swamp woman." He was about to say more but at that moment the waitress appeared by the side of the table to take their orders.

While they ate, the topic of conversation changed to the usual things, business and Lee's divorce. Jackson was half grateful that the talk wasn't about him and Josie.

On the one hand, he wanted to shout out his love for her to the world, but on the other hand it felt good just to keep it to himself with these three men who seemed to only refer to her as Josie from the swamp. Dammit, why couldn't she just be Josie?

He only brought her up when they were almost finished with their meals. "Since you guys haven't had a chance to meet Josie yet, I'd like to invite you all to my place this Friday night for drinks. Brian, bring your wife and, Sonny, bring whoever you're dating. Lee, bring your sorrows and we'll help you drink them away."

Lee laughed. "There isn't enough booze in the world to take my sorrows away, but I'll be there."

"And I'll make sure to get a babysitter so we can be there," Brian said.

"I can't wait to meet the woman who has taken you off the dating market, so I'll definitely be there, too," Sonny added.

"Great, it should be a good night," Jackson said, pleased by the prospect of them all getting to know Josie. "It will be just drinks and some crackers and cheese and some laughs."

"Jackson, you seem to be moving pretty fast with this Josie," Lee said. "I would just suggest you take things slow with her. Don't jump into anything too quickly." He laughed. "Look at me, the man who is getting divorced is giving relationship advice."

Jackson laughed. "Things have been moving pretty quickly between us," he admitted. "But we've spent a lot of time together in a short period of time. I can't help the way I feel about her."

It was just after two o'clock when the men parted ways and Jackson headed home. He was looking forward to getting everyone together on Friday night. Those three men were his closest friends and it was important to him that they all get to know the woman he intended to have in his life for a very long time to come. He was sure Josie would charm them all with her quick wit and intelligence.

He was meeting her at their tree trunk in a couple of hours and he hoped she was in for Friday night. Their tree trunk… It was funny that he claimed a fallen dead tree trunk as theirs alone. But that place had become so important to him. It was close to where they had met and they had spent many hours there since then just talking about anything and everything.

Their conversations made him believe he knew her better than he had ever known a woman and he had laid open his life to her. The one thing they hadn't talked about was their feelings for each other, but that would come in due time. He wasn't going to be able to hold his feelings for her in for very much longer.

That night she took him to her place where she made him grilled fish and fried potatoes for dinner. As always, their conversation was light and easy through the meal.

After dinner and cleanup, they were seated

on the sofa when he told her about the plans for Friday night. "That sounds like fun," she said. "I can't wait to finally meet your friends."

"And I can't wait for them to meet you," he replied.

"Tell me more about them." She leaned closer to him and a lick of hot desire shot off inside him.

He tried to tamp it down. "First there's Brian. He's married to Cynthia who was his high school sweetheart and they have a boy and a girl. When we were young and running wild on the streets, he was usually the voice of reason."

"So, he's the one who kept you hooligans out of jail," she replied teasingly.

"Exactly. Then there's Lee. He's going through an acrimonious divorce right now. He's always been more than a little bit dramatic. He's the type that if he gets a cut on his finger, he assumes it's going to get infected and he's going to die. Right now, he's going through the world's worst divorce." Jackson frowned. "The only thing that worries me about him right now is how angry he's become with the divorce."

"Do you think he might go after his wife in some sort of a physical kind of way?" she asked.

"I would certainly hope not. I really can't imagine him doing anything like that. He's never shown any signs of being capable of hurting anyone."

"Well, that's good." She shifted positions and her scent eddied in the air all around him, restirring the lust inside him.

"Finally, there's Sonny. He's the quieter one of the bunch. He's just an all-round nice guy. He's single and still looking for his forever woman. Anyway, I'm eager for them to meet you."

"And I'm eager to meet them since they all mean so much to you," she replied.

It wasn't long after that when he decided it was time for him to leave her place. For some reason, tonight he was having trouble keeping his desire for her in check and the last thing he wanted to do was do something to offend her in any way.

He knew with her history he had to take things very slow with her physically and he was more than willing to do that for he was certain she was more than worth the wait. When it came to his physical desire for her, he just needed to take his cues from her.

She walked him to the tree trunk. "Will I see you again tomorrow?" he asked.

"No, tomorrow I'll be busy checking lines and then tomorrow evening I'm going to take a load of fish into town. But I'll be ready for you on Friday if you're picking me up. Or I could drive to your place."

"I'll pick you up," he replied. "The gang is going to be at my place around seven, so why don't I pick you up around six? That will give us some time to visit before they all get there."

The moonlight overhead stroked the beautiful planes of her face as she smiled at him. "Then I'll be ready at six on Friday night."

"Great. Can I kiss you good-night?"

Her smile grew brighter. "I'd like that."

She leaned into him and he wrapped his arms around her. She fit so neat against him, as if she'd been made especially for him. The kiss began as something soft and tender, and then quickly escalated to something a bit more wild and hungry.

The earthy smell of the swamp coupled with her fresh slightly mysterious scent dizzied his senses. He felt half drugged by the heat, the place and the woman in his arms.

The kiss continued for only a short period of time and then he pulled away from her. "Oh, Josie. I want you so badly," he said with a deep sigh.

"And I want you," she replied softly. "Maybe on Friday night after your guests leave, we can have the romantic night we tried to have before."

"Only if you're ready for that," he said. "I certainly don't want to pressure you in any way."

"I'm ready, Jackson." Her eyes shone brightly as she looked up at him. "I really believe I'm ready."

His heart swelled as he saw what appeared to be raw desire shining from her beautiful eyes. "We'll play it by ear," he finally said. "In the meantime, I'll see you at six on Friday night."

"Okay. Good night, Jackson."

"'Night, Josie."

He got back in his car and drew in several deep long breaths. He'd been looking forward to Josie meeting his friends on Friday night but now he had something else to look forward to. That was the night that they hopefully would take their relationship to the next level.

Chapter Seven

The next morning Josie decided to sit and fish for a while before she ran her lines. It had taken her a long time to go to sleep the night before and the thoughts that had kept sleep at bay still plagued her this morning.

She was so confused about Jackson. She believed she was in love with him and she'd never wanted that to happen. Last night when he'd kissed her good-night, she had wanted him more than she ever had. She wanted to be in his bed and feel his naked body against her own. She'd wanted him to kiss her until she was utterly mindless.

Without a doubt, he would be a tender, giving lover. She knew he'd take his lead from her and that only made her want him more. Would he make love to her and then go back to dating the kind of woman who would be more appropriate as a wife for him? She didn't believe so. She didn't believe she was just a conquest to win for him. But she just couldn't be sure. And that lingering doubt continued to confuse her.

She jumped up as she felt a bite on her line. She tipped the end of her pole to give it a little jerk and then began to reel in. The fish on the line felt big and feisty and when she finally got it in, it was a huge catfish.

"Now that's a fine catch." The familiar voice came out of the foliage next to her and half scared the hell out of her.

"Dammit, Gator, how did you manage to sneak up on me?" she said as the old man stepped out of the nearby brush and into her view.

He grinned at her. "You was busy landing that big fish and I was just creeping quietly."

"So, how's life treating you?" she asked as she took her hook out of the catfish's mouth and put the fish into a basket in the water.

"Not too bad. Mind if I sit with you for a spell?" he asked.

"Not at all. You know I always welcome your company," she replied.

He set down the walking stick he always carried with him and then eased himself to the ground. He was quiet as she rebaited her hook and cast the line out into the water. "How's life treating you?" he then asked.

As usual, the old man was clad in an old

T-shirt, baggy jeans and alligator boots. The boots were made from the same alligator that had taken off three of his fingers.

"I can't complain," she replied. She returned to her seat on the bank.

"You seem to be spending a lot of time with that Jackson Fortier."

"I have been," she replied. "You been spying on me, Gator?" she asked teasingly.

He laughed and his dark eyes sparkled merrily. "You know I like walking about and on more than one occasion I've seen the two of you together. I keep my eyes and ears open around here, but I'd never spy on anyone."

"You ever been in love, Gator?" she asked. In all the years she had known the old man, he had always been alone.

"Oh, a million years ago I fell in love with a girl who was a neighbor of my ma and pa." He stared out across the water where the morning sun glittered gold. "Her name was Rosa and she was the prettiest, the sweetest woman in all of the swamp. Unfortunately, her and my baby boy died in childbirth."

"Oh, Gator, I'm so sorry," Josie said. "And you never found anyone else after her?"

Gator looked at her and all his features crinkled up in a smile. "Nah. I never wanted anyone else after that. After all these years, the memories of Rosa and her love still burns in my heart. Besides, I've become a strange old man who now feels married to the swamp and the gators I catch."

Josie returned his smile and then jumped up as she had another fish on her line. For the next twenty minutes or so, she and Gator small-talked while she caught three more fish.

"They're definitely biting good today," Gator said.

"They are, but I'm about done here. I still need to run my lines."

"Back to Jackson...you see a future with the city slicker?" Gator asked as he rose to his feet.

"Maybe," she replied. "I don't know for sure." There was no way to describe to Gator how confused she was about the man. Her love for him also battled with the fact that she'd been using him all along. Then there was her fear that she was from the swamp and would never be right for Jackson.

"And how do you think that would work out?" Gator looked at her and in the depths of his dark eyes, she saw age-old wisdom. "You got the swamp deep in your blood, Josie."

"I know that, but Peyton was a town woman and Beau was from the swamp. They've made it work between them," she replied.

"But Peyton ran the swamp as a young girl.

She loved Beau, but she also loved the swamp as well. Jackson doesn't have the same ease around here."

He leaned down and picked up his walking stick and when he straightened, he smiled once again. "I just don't want to see you get hurt, Josie. I had great respect for your parents and I guess I just want you to be careful with your heart."

He cleared his throat as if not used to talking about such things of the heart. "And now I'll just take my leave." Without saying anything more, he turned, walked away and quickly disappeared back into the brush.

Josie packed up her fishing supplies. She felt as if the world had gone a little mad. She'd never seen the softer side of Gator before today.

Normally, he was just a tough old man who wandered the swamp and hunted for alligators. She never even noticed his missing three fingers as he managed to function as well as any ten-fingered person. And now he was giving her relationship advice... Definitely a little wild.

The morning passed quickly as she ran her lines and then took all her fish back to her place and put them in the big basket in the water. She had quite a haul to take into town later in the day.

She was looking forward to meeting Jackson's friends and she was desperately hoping she didn't recognize any of their voices. She would hate to find out that one of Jackson's closest friends was her attacker. It would break his heart.

Gator's words floated around in her head throughout the afternoon. He was right that the swamp was deep in her blood. She couldn't imagine living anyplace else. And she also knew that the swamp was definitely not in Jackson's blood.

In the depths of her heart, she still didn't believe there was a future with Jackson. After Friday night, it was time for her to part ways with him. It would break her heart more than a little bit, but better hurt now than when she was in any deeper with him.

She'd met men at the café with him and then a lot more men at the gala. She now didn't believe that she would be able to identify her attacker through him unless it was one of his friends. But really, what were the odds of that? So, it was time...past time to tell him goodbye.

The afternoon had turned cloudy and gray and when she loaded the fish in her old pickup, it was just after seven o'clock and dark with a false twilight.

She didn't want to think about Jackson anymore tonight. She just needed to focus on the job at hand and not anticipate the heartache that she knew was right around the corner.

The owners of the places she sold her fish to always preferred she wait until after the dinner rush to come by, so it was always late in the evening when she parked outside their kitchens and sold to them.

The first place she went was to the café. She pulled up in front of the back door where light spilled out into the alley and two young men in hairnets stood just outside smoking cigarettes.

Josie got out of the truck and opened her tailgate. "Can one of you guys tell Marie that Josie is out here?"

"Sure." One of them tossed down his cigarette and ground it out with his heel, then disappeared back into the café kitchen.

The fish were displayed in big coolers filled with just enough water to keep them alive. It wasn't long before Marie Boujoulais came outside. The large woman had a plump face, a sweet smile and a shock of white hair.

"Evening, Josie," she said with a big smile. Despite her smiles, Josie knew the older woman had a will of steel. She ran the restaurant with an iron hand, yet everyone who worked for her adored her.

"Evening, Marie. I think you'll be happy with what I have for you tonight. I've got a beauty of a catfish caught fresh this morning, along with more nice fish."

"Let me get a good look at what you have." Marie moved closer to the back of the truck.

Marie had always been very kind to Josie, but she loved to dicker and drove a hard bargain. Still, Josie was a savvy business woman and wasn't about to allow Marie to get one over on her.

It took about fifteen minutes for the two to finally agree on what fish Marie wanted to buy and for how much. The fish were unloaded and then from there, Josie drove to Tremont's.

She once again pulled up to the back kitchen door. It was Joseph Tremont, a dapper older man who owned the restaurant, who came out to buy from her. He never argued over Josie's prices and bought what he wanted.

Finally, the last stop was the grocery store. The back door was located at the top of a shipping dock. Complete darkness had now fallen as she climbed the stairs to go into the back door, which led into a large storeroom.

To the left was the butcher area. It was enclosed in glass and there was a bell for her to ring to get the attention of Ed Moren, the head butcher.

He immediately came out and greeted her

with a wide smile. "It's good to see you, Josie. How are you doing?"

"I can't complain," she replied.

"I'm about out of all my fish supply so I hope you've got plenty for me."

"I've got an ice chest full for you out in my truck," she replied.

"Let me grab a couple of my men and one of our chests and we'll meet you out there," he said.

Minutes later, the fish had been removed from her cooler and she'd been paid. She hurried down the steps to get back to her truck. She was ready to get home before it rained and the scent of rain was definitely in the air.

She had just reached the driver's door when she felt a looming presence behind her. Before she could turn to see who was there, a hard punch slammed into the center of her back. Her breath whooshed out of her and she grabbed the truck door handle to keep from falling to the ground.

Another fist banged into the side of her head, making her brain reel with dizziness as pain seared through her. Wha-what was happening? Who was hitting her? And why? Before he could hit her again, she managed to whirl around. It was a man in a black ski mask, the same man who had chased her through the swamp. Oh, God, what did he want from her? Why was he doing this to her?

Her brain couldn't work properly as terror clutched her. He punched her in her belly and once again all the air left her lungs and she went down to the hot asphalt.

She scooted back from him and at the same time she fumbled to get her knife out. She managed to pull it out and held it out before her. He didn't even hesitate, but kicked her hand and the knife went skittering and spinning away from her.

He booted her in the head once again. A sky full of stars shot off in her vision, momentarily blinding her. He kicked her again in the stomach. Pain seared through her and she felt like she was going to throw up.

God, if she didn't do something quickly, he was going to beat her to death. How did she protect herself against a raging bull? She cast a quick glance around, seeking some kind of help. But the parking lot was empty. There was nobody around to help her.

She finally found her voice and screamed, but the sound was thin and faint amid the sobs of pain that also released from her. She screamed again and this time it was a little bit louder.

He began to pummel her, fists to the side of her face and head in a fury. She screamed over and over again, fearful that he was killing her. Tears of pain blinded her as she moved around on the ground in an effort to get away from him.

She smelled his rage as he continued to hit and kick her. Finally, she curled up in a fetal position in an attempt to survive, but that didn't stop him from the attack.

"Die, you bitch," he growled. "You need to die right now, you swamp scum," he said as he kicked her yet again.

She screamed once more, but it sounded to her ears like a mere whimper.

"Hey...what's going on out there," an unfamiliar voice yelled from the loading dock.

Just as quickly the attack stopped and the sound of running footsteps was the last thing she heard as darkness completely claimed her.

HE RAN AS fast and as furiously as he could away from the parking lot. His heart pounded hard in his chest and his breathing released from him in short deep gasps.

Dammit. He was so ticked off that some damn stocker boy had halted his beatdown on the swamp slut. If he'd had just a few more minutes with her, he would have been able to kill her or at the very least turn her into a vegetable that had to be fed and babbled nothing but nonsense. He could only hope he'd done enough damage to her that she would just die from all her injuries.

It had been a gift from God that he'd been on his way to the grocery store and saw her truck going into the back parking lot.

He'd parked in the front lot and then ran around the store and hid in the deep shadows behind one of the trash dumpsters in the back. He'd watched as she conducted her business with the butcher and then when she'd come back out to leave, he'd pounced on her.

With his first punch, an enormous rage toward her had taken over him. How dare she come out of the swamp and hook up with his best friend. How dare she play in his playground when she should be deep in the swamp where she belonged.

He finally stopped running and leaned against a tree trunk in somebody's dark front yard. He bent over with his hands on his knees to catch his breath and then checked his knuckles to see what kind of damage he had done to himself.

Thankfully, he had big meaty hands and he didn't think they looked too bad despite the numerous times he had hit her. Besides, he had kicked her more than he had punched her.

God, it had felt so good to unload on her. Beating her felt almost as good as that night when he'd encountered her in the swamp.

He began the long trek back through a neighborhood so he could get to the front door of the supermarket. He still had to buy some groceries before heading home.

He hoped it had been enough. He hoped like hell that he'd beaten her hard enough that she would die. He wanted so much for her to be dead. She could destroy his life. But he absolutely couldn't allow that to happen.

If his beatdown of her tonight hadn't killed her, then he'd come up with another plan to assure her death. He entered the grocery store and grabbed a cart. He smiled at one of the checkout girls and then went up the first aisle.

Oh, yeah, one way or another, the swamp slut would never get an opportunity to identify him as her attacker.

JACKSON HAD JUST gotten into bed when his cell phone rang. The caller identification was an unfamiliar number, but he decided to answer it anyway.

"Is this Jackson Fortier?" a feminine voice asked.

"It is," he replied.

"This is Amy Stein, I'm a nurse here at the hospital and we have a patient here who is requesting your presence."

Jackson frowned, wondering if this was some kind of a mix-up. "Uh…who is the patient?"

"Josephine Cadieux."

He shot up in the bed. Josie? "Why is she at the hospital?" A million things raced through his head, none of them good. "What is her condition?"

"I'm sorry, I can't discuss that with you. I was just given instructions and told to let you know that she's asking for you."

"Okay, thank you." Jackson hung up and flew into action. He dressed quickly, grabbed his keys and ran out of his house. As he drove toward the hospital, his nerves were taut and he felt sick to his stomach. What could have possibly happened to her? Why in God's name was she in the hospital and what was her condition?

Had she fallen and broken a bone? Had the Honey Island Swamp Monster attempted to make her his fourth victim and somehow she'd managed to escape from him but was wounded? Jeez, how wounded was she?

At least she'd been able to give them his name, but that hardly made him feel better. Was it an accident that had put her in the hospital or something far more nefarious?

He wheeled into the hospital parking lot, halted his engine and then bolted from the car. He flew into the emergency waiting room and immediately approached the desk. A woman he didn't know was seated behind a glass window. She opened the window and smiled at him. "May I help you?"

"Josephine Cadieux was brought in earlier. A nurse called me and said she was asking for me."

"Ah, yes, you must be Jackson," she replied. "She's in bay three. You can go on back." She punched a button and double doors allowed him to enter into the proper emergency room. There were only four bays inside with curtains hung as a measure of privacy.

The first two bays he passed were empty. He entered the third and stopped in his tracks. She was in the bed and her eyes were closed. An IV was in her wrist and she looked small and frail. He'd never seen her so utterly still and it broke his heart.

He quietly walked over to a chair at the side of the bed and sank down. What was going on? What had happened to her? She turned her head toward him and he saw a darkening on the side of her face. What the hell? It looked like she'd been hit and hit hard.

Her eyes fluttered open. She stared at him for a long moment and then began to cry. "Oh, baby, don't cry." He jumped to his feet and hovered over her, wanting to pull her into his arms but afraid to until he found out what had happened to her and how badly she was hurt.

Instead, he sat back down and scooted his chair closer, then took her hand in his. "Josie... honey, please don't cry."

"Oh, J-Jackson. It...it was so terr-terrible," she said amid her tears.

"What, honey? What was terrible? Tell me what happened to you?" he asked.

At that moment, Dr. Etienne Richards walked into the bay. The doctor greeted Jackson with a friendly nod. The two men had occasionally double-dated in the past and hung out on other social occasions. Josie finally managed to get her tears under control.

"Just as I suspected, Josie, along with the concussion, you have three cracked ribs, but thankfully there doesn't seem to be any other internal damage," he said.

A concussion? Three cracked ribs? "Can somebody please tell me what happened?" Jackson asked.

"Apparently, somebody tried to beat the hell out of Josie at the grocery store this evening," Etienne said.

"What?" Jackson looked from Etienne to Josie.

"He was trying to kill me, Jackson." Tears filled her eyes once again. "I... I swear he wanted to kill me. He...he told me to die wh-while he was beating me."

"Who, honey? Did you see who did this to you?"

"A man in a black ski mask," she replied. Her lips trembled and her eyes darkened.

"Like the man who chased you through the swamp," Jackson replied. His blood boiled at the thought of Josie being hit by anyone. It was now apparent to him that somebody was targeting her specifically. Why?

He had a lot of questions about what had happened tonight, but now wasn't the time to ask them. She was obviously in a lot of pain and now it was time for the doctor to speak.

"I'm going to keep you overnight," he said. "We'll monitor you to make sure there aren't any more issues. Unfortunately, there's nothing I can do about your cracked ribs. They'll just have to heal up on their own. I will give you some pain medicine, but because of your concussion, it will have to be a fairly light dose."

Etienne looked at Jackson. "You can see her tomorrow. I'm going to get her moved to a hospital room and right now, what she needs more than anything is rest and that means no visitors until tomorrow."

Jackson nodded his understanding. While he didn't want to leave her side, he wanted to do what was best for her. He stood and leaned over and gently kissed her forehead. "Josie, I'll see you tomorrow."

"Okay." She released a shuddering deep sigh and closed her eyes.

Jackson motioned for Etienne to step out of the bay with him. He waited to say anything until they were far enough away that Josie wouldn't hear them.

"Were the police called about this?" he asked the doctor.

Etienne nodded. "Officer Ryan Staub was here right before you arrived. He questioned her for a few minutes and then left to go check out the parking lot where she was attacked." He shook his head. "I've got to tell you, Jackson. Somebody really did a number on her and if the attack hadn't been interrupted, I don't even want to think about all the life-threatening injuries she could have suffered."

Jackson's heart squeezed tight as he thought about Josie's pain. He hoped like hell the police caught the person responsible. "What I'm worried about right now is her safety going forward. I know there's no real security here at the hospital, so I'd like to sit outside of her hospital room door for the night. Would you have a problem with that?"

Etienne frowned. "I guess that wouldn't be a

problem, as long as you stay out of her room and let her rest until morning. Jackson, she's been through a tremendous trauma and her mind and body needs a time-out."

"Can you tell me what hospital room you're putting her in?"

"It's going to be room five. It will take us about twenty minutes to get her transferred there."

"Then I'm going to run home real quick and I'll be right back," Jackson replied.

He didn't wait for any more conversation but rather he turned on his heels and hurried out of the emergency room. He drove back home as fast as he could. The first thing he did was make himself a cup of coffee, which he poured into a to-go cup. The second thing he did was grab his gun from his nightstand.

He slid on his holster and put the gun where it belonged and then pulled on a sports jacket to hide the fact that he wore the gun.

He carried his coffee to his car and then headed back to the hospital. As he drove, a million questions roared through his head.

Why had some man targeted Josie? The same person had gone after her twice now. Why would anyone want her dead? Who had stopped the attack? And had they seen something that might lead to the identity of the person who had beaten her?

Gravois and his men better be fully engaged in investigating this. Jackson tightened his hands on the steering wheel. If he caught the creep before he was arrested, he would beat the hell out of the man for hurting Josie. Jackson would make sure the man felt as much pain as Josie had.

His heart squeezed tight as he thought of her condition. He couldn't imagine the pain she must have gone through…must still be going through. How many times had she been hit? How many times had she been kicked? He couldn't imagine a man doing that to any woman. But why Josie?

The thing that bothered him the most was if that man meant to beat her to death, then he hadn't succeeded. That meant he was probably going to try to kill her again.

Not if Jackson could help it. He had a gun and a plan that would assure that nobody got close to Josie a second time.

When he got back to the hospital, he double-checked that his sports coat hid his gun. On the front of the building was a sign that no guns were allowed inside, but there wasn't adequate security here. The creep could just waltz in and find her and try to finish the job he had started.

He walked in through the main entrance and found room five where a folding chair was sitting just outside it.

Before he sat, he peeked inside. She was in the bed and appeared to be asleep. Assured that she was okay, he sank down in the chair and took a sip from his coffee cup.

Again, a thousand questions rolled around in his head, the main recurring one was who was responsible for this? If it was the same man who had chased her through the swamp, then he had to have somehow followed her to find her at the supermarket. Who…and why?

He leaned his head back and released a deep sigh. He was still shocked and angered by the events of the night. It was too late tonight to make any phone calls, but first thing in the morning he intended to phone Gravois to see exactly what was being done.

He also had to remember to call his buddies to cancel tomorrow night. There was no way Josie would be in any shape tomorrow for a social gathering.

In fact, it was going to take her some time to heal. God, he wished he would have been there with her. Then none of this would have ever happened. Thank God her attacker hadn't had a gun or a knife. This thought shot an icy chill up his spine.

He must have fallen asleep for he jerked awake at the sound of somebody coming down the hallway. He relaxed when he saw it was a nurse. She smiled at him and then went into Josie's room. As she went in, Jackson got out of his chair and he stood at the doorway and watched her as she checked Josie's vitals. Once she was finished and had left the room, he relaxed again in the chair.

When he finally opened his eyes for good, it was to daylight creeping through the nearby windows and the sounds of the hospital waking up. He stood and stretched and peeked into the room where Josie still appeared to be sleeping.

He felt surprisingly refreshed, considering that his light sleep had been interrupted several times by hospital staff coming or going down the hallway. He'd have liked a cup of coffee, but he wasn't about to leave his post. Anybody could walk into the hospital and find her. He didn't want to leave her unguarded for a minute.

It was only when a pleasant older woman wheeled in a cart that smelled of breakfast that he followed her into the room. "Here you go, sweetheart," the woman said as she set a tray of food on the table that swung over the bed. "You've got some scrambled eggs and bacon and an orange juice and coffee."

"Thank you," Josie replied. She raised the head of her bed and grimaced slightly.

"I'll be back later for your tray," the woman said and then she left the room.

Jackson sat in the chair next to the bed and eyed her worriedly. The side of her face was definitely bruised and he imagined she was also badly bruised beneath the blue-flowered hospital gown. "Josie…baby, how are you doing this morning?"

"Okay, except I feel like several big trucks ran over me."

"Honey, I'm so sorry this happened to you."

Her eyes flashed darkly. "He was filled with such rage, Jackson. He came at me out of nowhere and beat and kicked me. My knife was no defense at all. The minute I pulled it, he kicked it out of my hand. He kicked and hit me in such a flurry that I couldn't do anything to protect myself."

"Baby, don't think about it right now," he said. "Thank God you survived."

"If it weren't for a stocker who saw what was happening and yelled, I truly don't believe I would have survived. He would have killed me. He would have beat me to death."

"Thank God for that stocker, now eat your breakfast before it gets cold," he said.

She frowned. "I'm really not very hungry."

"Josie, you need to eat to keep up your strength. You have a lot of healing to do."

She picked up her fork and took a bite of her eggs, then took a drink of her orange juice. "You want my coffee? I'm not in the mood for it."

"If you're sure you don't want it, then I'll drink it."

"Go for it," she replied.

He had just taken his first drink of the hot brew when Etienne walked in. "Good morning," he said in greeting and immediately looked at Jackson. "How are you faring after last night?" he asked.

"I'm a little stiff, but I'm all right," Jackson replied.

"Wait…what did you do last night?" Josie asked in obvious confusion.

"He sat outside your door in a folding chair all night," Etienne said. "Now that's what I call devotion."

"Oh, Jackson," she said and tears filled her eyes.

"Hey, it was no big deal. I was just worried about you," he said quickly, not wanting to see her cry. "Please, don't worry about it."

"And how's my patient today?" Etienne asked Josie.

"I've definitely been better," she said. "But I'm ready to go home."

"Whoa, I'm not quite ready to release you yet," Etienne protested. "How about we keep you a little while longer and see how you're doing after lunch today."

"Okay," Josie replied.

"Then let's just do a quick checkup right now." Etienne listened to her heart, used a flashlight to look into her eyes and then left the room.

"As soon as he releases you, I'll take you home, but you aren't going to stay there," Jackson said. "We'll pack up a couple of bags for you and then you're coming to my place to stay while you heal."

"Jackson... I..."

"Please don't argue with me, Josie." He took her hand and squeezed it tight. "Somebody definitely tried to kill you last night and he didn't succeed, which means he'll come after you again. You need a bodyguard and I want that position. I'll make sure nobody hurts you again."

She stared into his eyes and tears filled hers. Was she going to reject his offer? He knew she was not only a strong woman, but a prideful one as well. "Josie, please," he said softly. "If nothing else, do this for me."

"Just for a couple of days while I get my strength back," she finally agreed.

"Good, then it's settled." He squeezed her hand one more time and then released it.

She'd agreed to a couple of days, but he intended to keep her with him until the police
caught the creep that was after her. And after
that, he was hoping to keep her with him forever.

Chapter Eight

It wasn't just the physical pain that had Josie uncomfortable, but it was emotional pain as well. She knew who had attacked her the night before. It was the same man who had raped her months before. She knew that because he had smelled exactly the same and she'd recognized his voice... The voice that had haunted her dreams for what felt like forever.

Once she got settled in at Jackson's, she intended to tell him that. More, she knew it was time she come clean with him about why she'd started her relationship with him in the first place. She knew it was going to hurt him, but he deserved to know the truth before he offered her any more help.

She couldn't believe that he'd sat outside her room all night long. He was obviously worried about her safety. His vigilance through the night touched her heart more deeply than anything had in her entire life.

She now turned on the television to pass the time until the doctor would return and hopefully release her. However, the TV didn't stop them from talking and they had only been talking a few minutes when she saw the gun at Jackson's waist.

"You have a gun?" she asked in surprise although it was a rhetorical question. "Why do you have it here?"

"I was worried about the person who attacked you last night creeping into the hospital to finish the job, so I ran home and got my gun and then came back to sit outside your doorway." His eyes narrowed slightly. "Nobody was going to get into your room last night except hospital staff."

"Jackson, I'll never be able to thank you enough," she said, her heart once again touched by his words and actions.

He cast her one of his gentle smiles. "You don't have to thank me, honey. I don't want you to ever get hurt like this again and I'm here to make sure that nothing else ever happens to you."

They chatted a little bit longer and then she must have fallen asleep.

She was back in time…back to that horrible night. A dark bag fell over her head, half-choking her. Fear shot through her as she was shoved from behind. She was flipped over as if she weighed nothing at all and then soft male hands grabbed hers with the intent to tie her up. No…no! This couldn't be happening.

"Honey… Josie…wake up." The male voice sliced through the nightmare. The soft sweetly familiar voice she knew. She opened her eyes to see Jackson standing over her, a worried expression on his handsome face.

"Oh, I'm sorry… Did…did I scream out?" she asked with embarrassment.

"No, not at all. But it looked and sounded like you weren't enjoying your nap."

"I wasn't. I was having a nightmare." She moved her bed so that she was sitting up once again. "Thank you for waking me. How long was I asleep?"

He sat back down in the chair. "About an hour and a half."

"Really?" She shook her head. "I almost never nap."

"You'll probably be napping a lot in the next couple of days. That's the way your body is going to heal itself." He held her gaze for a long moment. "Josie, I only wish I knew who attacked you, because I'd beat the holy hell out of him for what he did to you."

"Thank you, Jackson. I appreciate the sentiment." She broke the eye contact with him. If she looked into the depths of his eyes for too long, she would cry again. He loved her. She saw it in his beautiful eyes and felt it in his every touch.

He loved her and she thought if she looked deep in her heart, she would realize she was in love with him, too. But she didn't want to love him.

He was from the town and that scared her. She didn't believe a long-term relationship between them would ever work out. She probably didn't have to worry about it anyway because once she told him the truth about why she'd started pursuing him, he'd probably hate her. She'd be surprised if he took her back to his place to heal and she wanted to be at his house more than anything, at least for a little while.

For the first time in her life, she needed somebody. The attack last night had shaken her to her very core and she was more afraid than she'd ever been. And despite everything else that was whirling around in her head, she wanted…she needed Jackson.

"Do you want to talk about your nightmare?" he now asked.

"I don't have them very often and it's always the same thing. I relive the night of the assault against me, but I don't want to talk about that anymore."

"How about we talk about favorite animals. I've always been partial to the aardvark."

She laughed, and then immediately groaned and wrapped her arms around her middle. "Oh, please don't make me laugh. It makes my ribs hurt."

"Sorry," he replied. "The last thing I want to do is make you hurt more than you already do."

They wound up just small-talking until lunch arrived. "Jackson, help me eat this," she said. "You must be starving."

"I'm okay. I'll eat later when we get you settled in at my place."

If he decided to follow through on the plans after she confessed to him.

It wasn't long after lunch when the doctor came back in. He released her with the condition that she stay in bed and rest for the next week to ten days and after that do only what her body allowed her to do.

Jackson stepped out of the room as a nurse came in to help her dress. A shiver of revulsion shot through her as she pulled on the short-sleeved blouse that was now ripped and dirty. Her jeans had fared better, but were filthy from the scuffle on the parking lot asphalt.

She left the room armed with a handful of paperwork, a prescription for pain meds and a deep dread of what was to come with Jackson.

He cast her a big smile as she walked out of the room. "Okay, toots, let's blow this joint," he said and took her hand in his. "While you were dressing, I pulled my car up front so you won't have to walk too far."

"Thank you," she replied. She was definitely grateful, for every step she took shot pain throughout her body. In fact, just drawing too deep a breath caused her ribs to scream in protest. When she'd dressed, she noticed all kinds of bruises all over her.

She eased down into the passenger seat of his car and released a deep tired sigh. The first thing they did was drive through the pharmacy to get her pain meds and then he headed to Vincent's parking lot so they could go to her place to pack a few things.

Aside from her physical pain, with each mile that passed, her nerves jangled louder and louder inside her. Jackson had always been so very kind to her, among other things, and she knew what she was going to tell him would hurt him and probably hurt him deep. But it was now necessary to come clean to him. Her conscience couldn't hold it in any longer.

When they reached Vincent's, he parked the car and then hurried around to her side to help her out. "I wish I could carry you in, Josie. I wish you didn't even have to go to your place."

"But I do," she replied. She forced a reassuring smile to her lips. "I'll be fine, Jackson. We're just going to have to walk very slowly."

"That's no problem for me," he replied.

Together they entered the tangled growth and forged ahead. She went slowly, each step shooting pain through her. She fought back tears as she realized just how weak and injured she felt.

By the time they reached her shanty, she collapsed on the sofa in exhaustion and pain. Jackson sank down beside her. "Baby, is there anything I can do for you?" he asked, his blue eyes filled with concern.

"No, thanks. I just need a couple of minutes to rest before we head back out," she replied. *If* she left with him, she reminded herself.

"Take all the time you need," he said. "What you do need to do as soon as possible is take one of those pain pills and crawl into a nice soft bed."

"That sounds like heaven right now. But before I can do that, we need to have a talk," she said. Dread built up inside her and pressed tight against her chest.

"Okay…a talk about what?" He looked at her curiously.

"I know the person who attacked me last

night. It was the same man who raped me." She looked away from him. "I told you he was somebody from the swamp, but he's not. He's a person from town."

"How do you know that?" he asked, obviously surprised.

She looked back at him. "I know because he has soft hands. Nobody who lives and works in the swamp has hands like that. And I also know because of the way he smells. He smells of expensive cologne. It's a scent of balsam and patchouli. I'll never ever forget it. And both times I heard his voice."

He gazed at her in open confusion. "Then why did you tell me it was somebody from the swamp?"

She released a deep sigh, hating what she was going to tell him next. "Jackson, you know that as somebody from the swamp, I was never going to be in a place to identify him if he was from town. I wasn't welcome in the places where he would be."

Once again, she looked away from him, her heart beating a million miles a minute. "You were like a gift from God, dropped right into the swamp for me."

She gazed back at him. "I started dating you because you were absolutely perfect. I hoped you would take me to those places where I could find my assailant."

The shine in his eyes dimmed. "So basically, you've been using me all along." The hurt in his eyes twisted her heart. Why had she even decided he needed to know this? She should have just broken up with him and never let him know the truth.

"Oh, Jackson, I won't lie. I started out with the intention to use you, but then I grew to care for you and I wanted to spend time with you no matter what we did together. It...you became more than just catching my assailant."

It was true, he had dug himself deep into her heart but eventually she knew she had to let him go. "I'm sorry, Jackson, but I was using you." She reached out and placed her hand on his arm as tears filled her eyes. "I'm so very sorry." A deep sob escaped her.

"Don't cry, Josie. It will only make you hurt more," he replied on a deep sigh. "I just want to know why you decided to tell me all of this right now?"

She swallowed hard against her tears. "I didn't want the lie to be between us anymore. I care about you deeply and I thought you had the right to know."

"So, now you've told me and I think you

should go pack a bag before you get more tired and in pain."

"Are you sure you still want me to go with you?"

"Josie, I care about you very much and of course I still want you to go with me. We'll get you healed up and then I'll help you find the man who assaulted you. Now go, get a bag or whatever you need to be away for a while."

She got up from the sofa and then hurried to her bedroom. Once there, she sank down on the side of her bed and began to cry again.

This time the tears were because of Jackson's never-ending kindness to her, his willingness to take her in despite the fact that she had just told him she had been using him.

Her emotional pain right now was almost as bad as her physical pain, but she pulled herself together and went to her closet. She grabbed a large duffel bag and began to pack what she thought she'd need for a couple days away.

It didn't take long for her to finish. She then went into the bathroom and added her toiletries to the bag. Once that was done, she carried it out into the living room.

Jackson immediately jumped up from the sofa and took the bag from her. "All ready?"

"More ready than you know." She should feel guilty again for going to his place to heal. But she'd never felt so physically and emotionally broken. She also felt more vulnerable than she ever had in her life.

The man who had raped her months ago had tried to kill her last night. There was no doubt he'd wanted her dead. Somehow, she had threatened him. He had to have seen her around town with Jackson and knew she'd entered his world. He wanted to make sure he remained hidden and she jeopardized that.

Together, they left her place. He was unusually quiet and she wondered just how badly she had hurt him. She couldn't think about it now. Maybe it was good she had told him. Maybe this would redefine their relationship so that when the end finally did come, neither of them would be hurt.

By THE TIME they reached his car to go home, Jackson was still trying to process what she had confessed to him. Had it all been a lie?

Had her laughter with him been forced? Had the deep conversations they'd shared only been a bore to her all along? Had the passionate kisses they had shared only been an act on her part?

The fact that Josie needed him now didn't escape him. She was hurt and needed him to help care for her. He'd be there for her because despite what she'd told him, he still loved her and he knew the next few days would be rough ones for her.

He glanced over to her now. She had her head back and her eyes closed. The vivid bruise on the side of her face made his heart squeeze tight and a deep anger rose up inside him. He still couldn't believe somebody had attacked her with such force.

According to her, it had been the same man who had raped her…a man from town. She obviously hadn't run into him on the night of the gala, otherwise she would have identified him.

Maybe what Jackson needed to do now was sit and write a list of everyone she'd encountered at the party and write down all the men who hadn't been there. It would be a daunting task, but he was determined to help her find the person who haunted her dreams and gave her nightmares. He was determined to help find the man who had tried to kill her.

He pulled in and parked at his place. "Josie, we're here."

She straightened up and released a weary sigh. Together, they got out of the car. He grabbed her bag from the back seat and then they headed toward the front door.

"I want you to go in and get relaxed," he said as he unlocked the door.

"Before I do anything, I'd like a shower. I feel dirty. I still feel like his hands are all over me," she replied.

"I'm so sorry, Josie. We can definitely arrange a shower," he replied. He led her toward his guest room and set her bag on the foot of the bed. "Why don't you give me your pain pills and I'll bring you one with a glass of water."

"That sounds wonderful," she replied. Her face was unnaturally pale, her features taut and it was obvious she was in a lot of pain.

She gave him the pill bottle and he took it into the kitchen where he shook one of them out, got a glass of water and then carried them both back to her.

She took the pill and then handed him back the glass. "Thank you." Her gaze held his. "Jackson, thank you for all of this." Tears filled her eyes.

He placed a gentle hand on her shoulder. "Go take your shower and we'll get you settled in. You can use the shower in the bathroom across the hall. Towels are in the linen closet and there is soap there and shampoo under the sink."

"I can't wait to get out of these clothes," she said. "And to feel clean again," she added as she headed to the bathroom. Once she disappeared, he went back into his bedroom and grabbed an extra pillow, a navy throw blanket and a clean sheet.

He carried them all into the living room where he made up a bed on the sofa in case she wanted to rest here instead of in the bedroom. Surely, she wouldn't want to spend all day and all night alone in the bedroom.

He then sank down in the chair opposite the sofa and tried to turn off his whirling thoughts. But it was impossible. Had she always only seen him as a stooge to use? There was no question that his heart hurt a lot, but that hadn't stopped him from wanting to care for her while she was so hurt.

Still, he found himself second-guessing each and every moment the two of them had spent together. Was it possible she'd never really cared for him at all? Was she still just using him?

It didn't take her long in the shower and then she came out wearing black leggings and an oversize blue T-shirt. She still looked pale and weary with pain.

He stood. "Josie, I thought since it's still so early you might want to rest out here, but if you're ready to get into bed, I'll help you turn down the covers."

"No, I'd really like to sit out here with you."

"I don't want you sitting. You need to lie

down and as you can see I've got the sofa waiting for you," he replied.

She nodded and stretched out. When she was prone, he covered her up with the blanket and she released a deep sigh. "I'll never be able to thank you enough, Jackson."

He returned to his chair. "Josie, you don't have to keep thanking me. I'm doing this because I want to and because I think you need somebody right now."

"I hate that I'm so weak. I've always been a strong woman who didn't need anyone," she said angrily. "I hate who I am right now."

"I'm assuming you've never been beaten up before," he replied.

"Never. No man has ever laid a hand on me until this man. I think he must have seen me with you and it worried him. That's why he attacked me last night."

"That means he thinks you're getting closer to identifying him, although it pisses me off that being seen with me got you beat up. That also means somebody I know is a rapist." He frowned at that thought. Who could it be?

She didn't say anything in reply. "Why don't we stop talking about all this and I'll put on a movie or something that will let you rest your mind a bit. Or maybe you just prefer the silence," he said.

"A movie would be nice," she replied. "I don't get a chance to watch television or see any movies at home."

He found a movie that he had seen before and that he thought she might enjoy. He turned it on and then settled back in his chair.

Within fifteen minutes, she had fallen asleep. He quietly got up and went into the kitchen. It was going to be dinnertime soon and he decided rather than cooking a big meal, he would fix her a bowl of chicken soup. If she wanted something else, he would figure it out when she woke up. He could always order something and have it delivered.

He then went back into his bedroom, where his voice wouldn't wake her, to call his friends and tell them that tomorrow's gathering wasn't going to happen. They were all shocked at what had happened to Josie and each of them sent her their best.

He returned to the chair in the living room, his thoughts still on his group of friends. Was it possible one of those men was Josie's assailant?

He simply couldn't believe it. There was no way. He knew those men. Brian was happily married and Sonny could probably sleep with any single woman in town. He might have considered Lee because of the man's anger right now, but at the time the attack had occurred Lee had had no idea his marriage was over.

Still, they were three men she hadn't met yet. He'd be glad when she did get to meet them so they could be excluded from the list of potential suspects. The very idea of any one of them being guilty made him feel sick to his stomach.

With that thought in mind, he got up once again and went into the kitchen where a built-in desk held his laptop on the top and in the drawer several notebooks and pens. He grabbed one of the notebooks and pens and then returned to his chair in the living room.

While she was still sleeping, he began to write down the names of all the men who had been at the gala. He believed her attacker had to be of his social status. He was certain the blue-collar workers in town didn't wear expensive cologne or have soft hands.

He'd written down about fifteen names when Josie stirred and came awake. "Hey, sleepy-head," he said.

"I can't believe I fell asleep again," she said.

"I imagine that pain pill had something to do with it," he replied. "Besides, sleep is good for you right now." He set the notebook and his pen on the end table next to his chair. "It's about dinnertime. I was thinking maybe a bowl of chicken noodle soup might sound good to you. My mother always told me it was not only good for the soul but also had magical healing power."

She cast him a faint smile. "Then how can I possibly turn it down?" She sat up and slid her legs off the sofa. "What can I do to help?"

"First of all, we didn't go over the rules of your stay here with me before you went to sleep," he said.

"The rules?" She looked at him in obvious confusion.

"The rules are you stay down and I wait on you hand and foot. Now get back down and I'll have your dinner ready in just a few minutes," he said.

He got up from the chair and hurried to the kitchen where the two cans of the soup awaited him on the countertop. He poured one of the cans in a bowl for her and the second one in a bowl for himself.

As they microwaved, he got out a tray and crackers and spoons. Once the soup was hot, he filled the tray with the bowls and crackers and then carried it back into the living room where he set it on the coffee table.

"What would you like to drink?" he asked. He couldn't help but notice how beautiful she looked despite having just awakened. Her hair was tousled and she wore no makeup, but that only added to her attractiveness. The only thing he hated to see was the dark bruise on the side of her face.

"Nothing to drink for me," she replied. "The soup looks good."

"Yeah, I worked on it all afternoon. The most difficult issue was finding a chicken and when I finally found one, I had to sweet-talk it into my arms without it knowing I was going to stick it in a pot."

A burst of laughter escaped her and she immediately held her sides. "Oh, Jackson, you are good for my soul."

Did she mean that or was she just sweet-talking him because she needed him right now? He shoved the thought out of his head. He couldn't focus on things like that right now, otherwise he'd make himself go crazy.

When they were finished eating, he took the dishes back to the kitchen and put them in the dishwasher and the crackers back into his pantry.

He then returned to the living room. He switched the television to a show for them to watch and the evening hours went by quickly.

It was about eight thirty when she indicated she was ready to go to bed. He went back into the bedroom with her and turned down the bed as she went across the hall and into the bathroom.

He flipped on the small lamp on the night-stand and she reentered the room clad in a sleeveless light blue nightgown that fell to her knees. As she swept past him, he caught her scent, that ever-present evocative fragrance of floral and fauna and mysterious spices.

"Get into bed and I'll bring you another pill," he said.

She nodded and he turned and hurried back to the kitchen where he got a pain pill and a glass of water.

She took the pill and then settled back in the bed and released a deep sigh. "You can turn off the lamp whenever you're ready," he said and moved back to the doorway. "If you need anything at all through the night, don't hesitate to wake me. Otherwise, I'll just see you in the morning."

"Good night, Jackson."

"Sleep well, Josie."

He left her room and went back into the living room. He watched television for another hour or so and then shut it off, made sure the place was locked up tight and then headed for his own room.

The light in her room was still on but she was once again sleeping. He stood at the threshold of the room and simply gazed at her. His love for her ached deep inside him. He no longer knew what to do with the emotion, because he had no idea what she really felt about him.

He finally walked into his bedroom and sank down on the edge of his bed. Her confession about why she had been interested in him in the first place rang in his ears and through his heart.

She'd said she'd grown to care about him, but how much? And was that even true? He had a feeling he'd better hold on to his heart. It was time he figured out how to stop loving Josie.

Chapter Nine

Josie awakened to the scent of bacon and with pain rocking through her entire body. She remained in bed for several long minutes, grateful that Jackson was apparently fixing breakfast and would have a pain pill for her.

Thankfully, she had slept without dreams, but the sleep hadn't left her feeling well-rested and refreshed. In fact, she hurt more this morning than she had the day before.

She finally pulled herself out of the bed, grabbed a pair of shorts and a T-shirt from her bag along with her toiletry case and then went across the hall to the bathroom.

She changed her clothes, brushed her teeth and hair, and then ready to face the day she headed for the kitchen. Every step she took was still painful. Although most of the beating had been to her head and stomach, her whole body ached.

"Good morning," Jackson greeted her cheerfully when she stepped into the kitchen.

"Good morning to you," she replied and sank down on one of the chairs at the table.

"Coffee?" he asked.

"Please, and a pain pill would be great," she replied.

"Coming right up." He got her the coffee and pill and then returned to the stove and began removing bacon strips from the skillet.

"I certainly don't want to get dependent on this medication," she said after taking one of the pills.

"Give yourself a break, Josie. You only got out of the hospital yesterday and right now you need them," he replied. He looked very handsome this morning in a pair of jeans and a royal blue T-shirt that reminded her he had a very hot physique.

"Now, tell me how you like your eggs," he said as he got the eggs out of the fridge. "How about a nice cheese and mushroom omelet?"

"That sounds wonderful," she replied. "I didn't know you were such a man of many talents. When did you learn to cook?"

"My mom is a great cook and she made sure I knew my way around the kitchen by the time I was a teenager. She told me it was a survival skill that every man should know."

"Your mother is obviously a smart woman," she replied. She sipped her coffee and watched as he prepared the omelet, along with toast.

Once the large omelet was done, he cut it in half, placed each half on separate plates and set them, along with bacon and toast, on the table.

"This is delicious," she said after taking her first couple of bites.

"Good, I'm glad you like it. How did you sleep?" he asked.

"I slept like a baby," she replied. "The bed is very comfortable."

"Good, I'm glad you slept well." His gaze was so warm, so caring as it lingered on her. How could he look at her that way after what she had confessed to him?

She broke the eye contact and focused on eating again. "You know, I've been thinking about the list of potential suspects," he said after a few moments, drawing her attention back to him and away from her plate.

"What about them?" she asked.

"Yesterday while you were napping, I started writing down all the names of the men you met at the gala and then I thought about it after I went to bed last night and realized I probably don't have to worry about the married men in town."

She frowned at him. "And why is that?"

"I would assume that most married men are having intimate relationships with their wives and so wouldn't need to go out and seek sex anywhere else."

She set the piece of toast she was about to bite into back on her plate and released a small laugh. "Oh, Jackson, rape isn't about sex."

He looked at her in obvious confusion. "If it's not about sex, then what's it about?"

"Power," she replied. "It's all about power and control. That's what a rapist gets off on. It's about overpowering a woman and taking away her choices. The sex really has very little to do with it."

"I never really thought about it that way before, but now that you told me that, I guess it makes sense. So, my list will include both single and married men."

"Sounds like a lot of work," she said.

"I don't consider it work at all. Just call me Sherlock Holmes. I'm determined to find this guy for you, Josie. He needs to be in jail for what he's done to you."

She reached up and touched the side of her face. Her bruise looked worse today than it had yesterday. It was a vivid purple and ached relentlessly.

"You wear the color well," he said.

"Purple has always been one of my favorite

colors," she replied dryly. She picked up the piece of toast once again and for the next few minutes they ate the breakfast in silence. When they were finished eating, he insisted she go back to the sofa and relax.

For the next three days, they fell into an easy routine. He fixed her meals and when she wasn't eating in the kitchen with him, she was on the sofa.

They shared long talks and watched movies together. She napped in the afternoons, unable to help herself. However, the naps got shorter when she quit taking her pain pills and started to feel a little better. The one thing they didn't discuss was their feelings for one another.

She thought she sensed a little distance coming from him, but she couldn't be sure. He was still very attentive and determined to take care of her and if he had distanced himself a little from her, she certainly understood why.

The better she felt, the more she wanted him to take her in his arms and tell her he forgave her and to assure her that she was forever safe from the man who hunted her.

She so wanted the warmth of his close embrace, and if she were perfectly honest with herself, she wanted to see the flames of desire back in his eyes as he gazed at her.

She knew her emotions were all over the

place where he was concerned. At this point, she was trying not to overthink things. The best thing she could do was finish healing up and get back to the swamp. Surely, in the swamp she would be able to think more clearly about everything.

Meanwhile Jackson had continued making the list of all the men she'd met at the gala and had moved on to making a list of all the men she had yet to meet in town.

It was just a little after seven in the evening of the fourth day that she'd been at his place when Gravois showed up. Jackson led the lawman into the living room where Josie was on the sofa.

Josie knew that Jackson had called the man several times over the past couple of days but each time he'd been told that Gravois was unavailable.

She sat up so he could sit on the other end of the sofa while Jackson sat back in his chair. "Just the man I've been wanting to talk to," Jackson said once they were all settled.

"I'm sorry I haven't contacted you sooner." He looked at Josie. "And, Josie, I hope you are feeling better."

"How is she supposed to feel any better when there's somebody out there who wants to kill her? Somebody who tried to beat her to death just a couple of nights ago?" Jackson asked, his voice deep with a touch of anger. "I hope to hell you brought us some news about the assault."

"Unfortunately, I have no news for you. I spoke to Mac Aris, the stocker who stopped the attack, but the only thing he saw was a man running away from the scene," Gravois said. "He described him as medium height and weight and clad all in black, but could tell us nothing more specific. He was the only witness I could find and without a better description, there isn't much I can do. I'm sorry I don't have better news."

"Did you and your men go over the parking lot where this happened?" Jackson asked.

"We went over every inch of it, hoping that the perpetrator might have dropped something that would lead to his identity, but we found nothing except trash," Gravois replied. "Like I said, I'm sorry I don't have anything for you, but it isn't like we didn't try."

"And I guess you never had anything for Josie when she was raped." Once again, Jackson's voice held a tightly suppressed but discernable anger.

Gravois looked at him in surprise. "That was a long time ago."

"I remember it as if it were yesterday," she said, finding her voice for the first time since Gravois had arrived.

"What exactly did you do when Josie came to you and told you she'd been assaulted that time?" Jackson asked.

"Well, I did the best I could to investigate it," Gravois replied defensively.

"And what exactly did that investigation entail," Jackson pressed as she eyed the man with distaste.

"Well…uh… I would have to go over my notes about that," he replied, obviously flustered by the question. "I just came over now to check in on Josie and update the two of you." He stood, obviously eager now to leave.

Jackson got up as well and walked Gravois to the front door. Josie remained sitting up and exhaled a deep breath of resentment.

Did she believe Gravois had done everything possible to catch the man who had beaten her? The answer was no. Did she believe the man had done anything to investigate her rape? Absolutely not. He hadn't even asked for her clothing to collect DNA.

She heard Jackson's and Gravois's voices coming from the entryway, but they were only a deep mumbling as she was too far away to hear their exact words.

Not that any of it mattered. Gravois wasn't about to change his lazy ways, not for a mere swamp slut. She'd told him that night when she'd gone to the police station that she was certain her assailant was a man from town and Gravois wasn't about to arrest one of his own.

She heard the front door close and then Jackson came back into the room. "I'd love to see that man leave town and never come back," he said as he sank back down in his chair. "As soon as all of this is over, I'm leading a recall effort to get him out of office for good. He's nothing but a disgrace and it's past time for him to go."

She was surprised that Jackson's anger warmed her inside. She knew it was on her behalf and that he was fighting for justice for her. In fact, over the last couple of days, a desire for him had built up inside her. As her body healed, it yearned for something more… It yearned for him.

His scent was everywhere in the house, on the blanket she used to nap on the sofa, on the sheets she slept on each night. It was a redolent smell of clean masculinity and ocean fresh air. It was a smell that made her feel safe and protected and welled up a desire for him that she couldn't deny.

For the next few minutes, he talked to her about what was needed to get Gravois out of office. "Who would take his place?" she asked curiously.

"We would have to have a special election

and it depends on who runs for the position." He frowned. "I think the whole department stinks. Gravois told me before he left that he had placed ads in the Shreveport and New Orleans papers seeking a new hire for the department. Maybe a new guy coming in fresh will make a good chief of police."

"It would be nice if he came in with no prejudices and gave equal justice to the townspeople and to the people who live in the swamps," she replied.

"We're not going to put up with anything else but that," he replied firmly.

She offered him a smile. "You've become quite a justice warrior."

He returned her smile. "Thanks to you. You've opened my eyes to a lot of things, Josie. What was acceptable before is no longer acceptable now. There has to be changes made."

For a long moment, their gazes remained locked and in the depths of his beautiful blue eyes she saw a flickering flame that called to a heat that filled her.

He broke the eye contact and picked up the remote for the television. "Ready to watch something?"

She didn't want to watch television. She wanted Jackson to take her into his arms and kiss her until she was mindless. She wanted him to make love to her. Her body, soul and mind were ready for it to happen tonight.

"Actually, I'm ready for bed," she said and got up from the sofa. Her heart took on an accelerated rhythm. He immediately got up from his chair. Each night when she'd gone to bed, he'd walked her to the bedroom door to tell her good-night.

Together, they went down the hallway and when they reached the door, she turned back to face him. "Good night, Josie," he said. "I hope you sleep well."

She took a step closer to him, her heart now thundering in her chest. Since she'd told him that initially she'd been using him, maybe he wouldn't want her anymore. But she definitely wanted him right now.

"Jackson, I told you I was ready for bed, but the last thing on my mind is sleep." She took another step toward him, now standing so close to him their bodies almost touched.

"Josie." Her name fell from his lips on a whispered sigh as the fire in his eyes ignited.

"I want you, Jackson," she said boldly.

"Josie, you're hurt," he replied faintly.

"I'm better now, Jackson, and I want to make love with you." She reached her arms up and placed them on his shoulders. With a small groan, he gently pulled her into his embrace. "Kiss me, Jackson," she whispered softly. "Please kiss me."

He touched his lips to hers in a tender kiss that not only stirred her desire for him, but also touched her very heart. She deepened the kiss, dipping her tongue in to swirl with his.

The kiss went on for several long moments, and then she broke the embrace, grabbed his hand and led him into the bedroom. The lamp next to the bed was on, creating a small golden pool of illumination that couldn't begin to compete with the flames that burned in his eyes... the flames that burned deep inside her.

Once they were by the bed, she stepped back from him and pulled the T-shirt she wore over her head. She tossed it to the floor next to them and then moved back into his arms.

This time when he kissed her, she tasted his wild hunger for her and that only stoked the flames of want higher inside her. His warm hands caressed the bare skin of her back, shooting shivers of delight through her.

Despite her excitement, she felt safe...so wonderfully safe in his arms. There were no alarm bells ringing in her head, no hint of a flashback or anything to stop her from the physical act of making love with Jackson.

They finally broke apart and she reached behind her and unfastened her bra. It fell to the floor in front of her. "Oh, Josie, you are so beautiful," he said softly.

"I want to feel your naked chest next to mine," she said. Once again, she stepped close to him and began to unbutton his shirt. She held his gaze as her hands undressed him. The intense eye contact felt almost as intimate as the actual act of lovemaking.

Once his shirt was unbuttoned, she shoved it off his broad shoulders and it fell to the floor behind him. His chest was magnificent, firmly muscled and solid.

He stood before her yet made no move to touch her in any way. It was then she realized he was allowing her to take the lead. The fact that he was thinking about her despite his own physical desire once again touched her heart deeply.

She slid her shorts down her legs and then, clad only in her panties, she got into the bed. He hesitated only a moment and then took off the slacks he'd been wearing, leaving him wearing only a pair of black boxers. He joined her beneath the sheets and their bodies came together as he took her lips with his in a searing kiss.

His bare skin felt wonderful against her own and as his hands cupped her breasts, she wanted more…so much more. She rolled over on her back as his lips left her mouth and slid down her neck in nipping kisses.

Finally, his mouth reached one of her nipples. He licked and sucked, creating a coil of electricity that raced from her breasts to the very center of her.

She was quickly lost in him…in them. As he continued to give attention to her nipples, she ran her hands from his rich soft hair down his back, loving the play of his hard muscles beneath his soft skin.

He moved one hand down to her stomach and then stopped, as if hesitant to go any farther. "Touch me, Jackson," she whispered breathlessly. "It's okay. I want you to touch me everywhere."

He released a groan at her words and his hand slid farther down her stomach. He reached the top of her panties and ran his hand from one side to the other and back again, teasing and tormenting her. He finally touched her where she most wanted, moving his fingers to dance over the silk of her panties.

She gasped as sheer pleasure rocked through her, but it still wasn't enough for her. She pushed against him and he immediately stopped what he was doing. She shoved her panties down and kicked them off, then pulled him back toward her.

This time when he touched her, wild sensations sparked through her and shot a growing tension that had her panting for release. Higher and higher she climbed, and when that release finally came, she cried out his name in deep gasps.

Still, even then, she wanted more from him. She plucked at his boxers, wanting them off him. He complied and took them off and she pushed him on his back. He was fully aroused and she encircled him with her hand, loving the pulsating hardness of him.

"Josie, you're driving me wild," he said with a deep groan.

In answer, she crawled on top of him and once in position, she then lowered herself onto him. He groaned again and she moaned with pleasure. For several long moments she didn't move, simply reveling in the way he filled her up so completely.

When she did finally move, his hands held onto her hips as she rose up and down on his hard length. Once again, their gazes locked as they shared the utter intimacy of the moment.

She pumped up and down, faster and faster as a new tension inside her rose higher and higher. Her climax slammed into her at the same time he cried out her name and found his own release.

She collapsed on her back next to him, unable to speak as she waited for her breathing to return to normal. He was also catching his breath and neither of them spoke for several long moments.

He then rolled to his side facing her. "Are you okay?" he asked with a touch of concern in his voice.

She smiled at him. "I'm more than okay."

He reached out and gently shoved a strand of her hair away from her cheek. "You're an amazing woman, Josie."

"This amazing woman will be right back," she replied and rolled out of the bed. She grabbed her nightgown and hurried into the bathroom across the hall.

She hadn't thought she would ever make love again. She'd believed that part of her had been stolen away from her, taken in a single night of violence.

She knew without a doubt that Jackson was the reason she'd found her desire again. It had been his kindness, his tenderness and the wealth of love that shone from his eyes that had made her feel safe enough to go there again.

Pulling her nightgown over her head, the press of tears burned at her eyes. She swallowed hard against them and then left the bathroom.

Jackson wasn't in the bedroom. His boxers were missing from the floor so she assumed he'd gone back to the bathroom in his bedroom.

She got back into the bed and a moment later he appeared in the doorway. She hadn't wanted to bask in the afterglow of their lovemaking and she didn't want to spend the rest of the night with him holding her.

She didn't want his arms around her or his breathing to mingle with hers as she drifted off to sleep. It would be far too painful for her to have those memories.

He remained at the threshold, obviously waiting for her to invite him back in. "Jackson, if you don't mind, I'd like to sleep alone."

"Of course," he replied instantly. "Josie...did I hurt you?"

"Not at all, but I'm still a bit achy and just prefer to be alone to finish out the night."

"Then I'll just say good-night and I'll see you in the morning," he replied.

"Good night, Jackson." The minute he was gone from the doorway, she reached out and turned off the lamp. The room was dark except for the faint moonlight that shone through the window.

The tears that had burned at her eyes in the bathroom now seeped out once again. She wished she could have let him come back into the bedroom to sleep with her, but as crazy as it sounded after what they had just shared, she hadn't wanted the memory of falling asleep in his arms. What had happened tonight had been wonderful, but she could never ever allow it to happen again.

As much as she loved Jackson and as much as he thought he loved her, she knew once she was completely back on her feet, it was time for her to return to the swamp where she belonged.

If she continued in the relationship, there was no doubt in her mind that he would hurt her. Eventually the novelty of dating a woman from the swamp would wear off. He'd begin to notice the differences between them and not how alike they were. It was possible over time that the peer pressure of the prejudice in town would begin to weigh on him.

He was from the town and there was no doubt in her mind that ultimately he'd go back to the town to find his forever love. A deep sob escaped her and she rolled over to bury her face in the pillow as she began to weep.

For the first time in her life, Josie almost wished she wasn't from the swamp and that only made her cry harder.

Chapter Ten

Jackson awoke early, his thoughts immediately filled with the woman in the other bedroom. Making love with her had been more wonderful than he'd even dreamed. He certainly hadn't expected it to happen last night. She'd been so passionate and giving and he didn't think he could love her any more.

Surely, she loved him, too. Surely, she wouldn't share the intimate act of lovemaking with him if she didn't love him at least a little bit. But he was almost afraid to believe anything about her feelings toward him.

All he could do was be there for her until they caught the man who wanted her dead. There would be time for him to tell her how he felt about her later. With this thought in mind, he got out of bed and hurried into the bathroom for a shower.

Maybe if she was feeling well enough, they'd go to Tremont's for lunch. If there was any man inside the restaurant that she hadn't met at the gala, then he would introduce her to him.

In fact, it would probably be good for them to dine there for lunch and dinner every day. If Josie was right, and it was possible her assailant was from Jackson's social network, then eventually he would show up at Tremont's.

Once he'd showered, he pulled on a pair of black slacks and a short-sleeved black and gray shirt and then he headed for the kitchen. Maybe she'd like some French toast this morning. He had no idea if she liked the dish or not, but he was betting that she did.

The first thing he did was start the coffee brewing and while it worked, he got out the dishes he would need to make the French toast. He also set the table with two plates and the required silverware.

By that time, he was able to pour himself a cup of coffee and then he sank down at the table to wait for her to get up. He liked the look of two plates. He loved having her here in his home with him. She fit. Despite the differences of where they came from, he believed they were meant to be together.

However, once again he was completely confused by her. She'd already confessed she'd only been using him when they first began to see each other. Was she still just using him? There was no question she'd needed somebody after being attacked.

She still wanted to catch her assailant and he was her ticket into the world where she needed to be. Had she made love to him last night just to keep him on the hook?

That thought shot a deep pain through him. He'd been looking for love for a very long time. He'd always wanted to be married and share his life with a special woman. He'd found that woman in Josie. But was he the man for her? Or was he just a man of convenience for her right now? Was he just a fool?

He shoved these troubling thoughts aside and stared out the nearby window where the sun was just beginning to peek up over the horizon. He still hoped to arrange a night when his buddies could come over to meet Josie. It was Wednesday now—maybe she would feel up to it by Saturday night.

He was halfway through his second cup of coffee when she walked into the kitchen. It was obvious she had just showered. Her hair was still damp and she brought with her the scent of soap and shampoo mingling with the fragrance that was hers alone.

"Good morning," he said and quickly jumped up out of the chair.

"Good morning to you," she replied.

"Have a seat and I'll pour you coffee."

"You're spoiling me, Jackson," she said as he got a cup down from the cabinet and went to the coffee maker.

"You deserve to be spoiled," he replied and set the hot brew in front of her. "I was thinking French toast for breakfast. How does that sound?"

"It sounds delicious."

He was aware of her gaze on him as he started preparing their breakfast. "How did you sleep?" he asked.

"I slept okay. What about you?"

"Like a baby," he replied. He whipped the egg yolks and added milk, wondering if they needed to talk about what they had shared the night before. He decided to wait to see if she brought it up.

Within minutes, breakfast was on the table. While they ate, she was quiet and appeared to be deep in her own thoughts. They were almost finished when he finally broke the silence.

"The bruise on your face is almost gone," he observed.

"Overall, I'm feeling much better and I think it's time for me to go." Her gaze didn't quite meet his.

"Go where?" he asked in surprise.

"Back to my place," she replied.

"Josie, look at me," he said softly, wondering what on earth was going through her mind. Slowly, her dark eyes met his. "Honey, what are you thinking? Somebody is trying to kill you and now isn't the time for you to leave here. I can only thank God that when he encountered you in that parking lot, he didn't have a gun or a knife."

He reached across the table and took one of her hands in his. "In fact, I was just thinking this morning that our next course of action should be to spend lots of time at Tremont's. I believe relatively soon, the man we're looking for will come in there to eat or drink."

He squeezed her hand. "Please don't give up now, Josie. I believe we're so close to finding this guy."

She stared at him for a long moment and then slowly nodded her head. "Okay, I'll stay another day or so," she relented. "Now let me help you clean up the dishes."

A few more days? Had last night meant absolutely nothing to her? Was she so eager to escape him now that she would prefer to face a killer all alone? Damn, could she confuse him any further?

Don't get into your head too much, a small voice whispered inside his brain. In the end,

he had very little control over the situation...
over her.

All he could do at this point was work as hard
as he could to introduce her to as many men as
possible. He now had about a one-week deadline to catch the man who had tried to kill Josie.

"By the way," he said as they went into the
living room, "I thought since you were feeling
better, I'd plan on Saturday night to have my
friends over. How do you feel about that?"

"That would be fine," she replied. She sank
down on the sofa and he sat in his chair.

"And how about lunch today at Tremont's?"

She immediately frowned. "I really don't
have the clothes to go there."

"Honey, you rock a pair of leggings and any
top you put on. You'll be fine no matter what
you wear," he replied. "Besides, look at it this
way, we're partners and we're on a secret mission to catch a potential killer."

"Okay then, I'm in," she replied.

They agreed on eleven o'clock for lunch and
then she excused herself and went into her bedroom. He immediately got on the phone to call
his buddies and set up things for Saturday night.
He got hold of everyone and it all fell into place.
After that, he went into his office to check on
emails and updates on several projects he was
involved in.

When he was finished with all that, he went back into his bedroom and pulled on his gun holster and gun and then grabbed a lightweight casual sports coat and carried it back into the living room. Once there, he pulled on the sports coat over his gun. He wasn't about to go out in public with Josie without his weapon for defense.

Josie remained in her room until quarter to eleven and then she came back into the living room. She was clad in black leggings and a short-sleeved black and white blouse.

"You look gorgeous, Josie," he said.

"Thank you, but I don't feel very gorgeous right now. I threw this blouse into my suitcase to bring here because it was comfortable, not because it was particularly stylish."

"Well, whatever the reason, it looks very good on you," he replied. A flashback of her naked and on top of him suddenly shot through his mind. It instantly evoked a new desire for her, a reminder of the depth of love he had for her in his heart…in his very soul.

"Shall we go?" he asked. Once again, he had to remind himself that she was the one in control. If she didn't love him, then he would just have to figure out how to live without her.

It was precisely noon when they arrived at the restaurant. He was pleased to see that the parking lot was fairly full. His nerves began to tighten all his muscles.

Was it possible that today would be the day they'd find Josie's attacker? Would it be somebody Jackson had shared drinks with? Would it be somebody he'd sat across a lunch table from?

As they walked in, his gaze went to the bar to see who was sitting there. All six men who occupied the seats there had been at the gala and Josie had already met them.

As the hostess seated them at a two-top toward the back, he checked the diners to see who Josie hadn't yet met. He stopped briefly at a booth where Patrick James and his wife sat.

Patrick was a young guy who worked at the bank. Jackson had done business with him several times in the past and he didn't remember seeing them at the gala. "Hey, Patrick, good to see you," Jackson now said to the man.

"Jackson, good to see you, too," he replied. "You remember my wife, Brianna."

"I do, and this is Josie Cadieux."

"Nice to meet you both," Josie said.

"We missed you at the big gala," Jackson said.

"Yeah, we were sorry to miss it but Brianna wasn't feeling well that night," Patrick said. "But there will be other galas."

"That's for sure. And now we'll just leave you to enjoy your meal," Jackson said.

Moments later, Jackson and Josie were seated. "Not him?" Jackson asked.

"Not him," Josie confirmed. "I'll never forget the sound of his voice." She released a deep sigh. "I feel like we're looking for a needle in a haystack."

"But the haystack is getting smaller and smaller," he replied, wanting to chase the darkness out of her eyes.

"It would help if I believed Gravois was doing a real investigation into everything," she said. "And if he's not interested in my case, then I wish he would do more to catch the swamp monster."

"At least he's looking to hire some new people. Maybe fresh eyes on that case will result in it finally being solved," he replied.

"That would definitely be great. I worry every day that it's just a matter of time before another swamp woman will be killed."

"I hate to tell you this, Josie, but right now all my attention and energy is on you and what's happening in your life," he said.

At that moment, the waitress appeared to take their orders. They both ordered club sandwiches and sweet tea to drink. "Josie, I don't want you to go home until after we catch the guy who tried to kill you," he said once their meals arrived. "I don't care if it takes a week or a month. As long as you're with me, you'll be safe."

"Jackson, you brought me back to your house to heal, and I've done that," she replied.

"That's true, but I also brought you to my house to protect you from harm and I still want to protect you," he stressed. "Josie, please consider staying with me until we catch this guy."

She frowned and dragged one of her French fries through a pool of ketchup on her place. "I'll consider it," she finally said. "But, sooner or later I need to go home. What happens if we never catch this guy?"

"I believe we will," he replied with determination. "If we have to go door-to-door and have each man talk to us so you can recognize his voice, then that's what we'll do."

She smiled at him. "I'm not sure what I did in a previous life to deserve you, Jackson."

"Honestly, Josie, it's just the opposite. You've already changed my life for the positive in so many ways. I look at things so differently because of you and you've made me a much better man."

"This conversation has gotten way too serious for a lunch date," she replied with an uncomfortable laugh.

"You're right. So, let's talk about favorite animals. I'm personally drawn to the aardvark." He knew he'd make her laugh and she did.

From that point on, the conversation was lighter, but as they talked and enjoyed the food, he kept scanning the crowd for men she hadn't met.

They were almost finished eating when Sonny came in. He had Loretta Hannity, his latest in a long string of girlfriends, by his side.

Jackson motioned to him and the two headed toward them. "Josie, this is my buddy, Sonny Landry and his friend Loretta Hannity," he said.

"Josie, it's great to finally meet you," Sonny said. "I've heard so much about you."

"I've heard a lot about you, too," Josie replied with a smile.

"I'm sure it was all lies," Sonny returned with a laugh.

"Loretta, don't let this guy lead you into trouble," Jackson said.

"Don't worry, I'm trying to keep him out of trouble," Loretta said with a small laugh. "Josie, it's nice meeting you," she added.

"You, too," Josie replied.

"I guess we'll see you guys on Saturday night," Sonny said.

"We're looking forward to it," Jackson said.

The two moved on to their seats and Jackson

looked at Josie intently. "Not him?" he asked, half holding his breath.

"Not him," she replied.

He released a relieved sigh. The last thing he'd want to find out was that one of his close friends was Josie's monster. The only other man he saw that Josie hadn't met on the night of the gala was dependent on a walker. There was no way he was the man they sought.

"We'll come back for dinner," he said once they were in the car and headed back to his place.

"I intend to pay you back for all the meals out," Josie said. "I have cash at my place to repay you."

"You know I don't care about the money, Josie. I have more money than I'll ever spend in my lifetime. I'm not worried about the cost of eating out."

"I care," she replied. "You should know by now that I pay my own way, Jackson."

"As you wish," he finally said. He had forgotten that she was such a proud woman, something he admired in her.

They got back home and settled in for an afternoon of movie watching. They still hadn't spoken about what had happened between them the night before. It was obvious she didn't feel the need to discuss it. Was that because it had meant nothing to her?

Eventually when she went back home, would they resume the same relationship they'd had before all this happened? Could that even happen? He missed sitting on that fallen tree trunk in the swamp and talking to her about everything and nothing.

Would they be able to go back to that time where they were building their relationship? Could they recapture the innocence of that time in their lives? His worse fear was that she would go back to the swamp and never want to see him again.

JOSIE TRIED TO focus on the comedy movie that was playing on the television, but her head was filled with questions that churned around and around.

Was it really possible that they'd come across her attacker by dining at Tremont's? Would it... could it be that easy? What if the man didn't eat there? The mission they were on suddenly felt totally futile.

And then there was the fact that she was continuing to lead Jackson on, letting him believe there might be a relationship between them after this was over...if it was ever over.

The absolute worst thing she could have done

was make love with him. She'd allowed her desire for him to override her good sense. She was sure it had given him hope that they would be a couple after this was all over. Still, even knowing that, she was glad she'd had the opportunity to share such intimacy with him.

She would keep the memory of him forever in her mind...in her heart. In the evenings when the bullfrogs sang their deep-throated songs and the soft waves of the water rhythmically slapped against the shanty, when a deep loneliness swept through her soul, she would remember the town man who came into the swamp and loved her for a little while.

"I thought we'd head back to Tremont's for dinner about five," Jackson said, breaking the silence that had built up between them.

"This all feels so futile," she replied and turned to look at him. "Jackson, what if he never comes in to Tremont's to eat? What if you're just wasting all this money and time and I'm never able to identify this man?" She was aware her frustration, her anger at the situation was rife in her voice.

"Josie, I know this is all very upsetting to you. But you promised me, at the very least, that you would give this a week. We're getting together with my friends on Saturday night and after that we'll see where we are and how we move for-

ward, okay?" His gaze caressed her with softness that instantly soothed some of the anger
that had momentarily gripped her.

"That gives us tonight, tomorrow and Friday
to eat at Tremont's," he continued. "These are
the busiest times at the restaurant. So, are you
still with me?" This time there was a soft plead-
ing in his eyes.

"Okay, I'm still in," she finally replied. She
feared going back home, knowing there was
somebody out there who wanted her dead, but
she also feared staying here with Jackson and
falling deeper and deeper in love with him.

When it was close to when they were leaving
for dinner, she went back into her bedroom to
change her blouse from the one she'd worn at
lunchtime to something different.

When she'd packed to leave the swamp, all
that had been on her mind was bringing with
her the most comfortable clothing she had. She
definitely hadn't thrown in any special blouses
for dining out at a fancy restaurant.

She found another top that would be adequate
and shook it in an attempt to get most of the
wrinkles out. She now believed they were chasing the moon, set on an impossible quest that
would only expend their energy and hopes.

Still, she had given Jackson a week or so, and
she would stand by her word. She'd never bro-

ken a promise in her life and the last thing she wanted to do was break a promise she'd made to Jackson. But there was no question it would be difficult to continue to stay here with him.

She found herself wanting him again. She wanted his big strong arms to hold her close. She'd never felt as safe as she did with him. When she was in his embrace, all the ugliness of the outside world melted away and there was only him and his soft blue eyes.

One more week and she'd be back in the swamp. At least she knew the man who was after her didn't know the location of her shanty. She'd wait a couple of weeks before she attempted to sell her fish again. She wouldn't venture out of the shanty for a while.

She knew that Jackson would continue to put pressure on Gravois when she was gone, but there was no way they'd find the man without her. If the creep did find her shanty, she'd just have to make sure she was ready to fight for her life.

When she was finished dressing, she returned to the living room where Jackson was waiting for her. He smiled at her…that soft smile that always stirred her on so many levels inside.

"As always, you look positively beautiful," he said.

She frowned and plucked at the front of the

blouse. "I don't feel very beautiful. I certainly don't feel like I'm ready to walk into a fancy restaurant for dinner."

"What are you worried about, Josie? That a bunch of bigots might judge you?"

His words made her laugh. "You're right. I don't give a damn about how people talk about me." The laughter died on her lips. "But I do worry on your account."

"Well, don't. I don't give a damn how people talk about me, either." He took her by the arm. "Now, let's go have a nice dinner together."

For some reason, tonight felt different. It felt more like a date than a mission. As they drove there, Jackson kept the conversation light and entertaining, and she found herself relaxing and just enjoying his company.

By the time they were seated at a booth inside the restaurant, some of her tension had returned and twisted tight in the pit of her stomach.

She looked around and recognized most of the men inside. She noticed Jackson gazing at their fellow diners as well. The two men she didn't recognize were too old to have given her the kind of beatdown she'd received. Jackson must have thought they were too old as well for he didn't say anything about introducing them to her.

When the waitress arrived, he ordered the

steak and she got the baked fish. Once their meals had been served, their conversation continued to be light and easy, but his gaze on her was intent and filled with a flirtatious sparkle.

As they ate, his gaze also continued to scan the crowd, making her remember the real reason they were here. She prayed they'd find the guy tonight. Then tomorrow she would be able to return to her life in the swamp before Jackson had ever entered into it.

However, it didn't happen. When they left the restaurant two hours later, a wave of hopelessness swept through her. Once again, she felt as if they were just wasting their time and energy.

"Stop it, Josie," he said softly when they were in the car and headed back to his place.

She looked at him in surprise. "Stop what?"

"Stop doubting the process and falling down into a dark hole," he said.

"How do you know that's what I'm doing?"

He flashed her a quick smile. "Because I know you and I've learned some of your moods. Josie, I know how badly you want to find this man. Okay, so we came up empty-handed today, but I have hope that we'll get him tomorrow."

"Have you always been such a wide-eyed optimist?" she asked curiously.

He hesitated a moment before replying. "I never thought about it before, but yes, I've pretty much always seen the glass half-full. I think that's the way you saw the world before all of this happened to you."

He pulled into the driveway, stopped the engine and then turned in the seat to look at her. "Josie, I desperately want to give your life back to you…the one where you didn't have a worry in the world and didn't have to live looking over your shoulder. I… I want to be the hero in this story. I want to be your hero."

"Oh, Jackson." She reached out and stroked the side of his beautiful face. "You are my hero in so many ways." She dropped her hand. "Never feel like you haven't been my hero."

He slowly nodded and then together they got out of the car and went inside. She sank down on the sofa and he sat in his chair. "Whew, I think I ate too much," she said, hoping to lighten the mood once again.

"Yeah, me, too," he agreed. "But I always eat too much when I go to Tremont's. The food there is very good."

"I know my fish tonight was excellent," she replied.

"So, want to watch a little television before bedtime?" he asked.

"Sure."

Minutes later, they were watching a crime drama that immediately intrigued her. It was good to focus on somebody else's drama for an hour or two instead of being consumed by thoughts of her own.

"I would have sworn the killer was the nephew," she said once the show was over. "It was shocking to find out her own brother killed her."

"Yeah, I was surprised, too. I was leaning toward the boyfriend being the guilty party," Jackson replied.

She grinned at her. "Then that proves it. We both stink at solving a murder."

He laughed. "This just proves that we stink at solving this particular case. I refuse to wear a loser badge over this. Do you want to watch one more and see if we do any better?"

"Sure," she agreed.

He turned on another hour-long crime show and once again she lost herself in the drama playing out on the screen.

She didn't want to think about the fact that a man wanted her dead. She also didn't want to think about the heartache that she knew was in her future where Jackson was concerned.

In just a couple of days, she would leave here and she knew she would probably never see Jackson again.

Chapter Eleven

Jackson was almost as upset as Josie was as they came home from the restaurant on Thursday night. It had been another futile night. He'd introduced her to three more men she hadn't met at the gala, but unfortunately none of them had been the one they sought.

His biggest fear was that she intended to leave his place and her potential killer would still be out there plotting and planning on how he could get close to her, on how he could murder her.

They now sat in his living room, once again watching television. But despite the entertaining comedy that played on the screen, he couldn't keep his gaze away from her.

His love for her positively ached inside him. He knew her plans were probably to leave here and go home on Sunday and he dreaded when that time came.

He couldn't imagine how empty the house would feel, how very empty his life would feel without her in it. But he had known all along that eventually his time with her would run out and she would have to go home. He just didn't want her to go.

He now glanced at her once again. She was clad in a pair of navy leggings and a red and navy blouse. Her hair fell around her shoulders in a veil of silky darkness and he wanted nothing else than to reach out and stroke her beautiful hair.

Still, it was so much more than just her physical beauty he would miss. He would miss her sharp wit and intelligence. He was going to miss their long conversations and shared laughter.

What he hoped was they would continue their relationship when she went home. Her making love with him the other night had given him new hope that they could get through everything and still have a wonderful future together.

His only hope right now was that tomorrow they would identify her attacker. Tremont's was always super busy on Fridays, not so much at lunchtime, but the place rocked with people on Friday evenings.

Surely, her attacker would come in then to eat and socialize. Jackson had made reservations to assure that he and Josie would have a table or booth waiting for them when they arrived.

"I'm looking forward to Saturday night," he said during a commercial.

She turned and smiled at him. "So am I. I'm looking forward to meeting these hooligans you call your best friends."

He laughed. "I'll have you know that we've all grown out of the hooligan days of our past."

"Ha, I'll be the judge of that after Saturday night," she replied.

"Hopefully by Saturday night we will have identified your attacker and all will be well. I have a good feeling about tomorrow night. I think he'll show up for dinner at the restaurant and then Saturday night we'll have a big celebration because he's in jail."

The laughter that had momentarily lit her eyes darkened. "I'd like that but I'm certainly not getting my hopes up too high."

It didn't happen at lunch on Friday and all Jackson could hold onto was the fact that it had to happen at dinner. Josie was quiet Friday afternoon when they got back to the house after lunch.

He didn't know what to say to her to keep her hopes up because he was having trouble holding onto his own. He was desperate to keep her here as long as any danger surrounded her. But he was also aware that she was a strong-minded woman who would do what she wanted and if she wanted to go back to the swamp, then there was absolutely nothing he could do about it.

It was on the local news that another young woman from the swamp had been killed by the murderer that everyone called the Honey Island Swamp Monster.

Her body was found in the alley behind the bank. According to the report, she was stabbed to death and her throat and face were ripped out by a claw of some sort. The injuries were so bad they had yet to make an identification of her.

"Dammit," Jackson said as he hit pause on the television. "I was hoping this wouldn't happen again until Gravois and his team caught the monster."

"Like that's really going to happen," Josie replied derisively. "He's never going to catch anyone for anything."

"I just can't figure out how this murderer is getting away without leaving a single clue behind," he said. "These are obviously heinous crimes with plenty of blood. How is this monster getting away without leaving behind a footprint or something?"

"Who knows," Josie replied.

"I'll give it a couple of days and then I'm going to be all over that man's ass again," Jackson said as a rich anger rocked through him. "He didn't help you when you first went to him, he's done nothing since somebody tried to kill you and now this, another poor woman dead."

"I wonder if he knows who the Honey Island monster is and I also wonder if he knows who's after me."

Jackson looked at her in surprise. "What do you mean? Why would you wonder that?"

She shrugged. "I think both men are from town and I wonder if he's protecting somebody he knows. He's made it pretty clear that he doesn't really care about the people in the swamp."

"I know Gravois is lazy and prejudiced, but I can't imagine him covering for such a vicious killer as the Honey Island Swamp Monster."

"We may have to agree to disagree on that," she replied. She frowned. "I wonder if I knew her, if she was one of my friends."

"If that's the case, then I'm sorry for your loss," he said softly.

Her comment about Gravois stayed in his mind the remainder of the afternoon. Was it possible that the lawman was covering up for somebody? Maybe one of his wealthy friends? He didn't think a lot of Gravois, but he didn't want to believe the man was capable of that.

Would Gravois allow somebody to kill Josie? Was it possible he knew who attacked her but he didn't want to identify the person because he was a friend of the lawman? If Jackson found out that was true, then he'd not only see the man out of his office, but he'd do everything in his power to see him in jail for a very long time to come.

It was about four o'clock when Josie got up off the sofa. "Do you happen to own an ironing board and iron?" she asked.

"Actually, I do." He got up from his chair. "They're in my bedroom. I'll go get them for you."

"Thanks, the blouse I'm wearing tonight is all wrinkled from being stuffed in the bottom of my bag. It could definitely use the lick of a hot iron."

She stood close to him as he set the board up in her bedroom. As always, her nearness stoked a flame deep inside him. His heartbeat accelerated and all he wanted to do was take her in his arms and repeat what they had shared together before.

He plugged in the iron and then, to leave the room, he had to walk close to her once again. He stopped in front of her, his love burning hot in his lungs and in every fiber of his being.

"Josie, I… I want to kiss you," he said, his voice husky with his desire.

"I… I'd like that," she whispered.

He gathered her into his arms and took her

lips with his in a tender kiss that held all the love for her that burned in his heart. She raised her arms around his neck and leaned into him.

It was Josie who deepened the kiss, sneaking her tongue into his mouth to swirl with his. He tightened his arms around her, wanting…needing to hold her close forever.

However, it was also Josie who broke off the kiss and took a step back from him. "Thanks for the iron," she said, her gaze not quite meeting his.

"No problem," he replied, his desire for her still burning hot through his veins.

"I should be ready to go in about half an hour. Does that work?"

"Perfect," he replied. "Then I'll just get out of here and let you get ready."

He left the room and she closed the door after him. He went back into the living room and paced the floor, waiting for some of his sexual tension to pass. He was wound so tight he felt like he might explode. The woman utterly confused him. Her kisses said one thing, but her mouth and actions said something else altogether.

He was surprised when a knock fell on his door. Maybe it was Gravois with some good news for a change. Or maybe it was somebody else with a more nefarious intent. He grabbed his gun from the end table just to be on the safe side and then went to the door.

He looked through his peephole and then unlocked the door and pulled it open. "Hey, buddy, what are you doing here? The party is tomorrow night."

"More importantly, what are you doing? Give me that before you shoot all your toes off." Brian grabbed the gun from Jackson. "And I know the party is tomorrow night, but I stopped by to tell you we can't come. The wife had made plans that she neglected to tell me about until this morning."

"Well, come on in and sit for a few. You can at least meet Josie."

Brian followed him into the living room where he sank down on the sofa and placed the gun on the end table next to him. "So, where is the lady of the hour?"

"She's getting dressed. We're going to Tremont's tonight for dinner." Jackson sat in his chair facing his friend. "It seems like forever since I last saw you. What's up in your life these days?"

"Oh, Cynthia has been keeping me busy around the house. She's decided our place needs a total remodel and she's driving me more than a little bit crazy."

Jackson laughed. "I know Cynthia is hard-headed. She always was. I remember even in high school she ran you around in circles."

"You don't know the half of it," Brian replied with a deep sigh.

"Do you want a drink?" Jackson asked.

"Sure, I wouldn't mind a small shot of whiskey."

Jackson got up from the chair. "Coming right up." He went to the bar and poured the shot and then carried it back to Brian.

"Thanks," Brian replied. "So, how are things going with you? I was sorry to hear about Josie getting beat up. I heard that it was pretty bad."

"Somebody tried to kill her, Brian, and that somebody is still out there somewhere," Jackson said. "That's why she's been staying with me. I'm trying to protect her and keep her alive."

"So, Gravois doesn't have any clue as to who it might have been?" Brian asked.

"Of course, he doesn't. He doesn't know where his own ass is on most days," Jackson replied scornfully. "And now I heard this afternoon on the news that he has another murder on his watch."

"The woman from the swamp, yeah, I heard about it on the morning news." Brian shook his head. "It's too damn bad."

"Yeah, and Gravois is probably sitting on his

ass in his office and doing as little as possible about it."

"I heard yesterday he's hired some special private investigator to come in and work on the Honey Island monster murders."

"I hope you're right because somebody needs to be investigating those murders for real," Jackson replied. "If he hired somebody, then it would be the first smart thing he's done since he's been in office."

"You got that right." Brian swallowed his shot and then set the empty glass down on the coffee table.

"Want another?" Jackson asked.

"I'd love one, but I better not. I'm driving and I've got a lot to do when I get back home. Cynthia wants me to take the kids to the park so she can have a little time to herself."

"Well, that should be fun," Jackson replied.

"Yeah, I always enjoy having father time with them."

"I can't wait until I have some kids of my own," Jackson replied.

"I'm sure you'll be a good dad."

Jackson smiled at his friend. "Josie should be out here any minute now. I'm really eager for you to meet her."

Brian returned the smile. "After all the things

you've said about her, I'm definitely eager to meet her, too."

The two continued to visit for several more minutes and then heard the sound of the bedroom door opening. Brian stood, as did Jackson as Josie entered the room.

She looked utterly lovely clad in a pair of navy leggings and a tunic-style red blouse. The color emphasized the darkness of her hair, which fell rich and shiny across her shoulders.

Her features radiated surprise that they had a guest, but she offered a friendly smile at Brian. "Josie, this is my good friend Brian Miller," Jackson said. "And Brian, this is Josie Cadieux."

"Nice to officially meet you, Josie," Brian said.

Josie's smile froze on her face as she stared at him. "You," she finally said in a mere whisper.

Jackson looked at her and then gazed back at his good friend in stunned surprise. What? What was happening here? Brian?

"You're the man who raped me...the man who beat me," Josie said, her voice trembling with emotion. "It's him, Jackson. I swear it's him."

"Brian?" Once again, Jackson stared at Brian. Surely, there was some kind of mistake here. Surely, this couldn't be true.

"Oh, Josie. I was so hoping you wouldn't

be able to identify me," Brian said. "But this changes everything." He picked up Jackson's gun from the end table and pointed it at her.

JOSIE FELT AS if all the blood had left her body. The moment she heard his voice, she knew with a certainty that it was him. As she stared at the man who had raped her...the man who had nearly beaten her to death and now had Jackson's gun in his hand, icy chills raced up her spine.

"Brian, what in the hell are you doing?" Jackson asked with obvious surprise. "Put the gun down and talk to me."

"Sorry, I can't do that, Jackson," he replied.

"Is this all true? Did you rape Josie? Are you the one who tried to kill her?"

Brian ignored Jackson and instead motioned to Josie. "Move over there next to Jackson," he said.

She didn't move. She couldn't. Her body was frozen in place. Imminent danger snapped in the air and she couldn't even breathe. "Move," Brian yelled. He turned the gun on Jackson. "Move or I shoot him right now."

That snapped the inertia that had momentarily gripped her body. She quickly stepped over to stand next to Jackson. Oh, God, she had brought this danger into his life. What did

Brian have in mind? She knew he intended to kill her, but what about Jackson? What did he intend for him?

"Brian, what the hell?" Jackson now said, obviously upset.

"It's all true, Jackson, but it wasn't my fault," Brian said. "Cynthia had been ragging on me all day long and that night I'd had enough. I was filled with an enormous rage and I decided to go to the swamp and take the first woman I found. That woman just happened to be Josie."

She could feel Jackson's rage growing. She felt it in the tenseness of his body next to hers. She heard it in his heavy, erratic breathing.

"How in the hell did I know you were going to hook up with a piece of swamp trash," Brian continued. "Jackson, I can't let her ruin my life. She'll ruin my marriage and my reputation. I've worked too damn hard and long for it all to be ruined by swamp trash." Once again, Brian's voice was strident.

"You brought her into our world, Jackson, and that was your big mistake. Now I have to take care of both of you."

"What does that even mean, Brian?" Jackson asked. "What do you intend to do now?"

"It will be tragic…a murder/suicide," Brian said, once again making chills shoot through her. "You made it easy for me by handing over your gun to me. It will be the weapon that Josie kills you with and then blows her own brains out. It will be a cautionary tale for men who want to hook up with the swamp and invite that stink into their lives and people will talk about it for years to come."

A murder/suicide? Josie's brain worked hard to wrap around what was happening right now. She stared at Brian in horror. A murder/suicide? That meant he not only intended to kill her, but Jackson as well.

"Brian, think about it. I'm your good friend… one of your very best friends." Jackson took a step toward the man. "We have always had each other's backs. I'll help you get through this. We'll get you the best attorney that money can buy."

Brian laughed, the sound utterly maniacal. "I don't need an attorney because there's only three of us who know about this, and two of us are going to be dead."

"Don't hurt Jackson," Josie said as tears filled her eyes. "Please…he has nothing to do with any of this. He's innocent and he doesn't deserve to die." A deep sob escaped her. Her tears weren't for herself but rather for Jackson, who had only been good and loving toward her.

"Kill me, but please leave him alone," she continued frantically. "Shoot me, you can tell the police it was an accident. Jackson will cover for you, he's one of your best friends."

"You stupid whore, he's crazy in love with you. He's not going to cover for me," Brian half shouted. His face was red and sweat had begun to shine on his forehead.

"So, what's your plan, Brian?" Jackson asked, his voice surprisingly cool and calm in the madness that surrounded them. "Are you going to shoot me first, or Josie first?" Jackson took another step closer to the gunman. "How exactly is this going to go down? You might be many things, Brian, but you aren't a cold-blooded killer."

"Yes, I am," Brian replied. "You have no idea what I'm capable of. I enjoyed beating her, Jackson. I enjoyed hitting and kicking her as hard as I could."

At that moment, Jackson launched himself toward Brian. He smashed into Brian's chest. The gun fired off as the two men fell to the floor.

Josie screamed and, as the gun skittered across the floor, she picked it up. "Stop it," she shrieked. When the men continued to grapple with each other, she fired the gun into the ground.

Both men stopped fighting. Brian got to his feet and Jackson rose to his knees. "Watch him, Josie," Jackson said as he did a quick pat down of Brian. He found Brian's gun in his pocket and tossed it so it slid across the floor and landed at Josie's feet.

She kicked it behind her, her sole focus on the man who had stolen what wasn't his to take from her. She was vaguely aware of Jackson sitting back down on the floor and taking his cell phone from his pocket.

"You don't want to shoot me, Josie," Brian said smoothly as he took a small step toward her. "You aren't a killer."

"Stay where you are," she warned. "You have no idea what I'm capable of," she said, throwing his words back at him. "I promise you, there's nothing more I'd like to do than shoot you for all you've done to me."

Her eyes narrowed and it was just her and the man who had tried to kill her. "If I could, I would stomp on your head and kick you in the ribs until they all broke, but since I can't do all that, I'd be more than happy to shoot you."

For the first time since she'd entered the living room, Brian looked afraid. "Josie, the police are on their way." Jackson's voice filtered through to her brain.

"As slow as Gravois is, I still have time to kill him," she replied.

"Please…please don't," Brian said as he raised

his arms up in the air in surrender. "Please, Josie, I… I have two small children."

"You were going to kill us and then take them to a playground to play. You're sick, Brian," Jackson said.

"Were you thinking of your children when you dropped that bag over my head? Were you thinking of them when you pushed me down to the ground?" she half screamed as she remembered all the details of the assault.

"Please, I'm sorry. I'm so sorry about everything," Brian replied with a whimper. "I told you it wasn't my fault. It just…just happened. Please, Josie, don't shoot me."

The sound of sirens filled the air. Myriad emotions raced through her. He disgusted her. Just looking at him made her feel sick to her stomach.

There was a part of her that wanted to kill him, but there was a saner part of her that knew he'd be facing his own living hell in the weeks and months to come.

Within minutes, Gravois and two of his officers burst into the townhouse. He stopped short and looked at the scene.

"Thank God you're here," Brian exclaimed. "They called me over here and accused me of raping Josie and trying to beat her up, but it wasn't me." He pointed a finger at Josie. "That crazy bitch is threatening to kill me."

"He did it," Josie said. "He did it, Gravois, and he came here to kill us so nobody would ever know it was him, so nobody would tell the truth about him."

"Gravois, what Josie says is true," Jackson said from his seat on the floor. "He came here to kill us and he shot me with my own damn gun. Arrest him, Gravois. He's a rapist and an attempted murderer."

As Jackson's words filtered through her overworked brain, she shot him a surprised look and suddenly noticed a pool of blood coming from a wound someplace on his left side. He'd been shot? Oh, God, Jackson had been shot?

She couldn't tell exactly where he'd been shot and where all the blood was coming from, but the sight of it terrified her.

"Oh, Jackson," she cried. Her heart squeezed so tight she could scarcely breathe. "Get an ambulance," she shouted. She handed the gun to Gravois and then ran to Jackson's side and began to cry in earnest.

"How bad is it?" she asked amid her sobs. "I'm sorry, Jackson. I'm so sorry. I never meant for you to get hurt. This wasn't supposed to happen."

"I know that, honey." He smiled at her, but

she saw the pain deep in his eyes. She took his hand in hers and squeezed it tight. He looked over to where Gravois was placing Brian in handcuffs.

"They're both lying," Brian yelled. "They're both crazy. Listen to me, Gravois."

"You can tell it to the judge," Gravois replied. With Brian handcuffed, he nodded to one of the patrolmen. "Take him out and lock him in the backseat of my car."

"Just let me go," Brian appealed. "Please, I'm innocent. They're both lying. You'll be sorry about this, Gravois. I have a lot of money and power in this town."

"You'll have nothing when this news gets out," Jackson replied in obvious disgust.

Brian continued to profess his innocence as he was led out of Jackson's house. By that time, the ambulance had arrived and two paramedics pushed in a gurney.

Josie's head was still spinning and she continued to cry as they loaded up Jackson and swept him away. She wanted to go with him to find out how badly he was wounded, but Gravois told her she needed to stay there to be questioned.

An hour or so later, she had told the lawman everything that had occurred from the moment she had recognized Brian's voice. Afterward, Gravois agreed to take her to the hospital where he also needed to find out about Jackson's gunshot wound. Although more than anything she wanted to get to Jackson, she also wanted to give Gravois all the information he needed to keep Brian under arrest.

Once she was in Gravois's car, all her thoughts about Jackson filled her head. Had Brian halfway succeeded in his plan? Had Jackson's gunshot wound been a fatal one? Once again, her heart constricted so much she could scarcely draw a breath.

Jackson couldn't die. She prayed that he was going to be okay. If he did die, then his death was on her hands. First of all, she'd used him and then she'd invited danger and death into his life. Oh, God, he couldn't die.

When they reached the hospital, she bolted from the car and hurried inside to the emergency room desk. "Jackson Fortier," she blurted out. "He was just brought in with a gunshot wound. I... I need to talk to somebody. I need to know how he's doing."

"And you are?" the nurse at the desk asked.

"Josie... Josephine Cadieux," she said.

Gravois came up behind her. "And I need to speak to the doctor in charge of his case."

"I'll let the doctor know you are both here," she replied. She stood and disappeared through a doorway. She returned only moments later.

"He said for you both to have a seat and he'll be out when he can."

Josie turned and then sank down in one of the green plastic chairs. Gravois sat down next to her. "I never would have believed this of Brian. He's always appeared to be a fine, upstanding family man."

"I guess you can never know what's in the minds and hearts of people," she replied.

"Why didn't you shoot him?" Gravois asked curiously. "You had the gun in your hand. Before we arrived, why didn't you just pop him one?"

"Trust me, I thought about it long and hard. But first of all, it would be me stooping down to his level and second of all, his death by my hands would have been a deep stain on my very soul."

They fell silent after that. The minutes ticked by agonizingly slow. What was taking so long? Oh, God, how badly had he been hurt? She didn't even know where the bullet had hit him. Had it hit his heart? His lungs? Had it been a deadly shot?

She leaned her head back and once again prayed that he was going to be all right. It was about an hour later when Dr. Etienne Richards came out to speak to them.

Josie jumped out of her chair. "How is he?"

"He was very lucky. The bullet traveled in and out of his upper outer thigh. It was a clean shot that involved no further muscle damage. I've got it cleaned up and stitched and I've given him some pain meds. I intend to keep him for the night but, barring any complications, he should go home tomorrow."

Josie released a shuddery sigh of relief. Thank God it hadn't been worse. Thank God he was going to be just fine.

"Can I see him?" Gravois asked.

Etienne frowned. "I gave him enough pain meds to let him sleep. Can't your questions wait until tomorrow morning?"

"I suppose they can," Gravois said. "I'll be back in the morning."

"Can you do me a favor?" Josie asked the lawman.

"What's that?" he asked.

"Can you take me to Vincent's parking lot?"

"I suppose I can do that," he replied.

"I would really appreciate it." Minutes later, she was in the passenger seat of his patrol car and headed to Vincent's.

It was over. Finally, her bogeyman had finally been caught and she was no longer in any danger. It was all over. Jackson was going to be fine and now it was time for her to end it all.

The kindest thing she could do for Jackson

was disappear from his life. He could then find a woman from his social standing to marry.

Yes, it was time for her to leave him. It was time she went back to the swamp where she belonged.

Chapter Twelve

Jackson opened his eyes, momentarily disoriented as to where he was and what the time was. As he looked around his surroundings, it all came rushing back to him.

He remembered everything that had happened with Brian. Brian... He still couldn't believe his good friend had shown up at his house with the intent of killing both him and Josie. He couldn't believe he was responsible for everything that had happened to her.

Brian's betrayal stung deeply. He'd known him since they were boys. When had his friend turned into a monster? When had Brian become capable of all the things he had done?

For God's sake, he'd plotted a murder/suicide when he came to Jackson's house. And Jackson had made it half easy for him by allowing Brian to get a hold of his gun.

Thank God things had gone down as they had and Jackson had come out of it with only a wound to his thigh. Hopefully, Brian would go to prison for a very long time for all the crimes he'd committed and the ones he'd intended to commit.

Josie. Where was she right now? He hoped she was at his place, waiting for him to come home. She was free now…free of any fear, free of all the danger. They could now have a life not looking over their shoulders. Hopefully, she'd tell him she was in love with him and they could plan a future together.

He moved his leg and winced as pain shot through him. Thankfully, the bullet had gone in his thigh and not through his heart. He knew he had taken a chance in rushing at Brian, but there had been no way he was going to allow the man to harm Josie. Brian crowing about how much he'd enjoyed beating Josie had been the catalyst that shot an uncontrollable anger through Jackson and he'd made his move.

He'd only been awake a little while when an older woman pushed a cart in with his breakfast. He was happy to see it since he'd missed dinner the night before.

He turned on the television and then ate the scrambled eggs and bacon that was on the plate. He sipped his coffee and had just eaten a cup of fruit when Etienne walked in.

"Ah, my friend, you look much better this morning than you did last night," he said.

Jackson grinned at him. "I'm definitely feeling better this morning except my thigh is hurting me pretty good."

"That's going to hurt for the next couple of days or so, but hopefully you're a quick healer and it won't bother you for too long."

"So, what's the plan? Can I get out of here?"

"Give us a few minutes to get your discharge papers ready and then you can go. But before that happens, let me change the dressing on your thigh and explain some wound care to you," Etienne said.

An hour later, Jackson was dressed and sat on the edge of the bed, waiting for Sonny to pick him up and take him home. He was eager to get home to Josie. He only wished she had a cell phone. More than anything, he just wanted to hear the sound of her voice. He wanted to hear her with no fear in her tone. He was eager to see her with a bright, happy smile on her face.

Minutes later, Sonny walked in. "What the hell, man?" he said as Jackson stood up from the bed. "I leave you alone for a few minutes and you go and get yourself shot. I already heard a lot of rumors this morning so I need you to fill me in on all the real details."

"I'll fill you in on the way to my place," Jackson replied. His thigh burned and hurt as he walked out of the hospital to Sonny's car in the parking lot, but he was definitely glad to be alive.

Once in the car, he told Sonny everything. He explained about Brian raping Josie and that it was Brian who had beat her up. Finally, he told Sonny about the confrontation that had taken place in his house the night before.

"I heard he'd been arrested, but I had no idea for what. God, it's all so hard to believe," Sonny said. "I mean, I thought I knew Brian."

"Yeah, that makes two of us, but he obviously had some inner demons that none of us knew about or saw," Jackson replied. "He came to kill me, Sonny. He was prepared to kill both me and Josie in some crazy suicide/murder plot."

"I still find it hard to believe. This is definitely going to rock the whole town," Sonny said.

"I know. I feel bad for Cynthia and the children. Unfortunately, they're also victims in this," Jackson replied.

Sonny pulled into his driveway. "Do you need anything? I could make a run to the store for you if you need something."

"No, I'm good. I've got a script for pain pills, but I don't intend to get it filled unless I really need to. But I do appreciate the ride home." Jackson opened the car door.

"No problem. Don't hesitate to call me if you need anything," Sonny said.

"Thanks, Sonny," Jackson said, now eager to get inside and see Josie. He got out of the car and Sonny backed out of the driveway and zoomed down the street.

Slowly, Jackson walked to his front door. It was unlocked. "Honey, I'm home," he said as he walked in.

There was no greeting in reply. "Josie?" He walked into the living room, but she wasn't there. He walked back to the bedroom, but she wasn't there, either.

She wasn't any place in the house. He sank down in his chair and listened to the silence that surrounded him. Surely, she'd be back. Her bag and clothes were still in the bedroom.

Maybe she'd just taken a walk and would be back soon.

He'd been home about an hour when there was a knock on the door. It was Gravois. "Sorry to bother you but I need to get a full statement from you about what happened here last night," he said.

Jackson ushered him in and the two men sat. "Mind if I record this?" Gravois asked and placed his phone on the coffee table.

"No, I don't mind at all," Jackson said. He would do whatever was necessary to see to it that Brian went to prison for his crimes against Josie.

It took about half an hour to get through the night's events. Gravois occasionally asked a question to make sure the record was clear.

"Well, your story and Josie's are the exact same," the lawman said when they were finished.

"That's because we're both telling the truth about Brian and what happened. By the way," Jackson said as he walked the man back to his front door, "did you ever identify the new victim in the swamp murders yet?"

"Yeah, her name is Lisa Choate. She was twenty-two years old and worked as a housekeeper for May Welles. And don't worry, I just hired some hotshot investigator from Shreveport. His name is Nick Cain and he comes with great credentials and he is supposed to be here in two weeks' time."

"That's good. Maybe a set of fresh eyes will solve the cases." It was the kindest thing for Jackson to say rather than saying Gravois's lazy ass wasn't working too hard for a solve. "By the way, what happened to Josie when I was taken to the hospital? I'm assuming you saw her after I was taken away by the ambulance."

"She rode to the hospital with me and we spoke to the doctor to make sure you were okay and then she asked me if I would drop her off at Vincent's, so I did. I haven't seen her since then."

Jackson's heart fell. So, she'd gone back to the swamp. He told Gravois goodbye and the lawman left. When he was gone, Jackson returned to his chair.

He couldn't believe that she hadn't waited until he was home. He couldn't believe she'd left without a goodbye to him. What did it mean? Surely, she meant to come back here. At the very least she'd need to come back for her things.

He hadn't yet told her he loved her. He'd had so many chances to tell her, but ultimately he hadn't. There were so many things left unsaid between them. All he could do now was sit and wait to see if she returned.

However, three days later she still hadn't come back and the desire to see her, to speak to her became all-consuming to him. He couldn't believe she hadn't come by to see how he was doing. He couldn't believe she had left without even saying goodbye to him.

Finally, on the fourth day and with his thigh feeling a little bit better, he drove out to Vincent's and parked.

He got out of his car and headed into the

swamp. He really didn't know how to get to her shanty, but he made his way to their tree trunk and sank down.

The fragrance of the swamp surrounded him, reminding him of her. He hoped she'd come by. He felt as if he were in withdrawal, needing a hit of Josie to make him feel better.

However, she didn't come that day, nor the day after and not the day after that. He sat on the trunk for hours each day, hoping and praying he'd see her again.

Finally, on the fifth day, she appeared. She stopped dead in her tracks at the sight of him. "Jackson, what are you doing here?"

"I've been here for the past four days, hoping to see you. Please, Josie. Come sit and talk to me," he replied.

Her reluctance was obvious as she moved slowly and finally sank down next to him. He felt her body heat and smelled the familiar scent of her and all his love buoyed up inside him.

"How's your leg?" she asked.

"Healing up nicely. How have you been doing?" There were so many things he wanted to say to her, but he didn't even know where to begin.

"I'm doing okay," she replied. "The fishing has been great lately."

"That's good." A long moment of tense silence rose up. "Josie, were you not going to tell me goodbye?" he finally asked.

She released a deep sigh. "Oh, Jackson, I thought it was better this way. I figured it was time for you to get back to your life and for me to get back to mine. I just thought it was best if I ripped the bandage off and left."

"But I want you in my life every day and always." He gazed deep into her eyes. "Josie, I'm so in love with you."

She immediately looked away. "Jackson, go back to town and find a nice town woman to love."

"Why on earth would I want to do that? I don't want a nice town woman to love." He thought about the kiss they had shared the day they'd last been together, right before Brian had shown up. "I want you, Josie. I love you and I think if you look deep in your heart, you love me, too."

She looked down at the ground. "I'm sorry, but that just isn't true," she replied softly. "Jackson, I'm very grateful to you, but...but that's all."

"Josie, look me in the eyes and tell me that's not true. Look me directly in the eyes and tell me you aren't in love with me."

Slowly, she raised her gaze to meet his. There was pain in the depths of her beautiful eyes. "It really doesn't matter how I feel. Don't you see? Jackson, it would never work between us."

"Why wouldn't it? Josie, there is absolutely nothing standing in our way now. You're out of danger and now we can fully pursue a relationship together."

He reached out and took her hand in his. "Josie, I'll never love a woman as much as I love you. I want to marry you. I want you to have my babies and build a family with me."

She closed her eyes and tears trembled on the tips of her long dark lashes. "Jackson, don't you get it?" She opened her eyes and the tears trekked down her cheeks. "You're town and town men don't marry swamp. We're fun dalliances for them. We're exotic playthings, but we definitely aren't marriage material."

He stared at her for a long moment. "Oh, this is rich. You talk about how prejudice the townspeople are, but you're the one prejudice against town men."

"I... That's no-not true," she sputtered.

"But it is true. You've just painted a whole group of people that includes me with the same brush. I don't know what all town men are like, but I'm me and I know what I want. I don't give a damn about town or swamp. That has nothing to do with who we are at our core. Love is what matters."

"Jackson, I'm so afraid that in the end you'll hurt me. I'm afraid you'll realize I'm not enough, that I'll never be enough for you. I love you so much but I don't want to get hurt," she replied.

"Say that again," he said softly.

"Say what again? That I'm afraid?"

"No, the other part. The part where you love me so much." Her words filled him with an enormous joy.

"Jackson, I do love you."

"Then, Josie, don't be afraid. Trust me when I say I want you… I need you in my life forever. Hell, woman, I took a bullet for you. What more could you want from me?" he asked teasingly.

"That's not funny, Jackson. I was so scared that night when I realized you'd been shot." Once again, tears filled her eyes.

"Don't cry, Josie. It's all over and we're both alive and now all I want to know is if you'll be with me forever."

She frowned. "But how would this even work? Jackson, you know the swamp is in my very soul."

"I know that," he assured her. "What I envision is that we have the best of both worlds. We work it out like Peyton and Beau have. We spend a week or so in the shanty and then a week or so at our townhome. We can figure it out, Josie. Just give me a chance, please give us a chance."

She stared at him for several long moments. "Okay," she whispered softly.

"Really?"

"Really," she replied. "I love you, Jackson and you have proven to me over and over again what kind of a decent man you are. I'm… I'm willing to take a chance on us."

He stood and pulled her up to a standing position in front of him. Her eyes were now clear and shiny and this time in the depths of them he saw his forever.

"Can I kiss you, Josie?"

"I'll be mad at you if you don't," she replied.

He wrapped his arms around her and pulled her close against him. She came willingly and he took her lips with his. The kiss was deep and filled with emotion.

He tasted her passion but more importantly, he tasted her love for him. It reached inside him and filled up his heart and his very soul. He would spend the rest of his life loving Josie and he would make sure that every day she knew how very much he loved her.

They weren't town and swamp. They were just two people in love. The kiss ended and he smiled at her. "So, how soon are you going to marry me?"

She laughed. "How soon do you want to marry me?"

"Today...last week," he replied.

She laughed again. "You might give me time to wash my hair. I'm only planning to marry once so I want to look my best."

"Seriously, how about we plan a small wedding in about a month."

She released an audible sigh. "That sounds perfect to me because I don't have much when it comes to friends and family," she replied. "But I wouldn't want to cheat your parents out of the wedding they want for their son."

"Okay, then we'll have the wedding in a month and a week," he replied. "And I was thinking, maybe we should get a pet before we start having babies. How about we start with a baby aardvark?" he said.

Her laughter would forever be the music in his life. Her happiness would be the chords that rang melodically in his head forever. He kissed her again and he knew they were going to have a wonderful future together filled with laughter and love.

Epilogue

Josie sat next to Jackson on the bank, their fishing poles in the water before them and his arm around her shoulder. It had been a little over a week since they had professed their love to each other, eight glorious days of spending time with him in the swamp. Tomorrow they would return to the townhouse and spend about two weeks there.

Josie had never been as happy as she was now. Over the past days, they had talked about and planned their future together and during the nights they had made sweet, passionate love.

Brian had been charged with a handful of crimes and the judge had remanded him without bail. Brian had a lawyer who was working on overturning that, but it wasn't a high-dollar attorney that everyone had assumed he would get.

The gossip on the street was that Brian was completely broke. Many of his businesses had failed and he and his family had been, in recent months, living on credit cards.

However, Brian was the furthest thing on Josie's mind today. Josie couldn't believe she had intended to deny herself the pleasure of loving and being loved by Jackson.

The real turnaround for her had been the moment when Jackson accused her of being prejudice against all town men. He had been right. She had allowed Gentry's betrayal of her to paint all the men with the same heartless color.

There was no fear in her heart now. She didn't fear Brian anymore but most importantly, she didn't fear Jackson's love anymore.

"That new guy is supposed to show up any day now to start working for Gravois," he now said.

"I hope he's as good as Gravois has said he is," she replied.

"I'm hoping he can really dig into the monster murders and find the person responsible."

"That makes two of us," she replied. "It's past time the monster was caught."

"Oh…speaking of monsters… I've got one," he exclaimed and jumped to his feet.

"Set the hook, honey," she said and laughed as he reeled as fast and furiously as he could.

He finally got the catfish up on the bank. He looked at her with a boyish excitement. "He's a good one, isn't he? He's the biggest one I've ever caught, right?"

"Yes, he's a good one," she replied with a laugh. She got up and watched as he set his pole to the side and then took the fish off the hook and tossed it into the basket in the water. They planned to sell the fish they'd gathered through the week tonight, before returning to the townhouse tomorrow.

When he was finished with the fish, she wrapped her arms around his neck and he immediately drew her close to him. "You're becoming quite a fine fisherman, Mr. Fancy Pants," she said.

He grinned down at her. "I wouldn't be interested in fishing without my beautiful fishing partner next to me."

"I appreciate that you come fishing with me," she replied.

"Don't you get it yet, Josie? For the rest of our lives, I'll go anywhere you want, I'll do whatever you want because I love you so very much." His gorgeous blue eyes bathed her with his love. "Can I kiss you, Josie?" he asked teasingly.

"I'll be sad if you don't," she replied.

"Since I never want you to be sad…" He took her lips in a tender kiss that spoke of his love and devotion to her.

She knew deep inside her soul that their

love was going to last a lifetime. She thanked the stars above for sending her Jackson. She couldn't wait to have his babies and build a forever life with him.

* * * * *

Don't miss the stories in this mini series!

THE SWAMP SLAYINGS

Monster In The Marsh
CARLA CASSIDY
January 2024

Wetlands Investigation
CARLA CASSIDY
February 2024

The Sheriff's To Protect

Janice Kay Johnson

MILLS & BOON

An author of more than ninety books for children and adults with more than seventy-five for Harlequin, **Janice Kay Johnson** writes about love and family and pens books of gripping romantic suspense. A *USA TODAY* bestselling author and an eight-time finalist for the Romance Writers of America RITA® Award, she won a RITA® Award in 2008. A former librarian, Janice raised two daughters in a small town north of Seattle, Washington.

Visit the Author Profile page
at millsandboon.com.au.

CAST OF CHARACTERS

Savannah Baird—Newly parenting her vulnerable niece, she rushes Molly home to her parents' ranch despite unhappy memories. When danger follows, the sheriff, who'd broken her heart, is her only bulwark against the men certain she possesses something dangerous her brother had stolen from them.

Sheriff Logan Quade—Recently returned home to help an ailing parent, Logan doesn't expect to see Savannah. Their history makes trust difficult, but he doesn't hesitate to protect Savannah and Molly.

Molly Baird—All she knows is that Daddy had to go away and now she lives with her auntie Vannah. How can ruthless men see her as a bargaining chip?

Jared Baird—Working undercover, sensing danger, Jared trusts only his sister to keep his young daughter safe—and to pass on his last, critical trove of information to Donaldson.

DEA agent Cormac Donaldson—He's dedicated years to shutting down a drug-trafficking organization. Now his undercover informant is murdered, leaving behind a young child. Might she unknowingly hold a last message from Jared?

Gene Baird—He's a hard man. But when Savannah comes home with Jared's daughter, trouble nipping at their heels, Gene will do anything to atone for long-ago mistakes.

Chapter One

The phone call came out of the blue, as Jared's always did. About to start work, Savannah Baird had just turned off her ringer, so it was pure chance she saw his name come up before she stowed the phone in the pocket of her fleece vest. The timing was lousy, but since she heard from her brother only a couple of times a year, she never sent him to voice mail. She wasn't all that sure he'd *leave* a message.

She accepted the call, said, "Hey, Jared," and then to the groom on the other side of the fence holding the young Arabian horse's reins, "I have to take this. Can you walk him?"

He nodded.

Jared said, "You there?"

"Yes." Savannah turned away from the fence and headed into the cavernous covered arena, currently empty, where she could sit at the foot of the bleachers. "How are you?"

"Uh…tell you the truth, I'm in some trouble."

His hushed voice scared her right away. She

pictured him hunched over his phone, his head turning to be sure he was still alone. The picture wasn't well formed, since she hadn't seen him since he was a skinny sixteen-year-old. The couple of photos she'd coaxed out of him via text refused to supplant in her head the image of the boy she'd known and loved so much.

"What kind of trouble?" she asked.

"Better if I don't tell you that, except..." Now he sounded raw. "I'll try to run, but I think they're suspicious."

They had something to do with illegal drugs. That was all she knew, except a couple of years ago he'd said something about redeeming himself. She thought Jared really had gotten clean, but too late; he'd been caught up in a shady business and not been allowed to escape. Or maybe he didn't want to. Unless he was attempting to bring down his employer? Savannah had never dared ask, afraid if she did, he'd quit calling at all.

Now he said with unmistakable urgency, "I should have told you this before. I have a daughter. Almost five. Her mother has problems and got so she couldn't take care of her. I'm all she has." He made a sound she couldn't identify. "Vannah, will you take Molly, at least until I straighten things out? I have her stuff packed. She's a good kid."

Staggered, all Savannah could get out was "A daughter? In five *years*, you couldn't tell me?"

"I lost touch with her mother. I kept thinking…" He huffed. "It doesn't matter. She's mine, and I don't know what they'd do to her. At best, she'd end up in the foster care system."

Savannah knew who was at the root of his problems: their parents. Specifically, their father, who hadn't just been hard on Jared, he'd seemed actively to dislike him, while their mother's efforts to protect her brother had been ineffectual. Meanwhile, *she'd* been Daddy's little princess. The contrast had been painful, and nothing she'd been able to do had ever made any difference. The astonishing part was that he mostly hadn't blamed her.

Now there was only one thing she could say.

"Of course I'll take her. Can you bring her to me? Or…where are you?"

"Still in San Francisco. Can you come here?"

"Today?"

"Yeah." The tension in his voice raised prickles on her arms.

She glanced at the phone. "Yes. Okay. It's early enough. I should be able to drive to Albuquerque and get an afternoon flight. When and where shall we meet?"

"Call me when you get in." He paused. "No. If things go bad… Ah, come to Bayview. It's not the best part of the city, but we can make the handoff fast." He gave her an address.

Never having been to the City by the Bay, she

had no way of envisioning the neighborhood. Thank goodness for GPS.

"Yes, sure. I'll rent a car."

"Thank you. Molly is everything to me." His voice roughened. "Make sure she knows I love her. I'd have done anything for her. I just wish I'd done it sooner."

"Don't sound like that! You're smart. You'll get yourself out of…of whatever mess this is. In fact, why don't *you* come with me, too? You know I'm working in really remote country in New Mexico."

"Maybe I'll try."

He didn't believe himself. She could hear it in his voice. Now even more scared, she clung to the phone. "Jared?"

"I love you," he said and was gone.

The beginning of a sob shook her, but she didn't have time for fear. She had to talk to her boss, the owner of this ranch dedicated primarily to breeding Arabians and training them for show as well as cutting, barrel racing, roping and the like. A stallion that stood stud here had been a national champion four years ago. Ed Loewen had made his money in software, using it to follow his dream. He wouldn't be happy that she had to take off with no notice, but he had kids and grandkids of his own. He'd understand.

Not that it mattered. She would go no matter what.

In fact…she hustled back to the outdoor arena and let the groom know she wouldn't be riding Chopaka after all. Then she jogged for the house.

Savannah's first stop after picking up the rental car was a corner convenience store to buy a can of soda and a few snacks. She added extras in case Molly was hungry. Then, the afternoon waning, she followed the voice coming from her phone. Take this exit onto another freeway. Stay in the second lane from the right. Exit. Left onto a major thoroughfare. Traffic grew steadily heavier.

Once she broke free of it, she was winding through the city itself. Another time, she would have paid more attention to the Victorian homes or tried to catch glimpses of the bay or the graceful arches of the Golden Gate Bridge. But the light was going, and fog rolled in off the ocean, making visibility increasingly poor. She couldn't have said when she realized that she'd entered an area of a very wealthy city that "isn't the best." Vacant storefronts and graffiti were the first clue. Small groups of young men with the waistbands of their pants sagging below their butts clustered in groups at corners. None of them would get far slinging a leg over the back of a horse, she couldn't help thinking. Or running. When she slowed for lights, she didn't like the way heads turned and she was watched.

Why here? Did Jared live in the neighborhood?

If this was his home address, why hadn't he said? But her gut told her this was nowhere near his usual stomping grounds. He wouldn't want anybody he knew to see him transferring his darling daughter to another person.

The daughter, she thought uneasily, who could be used to apply pressure on him. Probably not his sister; whoever lurked in his secretive world had no reason even to know he had a sister.

I'm imagining things, she tried telling herself stoutly, but it didn't help much as night closed in, muffled by the thick, low fog. She could see lights on porches and lit windows in the few businesses still open as if through a filter. She imagined Jack the Ripper's London had looked rather like this.

Oh, for Pete's sake—her real problem was that she'd never spent time in a major city. The buildings crowding in, the sense she was wandering a maze, made her feel claustrophobic.

GPS instructed her to make another turn. Without the guidance, she might have passed the street. The next storefront she saw had Gone Out of Business spray-painted on plywood nailed up to cover a window.

GPS was telling her she'd reached her destination. Not the store that had gone out of business, but two doors down. A dry cleaner's, closed for the day. No other car waited for her at the curb.

With a shiver, she signaled and pulled over, her

eyes on her rearview mirror. She seemed to be completely alone on this block. Had Jared been held up? If only there was a streetlight closer; the recess in front of the door was awfully dark. Except...something huddled there.

Oh, God. Savannah was out of her car without having conscious thought, rushing across the sidewalk toward the child who crouched in the door well, hugging her knees and peering up at Savannah.

A small, shaking voice said, "Are you Auntie Vannah?"

Savannah choked back something like a sob. "Yes. Oh, honey. You must be Molly."

The head bobbed.

"Where is your daddy? I thought he'd be here."

The face she could see was thin and pinched. "He...he had to go. He promised you'd come. He said I shouldn't move *at all*. And I didn't, but I was *scared*."

"I don't blame you for being scared, but I did come." Tears wanted to burn her eyes, but she blinked them back. "Once we're in the car—" *locked* in the car "—I'll call him." She summoned a smile. "The pink suitcase must be yours."

"Uh-huh," her niece said in her childish voice. "Daddy left this for you."

This was a duffel bag that didn't appear to have much in it. Did it contain a few changes of clothes for himself in the hopes he could wait and hop into Savannah's car for a getaway? Or was it really packed with more for this little girl? She'd look later. Her priority now was Molly and getting her safely away.

Savannah helped her up and, without releasing her hand, led her to the car. At Molly's age, she should probably sit in the back, but Savannah lifted her into the front seat anyway. She wanted to be able to see her face, to hold her hand. Then she popped the trunk and stowed the two bags before rushing to get in behind the wheel and hit the lock button.

Just as she did, a car with lights that seemed to be on high beam approached, hesitated, then passed.

Savannah started the car. "Let me drive a little ways."

A few blocks later, she found a small grocery store with several cars parked in a small lot. Feeling a bit safer, she joined them, set the emergency brake and said, "Okay, let's call your daddy."

Molly watched anxiously, listening to the multiple rings, then the abrupt message.

"Jared. I'll call you when I can."

Savannah said, "I have Molly. Will you *please* call? As soon as you can?"

She waited for a moment, as if he'd magically hear and rush to answer. Since it wasn't as if he was listening to messages in real time, she set her phone down and focused on this child who had just become her responsibility.

A little girl who had no one else.

It was chilly enough this evening that she wore a pink knit hat pulled over her ears, but Savannah could see that she had long blond hair. It must be Jared who'd braided it into pigtails, although strands were escaping. She couldn't be sure, but thought Molly had blue eyes, like he had. Savannah's had been blue when she was young, but eventually turned more hazel, just as her pale blond hair had darkened.

Otherwise, she couldn't see Jared in the scared face looking back at her, but that was hardly surprising with the inadequate light and the stress they were both feeling.

"Your daddy is my big brother. He probably told you that."

Molly nodded.

"He wants you to come home with me, at least for now. Until we hear from him." When, not if. "So right now, we're going to get a room at a hotel near the airport, and I'll buy us tickets to fly in the morning back to New Mexico, where I live."

What would she do with a child this age while she worked? she wondered in sudden panic, but that worry could wait.

"Okay?"

"Daddy said to do what you told me," Molly said as if by rote.

Savannah smiled. "Are you hungry?"

"Uh-huh."

She reached to the floorboards on the passenger side and produced the grocery sack. "I have some snacks in here to hold you. Once we find a hotel, we'll get dinner." There had to be some restaurants open late in the vicinity of the airport.

Molly peered into the bag and tentatively reached in, producing a bag of Skittles. Savannah's stomach grumbled, but she decided to wait until they were out of this neighborhood, at least. She felt as if eyes watched them.

Paranoid, but…why had Jared had to go so urgently he'd leave the little girl who was his "everything" alone in a dark doorway in a sketchy part of the city?

As soon as he called, she'd demand answers. In the meantime, she entered the address for a hotel she'd noticed by the airport into the maps app on her phone. She gratefully followed instructions even as she flickered her gaze from one mirror to another as well as to the road ahead, watching for…she didn't know what.

MY NIECE.

Unable to sleep yet, Savannah had left the one nightstand lamp on. They had a room with a single queen-size bed because she'd asked Molly whether she wanted her own bed.

She'd shaken her head hard.

So there she lay, a small lump almost touching Savannah, as if she wanted the reassurance of cuddling, but wasn't quite brave enough to commit to it. After eating a tiny portion of her cheeseburger and fries at a Denny's, she had changed from saggy pink leggings and a sweatshirt that was too big for her into a nightgown Savannah found in the pink suitcase. Her toothbrush and toothpaste were in there, too, as well as a pink hairbrush with long blond strands caught in the bristles. Jared had packed several days' worth of clothes, but no alternative to the worn sneakers his daughter had worn, and only one toy, a stuffed rabbit that Molly had latched right on to, and now held squeezed in her arms as she surrendered to sleep.

Savannah knew she should go through the duffel bag, but she felt deep reluctance. When they got home was soon enough, right?

Except...it wasn't, and she wouldn't be able to sleep until she saw what he'd left for her. There had to be a message, right?

She eased herself carefully off the bed so she didn't awaken Molly. The bag felt absurdly light when she picked it up and carried it to the comfortable chair by the window. The zipper sounded loud to her ears, but the child didn't stir.

Most of what she pulled out initially was Molly's: more clothes, a pair of sandals, a couple of games in boxes and a yellow-haired doll with...

yes, a shoebox full of doll-size changes of clothes. Something bumped her hand, and she immediately recognized the shape and smooth texture of a cell phone. If this was Jared's, that meant it had been ringing in the trunk of her rental car when she called him.

It opened right away to her touch, and she explored to find that, indeed, a missed call from her showed at the top of a very limited list of other calls. There was the one he'd made *to* her, as well. The realization that he had abandoned his phone chilled her and made plain that he'd never even considered fleeing with her and Molly.

The fact that the phone wasn't password-protected had to be out of character for her brother. This was part of his plan, she assumed—the plan he hadn't confided to her. He'd cleared away any passwords he'd used to give her complete access to his phone. Why? What was she supposed to glean from the numbers and messages? His contacts list...was empty.

She looked down to see that her knuckles were white, she gripped the damn phone so tightly. It felt like her only connection to her brother.

I can pick it up again, she reminded herself. *Search it for any hidden messages.*

At the very bottom of the duffel bag lay a manila envelope. Savannah opened it apprehensively. The first words that caught her eye were *last will and trust*. Dear God, he'd expected to die. Or disappear and eventually be declared dead? She hoped it was the second alternative.

He'd left an investment account and the contents of a savings account to his daughter, Molly Elizabeth Baird. He named his sister, Savannah Louise Baird, to assume guardianship of Molly, giving her complete control over the money until his daughter reached the age of twenty-one.

Swallowing, Savannah flipped through the few other pages. The bank account contained fifty-two thousand dollars and change. The investments handled by a brokerage firm added up to over a hundred thousand more. Not a fortune, but enough to put Molly through college, say, or pay expenses in the intervening years.

No, Savannah decided right away; she didn't need to draw on his money. She didn't want to use money she was horribly afraid had been earned in the illegal drug trade. She'd honor Jared's trust, though, and invest it as well as she could for his daughter's sake.

After repacking the duffel, she sat staring at it. Jared had said goodbye. She refused to believe he meant to kill himself, which led her back to the two alternatives: he hoped to vanish…or he'd known before calling her that he was a dead man.

After a minute, Savannah walked silently to the hotel room door and checked to be absolutely certain she'd put on the probably useless chain as well as the dead bolt lock.

She felt even less sleepy than she had when she slipped from the bed.

Chapter Two

"What the hell are you doing?"

Logan Quade had hoped to be done mucking out the stalls before his father caught him in the act, but no such luck. Dad had undoubtedly heard his truck even though he'd parked at the barn instead of the house when he'd driven up at the end of the day. He straightened, leaning on the shovel. Weather was really turning. He was glad for his sheepskin-lined coat and leather gloves.

"Same thing you made me do every day growing up, football practice or no. Same thing I did yesterday." And would do tomorrow. He couldn't take over running his father's ranch; Dad wouldn't stand for it. But Logan had moved back to Sage Creek in eastern Oregon three months ago to help out his father whether he wanted help or not, and Logan fully intended to keep assuming as many of the heavy tasks as he could.

"You *have* a damn job!" His father scowled at him.

Yes, he did. Logan had agreed to take over as county sheriff for the remainder of the previous sheriff's term. That had given him an excuse to come home that Dad accepted, and something to do besides ranch work. He'd never wanted to follow in his father's footsteps and someday take over the ranch, which was a sore point between them since his sister was even less interested. Knowing the land would be sold after he was gone didn't sit well with Brian Quade. That knowledge would fester even if Logan's mother had still been alive, but he felt sure his dad would have listened to Mom and been more reasonable about taking it easier.

"I did my job," Logan said briefly. "I've made as plain as I can that I'll be lending a hand here. Your doctor says you can't do heavy labor, and I'm here to make sure you follow Dr. Lancaster's orders."

"Blasted doctor doesn't know what he's talking about," Dad scoffed. "I feel just fine! A little cough is nothing."

Not to mention obvious shortness of breath on any exertion. "Because you quit smoking and because I'm riding you about doing your exercises." How many times did they need to have the same argument that hadn't been laid to rest in the months since he'd moved back into his childhood home? "They don't restore your lungs to working order, and you know it!"

His father snorted. "What am I supposed to do, sit on my ass and watch soap operas so I can live a few months longer?"

Logan's spurt of temper died. He did understand. This was the life his father had chosen. He had zero interest in retiring to a senior community in Arizona, or taking up hobbies that didn't include any real physical activity. That didn't mean he could accept his son's help with reasonable grace, even though Dad had to know that COPD was a progressive disease.

"Dad," he said quietly, "I came home to help." The progression could be slowed, but, always stubborn, Brian Quade resisted dealing with the depression that was part of his problem. "I want to spend time with you, not know you're working yourself to death—literally—while I'm on the other side of the state hanging out with friends when I'm not on the job."

The job, for him, was being a cop. Specifically, he'd been a detective with the city of Portland police bureau. Just last year, he'd been promoted to sergeant, so that he not only worked investigations directly, he supervised ones conducted by other detectives. That experience, along with his hometown boy, star athlete status, had been why the county council had named him sheriff in the absence of any other good options. Logan's captain had promised to rehire him when the time came.

Unless, of course, he became addicted to the power of being in ultimate charge. He might have snorted himself if he hadn't been facing down his father.

Who grunted dismissively. "Shovel manure if you want. Mrs. Sanders says dinner will be on the table in forty-five minutes."

Dad had been subsisting on microwavable meals until Logan hired a housekeeper-slash-cook first thing. They'd fought about that, too, but Dad had quieted down about it once he became accustomed to decent food on the table most evenings again.

"I'm nearly done," Logan said. "Just have to empty this wheelbarrow." He'd drop hay into the mangers, too, and let the horses back into their stalls, but that was no secret from his father, who gave him a last flinty stare before he turned and stalked off back toward the house.

Logan watched him go.

At times he thought his father hadn't changed one iota in the past twenty years except for a deepening of the creases on his leathery face and the white that had gradually come to dominate dark brown hair. Then there were moments, like now, when he couldn't help noticing weight loss, frailty and a slowness in every movement, never mind the rasp of his breath. His stride wasn't the same.

A stab of pain felt too much like a knife inserted between Logan's ribs. He'd been happy enough with his job, his friends, the women he'd hooked up with for a few months at a time, but he hadn't realized how important it was to know that Dad was still here, that *home* was still here. His complacency had taken a serious jolt when his father grumblingly admitted to his diagnosis after he'd seen the doctor assuming he might have some bronchitis that could be cured with an antibiotic. A lifelong smoker, he'd hated giving up the cigarettes but had done it, and that took real guts.

Yeah, Logan understood. Dad had lost his wife, his kids had taken off into the world with no intentions of coming home permanently, and then he'd had to quit smoking. He'd never been much of a drinker, so what was left?

The indignity of having to admit he was failing, that was what. And worse yet, it was his son to whom he had to make that admission. The son who had the strength he'd lost, who was a decorated cop and now the county sheriff.

Maybe humility didn't come easily to either of them, Logan thought ruefully.

"OH, HONEY." Savannah sank down on her niece's twin bed. "Another nightmare?"

Two night-lights in the bedroom and the overhead light left on in the bathroom across the hall weren't enough to make Molly feel safe.

Many nights, Savannah ended up letting Molly get in bed with her. Even then, as often as not she awakened every couple of hours gasping or sobbing or, once, screaming. She could never quite verbalize who or what those terrible dreams were about. Savannah was getting madder and madder at her brother, even though she reminded herself regularly that the little girl had spent much of her short life with her mother, not her daddy.

The mother who couldn't take care of her child. Jared *had* stepped in, but had he been any more able to offer a sense of real security? Savannah wished she knew, but Molly wasn't even able to tell her how long she'd lived with her father versus her mother.

Now she rocked this little girl who felt too thin, just skin covering fragile bones, offering her warmth and murmured words. "You're safe, Molly. I won't let anything happen to you. I promise. I know the dreams are scary, but they'll quit coming eventually. Why don't you think about riding Toto again tomorrow?"

Toto was a fat gray pony living an easy life here on the ranch for the benefit of the frequently visiting grandkids. Molly had been entranced at first sight. Not surprisingly, she'd never even petted a horse before, never mind ridden one. Her upbringing presumably hadn't been the kind that included sunny Sundays at the zoo, where there might be pony rides, or friends' birthday parties that included ponies as well as cake. Savannah had been spending more time than she should leading the pony around and around the arena with Molly clutching the saddle horn for dear life but also looking thrilled.

"Can I get in your bed?" she whispered.

"Of course you can." Savannah gave her a big hug, scooped her up and carried her to the full-size bed in her own room.

"Will you sing 'Sunshine' to me?" Molly asked.

Savannah did almost every night. Apparently Jared had told his little girl that "You Are My Sunshine" had been Auntie Vannah's favorite song when *she* was a little girl. Of course, she knew the tune well enough to hum it. Who didn't? The truth was, though, she didn't remember her mother ever singing it and had had to look up the lyrics. She stuck to the chorus, since there was too much else in the song that was sad.

Now Savannah murmured, "You don't even have to ask," and softly began as she cuddled her niece under the covers. The stiff little body gradually relaxed.

Child behavioral experts would probably disapprove of her letting Molly sleep with her so often, but they dealt with kids whose night terrors weren't associated with a seamy underworld of drug dealing, a mother with unknown "problems" and a daddy who'd dropped her off at a dark strip mall to wait for an aunt Molly had never met before disappearing.

The two of them were getting by. Savannah thought her niece was starting to trust her, but both of them were waiting, too, for a call from Jared that might change everything. The bigger problem was her own exhaustion. She'd been shocked last night when she looked at herself in the mirror after brushing her teeth. The blue circles under her eyes more closely resembled a pair of black eyes. She felt dull, too, her brain foggy. A young mare had kicked her yesterday, something that wouldn't have happened if she weren't all but sleepwalking. Now she had a livid bruise on her lower thigh and a knee that hurt.

Savannah's boss hadn't said anything yet, but he'd been spending more time than usual watching her work, one boot propped on the bottom rail, arms crossed on the top one, face shaded by a dark Stetson. He had to know she wasn't giving the horses her best. She needed that almost-magical connection she'd always felt with horses, but her tiredness and indecision were interfering.

So far, she'd been lucky that the wife of one of the ranch hands was willing to take care of Molly during the day along with her own children, but Brenda was noticeably distressed every morning when Savannah had to pry Molly's hands off her and hand her over, crying quietly. Once Auntie Vannah was out of sight, Molly was good, Brenda reported; too good, too obedient, too anxious. If she napped at all, her nightmares came even more frequently than they did at night.

Jared, where are you? Savannah begged, her cheek pressed to the little girl's head. *What were you thinking? Can't you call and let us know what's going on?*

And then, *What am I going to do?*

There was an obvious answer, one she had been reluctant to even consider. She could go home. Take Molly to meet her grandparents. And, oh, she didn't want to confess she needed her parents.

Her own horribly mixed emotions concerning them weren't what worried her. The question was how her father would respond to the granddaughter they hadn't known about. If Savannah had been bringing home her own child, she had no doubt both her parents would welcome her with open arms and set about spoiling her. No matter what, she knew Mom would adore Molly from the minute she set eyes on her. Savannah *wanted* that for this fragile child.

But Molly was Jared's child. Even Mom had seemed to slump in relief when he ran away. Tension in their house kept anyone from talking about him. Over time, Savannah had the impression even Mom had shrugged off his existence and the dangers he faced as an unprotected teen-ager out in the world as if he was nothing to them. Would Molly be tainted by association with the unwanted son?

But Savannah knew she was going to have to find out. She needed help, and Molly needed more family. People who loved her and were willing to do anything to protect her. Savannah's parents had been begging her to come home for years, promising to expand the horse breeding and train-ing part of their business since that was what in-terested her most, reminding her that the ranch would someday be hers.

Lying there in the dark, aware her young charge had fallen asleep, Savannah let out a long sigh. She'd call Mom and Dad tomorrow. If she was ever dissatisfied with how Dad treated Molly, well, she would up and move again. She wouldn't let herself be turned into a coward the way Mom had been. She had a reputation as a trainer; she could get another job.

She just had to shake off her fear that a return to Sage Creek was the last thing Jared would have wanted for his daughter. Well, too bad; he'd given up any right to make decisions for Molly, hadn't he?

STILL WEARING HIS UNIFORM, Logan stopped at the pharmacy to pick up prescription refills for his father. He could have asked Mrs. Sanders to do it—she had taken over grocery shopping—but Logan wanted to keep an eye on how well Dad was taking his medications, and short of stealing into Dad's bathroom to count pills, staying on top of when they needed refilling seemed like the best option.

He was cutting through the store toward the pharmacy counter at the back when he saw a woman pushing a cart in the toy aisle. A kid sat in the cart. His stride checked. There was something about—

At that moment, the woman lifted a boxed toy from the shelf and, smiling softly, showed it to the little girl. Logan felt a warning flare in the region of his heart.

Damn. Savannah Baird was back in town. She always had left him feeling conflicted. Not that the reasons mattered anymore, he realized, since she obviously had a daughter. Probably there was a husband, too, who just didn't happen to be with them right now. He was surprised his father hadn't mentioned that she'd married.

He started to back up, which caught her attention. She stared, too, then said, "Logan?"

"Yeah, it's me." He sounded gruff for a reason. Jared Baird had been his best friend growing up. After Jared had run away—or just plain disappeared—Logan hadn't tried to hide how he felt about Jared's sister, the little princess in that household. The one who shone so brightly, no one seemed to see Jared. Logan had hurt her feelings and refused to care. He was solidly in Jared's corner.

"Are you...visiting your dad?" she asked tentatively.

They were adults now, and there was no reason not to be civil. He walked down the aisle toward her, evaluating how a beautiful, spoiled-rotten young woman, a rodeo queen and homecoming princess, had matured.

Really well, was his conclusion. She was still slim, maybe a little curvier in the right places, and her gray-green eyes were as pretty as he remembered. Her hair had darkened some, but he'd still call her blonde, pale streaks mixed with light brown. Maybe the streaks were courtesy of a hairdresser.

Refocusing on her question, Logan made himself say, "Dad's having health problems. COPD."

Her nod meant she knew what that meant. "I'm sorry."

"I quit my job and came home to help out on the ranch. If I weren't here, he'd keep on the way he always has, even if that cut years off his life." He shook his head. "He's fighting me the whole way."

She smiled. "As stubborn as ever, then."

"Yeah." He studied the kid, who watched him warily with big blue eyes. "What about you? This must be your daughter."

Some emotion crossed Savannah's face like a shadow. He might have read it better if he'd been looking right at her. He did know that she was hesitating.

"No," she finally said. "Molly is Jared's daughter." She smiled at the girl. "Molly, this is Logan. I'll bet your daddy talked about him, didn't he? They were best friends when they were boys."

What the hell? The shock rocketed through him. He'd assumed Jared was dead—in fact, had wondered if Jared had died during a confrontation with his own father and been buried all this time somewhere on the family ranch. Had he come home and not bothered to call?

The girl still wasn't sure about Logan, but she gave a timid nod. "Daddy said you went riding together all the time. That you lived near him."

"That's right. My father's ranch is on the same road as your grandmother and grandfather's ranch is."

She hardly blinked, finally shifting that slightly unnerving stare to her…aunt?

"Is Jared home, too?" Logan asked.

"No," Savannah said quietly. "He…asked me to take care of Molly. We're…waiting to hear from him."

What did that mean? Nothing as simple as Jared having to take a business trip, Logan guessed.

"I always assumed he was…" Logan glanced again at the little girl and amended what he'd been about to say. "Gone."

"Did you?" The tilt of Savannah's head and the sharp tone in her voice were a challenge.

One that irritated him. "You mean, you've known what he was up to all these years? You didn't think to say, by the way, Logan, *your best friend is fine*?"

"Why would I?" she responded coolly. "Now, if you'll excuse us, we need to pick up a few things."

As if he wasn't still there, Savannah turned her back on him, added the toy, whatever it was, to the cart and then wheeled cart and niece away from him.

Logan stood stock-still, stunned in some way he didn't entirely understand.

The girl who'd had a crush on him had grown to be a woman who looked at him with open dislike. And, damn it, she was even more beautiful than she'd been. Back then, he had tried hard not to analyze his intense reaction to her, but now…yeah, he'd been attracted to her. Nothing he'd have acted on even if he hadn't detested her, too; she'd been too young. Three years mattered then.

His mind jumped, as if he was playing hopscotch.

Jared was alive. Logan had had other friends, but there'd never been anyone he felt closer to than Jared. They'd been brothers at heart. Even after he started giving Jared a hard time about his drinking, the parties he went to, the experimentation with drugs, opening a distance between them, he'd have still sworn the bond was there. Until Jared took off without telling him, and then a year went by, followed by another and another.

Why would Jared have stayed in touch with the little sister whom Daddy had adored, the sister Jared had resented so much, and not with his best friend?

Maybe he hadn't, it occurred to Logan; maybe he hadn't contacted Savannah until he needed help with his little girl.

Logan shook his head, confused and, yeah, hurt. He had to pull himself together. He was a cop, and situational awareness wasn't optional. He didn't like knowing someone could have walked right up behind him without him noticing. Sure, he was home in Sage Creek. He hadn't personally made an arrest yet and had no reason to think he'd acquired any enemies.

Unless Savannah fell into that category.

A minute later, as he waited at the pharmacy counter for the guy to retrieve his dad's prescriptions that were ready, Logan had another thought. Only one person could give him answers to any of his questions—if he could convince her to talk to him.

He'd have been happy never to run into either of Jared's parents again, but he thought he might drop by the Circle B ranch in the next few days.

Chapter Three

That evening over dinner, Savannah paused in the act of dishing up a small serving of potato salad for Molly. They were still negotiating what foods Molly would and wouldn't eat—or, in some cases, had never seen before. Savannah wasn't sure about this one. Fortunately, her parents were patient with this new granddaughter who'd unexpectedly appeared on their doorstep. In fact, they doted on her, as they'd done on Savannah. They'd apparently dismissed the reality that Molly was actually Jared's child.

"I saw Logan Quade today," she said, going for casual. "Apparently his father is having health problems."

Dad said, "The county council appointed the Quade boy to be interim sheriff. Sheriff Brady had a heart attack and had to retire." He took a bite. "Carried quite a gut around with him these past ten years or so."

"Logan is hardly a boy," Savannah protested. She knew exactly how old Logan was—still remembered his birthday—but went with, "I'm thirty-one, so he must be…thirty-four."

Just like Jared, as they all knew.

"Young to take over the sheriff's department."

"You disapprove?"

He grunted and took the serving bowl from her to dish up a hefty helping of the potato salad for himself. "No reason to. Heard he was a sergeant with the Portland police department, so he must know what he's doing."

"Did Logan say what's wrong with his father?" Savannah's mother asked. She'd had lunch today with friends, so she wore her prettiest snap-front shirt and makeup, and had styled her hair in a smooth bob. The blond shade had to be courtesy of her hairdresser. Savannah remembered Mom's natural color as a light brown that had started graying as much as ten years ago.

"COPD."

Mom gave her husband a minatory look. "That's what comes of smoking."

Sounding irritable, he shot back, "You know I've never smoked over a pack a day."

Savannah was tempted to comment on how many cigarettes a year that added up to, but refrained. Because…she didn't care? No, that wasn't true; she loved her father. But she also knew nothing she could say would sway him. It never had before.

"I take it you haven't stayed friends with Mr. Quade?"

Dad looked surprised. "Sure we have. We see him regularly at the Elks Club and the Cattlemen's Association get-togethers. Noticed he'd quit smoking. He hasn't said a word about his health."

"Pride."

"It's not the kind of thing you want everyone talking about. Could be he likes his privacy."

She had to concede the argument. "Except if he'd let people know, they might have offered to help him out so Logan didn't have to come home so soon."

Her father grunted his opinion of that. "Ranch is going to be his."

The idea that Logan might not want the ranch was apparently inconceivable to Dad.

"Is he married?" her mother asked. "Does he have kids? I don't think Brian ever said."

"I didn't ask, and Logan didn't say."

In his usual blunt fashion, Dad put in, "Well, he was Jared's friend, not yours."

Savannah didn't need anyone to tell her that. Logan had always made that reality plenty clear.

Later that evening, after she'd tucked Molly into bed, knowing full well she'd wake up sobbing in a couple of hours, Savannah debated going back downstairs and pretending to watch TV with her parents.

Tonight, she couldn't make herself, and she knew why she felt so on edge.

The encounter with Logan bothered her more than she wanted to acknowledge. From the time she was a little girl, she'd adored her big brother—*and* his best friend. They had included her in activities sometimes, less often as the years went on and they thought they were big, tough boys and she was a nuisance who wore too much pink. Both boys were athletes; they'd played Little League baseball together, Pop Warner football, then naturally become stars of the high school baseball and football teams.

Until Jared had been suspended from both, Savannah reminded herself. By then, it wasn't that he was too busy for her. Nope, he was too angry, too secretive, too sullen.

Too resentful?

She'd convinced herself that he still loved her, that he didn't blame her for Dad's obvious bias or Mom's weak efforts to intervene. He'd seldom been around to hear Mom and Dad's low-voiced fights, as if they thought Savannah wouldn't hear what was being said. But she'd quit kidding herself that Jared still loved her when she saw the way Logan's lip curled at the sight of her, the way he shook off any attempt by Jared to include her in whatever they were doing, and later, after Jared was gone, by the way Logan pretended not to even *see* her once she was in high school, too. Jared had to have complained to his best buddy about his *perfect*, walks-on-water little sister. Why else would Logan's attitude toward her have curdled?

So even before Jared had taken off, she knew he must have come to hate her. Who could blame him?

She'd tried so hard to head off Dad's vicious swipes, to talk Jared down after Mom begged him to avoid aggravating his father. To pretend the near-violence that thickened the air when father and son were forced to share a dinner table or conversation didn't exist.

When Savannah pressed her, her mother had eventually admitted to her fear that Jared would be damaged by his father's treatment of him. Dad refused to see what he was doing to Jared and got increasingly angry when his wife pushed him.

"What can I do?" Mom had said helplessly. "I have no working history. If I leave your father, how could I support the three of us? Child support wouldn't be anywhere near enough. Grandma and Granddad wouldn't help. They didn't want me to marry Gene in the first place."

Savannah hadn't known that.

"I don't see how poverty would help Jared. If he would just…step lightly, quit baiting his father, he'd be fine! The tension isn't one-sided, you know! It's not *that* long until he graduates from high school. If only he'd listen to me."

As an adult, Savannah understood her mother's decision better than she had then, but the hot coals of anger still burned. Yes, the idea of leaving her husband must have been terrifying, but the choice she'd made had essentially been to sacrifice one of her two children. Although, really, by the time of that conversation, it had been too late to change Jared's increasing alienation and anger.

Savannah had kept trying. She'd rolled her eyes when either of her parents bragged about her achievements. She'd gone to every one of Jared's games that she could. She'd confronted her father, for what good that did. Later, she'd read enough to know that instinct had led her to play the role of peacekeeper in their family dynamic, except nothing she did was ever good enough.

What Mom had never understood was how that failure had damaged Savannah's confidence, too.

When Jared called her the first time, almost a year after he took off, she'd almost fallen to her knees in relief. She'd had a secret fear that her own father had killed Jared when a fight escalated into violence. She still remembered clutching the phone, tears pouring down her face, because he was alive. He wanted to talk to *her*. He hadn't called to mine her for news about what was happening at home. *I just wanted to hear your voice,* he'd said, sounding sad in a way that haunted her still.

But what good did it do to brood about a past she couldn't change? She was in the middle of a book she was enjoying. She'd curl up in the easy chair squeezed into her bedroom that had been her refuge as a teenager when she couldn't take her family for another minute. She found the book and had just sunk into the chair, curling her legs under her, when her phone rang. Surprised, she reached for it. The number was unfamiliar. Her heart jumped. *Please let it be Jared.*

She answered cautiously.

"I'm hoping to reach Jared Baird's sister," a man said. "Would that be you?"

Her heartbeat picked up. "Who is asking?"

"I'm sorry." He sounded sincere. "I'm Detective Alan Trenowski, San Francisco Police Department."

Should she deny any relationship with Jared? No, that ship had sailed. And…she needed to find out why a detective was calling. Except… Oh, God. How would she know if this was a lie, if *he* was one of the men Jared was fleeing? Or…had Jared been running from law enforcement? He wouldn't have wanted to tell her that.

"I…" She swallowed. "I'm Savannah Baird. Jared is my brother."

"Ah. Then I'm sorry to have to deliver bad news." The voice became gentle. "Your brother's body was pulled from the bay by a boater late this afternoon. He'd been shot."

Oh, Jared.

THERE WAS MORE, of course. Police assumed whoever had murdered Jared had dumped his body in the bay hoping tides would pull it out to sea, where it might never be found. They'd identified him from his wallet, left in the back pocket of his jeans. He'd also carried a cheap phone—the officer had started to say "a burner" before correcting himself—with only one person in the contacts: her. He'd labeled her as "sister" along with her name.

Plainly, he'd wanted to be sure she was informed if he was killed. In a way, that was the bad news: his killers had left the wallet and phone on his body so he would be identified and she'd learn of Jared's death.

Why?

Scary question.

She answered more questions from Detective Trenowski and also agreed to speak with him again in the morning. She told him which of Jared's possessions she had, including the phone—and how the phone lacked any real information. She explained how little she knew about her brother's life, but revealed her belief that in the past he'd been involved in the illegal drug trade in some way. She told the detective about that last phone call, how Jared had admitted to being in trouble. She remembered word for word what he'd said: *I'll try to run, but I think they're suspicious.*

Yes, of course she'd asked for an explanation, and all he'd say was *It's better if I don't tell you.*

There would be an autopsy, of course. Someone would be in touch when the body was freed for burial.

Savannah's hand shook as she set down the phone. She hunched in on herself, almost shocked at the power of her grief. She'd imagined a call just like this so many times, why was she even surprised? And yet she was. She'd *talked* to Jared only a few weeks ago. Found out she had a niece, now asleep in Jared's old bedroom.

I'll have to tell them, she thought. Would Dad care at all? Pretend to care? How would the news hit Mom, who must have spent years trying to convince herself that somewhere out there, Jared was doing fine? That someday he'd call.

Worse yet, she'd have to tell Molly that her father would never be coming back for her.

Shuddering, she curled forward and let herself cry.

That meant, of course, bloodshot, swollen eyes when she went downstairs. The stop in the bathroom to splash her face with cold water hadn't helped at all.

Only her mother glanced her way when she appeared in the opening leading to the living room.

Dad's gaze didn't leave the TV until Savannah's mother sat up so fast, her recliner squealed in protest. Then they both looked at her.

"Can you…turn that off?" Savannah asked, gesturing toward the TV.

Her father used the remote, plunging the living room into silence.

Until her mother almost whispered, "Is something wrong?"

Is something wrong? The absurdity quelled renewed tears.

"Yes. A police detective in San Francisco just called to let me know that Jared is dead. His body…was found today."

Her parents just stared.

"Why did they call you and not us?" her father asked, sounding a little huffy.

Was he really offended?

"He had my name in his phone contacts."

"Oh, no," her mother murmured.

Suddenly nauseated, Savannah almost turned to go back upstairs. She had to think about Molly, though. Unless she wanted to make a permanent break from her parents, she couldn't tell them how angry she was.

"Do they know how he died?" her father asked.

Her throat wanted to close. It was hard to get the next words out. "He was shot, his body thrown in San Francisco Bay."

Dad grunted. "I suppose it was the drugs." Because his death had to be solely Jared's fault, having nothing to do with the childhood tensions. Only...her father's voice carried a heaviness she didn't recognize.

"I...think he'd been straight for some years now," she said. "I'm sure he was when he called. He said something about 'them' being suspicious. He might have been, well, working undercover to bring them down."

Her mother stood up, cheeks already wet, and rushed past her, hurrying up the stairs. Dad half stood, then sank back down. "I thought she'd shed her last tears for that boy."

"Did you ever shed any tears for him?" Savannah asked quietly, not waiting for an answer.

A PLUME OF dust trailed Logan's department-issue SUV as he drove down the Bairds' long drive. A minute ago, Logan had passed a couple of ranch hands stretching barbed wire on the rough-hewn posts alongside the road. Both had glanced up and nodded. He didn't recognize either, but they were too young to have been around when he spent half his time at the Circle B. He couldn't tell if the work was routine or if a section of fence had gone down. This was the season, though; it was the kind of job that got done in late fall and winter, when other business slowed down. Last weekend Logan had helped replace sagging sections of fence on Dad's place. He had a long scratch on his left arm to prove it.

When he first reached the two-story white ranch house, so much like the one he'd grown up in, he didn't see anybody. The broad double doors at the barn stood open, the interior shadowed. Not a soul seemed to be around.

He hesitated between going to the house or walking around first, choosing the look-see. He'd rather not have to be polite to Jared's parents.

Just as he rounded a corner of the barn, he heard a woman say, "It's a long ways down, isn't it?"

He had no idea if Savannah could sing; she hadn't been in the school choir, as far as he knew. But her voice had always had a musical quality that triggered a reaction in him. He could close his eyes and imagine her in his bed, talking to him, that voice as sensual as her touch.

Irritated anew at any reaction to Jared's sister, he followed her voice anyway. Sure enough, there she was in an outdoor arena, her back to him as she gazed up at the girl, sitting atop a sorrel mare who looked downright somnolent. He kind of doubted this was a top-notch cutting prospect, although appearances could be deceptive. The girl—Molly—clutched the saddle horn in a death grip.

"I promise you Checkers won't take a step unless I'm leading her or you nudge her with your heels. Okay?"

The blonde head bobbed. The kid was nervous, then, but not terrified.

"Let me lead you around for a few minutes. Then I'll get on and we can ride double."

Unnoticed, Logan stayed where he was while Savannah led the ambling mare along the fence of the oblong arena. After a moment, he walked up to a spot beside the gate, crossed his arms on the top rail and watched as Jared's little girl noticeably relaxed. Her back straightened and she held her head up.

Not until they rounded the far end of the arena and faced him did they notice him—at the same moment he saw the remnants of tears on both their faces. What the hell?

He straightened, too, waiting for them to reach him. Then he tipped the brim of his gray Stetson. "Savannah. Molly."

Savannah's gaze took in his dark green uniform and the star pinned to his shirt, and probably the heavy belt holding the holster and other implements. "Sheriff. Are you looking for my father?"

"No, you. Happened to be nearby—" *happened* not being quite the right word "—thought maybe we could talk a little more."

Strain on her fine-boned face made her less obviously pretty than when he'd seen her in the pharmacy, but now he knew he wasn't viewing a careful facade.

"I was going to call you later," she said stiffly. "Um...give me a minute." She turned back to her niece. "I need to talk to the sheriff. I'll just tether Checkers, and we can ride some more in a little bit. In the meantime, why don't you go see if that first batch of cookies is out of the oven yet?"

The kid was a cutie, even scowling at him, and she lifted her arms so Savannah could swing her off the horse's back. Logan opened the gate, although only the girl came through it. Savannah looped the reins around a rail, then walked along the fence, Logan doing the same on the other side of it, until she could watch as Molly plodded toward the house, finally disappearing inside.

Then she looked at him, devastation in her eyes. "Jared is dead."

"What?" he said, almost soundlessly. Hadn't she told him, just yesterday, that—

"I got a call last night, from a San Francisco PD detective. Jared's body was pulled out of the bay. He'd been shot. They don't seem to know much yet, even where he was tossed in. Whoever killed him didn't take his wallet or phone. The phone was one of those cheap ones, you know."

Logan nodded. He seemed to be numb, but didn't know how long that would last.

"Which means—"

"They wanted him to be identified."

"Or…or at least didn't care if he was."

Considerate of a killer, he thought, but didn't say.

"Does this have anything to do with why he asked you to take Molly?" he asked.

She closed her eyes for a moment and took a deep breath before fixing that anguished gaze back on him. "I know it does. I don't remember what I told you—"

"Almost nothing," he said, more harshly than he'd intended.

She took a half step back, making him feel like a bastard.

"He's called me, oh, once or twice a year ever since he took off."

A slow burn of anger ignited. "He stayed in touch all that time?"

Her chin rose. "You think I should have told you?"

"You had to know I worried about him."

"How would I know that? Did you ever speak a word to me again?" Oh, she was steamed, too.

And in the right, he was ashamed to admit to himself. He hadn't even been civil. "I…regret that," he said roughly. "Too little, too late, I know, but I am sorry."

She searched his face, then sagged. "I didn't know that Jared wasn't calling you, too. And… I suppose I was being petty."

"You had reason," he said wryly.

She let that go. "Anyway, for the first few years, he was mostly stoned or maybe drunk when he called. Not falling-down plastered, but I could tell. Then… I think he was trying to get clean. He'd sound great a couple of times, then—" Her shoulders moved. "I'm pretty sure at some point he got involved in the drug trade. I don't know if he worked for a cartel doing business in this country or just a distributor. A couple of years ago, he said something about trying to atone. That worried me, because I wondered if he was endangering himself."

No question now that was what Jared had done.

"When he called a few weeks ago, he said he was in trouble. That they were suspicious. That's when he told me about Molly—I had no idea he had a child. I guess she'd been with her mother, but he said she couldn't take care of Molly anymore. I don't know how long ago it was that he took her. He begged me to meet him, to take Molly until he got in touch."

"You *met* with him?"

She told him about flying to San Francisco, reaching the address her brother had given her and finding only the little girl and a couple of bags.

"I think he knew all along that he didn't dare meet me. He just didn't want me to know—" her face contorted "—that he was really saying goodbye."

"Savannah." He put his hands on the rail with the intention of vaulting the fence, but she backed up again.

"No. I'm okay. I've expected this for years. It's just…harder when I really thought I'd see him again. And because of Molly. Telling her this morning—" A shudder passed over her, but her eyes met his again. "Now I'm wondering whether whoever killed Jared has any reason to track *me* down."

After years of being a cop, Logan had already leaped to wondering the same thing. What drug traffickers would want with Jared's sister was a mystery, but why else had they all but handed the SFPD a handwritten note saying *Here's who to contact to claim this body*?

And maybe answer a few questions?

Logan cursed, but silently.

Chapter Four

Savannah walked Logan to his car, a marked police SUV with a light bar and bristling with tall antennae. At five foot nine, she wasn't short for a woman, but he'd always been taller. Now she'd guess him to be six foot two or so, all of him lean and athletic, made bulkier by his coat.

And, heavens, she'd let herself forget—or was that *made* herself forget?—how striking he was. His dark brown hair was short enough to tame the waves she remembered. Icy gray eyes were as startling as ever in a thin, tanned face with sharp cheekbones and a mouth that had provoked her hormone-ridden teenage fantasies.

Her gaze slid to his left hand. No wedding ring, but maybe he chose not to wear one.

As if his marital status mattered.

Frowning, he said, "Have your parents accepted Molly?"

"Yes. I wasn't sure Dad would, but… I needed help. She's pretty traumatized. She clings to me, which made it hard to leave her when I had to work, and she has constant nightmares."

His big hand drew her to a stop. "That's why you look so tired."

She must look really bad. "Sleep is an issue," she admitted. "I think Mom would get up with her, but so far that isn't an option. Molly wants me. Apparently, only my singing will put her to sleep. I'm actually thinking—" Whoa. Why would she confide in *him*?

But with those pale eyes intent on her face, he prodded, "Thinking?"

"Oh, we have an empty cabin. Dad's cut back a little on the size of the herd and didn't hire as many hands this past year. This cabin was meant to house a worker with a family, but Joe Haskins—do you remember him?—is the only employee here right now fitting that criteria, and he's had his place ever since he started with us. I don't really want to keep living in my childhood bedroom and feeling like a guest in the rest of the house. Molly and I could be more of a family if we had our own place, but I could still rely on Mom to watch her during the day."

"I always thought you'd stay, since it was obvious the ranch would be yours." His tone was careful, but his opinion obvious.

"Whatever you think, I was mad at both of my parents. I wouldn't be here now if it weren't for Molly." Savannah took a step back. "Thanks for stopping by. I need to keep my promise and give her a longer ride before I start work."

"You're training for your dad?"

"Yes." She kept backing up.

He continued to watch her, his gaze unnerving. "Savannah."

She stopped.

"I'm the law around here. If you hear anything more about Jared, and especially from the people who decided he was a threat, you need to let me know."

The steel in his low, resonant voice irritated her, but Savannah also understood that if she or Molly were threatened, he'd be their ally. No question. Who else could she turn to?

"I'll do that."

Their conversation over, she turned and walked toward the house, not once looking back even after she heard the powerful engine start or the SUV recede down the ranch lane.

HER FATHER CLEARED his throat. "Your mother and I have been talking."

Bent over as she loaded the dishwasher, Savannah looked up in surprise. Her mother was putting away leftovers in the refrigerator, but turned a hesitant smile on her. So they'd planned this. Was it ominous that they'd waited for whatever discussion this was meant to be until they had separated her from Molly? Savannah could hear a song from *Aladdin*, the Disney movie the four-year-old was watching right now.

"What's that?" Savannah asked, straightening.

"There's no reason for you to put your life on hold because of your brother's whims," Dad said brusquely. "I don't know why he'd think he could put the burden of raising his child on you when you're not married or settled."

"I always thought Jared would come home again. Having his daughter here…" Mom choked up. "She's a sweetheart. She reminds me so much of you at that age, except for her being so…timid."

"Molly has reason for that."

"We know she does." Dad again. "If you keep moving, maybe meet someone, start your own family, that'll be hard on her. Would have made more sense for Jared to give us custody."

"We'd be really glad to have her," Savannah's mother said with quiet fervency. "We've missed you so much. It would almost be like starting over with you."

That stung. "Would you be hoping for a better result?"

Mom gasped. "How can you say that? Have we ever been less than proud of you?"

No. Her parents had glowed with pride in her, even as any praise for Jared was handed out grudgingly.

"I was…sort of kidding."

"Oh," her mother said, mollified. "We don't

mean any kind of criticism of you. You're wonderful with Molly, but our offer is sincerely meant. You must have noticed that she has even your father wrapped around her little finger."

Dad's face did soften whenever his gaze rested on his granddaughter. Thank goodness Jared had had a daughter instead of a son, a girl who looked enough like Savannah to be *her* daughter. Her parents had been good to Molly, relieving Savannah of a major worry. Molly seemed less reluctant to be left in her grandmother's care than she had Brenda's. That didn't mean Savannah was going to say—what?—*Oh, great, she's all yours.* And then take off, free as a bird?

"That's generous of you," she said carefully. "You know I moved home because she needs more family. Having her grandma and granddad here to give her what she needs is really important. But I love her. Jared entrusted her to me, and I plan to live up to that. As far as I'm concerned, Molly *is* my daughter now."

"Oh, well." Mom was clearly disappointed, but also nodding approval. "Just know, if you ever change your mind—"

"That won't happen, but thank you." She took a couple of steps so she could hug her mother, then smiled at her father. "It's been good to be home."

In some ways, but there was nothing to be gained anymore in reminding them of how they'd treated Jared, or even in pursuing the *why*.

Maybe this was the wrong time, but she took a deep breath. "Actually, I've been thinking I'd like to move with Molly into that empty cabin. Unless you have plans for it?" She looked to her father.

He frowned. "No, but why would you want to do that? This house is plenty big for all of us. We're family, for God's sake!"

"I know. But I'm thirty-one." Thirty-two in March. "I haven't lived at home since I left for college. In one way these last two weeks have been good, but…finding myself back in my old bedroom, mostly just helping around the house like I did when I was a teenager, I feel as if I've gone backward, you know? I guess I'd like a little more sense of independence, but staying here on the ranch would let Molly and me lean on you, too."

Her parents exchanged a glance. She could tell they didn't like her idea, but if pressed, they'd probably both have to admit they understood how she felt, too.

Wanting to let the concept of her and Molly moving out settle a little, she asked, "Dad, did you get a look at Akil? He's gorgeous."

The Arabian gelding had been sent here by an owner she'd trained for in the past. They wanted him for cutting, but so far he wasn't patient enough. It was possible that, in the end, she'd have to give them a dose of reality and suggest they find another focus for him, but it was equally possible that the trainer who had worked with him was the one lacking in patience.

Her father grunted. "Pretty enough, but you know I like quarter horses."

"Big butts," she teased, and he grinned.

"Damn right. You can *see* the power."

They had had nothing but quarter horses on the Circle B, but part of the deal they'd made before she came home was that she could take in other horses to train as a side business, as long as she had time for the animals bred and raised here at the ranch.

"Okay," he said abruptly. "No reason you can't have the cabin. I'll have Jeff look it over, make sure there are no problems before you move in."

"Oh, good." Now she hugged him. "I can probably buy beds and some of the furniture in town—"

"You don't have any in storage?" her mother asked, sounding startled.

"No, I always had furnished apartments. It'll be good to change that."

"Well, we certainly have more beds and dressers and the like than we need, so you can start with that," Mom said firmly. "Although it might be fun for Molly to make decisions for her own bedroom."

Savannah wrinkled her nose. "Expect pink. I guess that won't surprise you. You're lucky I never went through that stage."

"No, you didn't," her mother agreed. "You were a tomboy from the get-go. After having a boy, I was so looking forward to buying you cute clothes, and what did you insist on wearing?"

"Jeans and cowboy boots."

Mom sighed. "Even when you were chosen as the rodeo princess, you balked at being too girlie. Your words."

Savannah laughed. "Although there were homecoming and prom dresses."

"Except you hated shopping, and picked out the first thing that fit."

"Well, just think." Sound had quit coming from the living room, and she saw the little girl appear in the doorway. "You-know-who will *love* cute clothes."

Mom looked…hopeful. And clothes shopping was one task that Savannah would be delighted to leave in her mother's hands.

"PINK COWBOY BOOTS?"

Those were the first words out of Logan's mouth, partly because he didn't have any real excuse for having stopped by the ranch for the third time in four days.

After seeing him, Savannah had reined a glossy bay gelding to a stop at the arena fence where Logan hooked a boot on the lowest rung and crossed his arms on the highest so he could watch her in action. Her mount had the classic dished face of an Arabian.

A small herd of steers bellowed and shoved in a narrow holding pen to one side. Usually they'd be raising dust, too, but the temp last night had dropped well below freezing, and the ground was still crisp. Logan had felt ice that wasn't visible cracking under his boots as he walked from where he'd parked closer to the house. Ugh. The time to start throwing out hay for the herd was upon them, and Logan foresaw new arguments with his father.

Savannah laughed about his last comment. "You saw those, huh? Mom took her shopping yesterday."

"Doesn't bode well for her to want to grow up to be a rancher."

"No reason she can't herd cattle wearing pink boots and shirt, is there?"

"No, but they wouldn't end up near as pretty after roping calves or getting down to wrestle with them."

He liked that Savannah laughed again. "She'll have to learn that the hard way." She waved to a ranch hand who had been waiting for the command, and he lifted a bar to allow the cattle to jostle each other through the chute and into the arena. In typical fashion, they circled the arena at a trot a couple of times, searching for a way to make a break.

Savannah's horse quivered with his desire to take charge as the steers lumbered by, continuing to bawl their displeasure, but she kept him still with legs, hands on the rein and a quiet word.

Also as usual, the small herd finally clumped together at one end.

"Did you have a question?" Savannah asked him. "Otherwise, I need to get to work."

Logan shook his head. "Just checking on the two of you. I don't mind watching you in action. It's always a pleasure."

He'd swear she blushed, but she turned the gelding away before he could be sure. What he'd said was the honest truth. He was good on a horse, as were most ranchers in these parts and their children. Sure, ATMs were used for a lot of the jobs once handled by men on horseback, but they all spent plenty of time in the saddle, too. From the time Savannah was eight or nine, though, she'd taken his breath away when she rode.

As he watched, she reined the gelding right into the middle of the small herd, ambling along so as not to alarm the cattle. No, not as relaxed as he'd initially thought; the horse hunched his back once, skittered a couple of feet sideways a minute later, causing restlessness around him. Savannah had him cut through the herd, circle out, then do it again, over and over again, until he decided he didn't have to get excited.

Logan knew he should get back to work; with ice lurking in shaded stretches of the roads, there were bound to be more accidents than usual. This time of year, even locals forgot to be cautious. A long skid was a wake-up call that seemed to be necessary every winter. Those same locals couldn't seem to get through their heads that pickup trucks, bearing most of the weight in the cab, didn't handle well in icy or snowy conditions unless some weight was added to the bed. Sandbags, say, or bales of hay.

He'd planned to patrol this morning, since his deputies were spread too thin, but he couldn't seem to take his eyes off Savannah. She had that high-strung horse meandering along as if he had nothing more on his mind than finding a sunny spot to graze.

The gelding was momentarily startled when she set him to work cutting a single steer out of the middle of the herd. He moved a little too sharply, stirring up the herd. Once he'd edged the one steer into the open arena, though, horse and rider were a treat to watch when it came to preventing the steer from rejoining the others. Each attempt to break free was blocked, the Arabian spinning on his haunches, Savannah moving as one with him, hardly seeming to do a thing.

At last, she gave an invisible signal to her mount, and they stayed still and allowed the steer to rush back to the safety of the herd.

Waiting a couple of minutes, she started all over again, choosing a different steer, again from the center of the herd. In a cutting competition, taking one from the edge would result in poorer scores; what was called a "deep cut" was rewarded. Still a little too much movement from the cattle; riders were downgraded if the herd was stirred up.

He stayed to watch her repeat one more time, then made himself leave. Logan was frowning when he fired up the engine. His current fascination with this woman wasn't compatible with the disdain, even dislike, he'd felt for her all these years.

Having been burned so recently by another woman made his interest even more nonsensical. No, he hadn't been to the point of asking Laura to marry him, but they had been living together for a few months and he'd considered that the relationship might be going somewhere. He'd debated before asking her to move with him, and been stunned when she dismissed the idea as if it were a complete absurdity.

She'd been really peeved when he hadn't been in the mood a few hours later to hop into bed and have some presplit sex.

No, he hadn't been brokenhearted, but he hadn't enjoyed the experience of finding out how low he was on her scale of importance. You might say he was a little off women right now.

Which made more inexplicable this compulsion to keep a close eye on Jared's sister.

OF COURSE, the San Francisco police detective kept calling. She would have given a lot to be able to share anything the slightest bit helpful to his investigation into her brother's death. Clearly, he'd like to get his hands on Jared's phone, but hadn't pushed the issue yet.

He seemed surprised when he admitted that the autopsy tests hadn't found any illegal substances in Jared's blood. In fact, he'd appeared surprisingly healthy and fit for a man with a history of drug addiction. The pathologist agreed with Savannah's guess that Jared had been clean for a number of years now.

What she didn't know was why her brother hadn't cut himself free of the dark underworld of drug dealing. He'd given her hints, but stayed closemouthed during their phone conversations. Had he thought someone might be listening?

She did remind Detective Trenowski that she'd wondered whether Jared wasn't working undercover, although she had no idea who he was reporting to, if so.

"Was he going by his own name?" the detective asked.

Of course she had to say, for at least the dozenth time, "I don't know. Except, well, his driver's license was in his name, wasn't it?" Why hadn't she pushed for more answers? But she knew. She'd been afraid Jared would quit calling her at all.

"I might check with the DEA in case they've been pulling his strings," Trenowski said thoughtfully.

"Will you let me know?" she asked. Or was that begged?

"If I can," he said. "Ah, your brother's body has been released. Have you come up with a plan?"

She took a deep breath. There was something awful about choosing a funeral home from Yelp reviews, but that was what she'd done. She hadn't even discussed this with her parents. Mom had fretted that "those police" wouldn't let the family bury her son, but she'd also never asked when Jared's body would be released.

Ultimately, Savannah had decided on cremation. Jared's ashes would be mailed to her. She couldn't imagine shipping his body home to be buried in Sage Creek, not after he'd run away and never returned in all these years. Anyway, who would go to the funeral, if she'd arranged one? Logan and her. Oh, maybe there'd be a few friends from school or teachers who'd attend. Her parents undoubtedly would, but Savannah couldn't stomach any hypocrisy from her father.

No, it was better this way. Eventually, she and Molly together could decide what to do with Jared's ashes. Savannah wished she'd known the adult Jared well enough to guess whether he'd want his ashes spread in the ocean, the mountains… Not in the dry, sagebrush-and-juniper country where he'd grown up, she felt sure.

Logan asked about Jared's body, during his fifth or sixth stop by the ranch, and frowned when she told him what she'd decided. To her relief, though, after a minute he only nodded and said, "He wouldn't have wanted to be buried here."

"No."

They let the subject drop.

He asked, as he had every time he came by, whether she'd had any phone calls that made her uneasy, any hang-ups, any hint at all that somebody might be looking for her and Molly, but she shook her head at that.

Savannah hated the fact that she had started looking forward to seeing him, and that his crooked smile made her heart squeeze every bit as much as it had during the height of her teenage crush on him. The truth was, Logan might be presenting himself as an old friend, but he was a cop whose interest had been piqued, and who maybe was outraged on behalf of his old friend. When he stopped by here, he was Sheriff Quade, and she shouldn't kid herself otherwise.

Chapter Five

Her father's voice always had carried. Savannah was hanging towels in the bathroom after slinging the new matching bath mat over the tub curtain rod when she heard him snap, "This is a damn fool thing for her to be doing! But try to talk to her?" He snorted. "She's too independent for her own good." Logan and Dad had carried in her new sofa a few minutes ago.

Logan answered, his voice as calm and deep as always. "I don't know, Gene. I've got to sympathize, since I've moved back into my old bedroom, too. It's not just that my feet hang off the bed. It's having Dad keeping an eye on me, ready to jump on me if he's not happy with the way I do something. This seems like a good compromise for Savannah to me."

Bless him! She hadn't been sure how she felt about his appearance a couple of hours earlier to help her move in. She hadn't invited Logan, but he'd known which day they planned for the great move, and shown up bright and early. He'd even brought a completely unexpected housewarming present.

Shoving a big item in a sack at her, he'd said, "You may not need this. If not, the receipt is in the bag. I just thought..." Sounding embarrassed, he'd trailed off.

He'd bought a high-end coffee maker for her. Way to a woman's heart. She hugged the gift.

"I haven't bought one yet. Thank you, Logan. This is...really nice of you."

He'd given one nod and then said, "What can I do?"

Really, there wasn't that much, but he had helped Dad dismantle a couple of beds at her parents' house and carry frames, springs and mattresses downstairs and the quarter mile or so to the cabin. Mom had helped Savannah make up the beds once they were in place. Molly had brand-new bedding with purple unicorns galloping over rainbows along with matching curtains. She hadn't left her bedroom since. Savannah could hear her across the hall singing tunelessly to herself.

Didn't Dad know *everyone* could hear what he was saying?

Savannah had been doing well restraining herself where her father was concerned, but his attitude was rubbing her the wrong way. Now that she was home, he wanted his wayward daughter under his thumb, day and night.

Logan's low-key explanation of how she felt might be more effective than her efforts, though. Both men's voices had gone quieter, and she let herself relax and look around the bathroom. She'd gone with peach and rust in here, and thought she might paint the walls if it looked like she and Molly would be staying. The kitchen, too. Maybe a lemon yellow, she thought.

The scuff of a footstep had her turning sharply to find Logan filling the doorway with those broad shoulders. As always, she was hyperaware of his very presence.

"Looking good."

"Thanks."

He eyed the towels. "Is that color close enough to pink to please your little cutie?"

Savannah laughed. "We had a minor argument, but she's satisfied because she got to pick out her own bedding. Have you seen it?"

His grin was even sexier in such close quarters. "Yeah. She's singing 'Over the Rainbow,' except I don't think she knows most of the lines."

"I noticed. I've already looked it up on the internet so I can sing it for her. I bet it's now on her favorites list along with 'You Are My Sunshine.'" Her own answering smile wobbled. "I love seeing her so happy."

"Yeah." He could sound remarkably gentle. He glanced over his shoulder and lowered his voice. "Maybe this isn't the time, but I've been meaning to ask, ah, whether you've considered looking for her mother. Just to be sure she won't pop up someday wanting her daughter back."

"I haven't yet, but I should, shouldn't I?"

Creases deepened on his forehead. "I think so."

"The thing is… I don't want to trigger her interest."

He gripped the door frame on each side of him. "I can do the looking, if you want."

Savannah tried to decide how she felt about that. "I thought about hiring a private investigator. The trouble is, all I know is the woman's name from Molly's birth certificate. I have absolutely no idea whether she stayed on in San Francisco or moved to Chicago or anywhere else. Or how long it's been since she gave up Molly."

"I'll be glad to conduct a search," he said. "Law enforcement databases give me access to a lot of information."

"I…" She hesitated for only a moment. "Yes, thank you. Let me try talking to Molly again first, in case she can tell me anything at all. You'd think she'd remember whether she had to travel when Jared took her, for example."

"You would. I'm no expert on kids her age, but she seems pretty verbal to me."

"I think she is, too, except she clams up when it comes to talking about her mother or anything except the recent past. I think she'll need counseling, but maybe not yet when so much change has been piled on her."

"Understandable."

He just stood there, a big man who effortlessly dominated this small space. He had a way of watching her from those unnervingly pale eyes that awakened an awareness that she was a woman who hadn't been involved with a man for an awfully long time. Blame the crush she'd had on him as a boy, she told herself desperately. Yes, he'd grown up to be as sexy as she'd imagined he would, but this was the guy who'd looked at her with contempt when he happened to notice her in the high school halls, remember?

"Do you know where my mom is?" she asked briskly.

His gaze lingered on her for a minute longer before his arms dropped to his sides and he stepped back. "Up at the house. She says lunch should be ready in about ten minutes."

Savannah managed to offer a smile that was no more than pleasant. "I trust she invited you?"

"She did."

"Well, let me take a peek at the living room, and then we can head over to the house." She hesitated. "Thank you for what you said to Dad. He isn't happy about us moving out of the house."

"Not hard to tell."

She walked past him and into the small living room, which at present held only her new sofa, a new wall-hung television, and a small bookcase and antique rocking chair Mom had dredged up from the house. The curtains were ugly, but she planned to have blinds installed to replace them, and for her bedroom window and the kitchen and bathroom windows, too. Every once in a while, she had an uneasy remembrance of how she'd felt watched that night when she picked up Molly, about the car that had slowed and pinned hers in bright lights. The crime level in a rural county like this was nothing compared to a rough neighborhood in a big city, but she would still be happiest to know that nobody could peek in the windows.

"Auntie Vannah?" The high voice came from behind her. "Where's Grandma and Grand-daddy?"

"Getting lunch ready." Savannah scooped her up, twirled once, smacked a kiss on her cheek and said, "But you're not hungry, are you? Not even for mac and cheese. Or cookies."

Molly giggled as she hadn't been able to do in her first weeks with Savannah. "I'm always hungry!" she declared.

Logan grinned at her. "Then how come you aren't bigger? You should be at least this high." He held a hand a foot over the top of her head.

She sniffed. "I will be. When I'm five. Or maybe six."

"Five is coming up pretty soon, isn't it?"

"Uh-*huh*."

"January," Savannah said. "That really isn't far away."

"'Cept Christmas comes first," Molly informed them. "I want my own pony for Christmas."

They kept talking as they walked along a white-painted fence bordering a pasture where brood mares were kept. Not as many as Savannah would like to see in the future, but she was looking forward to foaling season anyway.

Molly would love seeing newborn foals.

Savannah smiled and turned her head to meet Logan's compelling gaze. After a moment, his mouth curved, too.

LOGAN HAD EXPECTED to find himself bristling when he had to spend any time with either of Jared's parents, but today had felt surprisingly comfortable. Or maybe he shouldn't be surprised. He'd spent a lot of time here as a kid, just as Jared had at his house. Things weren't as bad in the early years. Except for the irritation Savannah had let him see once, she seemed to be getting along fine with her parents, too—who showed signs of worshipping this new granddaughter as much as they had their daughter.

After an excellent lunch, Savannah walked him out to the porch to thank him again for his help. Looking down at this beautiful woman, no lon-

ger glaring at him, he did something out of the
ordinary for him.

He let impulse seize him.

"Any chance I could take you to dinner one of
these evenings?" he asked.

She looked startled.

Since he was undecided about his own moti-
vation, he added, "I've been hoping to hear more
about Jared. Sounds like you talked to him pretty
regularly over the years. I've spent a lot of time
wondering."

Her face softened again. "I can imagine. Why
he didn't call you, I can't imagine."

His jaw tightened. "I can." As annoyed as he'd
been to find out that his old friend *had* called Savannah on a regular basis, Logan tried not to lie
to himself. "That last year, he was getting into
things I didn't approve of. The drugs, especially,
but heavy drinking, too. He developed a flash
temper. You probably knew that. He was involved
in a lot of fights."

She nodded. The principal would have been
calling her parents to pick Jared up after a teacher
or the vice principal in charge of discipline had
broken up those fights. How could she help but
hear about it, and see her brother's black eyes and
raw knuckles?

"I came down hard on him." This was hard to
say. "Told him if he was using or drunk, I didn't

want to see him. I didn't think of it as tough love, but I guess that's what I was going for."

"Only, it didn't work," she said, pain in her voice.

For the first time, it occurred to him that she might have used a similar tactic with Jared.

"No. By the time he took off, we were hardly speaking, not spending any time together. I was probably the last person he'd have confided in."

She offered a twisted smile. "I tried to stand up for him with Mom and Dad, but…he wasn't exactly confiding in me, either."

"Dinner?"

The smile became more natural. "That sounds good. I guess you can tell Mom will be thrilled to have Molly to herself."

"It's obvious she's besotted. I think that's the word."

Savannah chuckled. "Dad, too, even though he's not much into hugs or explaining what's happening in the NFL games to her."

"And sometimes the Seahawks are especially hard to explain," Logan muttered. "Assuming your dad's a fan." The Seattle team wasn't having a good year.

She laughed again. "He is, and I really doubt that Molly would understand why he's yelling at the TV. Um." She nibbled on her lower lip. "I'm free any evening."

"Tomorrow?"

"That's fine. Shall I meet you in town, or...?"

She probably realized how silly that sounded, given that he lived just down the road. She didn't argue when he said a little dryly, "Why don't I just pick you up?"

Logan left after a moment that felt awkward to him. He wanted to kiss her, even just on the cheek, as if they'd always parted that way. But, no, they hadn't, and he still had some serious ground to make up...if he decided he wanted to upend a relationship that had him uneasy.

He'd have to see how it went.

A HALF HOUR into the evening, Logan discovered how good it felt to talk to Savannah and how much he liked having her confide in him.

They'd decided on an Italian restaurant, which had excellent food even by his tastes, altered by years spent in a cosmopolitan city. This had been a pizza parlor when he was a teenager, but clearly someone had bought it out and upgraded in the intervening years.

They did talk about Jared initially, Savannah showing him the few photos she had of an older Jared. Logan looked at them for a long time.

"I can email them to you, if you want," she offered.

"Yeah." He cleared his voice. "I'd like that."

She shared some of what her brother had told her over the years.

"The worst part was knowing that his addiction drove him into... I don't know exactly, whether he was selling illegal drugs or helping run them or what. Or maybe that was part of his rebellion, knowing how much it would offend Dad." She made no effort to hide how hard it had been to continue to love someone whose lifestyle she utterly opposed. "If I hadn't known the causes of his depression so well, I'd have been angrier at him. As it was, we never talked for long, and I tried not to say anything that might make him quit calling. At least I knew—" She shrugged.

"He was alive."

"If not well. Except sometimes he sounded really good. Another thing I never knew was whether he was fighting the addiction on his own, or whether he went through rehab once or a dozen times, but I would let myself hope. And I'd swear he *had* been completely straight the last few years."

Being a cop, Logan wasn't big on excuses for not doing the right thing. "Then why didn't he walk away?"

She was quiet for a minute, turning her wineglass in her hand, but finally lifted her gaze to Logan's. "I was never sure, but...he hinted a few times that he might be working undercover. He used the word *atone*."

"They were getting suspicious. Isn't that what he said?"

"Yes." Expression troubled, Savannah said, "Wouldn't you think he'd have told me? Or left something in the duffel that I could have taken to authorities?"

Instincts sharpening, Logan said, "Are you so sure he didn't?"

"He left a will naming me guardian and some paperwork about investments for Molly. His personal phone, too, but it has so little on it. There are the numbers of people he called, but...not many. No messages or texts. I wonder if he had any friends at all. I searched in hopes of finding more about Molly's mother, but failed unless one of those numbers is hers. Otherwise, nothing."

"Maybe he wanted to keep you and Molly out of the dark side of his life," Logan said slowly. That would have been his own inclination. "He wouldn't have liked the idea of endangering you."

"No." Savannah tried to smile. "That's what I tell myself."

"I suppose in coming home, you've dropped off the radar. Who'd know?"

"My former boss. I guess the IRS will when I file next year's taxes."

"The IRS knows all," Logan intoned.

He loved her laugh. From then on, as if by mutual agreement, they let the subject of her troubled brother go, instead talking about what had changed—notably, this restaurant—and what hadn't in Sage Creek. Which wasn't much.

"Well, I noticed they did finally build a new elementary school," Savannah conceded. "Do you remember what a *pit* that place was? The one building got condemned, so we weren't allowed in it, and everyone started to think it was haunted."

Logan's turn to laugh. "I hadn't heard that. Who was supposed to be doing the haunting?"

"Mostly teachers who'd moved away or died. Do you remember Mr. Barrick?"

"PE? God, yes."

"You know, the gym was in that building. It made sense he'd still be there terrorizing students." Humor brightened the color in Savannah's eyes.

"Him, I'd believe in. Except I think he just retired. He's probably terrorizing neighbors in Arizona or Florida, wherever he and his wife moved to."

She giggled. "Can't you picture him ruling over a homeowners' association? He could ride a golf cart around the neighborhood making notes about any landscaping violations."

He suggested a few teachers he could picture choosing to hang around as ghosts, and she added a couple more. Small as the school district was, they'd had many of the same teachers, from kindergarten up through high school, despite being three years apart.

From there, they moved on to mutual acquaintances—who was still around, who'd died, who'd gotten divorced, taken over a parents' business and so on. Since he'd been back in town longer, and stayed in closer touch with his dad than she had with her parents, mostly he updated her on the local scandals. They were both laughing when the check arrived.

He unlocked his truck and held the door open for her, only going around to get in behind the wheel once she was fastening her seat belt. As he steered the truck out of the parking lot onto the main street here in town, he was surprised at how busy Sage Creek was this evening. Dad had always claimed the town rolled up the carpet by eight o'clock, and it was mostly true. Restaurants, a few taverns, a bowling alley and something going on at the Elks Club provided the only evening entertainment.

Once they left town behind, darkness surrounded them. Only a few passing headlights intruded. Logan tried to retreat from the sense of intimacy he felt in this cocoon by starting a conversation again—and not the first-date kind they'd had in the restaurant.

"Jared was expecting a lot from you, asking you to take on his daughter," he said. "Given that you'd never met Molly."

"Didn't know she existed," Savannah said dryly.

"Yeah."

"He had to be so desperate he didn't think about it. What else could he do with her?"

"It must have been a shocker for you."

"That's an understatement." She was quiet for a minute. "Especially when we didn't hear from him, and it sank in that I was all she had. I had to quit my job. Molly was too traumatized to settle into the only day care available, and she had so many nightmares, I started feeling like a zombie. There were moments—" She broke off.

"Moments?"

"Oh, it doesn't matter. I'm lucky she's such a sweetheart."

"It's a surprise she is," he said, "given how much change *she's* suffered." Damn, they were almost to the ranch. He didn't like having such mixed emotions about this woman. Wanting to see her, get to know her again, lay his hands on her, while also having the equal and opposite reaction, thinking that the way she presented herself now could be a facade.

"We might be in the honeymoon phase," Savannah commented. "Her wanting to please me because she's scared of what will happen if she makes me mad. After all, she's been abandoned twice already in her life."

He'd read that was common behavior for foster kids in a new home, or new adoptees. The suggestion made sense.

That led to him speculating on how Savannah

would react if that cute little blonde girl started throwing screaming temper tantrums and yelling, *I want Daddy! I don't want* you!

With no experience at being a mother, did she even know?

He couldn't forget that the girl he knew had been the unfailing center of her parents' lives. If Jared was to be believed, she'd always gotten what she wanted when she wanted it. That hadn't changed; even though her father hadn't liked her moving into the cabin, she got her way. Went without saying she'd also been popular at school. Had she ever faced the slightest bump in her belief that *her* life would be one of sunshine and rainbows?

Look at her now. The minute she felt burdened, she'd run home to Mommy and Daddy.

She was good with Molly. He'd yet to see her be anything but patient. But how long would that last? How long before she needed to be the center of attention again, no matter who that hurt?

Chapter Six

Savannah was chagrined to realize how much she wished Logan had done more than kiss her lightly on the cheek before he left her on her parents' porch. As he looked down at her, his eyes had narrowed with the kind of purpose she recognized. His gaze had flickered to her mouth, she'd swear it had, and her pulse quickened. She might even have started to push up onto her tiptoes when his expression changed and he brushed his lips on her cheek. Then he'd said gruffly, "Good night, Savannah. I'm glad we did this." And darned if he didn't bound down the porch steps, walk to his truck, get in and drive away without more than a casual lift of the hand.

She stood there on the doorstep long enough that if her parents had been listening for her, they'd be wondering what she was doing. Or not wondering. She puffed out a breath.

She'd wanted Logan to kiss her, all right, but because it would be a fulfillment of her youthful crush, not because she liked and trusted him down to the bone. So…it was just as well they hadn't gone there.

She made a face. Uh-huh. Sure.

Her phone rang, distracting her. The number was blocked. She never answered calls that looked like spam. If it turned out to be anyone she wanted to talk to, she'd return the call after she heard the message. If she was lucky, it would be someone tracking her down to train a problem horse.

Blocked, though. That seemed strange. Especially after telling Logan her speculation that Jared might have been trying to bring down an organization with ruthless employee relations. As in: *you betray us, you're dead*.

Which Jared was.

Stepping into the house, hearing the TV in the living room and her mother's light voice, she realized there'd been no follow-up *ding* indicating the caller had left a message.

Well, who didn't get junk phone calls?

She almost dismissed her worry.

Still, after she and Molly walked back to the cabin and she tucked her niece into bed, Savannah was left restless, feeling a warm curl low in her belly, a sense of anticipation she hadn't had in a long time. Or ever? She hadn't had a steady boyfriend while she was in high school. None of the guys could compare to Logan, even after he'd left for college.

Truth to tell, her couple of later relationships that had gone far enough for her to share her bed had been a form of *settling*. Funny that she hadn't seen that, but the ranches where she'd worked were typically remote, and she had never been a big fan of hanging out in taverns. That left the pickings sparse, and she'd never been sure what kind of man she wanted. Some of the ranchers reminded her too much of her father, gruff, single-minded, not given to tenderness and lacking any sense of fun. Many of the hands seemed to have no ambition. Probably because of Jared, Savannah recoiled from heavy drinkers.

Somewhere in the back of her mind, she'd believed that, someday, she'd meet the right guy. It was more than a little disquieting to discover that Logan had been there all that time in the back of her head, too. He'd only been eighteen the last time she saw him except from a distance during his visits home, but no one she'd met since measured up.

Wonderful. She still had a thing for a man she deeply suspected hadn't gotten over despising her. Chances were really good that he'd been dropping by regularly out of loyalty to Jared, thinking that she and Jared's daughter might need his protection. He might have been briefly tempted to kiss her tonight, but he'd easily resisted that temptation, hadn't he?

Well, despite her occasional unease, she

thought it unlikely that they'd need him. He'd pointed out himself that she'd effectively disappeared, right? Her phone number was out there, but not her whereabouts. And why would anyone think she'd know anything about Jared's business?

Despite her perturbation when she went to bed, Savannah slept well. So well, she didn't wake up until her mattress started bouncing, as if she was in a boat in rough water.

She pried open her eyes to find Molly jumping up and down and giggling.

"Aargh!" Savannah lunged up, snatched her niece into a hug and growled into her ear. "You're making me seasick."

Molly beamed at her. "Grandma said maybe we could get a trampoline. That would be even *more* fun!"

"Yes, it would." Except Savannah had qualms about how safe they were. She'd definitely vet anything her mother considered.

And then she had a thought. "You didn't have a nightmare! Not even one!" Unless she'd slept through it, but she couldn't imagine.

"Uh-uh. I didn't wet the bed, either."

That had happened only a few times, but embarrassed Molly terribly.

Savannah hugged her even harder, then set her aside. "I don't know about you, but *I* need the bathroom."

"I already went, and I washed my hands, too," Molly told her.

"Good for you."

This move home had been the right thing to do, she thought as she got out the cereal, bowls, milk and a banana. Molly really was thriving, not only because she was gaining confidence that Auntie Vannah was solidly in her corner, but also because of her grandparents.

Even Jared might forgive them if he could see how good they were for his daughter.

And, yes, things wouldn't always go so smoothly, but they'd get through them.

She'd sent Molly off to get dressed and was loading the dishwasher when her phone rang again. The call looked just like last night's: *No Number*, her phone told her. That was weird, but she didn't want to lose a good training opportunity because she refused to listen to a sales spiel or whatever.

So this time, she answered with a "Hello."

"Have I reached Ms. Baird?" The voice was a man's and unfamiliar.

Could it be the police again?

"Yes," she said cautiously.

"I understand your brother died recently."

Her skin prickled. "That's true."

"He worked for me. Having him vanish was…a shock." He paused. "I'm sure it was worse for you."

"Yes."

"I don't know how much he's told you—"

"About his work? Nothing," she said quickly. "We were mostly estranged."

"I see. Well, he was undertaking some critical work for us that should have remained confidential. Unfortunately, it's clear that when he took off, he had information that should never have left, er, the company offices. It's my understanding that he met with you before his death."

Why would he have thought that? Did they have an informant on the police force who'd implied that she had lied to the detective and might really have seen Jared?

Scared, she shook her head hard at Molly, who appeared in the kitchen doorway.

To the man, she said, "I wish that was true. I'd have loved the chance to see him, but…he didn't show up."

"He gave something to you." On the surface, the tone was still civil, but somehow darker.

"His daughter. She's just a little girl. That's all he left for me—Molly and a pink suitcase with her clothes and toys." She immediately regretted telling him Molly's name.

"I'm having trouble believing that," he remarked coldly. The gloves were off.

"I can't help that," she said, going for offended in hopes of hiding her fear. "I hadn't seen Jared in eighteen years. That's a long time. We only occasionally spoke on the phone. I have no idea what he did for a living. I'm glad he felt he could trust me enough to raise the daughter he loved. I don't even know where Jared lived. I can't help you find whatever you're looking for."

"If you expect me to buy that—"

"I'm sorry. This has been difficult enough. I have nothing else to say." She ended the call, and silenced her phone with a quick flick of her fingernail.

Oh, dear God. Could she hope Jared's boss— and his minions—couldn't find her and Molly?

BY CHANCE, Detective Trenowski called an hour later to let her know Jared's cremated remains should arrive on her doorstep within the next day or two. He sounded alarmed when she told him about the phone call.

"I hope you planned to let me know about this," he said sternly.

She agreed hastily that she had, which was true. In fact, she'd just left Molly with Grandma and had sought the quiet and relative warmth of the tack room in the barn to hold this conversation. The soft sounds that reached her, rustles as horses moved around in their stalls or nosed hay in mangers, an occasional clomp of a hoof or a nicker, should have been familiar and comforting.

"You might want to consider getting in touch with local law enforcement," the detective suggested. "Just…let them know about the call and why it's worrisome. If you give them my phone number, I'll be glad to talk to them."

"Thank you," she said. "I'll do that." In fact, she'd intended to call Logan first. Why she'd been standing here waffling, she didn't know.

Logan answered his cell phone on the first ring. She could hear a vehicle engine and assumed he was on the road. "Savannah?"

"Yes. Um, after you dropped me off last night, a blocked call came in on my phone. I ignored it, but this morning, when it came up again, I answered. It was a man, saying he'd been Jared's boss."

"Damn it."

He already disapproved? "You think I should have kept ignoring whoever was calling?"

"No, I didn't mean that," he said quickly. "I'm annoyed at myself. I should have thought about having you download a recording app onto your phone."

"Oh. That would have been good. Except the guy didn't come out and say anything direct enough for you to act on."

"No, and technically you're supposed to tell someone they're being recorded, but at this point I don't care."

Law-abiding to a fault, she didn't, either.

"We'll do that as soon as I can get away," he added.

"Why would he call back?" she had to ask. "I

said, no, I hadn't seen Jared, that he'd never talked to me about his work, we were mostly estranged, and I apologized for not being able to help."

"Tell me what he said."

She reported the conversation the best she could and didn't like the silence when she was done.

"You didn't get the impression this guy was satisfied?"

"No," she said reluctantly. "The last thing he said was that he didn't buy what I was saying."

Logan swore. "I really wish I could have heard the conversation." He let out a long breath. "I can't do anything right now. I'm on my way to a vehicular accident. A head-on."

"Oh, no."

"I'll see if I can arrange some drive-bys, but you're pretty remote. You have a bunch of hands living on the ranch as well as your parents, right?"

"Yes."

"There's probably no reason to worry." He didn't sound as confident as she'd have liked, but he was right. It would be too obvious for anyone with hostile intentions to drive as far as the house and barns, and it would be a long, dark walk otherwise. Any unusual noise would arouse curiosity. Loud curiosity, when it came to the ranch dogs.

"Oh—the detective I've been talking to in San Francisco suggested I give you his number."

"Can you text it? I'm driving right now."

"No problem. I should let you go."

"Yeah." Logan's voice had changed, and she knew he'd arrived at the site of what might be a gruesome accident.

"Thank you for listening," she said.

He was gone without another word.

LOGAN DID MAKE a quick stop at the Circle B the next day to talk Savannah through downloading the app to record conversations, even though he leaned toward thinking that a repeat call was an unlikely next step—if there would be any. Jared must have had friends, even a girlfriend. It sounded like Savannah had been as clear as she could be in telling the caller she'd had no appreciable relationship with her brother in many years. What else could they do on the phone except issue threats, and why would they expect that to do any good?

He'd interrupted her in the middle of a working day. In fact, she was taking a quarter horse around some bright painted barrels in the arena when he arrived. Not yet at full speed, but even so, each turn around the barrel would look hair-raising to someone not accustomed to sticking on a quarter horse's back when he used those powerful hindquarters to spin. On the dime, as the saying went.

Logan was just as glad to have no reason to

linger when they were done. He hadn't resolved his confusion where she was concerned and had decided avoidance was the smartest tactic until he did. He was damn glad he hadn't kissed her the way he'd wanted to; he still harbored plenty of doubts about this woman.

He had a particularly busy week at work, too. The head-on collision had taken place on a county road rather than a state highway, unfortunately, so the responsibility for measuring distances and more, so that he could determine speed and trajectory for each vehicle, was his. He made the immediate decision to send someone else in his small department for training in accident reconstruction.

As was all too common, the speeder had been a seventeen-year-old boy, probably trying to impress his girlfriend. She survived; he didn't. If it had been the reverse, there would have been legal consequences, but beyond that, Logan doubted the kid would have ever gotten over his culpability in such a tragedy. The car had hit a pickup truck, severely damaged it, but it had been solid enough to keep the driver from serious injury. Since the kids were locals, a pall had swept over the entire county. The funeral was planned for next week, although the girlfriend would still be in the hospital.

Local residents were also facing a rash of thefts from mailboxes—hard to combat, given the vast number of miles of road in a rural county like this one versus the number of deputies Logan could deploy. And, yeah, that was a federal crime, but no federal law enforcement agency had time for an isolated, little-populated area like this.

To top it off, there'd been a break-in at the farm-and-ranch store. The list of items taken was long enough that the thief had spent as much as an hour "shopping" and probably had a pickup truck backed up to the loading dock in back. The lock showed some damage, but not enough. The camera aimed at the loading dock had been mysteriously disabled. That added up to a guilty employee or, conceivably, ex-employee who'd copied a key.

Not that he managed to put thoughts of Savannah aside. She was always there, for several reasons. Coming face-to-face with her in the pharmacy, not to mention their dinner together, had brought a whole lot back to him. Jared was tangled up in so many of Logan's memories of growing up. He'd turn his head and remember taking that trail on their horses, or when he went by the high school he would grimace at the memory of the two of them sharing a six-pack sitting on the bleachers late at night.

That was the first time he'd gotten drunk, although now he wondered if that was so for Jared, even though they'd been only…fourteen, Logan thought.

Dad mentioned Jared now and again, too. He went so far as to drive over to the Circle B to say howdy and meet the little girl who had Jared's eyes.

"Wouldn't mind a grandchild," he remarked after that.

Logan grinned at him. "Call Mary and nag her." He happened to know that his sister and her husband intended to have children but weren't yet ready.

His dad laughed.

This evening, he'd checked for a last time on his father, showered and stretched out in bed. Now he let his thoughts wander.

He'd contended with equally mixed feelings about Jared's younger sister back when they were kids and then teenagers. She had dogged their steps whenever they allowed it, and he'd secretly admired her determination and toughness on the occasions when she took on more than she should have and got dumped from a horse or banged up in some other way. Of course, if her parents were around, they'd rush to her side to fuss over her, and if Jared was around, he'd be chewed out for letting his sister get hurt.

Logan had been acutely aware of her later, when she developed a figure and he'd see her sashaying down the hall at school, her butt really fine in tight jeans, her honey-blond hair rippling down to midback.

By then he'd blocked any memories of fondness. He heard and saw Jared's hurt every time Mr. Baird made plain how worthless he thought his son was in comparison to his beautiful, smart, talented daughter. Logan convinced himself that she gloried in the praise and didn't care about the brother she'd pushed aside.

Now he thought he knew better. Mostly, Jared had been neutral about her. Loved her, even if he couldn't help resenting her, too. Logan just hadn't read it that way, still felt suspicious of Savannah's character.

Maybe because here she was, home again, to her parents' open delight. Why wouldn't she be eating it up? No sullen brother to get in the way.

That was probably unfair, but he couldn't seem to shake an opinion of her that had solidified by the time he was thirteen or fourteen years old.

No wonder his attraction to her disturbed him.

And yet…considering she was the first woman who'd seriously caught his eye since his return to Sage Creek, he wondered if he wasn't a fool to hesitate making a move on her. She had to have done a lot of growing up since he'd last seen her.

Maybe he'd stop by the ranch tomorrow, he thought. Why not get to know Savannah as a woman instead of a girl? A few dates didn't equal any kind of commitment, after all. Satisfied, he sought sleep.

SAVANNAH'S EYES POPPED open to near-complete darkness. She lay stiff, peering toward where she knew her bedroom doorway was. Was Molly having a nightmare? She'd made it without one last night, for the second time this week. But she wasn't screaming, and Savannah was sure she'd have heard even quiet crying.

She focused immediately on the heavy tread of feet on the front porch, a sound that was familiar but didn't belong in the middle of the night. Something must be wrong. That had to be Dad or one of the ranch hands—

She sat up and swung her feet to the floor, surprised to have heard no knock. Barefoot, she slipped out of her room into the hall. She could peek out through a crack in the blinds.

But when she reached the living room, she saw the doorknob turning and heard a thump when an attempt to open the door failed because of the dead bolt lock. Silence followed.

Heart racing, she tiptoed forward.

Rap, rap, rap.

It came from the window, not the door. Seconds later, she heard another thud that might be someone jumping off the porch. Not ten seconds later came another *rap, rap, rap*, this time from the kitchen window. The back door rattled but the lock held.

Pulse racing, she yanked open a drawer and put

her hand right away on the butcher knife. Maybe the cast-iron skillet would be better... No, she'd take both.

The next raps came from the bathroom, followed by Molly's bedroom. Terrified by this time, Savannah hovered in the doorway. Thank God, Molly was either still asleep or huddled in a small ball under her covers pretending nothing was happening.

Savannah dashed for the window, desperate to see out, but already her tormentor was knocking on *her* bedroom window. Was whoever this was trying to lure her out? Or was the message quite different?

We're right here, only a few feet away. We could break the glass and come in, and you couldn't stop us.

She should have gone for her phone instead of inadequate weapons, she realized suddenly. But the ranch dogs had started to bark, deep and threatening, and they were coming this way.

Chapter Seven

Savannah would have waited until morning to call Logan, but she couldn't stop her father. She was so shaken, so unnerved, she'd rather not have to describe every minute once again, but apparently she had no choice. Dad was even more upset than she was, if such a thing were possible. He'd always been protective of her, one reason he'd hated her moving away for work.

She sat at her kitchen table, Molly on her lap clutching her tight, face buried against the one person she evidently trusted. Dad had suggested Molly go back to bed, and since then she'd held on even tighter.

"I could have reported this in the morning," Savannah repeated. "You shouldn't have dragged Logan out of bed. What can he do? Whoever was out there is long gone."

"You know that for a fact?"

"Of course not!" She breathed deep a few times and regulated her voice. Dad meant well. "How could I? But after rousing the whole ranch, nobody but a crazy man would come back tonight."

Dad turned his head. "That must be Logan now." His relief was obvious.

Rocking slightly to comfort herself as much as the little girl she held, she wanted Logan; she did. But she'd have rather felt more together before she talked to him.

He knocked on the front door and then walked in without waiting for anyone to open it for him. His eyes went straight to her and Molly before turning to her father.

"What happened?"

Savannah opened her mouth to answer, but Dad didn't let her.

"Savannah says someone circled the house, trying the doors and then tapping on the windows. Dogs started barking, whoever he was ran. Back when the kids were teenagers, I'd have thought it was some kind of prank. Jared might have thought it was funny to scare his sister. But now? If those drug dealers know she and Molly moved into this cabin…" Face choleric, he didn't finish.

Logan's brows drew together. She met his eyes and was dismayed to see doubt. Maybe it was even valid. If this had anything to do with that phone call, how *had* the creeps who thought she had something Jared had stolen known she'd moved home in the first place, and then which cabin she and Molly lived in? But who else would set out to terrify her?

Feeling Molly trembling, Savannah said, "I woke up to heavy footsteps on the porch. At first I thought Dad had come over because something was wrong, or maybe one of the ranch hands, but...whoever it was tried the door, but didn't knock. Then he rapped three or four times on every window as he walked around the house. He tried the back door, too."

"Him?"

"I can't be sure. The footsteps sounded like a man's."

"You didn't try to get a look at him?"

"I...was going to peek out at the porch, you know, just through a slit in the blinds, but by then he'd moved on. I wasn't fast enough. Anyway, I didn't think finding myself face-to-face with him was a good idea. I ran to the kitchen so I'd have *some* kind of weapon in case—"

Logan's gaze lowered to the heavy skillet and the knife that sat on the kitchen table, then met hers again. Those icy eyes were intense. "Why do you think he ran?"

"Because he'd done what he meant to do? Or maybe because the dogs had started barking and were tearing this way?"

He didn't say anything for a long time. The distinctive lines on his face seemed to deepen.

Finally, he said, "You think this has to do with Jared."

"What else could it be?"

"It...seems strange."

She wished she could feel numb. "You think I'm imagining things."

"Imagining?" The pause left a lot unspoken. "No."

Then what?

She licked dry lips. "The message seemed pretty clear to me. 'We know where you are. We can get to you anytime.'"

"Isn't that unnecessarily dramatic, when they could just call and tell you the same thing?"

"This had...a lot more impact." She hoped her voice wasn't shaking.

He grunted, pushed back his chair and said, "I'm going outside to take a look around."

"Why are you bothering?" she said to his back.

He ignored her and went outside.

"He'd damn well better take you seriously and do his job," her father snapped. "Meantime, why don't you take Molly up to the house? With your mother there, at least she can get some sleep."

"She's scared. I think she'll do better here. She can sleep with me."

"You sure she wouldn't feel more secure with us?" His idea of gentle fell short, but he was trying.

"I don't believe whoever this was will come back tonight."

He scowled, of course. Her father wanted to believe he could handle anything. Calling in law enforcement would normally be a last resort, in his view.

He didn't argue, though, and they sat in frigid silence until the front door opened and closed again, and Logan walked back into the kitchen.

"Too bad there's no frost tonight," he said. "I don't see any footprints."

Of course there weren't any.

"I'll talk to the employees," her father said. "You'd think someone would have heard a part of this. If anyone working here was drunk and thought this was a joke, it'll be his last laugh."

She'd been getting to know the half dozen men. The ones Dad kept on through the winter were all long-term employees. The odds weren't good any of them had been wandering around on a dark night, but considering the vibe Logan was giving off, another witness would be good.

"With cold weather, you ever had a vagrant break into one of your cabins?" Logan asked.

"Never. We're too far out of town."

Logan focused again on Savannah. "Would have been better if you'd gotten on the phone right away," he commented, his lean face unreadable. "When we might have had a chance to catch the guy."

"Tell me," she said acidly. "How many deputies do you actually have patrolling in the middle of the night? One? Two? What are the chances one would have been anywhere nearby?"

His jaw tightened. "Why'd it take the dogs so long to get worked up?"

Molly burrowed more deeply into Savannah. *Had* she heard any of the noise? If so, she was too afraid to say anything.

Savannah stared at him expressionlessly. "Because there was nothing to hear, of course." She shook her head. "Tell me why I'd do this. For attention?"

Dad scowled at Logan. "You questioning my daughter's word?"

"I didn't say that."

But he was wondering. She could tell. *This* was the Logan who'd long despised her.

Nauseated and feeling more alone than she had since the night she'd found Molly abandoned in a frightening situation, Savannah squared her shoulders.

"I think it's time Molly and I go back to bed. Mom will be worrying," she added to her father. "Tell her we're fine."

"If someone was here, he won't be back tonight," Logan conceded.

Her father's face was set in deep lines, but he nodded and pushed himself to his feet. "We can talk more in the morning."

She held out a hand and squeezed his. "Thank you for coming, Dad. Good night."

Dark color ran over his cheeks. "Would I ever not come running if you needed me?" Obviously embarrassed, he let himself out the back door.

Unfortunately, Logan didn't follow him.

She reverted to her deep-breathing exercise.

"Sometimes it's my job to ask hard questions," he said. "Always had the impression you thrived on attention."

Her laugh had to be one of the least pleasant sounds she'd ever made. "You're wrong, but you've always thought the worst of me. I've never forgotten the way you curled your lip every time you saw me." There. He'd done it now. She shook her head and looked down.

"Savannah. I'm just trying to figure out how an intruder knew where you were staying. You don't get much traffic out here at the ranch. How could someone have been watching without being noticed? Are you sure your imagination wasn't at play here?"

"Please leave," she said tonelessly, bending her neck so she could press her cheek to Molly's head. "And… I'd rather you didn't come back, even if you are the sheriff. You'll never get over despising me because of Jared. We both know that."

"You're talking nonsense—" he snapped.

She raised her head again to look directly at him. "Is it?"

He took just a moment too long before saying,

"It is, but we'll settle that later. What do you plan to do tomorrow?"

"Buy a gun, and maybe throw out feelers for a new job."

"Savannah…"

Stone-faced, she stared him down.

He muttered a curse. "You're misunderstanding me."

She didn't let even a faint crack show on her face. Finally he bent his head in acknowledgment and walked out. She heard the throaty engine of his pickup, loud at first and then fading.

Tears hot in her eyes, she locked the front door, leaving the porch light on, and tucked Molly under the covers in her bed. "I'll be right back," she whispered and hurried to the kitchen for her makeshift weapons, setting them within reach in the bedroom. Then, cold all the way to the bone, she slipped under the covers with the little girl who scrambled to cuddle right up to her, knees digging into Savannah's belly.

If only she already had that gun.

She'd have to get a safe, too, of course. She wondered how long it took to unlock one and yank out the gun. Would she be quick enough?

Fear didn't keep her awake; no, the sense of betrayal did that all on its own.

ANGRY AND FEELING SICK, Logan drove away too fast. He'd let past convictions build doubt in his mind before he so much as heard a word she said, but when she'd stared at him with bottomless pain in her eyes, he'd known what he'd done. Woman and girl needed him, but Savannah wouldn't call him again no matter what happened.

Sure, he'd been concerned, after that phone call Savannah had taken from Jared's so-called boss. But he'd spent a couple of nights now convincing himself that there was nothing to worry about there. Nobody knew where she and Molly were, and she'd talked to the San Francisco cop about the situation. He had a lot on his plate, and he wasn't going to add to it with needless conjecture from a woman with a history of being the center of attention, especially since in all of his father's years of ranching, he'd never had a break-in. Obviously, the Circle B hadn't, either. In fact, that kind of crime was rare to nonexistent in these parts.

It didn't help that Logan had detested Gene Baird for years. His phone call had been all but frantic, because his precious daughter had been threatened. If Jared had been, he'd have probably growled, "Deal with it," and rolled over to go back to sleep.

Driving over here, Savannah on his mind, Logan remembered the rodeo princess, the homecoming queen. The center of attention, except now her pretty niece had taken that place.

The icing on the cake was that he couldn't help remembering what he'd said while they drove back from town a few evenings ago—and how she'd responded.

He'd suggested that her brother had expected a lot from her. She agreed it had been a shocker.

Especially when we didn't hear from him, and it sank in that I was all she had. I had to quit my job. Molly was too traumatized to settle into the only day care available, and she had so many nightmares, I started feeling like a zombie. There were moments—

He thought that was what she'd said, almost word for word. She'd backed off fast after that.

Moments that what? The only interpretation he could come to was that she had times when she quaked at the burden she'd taken on. Thought it was more than she could bear.

Even if that was true, did he really believe she'd do something so despicable as terrify an already traumatized child with a spotlight-grabbing stunt?

He'd *seen* her with Molly. No. He wouldn't believe it. Was he stuck in the past, assuming she was the pampered girl he used to know? Or had he really known her at all?

Throat so tight he couldn't have swallowed, he steered onto the shoulder of the road just short of his own driveway and put the truck into Park.

Would she accept an apology?

Logan couldn't imagine.

SINCE SAVANNAH HAD plans for the morning that didn't include working, and she and Molly were up plenty early, she made pancakes for breakfast instead of setting out the usual cereal and milk. She even tried to pour the batter to form some recognizable shapes, but without a lot of success. Dad had been skilled at that, she remembered suddenly. His horses looked like horses. He'd done that every so often, to her and Jared's delight.

The memory held a bittersweet sting.

Molly giggled when Savannah delivered a plate to her with two pancakes that were supposed to be, yes, a horse and a crescent moon, but she scarfed them down happily, eating more than she usually did.

Savannah finished her own breakfast—her pancakes looked more like blobs of sagebrush than anything, she decided—and then smiled at her niece. "Honey, I think it's time you tell me what you remember about your mom."

Molly's eyes widened in alarm. "I don't want to live with her," she whispered.

"No." Savannah reached over the table to clasp the small hand snugly in hers. "Never, never, never. You're *my* little girl now. I'll fight anyone who tries to take you away from me. You understand?"

Maybe she'd spoken more fiercely than she should have. Maybe she shouldn't have even hinted that anyone *might* try to take Molly. But those blue eyes stayed fixed, unblinking, on Savannah's face for longer than was comfortable.

Then she nodded.

"Good. I'm glad we've got that straight." She smiled, and Molly relaxed enough to smile back.

It took some more coaxing, but eventually the four-year-old did share confused memories of when she'd lived with her mother. Memories that horrified Savannah.

There had apparently always been other people living with them. Or else Molly and her mother had moved frequently to stay with anyone who'd take them in. Savannah couldn't tell. Molly's mommy had sometimes tried to be the mother she needed to be, but sometimes she slept a lot or just sat staring straight ahead and didn't even hear when Molly spoke to her. It sounded as if Molly had crept around trying not to attract any attention, because she knew the other, rotating members of the household thought she was a nuisance. She'd fed herself, mostly cereal and bread, when no one thought to offer her anything.

Then one day her daddy had swept in and taken her away. She *thought* they'd driven a long ways in his car, but she'd fallen asleep and didn't really know whether it was all night or not.

"I liked being with Daddy," she added, "'cept he worked a lot, and then I had to stay with Julie." Her nose crinkled. "This boy she took care of was mean to me, but Daddy said I couldn't go to work with him, and at least I could play and watch TV and stuff at Julie's 'partment."

"I see." Molly must have felt a déjà vu when her auntie left her during the day with Brenda. "Did you get to say goodbye to your mommy?"

Molly's eyes filled with tears. "Uh-huh. She looked sad, but she said I would be better with Daddy. Only... I was scared, 'cause I didn't know him." She sniffed. "Is Mommy dead, too?"

"I...don't know, but I do think she was right. You were better off with your dad, and now with me."

"I like living with you best," her niece said simply.

"Good." She half stood, scooped Molly up in her arms and sat back down. "*I* like living with you, too."

Nothing Molly had told her came as a surprise. The mother had very likely been a drug addict, too. How and why Jared came to learn about his daughter would remain a mystery, but she was glad to know he hadn't hesitated to leap into action, even if single parenthood didn't conform well with his lifestyle. He'd made Molly feel loved, though.

Unfortunately, Molly hadn't said anything that would help Savannah find the mother. Maybe that was just as well. She wouldn't be turning to Logan for help, that was for sure.

Savannah sent Molly to get dressed and stood up to load the dishwasher.

Her phone rang. She saw exactly what she'd expected: instead of a displayed number, her screen showed that the number was blocked.

Oh, God. Not answering didn't seem to be an option. *Please let Molly dawdle over picking out clothes.*

She answered the call and triggered the recording app, hoping she'd done it right and it would actually work. "Hello?"

"Ms. Baird." The voice was familiar from that last call. "I hope we didn't alarm you too much last night."

"You're kidding, right?"

"We need you to know that we're serious. That you can't hide from us."

This was hopeless, but— "You're barking up the wrong tree," she said. "I told you the truth last time. If Jared had something he shouldn't have had, I'm the last person he'd have passed it on to. I'd always been careful during our rare conversations not to ask what he did for a living.

If he wanted something done, he wouldn't have depended on me. We were virtual strangers."

"But, you see, I don't believe you," the man said, almost gently. "*You* were the last person he called. He entrusted you with his child. He knew you'd raise her the way he wanted you to. You can't deny that."

"I can't, but a little girl is different than…than whatever you're talking about. Of course I'd take my niece, no matter how I felt about Jared! Why can't you see that?"

"We have considered all other possibilities," the man assured her. He sounded so businesslike, it was surreal. "We're left with only one. You."

"My brother didn't give me anything. He left no instructions, only paperwork giving me legal custody over his daughter. You're wasting your time."

"It's ours to waste, but we are getting somewhat impatient." That voice took on an edge. "Last night was a gentle warning. Please take another hard look at every message your brother left you, every single thing he passed on to you along with his *precious* daughter."

The emphasis on *precious* scared the daylights out of Savannah.

"We'll call again," he said. "If you don't have an answer, we may have to apply some real pressure."

Her mouth opened, even though she had no

idea what to say, but she knew immediately that the caller was gone. The connection was dead.

Bad choice of words.

Disturbed, she sank down in a chair, dropped the phone onto the table in front of her and stared at it as if it was a coiled snake rattling its tail.

Chapter Eight

Hearing the sound of the toilet flushing from down the hall, Savannah didn't move. Her mind whirled. Now what?

Search everything Jared had left again, yes, but she'd already done that. The obvious item of interest was his phone, and she'd gone through it several times already, finding nothing. Who knew why he'd discarded it? Anyway, if she found something, what would she do with it? Hand it over to the creeps who were threatening her? She didn't think so.

Otherwise…she would definitely let Detective Trenowski know about the call, for what little good he could do her. Logan? She supposed she almost had to. At least he'd have to believe her, since he could listen to the wretched conversation himself—unless she had done something wrong and failed to record it. But what would he do, sheriff with authority over an inadequate number of officers already stretched too thin? Savannah had no doubt tracing the phone the call had been made from, assuming he could do that, would be useless. She'd recently become well aware of the cheap phones anyone who was criminal-minded or just didn't want to be found could use, toss and replace.

So. Pack up, the way she'd intended, and run with Molly for their very lives? Try to find someplace they could live off the grid, preferably with some protection? But she didn't know how her brother's "employers" had pinned down where she and Molly were so quickly. How could the two of them make a getaway sure they were unseen?

Especially since she'd sold her own car to another ranch hand back in New Mexico and was currently borrowing an old pickup used around her father's ranch. If she disappeared with it, of course, she felt sure Dad wouldn't call the cops to report grand theft auto, but she'd undoubtedly have to dump it somewhere so she and Molly could hop buses and zigzag across the West undetected until they found what appeared to be a safe roost.

And she couldn't let herself forget how happy Molly was here, with grandparents as well as her aunt. Savannah tried to picture leaving Molly, if only temporarily, with those grandparents, but aside from understanding that Molly would feel abandoned for the third time in her life, she couldn't forget the way that man had described

Molly as Jared's *precious* daughter. If that wasn't
a threat, she'd never heard one.

Staying here, Molly would still be vulnerable,
and what more powerful lever could evil men
find than the child whom Savannah loved?

Not a single option seemed to offer any hope
at all.

MOLLY BEGGED FOR her fine blond hair to be
French-braided, and then insisted on wearing
those pink cowboy boots even though she probably wouldn't go near a horse this morning, but
finally Savannah walked her to the big house.
She found only Mom in the kitchen. Molly ran
to her for a hug.

Mom looked worried. "Your father said it
sounded like someone was breaking into the
cabin last night?"

Molly visibly shrank.

Glancing meaningfully at her, Savannah said
only, "Or…taunting me. It was scary, but we were
okay, weren't we, pumpkin?"

The child's blonde head bobbed, but her body
language showed tension.

"I need to go into town to do some errands,"
she said. "You don't mind Molly staying with
you, do you?"

"Of course not!" Her mother beamed at her
granddaughter, although she still looked anxious.
"We can read some more, and bake pies, and—"

Molly had perked up, and they were still talking about how they could fill the day when Savannah left.

A gun store was her first stop. She tried out half a dozen handguns the owner recommended for women. She hadn't fired one since she was a kid and her father gave her and Jared lessons aiming at the classic bottles on fence posts. Target shooting had never appealed to her, and didn't now, but she was glad to find that she was still reasonably accurate. She also agreed to come in and spend some time in the range. For Molly's sake, she had to become comfortable with the gun in her hands.

The background check was quick in the state of Oregon, as was approval for a concealed carry permit, and she was able to leave with her new Sig Sauer P365 tucked in a holster and bagged along with a small gun safe that would sit cozily on her bedside table next to her clock and lamp. Just what she'd always wanted.

Had Jared carried a weapon on a day-to-day basis? she wondered. If so, it had been stripped from him.

For a dose of normalcy, she loaded up with groceries, stopped by the pharmacy and chose a couple of new games and toys for Molly, including a particularly cute stuffed sea turtle, then turned in their library books and picked out a dozen new ones to read to Molly, plus a couple for herself.

Somehow, the mysteries didn't appeal to her right now. She chose fantasies.

She thought seriously about making calls to horse owners in her contacts list, asking them to spread the word that she was looking for a job, but decided to leave that for another day. Part of her, the Savannah who was angry at Logan, not to mention feeling sick with roiling panic, still wanted to pack and go right this minute. But how? Even if she persuaded Dad or even one of the ranch hands to drive her and Molly someplace less obvious than town to catch a Greyhound bus, they could be followed.

Anyway, she kept thinking about the way Molly had run to her grandmother this morning, how much she loved her new bedroom and how she'd lit up when Savannah promised her a pony of her own. Then there were the horses Savannah had started to work with. Would those owners be willing to transport them to another ranch, even assuming she could find a place where she'd be able to take on outside horses? And how could *that* happen without any pursuers being led right to her?

Little as she wanted to move back into her parents' house, she'd do it if she believed she and Molly would be safer there. But would they really be?

And…if her worst fears were true, did she want to risk her parents, too?

Didn't it figure that, when she came out of the library, a sheriff's department SUV approached down the street. Not even giving herself a chance to identify the driver, she hustled for her pickup and leaped into the driver's seat. Maybe he wouldn't recognize the borrowed truck. She wasn't ready to talk to Logan…but it was too late. By the time she'd fired up the engine, the marked SUV swung abruptly into the library parking lot and braked in front of her, blocking her in.

LOGAN HAD DETOURED by the Circle B before going into work, but didn't stop to knock on doors or talk to anyone once he'd seen that Savannah's pickup was missing. After that, he'd been delayed with business at headquarters, but once he set out on the road again, he drove slowly through town looking for her. He'd begun to think he'd missed her.

His relief when he spotted her was powerful enough to awaken uneasiness again, but he blocked out that part. She hadn't packed up Molly and taken off this morning for points unknown. For the moment, that was enough.

He hopped out, walked to the driver side of her vehicle and twirled his finger to ask her to roll down her window.

Fingers gripped tight on the steering wheel, she just stared at him for a minute, and he wondered if she'd ignore his request. She'd probably consider it a demand.

Finally, she closed her eyes for a moment, then complied with obvious reluctance. "Sheriff."

"Where's Molly?" he asked.

"With Mom. Where else?"

"I called your dad, but he said he hadn't had a chance to talk to you this morning," he said.

Her mouth tightened. "No. Little as I like the idea, I did intend to call you."

"You did?" God. Something else had to have happened.

"First, why don't you spit out whatever it is you're determined to say?"

"You've never made a mistake?"

Her vividly colored eyes held his. "Plenty of them, but you didn't make a mistake. You've disliked me for most of your life, and you made that obvious again. At a bad time, too."

In one way, she was right, and he hated knowing that. What she'd forgotten or never guessed was the flip side, his fondness for the scrappy little girl who'd idolized him and her brother, the attraction that had plagued him the last couple of years of high school—and since she'd returned to town.

"I...had a moment of doubt." He didn't much like humbling himself, but if she wouldn't forgive him— He couldn't let himself think about that and went on. "I let myself...wonder."

Her short laugh held an edge sharp enough to slice vulnerable skin. "Uh-huh. Well, I'm sorry to say I didn't dream the whole thing. I got another call first thing this morning."

"Did you record it?"

"I did." She reached in her bag and then handed him the phone.

Since he'd installed the app, he pulled up the call quickly. The man's voice came from the phone, crystal clear. Logan's gaze never left hers as he listened, his body rigid.

"Ms. Baird. I hope we didn't alarm you too much last night." Her protest went ignored. "We need you to know that we're serious. That you can't hide from us."

The thrust of the call got worse and worse.

"Last night was a gentle warning. Please take another hard look at every message your brother left you, every single thing he passed on to you along with his *precious* daughter."

The implicit threat enraged Logan.

"We'll call again," the SOB said. "If you don't have an answer, we may have to apply some real pressure."

Either she hadn't had a chance to say anything more, or she'd been cut off. Logan cursed, but his outburst didn't help vent any of his tension. He handed the phone back to her.

"If you come into the station, I'd like to make a copy of that and put a trace on the original call."

"Like that'll do any good," she scoffed.

Unfortunately, she was right. Who in their right mind would issue a threat from a phone number linked to an identifiable business or individual?

"I plan to share this with the detective in San Francisco," she said. "I wanted to get my errands done first."

His gaze fell to the passenger seat and the floor in front of it, crowded with bags. He recognized one of them, printed like desert camouflage.

"You bought a gun."

"Yes, I did."

"You're lucky someone didn't break in if you left that in sight while you were in the library."

"You mean, there is crime in the county?" she exclaimed in mock astonishment, before dropping it and reverting to a flat "I made sure it couldn't be seen."

"You going to be able to lock it up?"

"Yes, Sheriff, I bought a gun safe, too. Now, if we're done?"

He gripped the bottom of her window frame, even though he knew full well he couldn't stop her from rolling up the window.

"Damn it, Savannah! I'm here for you. I came last night without hesitation. And, yeah, I screwed up, but, like your father, I'll come running anytime you need me. I swear it."

Her remote expression chilled him. "I'll keep that in mind, but I don't plan to need you." She looked pointedly at his hands. "I have to get home."

Home. Did that mean she didn't intend to leave? He thought he'd pushed it enough for the moment. Asking her future intentions probably wouldn't be smart.

After a moment, he let his hands drop to his sides and backed up. "Don't let hurt feelings put you or Molly at risk."

Now her stare blistered him, but she didn't say anything. He could only nod and walk back to his SUV, get in and drive away. Logan hoped like hell she didn't try to disappear the way she'd said she would.

Being brutally honest with himself, he wasn't sure how much of that hope had to do with keeping woman and child safe…and how much with this morass of emotions that kept surfacing where she was concerned.

APPARENTLY DETERMINED TO do his best to know where she was and what she was doing, Logan stopped by the ranch at least once a day during the following week. The only news she shared was that she'd received Jared's ashes, which she was currently storing in her closet so as not to disturb Molly. Most often, she was able to ignore Logan, although his very presence leaning on the fence surrounding the outdoor corral or sitting on the bleacher-style benches in the indoor arena challenged her ability to maintain concentration as she worked with horses she had in training. She could *feel* his eyes on her, even with her back turned. When she let her own gaze slide indifferently over him, he was always looking back. Watching.

Well, to hell with him. She couldn't ban him from the property, since she didn't own it—in fact, a couple of times her father joined him and they talked for a few minutes. And, no, she wouldn't cut off her nose to spite her face—one of Mom's pithy sayings—and reject the help she would likely need from local law enforcement, but that still didn't mean she had to talk to him. What annoyed her most was when she spotted him walking up to the house a couple of times and disappearing inside long enough to have a cup of coffee and probably charm Molly.

And, yes, she was petty enough to want him to stay away from Molly, too, but she knew talking to Sheriff Quade wouldn't hurt any child. He'd been astonishingly natural with Molly, surprisingly so considering he apparently didn't have any kids of his own. Maybe seeing him around and learning to trust him would even build Molly's sense of security. Savannah wished that was working for her. Instead…just the sight of him stirred up her tangled feelings for the boy he'd been and the man he was now. Examining them didn't seem to do any good. Afraid for herself and Molly and wishing she could trust Logan, she never had a peaceful moment.

Truthfully, her concentration when she was on horseback was poor even when Logan wasn't here, watching.

Once Molly had fallen asleep each evening, Savannah searched everything that Jared had sent with her. She got desperate enough to cut open the tube of toothpaste, hoping Molly wouldn't wonder too much why her auntie Vannah had replaced it. The doll, with its hard body, didn't seem to offer any possibilities, nor did the doll's wardrobe, although Savannah studied every garment carefully. Feeling even worse, she sliced seams on the stuffed animals that had come with Molly, running her fingers through the foam pellets in one case, the white polyester filling in the others. She felt nothing hard, like a thumb drive, or crackly, like paper. Having planned in advance, she'd sneaked into Mom's sewing room to borrow a needle and thread so she could stitch the poor stuffed animals back together again. She examined the duffel bag in case Jared had added a pocket that wasn't obviously visible. No to that, too. Molly's clothes, her coat, her shoes, got scrutinized. Oh, and the board games—a good place to disguise a code or password, maybe.

She didn't find a thing.

The week was so quiet, it was as if she'd imagined that last phone call. She wasn't at all reassured. *Disturbed* was a better description. The only times her phone rang, the callers were friends or trainers she knew. Meantime, whatever Dad had said to her, he'd instructed hands to keep an eye out for anyone who might be trying to slip onto the ranch unnoticed. Logan's regular stops probably had a similar intent, as did the occasional sheriff's deputy vehicle she saw out on the road and even, a couple of times, coming up to the house before circling and going back out.

The efforts to keep her safe continued to undermine her original determination to pack up and leave. People were watching out for her here. Molly loved the time she spent with Grandma, who was totally devoted to her, and she loved equally the short horseback rides Savannah took her on. So far, they had stayed in the open, close to ranch buildings. Trails that wound among junipers, along a stream lined with cottonwood, or over a crumbling basalt rimrock that was one of the more distinctive features here on the ranch, all were off-limits.

She'd put off buying Molly a pony in case they had to move on, but she couldn't explain why without scaring Molly even more than she already was. She kept repeating, "I haven't found the right pony yet."

Savannah drove to the gun range to practice several times, but felt uneasy the whole time she was gone. Mom had agreed to lock the doors when Molly was with her, but how hard would it really be for someone to break in? Dad was sometimes nearby in the barn or corrals, but more often, given the time of year, he joined his foreman and the hired hands checking fences and hauling feed out to far pastures with the tractor.

The next time she planned to go to the library, Molly begged to come. She'd attended the story time put on by the children's librarian and wanted to go again.

"I can pick out my own books," she declared, too.

Savannah laughed and capitulated.

During the story time, Molly sat cross-legged on the carpeted floor beside another girl who looked about her age. That girl was a lot bolder than Molly, whispering in her ear and giggling, Molly shyly pleased. After the story time was over, the girl tugged her mother over and said, "Can Molly come over and play someday?"

The woman chuckled. "I'm Sheila Kavanagh, and this is my not-so-shy daughter, Poppy."

Savannah introduced the two of them, and they determined that both girls would be starting kindergarten the next fall. They exchanged phone numbers and addresses, and made a date for Molly to go to Poppy's house first. Poppy had a Barbie house *and* car, while Molly could bring the Barbie horse and dolls her grandma had recently bought for her.

Not until they parted in the library parking lot did Savannah realize she'd just committed to something almost a week away. And yet…wasn't this what she wanted for Molly—the start of a friendship, a chance to be part of a small community in complete contrast to the scary places she'd lived in the past?

Maybe it would be better if she and Molly moved into the house for now.

Except…nothing else had happened. There'd been no follow-up at all, neither calls nor, as far as she could tell, any sign of a tail when she left the ranch. She hated as much as ever the possibility of either of her parents trying to stop a cold-blooded man—or men—determined to grab her *or* Molly. In the cabin, she could fire her new handgun at will. Which circled her back to staying in the cabin by herself, Molly tucked in an upstairs bedroom at the house.

Only listening to Molly's chatter with half an ear, she guiltily checked her rearview and side mirrors for anyone seemingly trailing them. This being midday, of course there were other cars on the road, so how was she supposed to tell?

But gradually, the other vehicles turned off. As she neared her own turnoff, an SUV closed in on her from behind, exceeding the speed limit. Tensing, Savannah watched it approach and debated pulling out the handgun she'd taken to carrying in a holster, but as far as she could tell, there was no one else in the vehicle but the driver. She stuck exactly to the speed limit, put on her turn signal…and the SUV swerved into the other lane and sped past her. As far as she could tell, the male driver didn't even turn his head.

He just wanted to drive faster than she'd been going.

Idiot. Most country roads in the county had yellow stripes down the middle and next-to-no shoulders. You'd find yourself in a ditch if you were even a little careless. Or tangled in a sagebrush-choked barbed wire fence, even more fun.

Speeders weren't uncommon, but she found her heartbeat had accelerated, and she felt shaky as she rattled over the cattle guard and drove slowly up the packed-earth ranch lane. Her gaze kept going to the rearview mirror. Maybe she shouldn't have turned where a passing driver could see her. Except…somebody had already found her, so it was a little late to pretend she and Molly didn't live here.

Another night came in which she slept only restlessly, prepared to turn the dial on the small safe to the last number in an instant. She'd rehearsed the act—opening the safe, snatching out the gun, flicking off the safety—dozens of times.

But morning came with no scares, no phone calls, only the routine of feeding herself and Molly, getting dressed, planning which horses she'd work with today. As she and Molly walked the distance to the house, she saw the green tractor pulling a trailer piled high with hay bales rumbling through a gate, then on through the pasture.

Mom was waiting for Molly, who said, "Auntie Vannah says we can ride later! After lunch."

Mom laughed as she tugged off the little girl's mittens and then hat, and started unzipping her parka. "That sounds fun, but I'll bet we can have fun right here, too. What do you think?"

Molly nodded vigorously. "I liked painting. Can we paint again?"

"Of course we can."

Savannah doubted her niece even noticed when she left. She paused on the porch, however, until she heard the dead bolt snap shut on the back door. Glad Mom was taking the threat seriously, whether she believed in it or not, Savannah headed for the barn. She actually liked mornings like this, when she would likely have it to herself. Despite her sheepskin-lined jacket and gloves, she was very conscious of the cold and light layer of frost. It wouldn't be a problem in the arena, though.

She'd left the metal barrels out yesterday in the corral, so she'd start with a mare she was training for a teenage daughter of a longtime customer. The prosaically named Brownie, whose coat was indeed an unrelieved brown, had real promise.

Savannah patted noses, distributed sugar cubes she'd pocketed earlier and worked her way down the aisle to Brownie, who hung her head eagerly over the stall door. As always, she'd start by cross-tying her and doing a light grooming.

Trying to dodge Brownie's head butts, she reached for the latch on the stall door. A soft sound came from behind her. A barn cat, maybe, or had one of the hands stayed behind? She had started to turn when a blow slammed her against the stall door.

Chapter Nine

Savannah saw the next blow coming. She managed to twist as she slid down the rough wood of the stall to the hard-packed floor in the aisle, cushioned with a couple of inches of shavings. She didn't know what the man looming above her was wielding, but it looked like a flashlight, only longer—

As he swung it, she kept twisting. She heard the weapon whistle through the air, but it connected only with her shoulder. It hurt terribly. He'd kill her if he struck her head—

Screaming now, she flung herself facedown and rolled toward the man's booted feet with some vague idea of knocking him off-balance. It didn't work. He dodged her even as he readied for another blow. She tried to grope for the gun she wore in a shoulder holster, but she'd zipped the coat. Lousy planning.

Smash. Her upper arm again. Oh, God, was it broken?

On a distant plane, she thought, *That might be*

a flashlight, but why does it have a ball on the end like a baseball bat to ensure a secure grip?

She gave up on screaming. All she could do was keep moving, watching for his backswing and responding desperately, trying to evade the blows. She got up as far as her knees once, but he kicked her backward. All she managed was to protect her head. The pointed toe of his cowboy boot lashed out again, this time connecting with her belly. She retched, tasting bile as she curled protectively around an agony in her midsection that had to be a broken or cracked rib.

The attack went on and on. She wound down. No one had heard her screams. Would he kill her?

When finally she had rolled into a ball and tried to protect as much of her body as she could, knowing tears and snot wet her face, the man nudged her hard with his toe.

She peered at him through a slitted eye. Her right cheekbone was on fire, so one of the many blows had struck her face after all.

He was dressed like any man around here: faded jeans, cowboy boots, heavy jacket—and a ski mask that covered his whole head. Only his eyes glittered. Brown. As if it mattered.

He crouched. "Appears you didn't pay attention to our first message. This is your last chance to give us what we need. Next time, we won't hold back." He was smiling, she was sure of it. "Be smart. We can get you anytime, anywhere. Expect a call."

He walked away.

Savannah would have shot him…if she could have made her battered body obey any commands at all. If the pain wasn't swelling until darkness crept over her remaining vision.

TEN O'CLOCK OR SO, Logan's phone rang. Driving hands-free since he was patrolling in place of an officer who'd called in sick, he answered immediately.

"Logan?" The low voice sounded…thick. "It's 'Vannah."

She might have said her full name. He couldn't tell.

With a bare glance in his rearview mirror, Logan braked hard enough to burn rubber and then spun the steering wheel to accomplish a high-speed U-turn midhighway. "Savannah? Are you hurt?"

"Yah. Barn."

Slammed by fear, he stepped hard on the accelerator and activated lights and siren. "I'm on my way. Ten minutes. Are you alone?"

"Yah," she said again. "Don't want… Mom… come out."

"I'm calling for an aide car, too. I should get there first."

Whatever she said, he didn't make out. "Savannah? Stay on the line."

But she'd quit speaking. No, disconnected.

He drove a hell of a lot faster than was safe.

The few drivers he'd passed going the other way rubbernecked. Exactly seven minutes later, he passed his father's ranch. He slowed but still skidded on the packed earth to turn into the Circle B. He accelerated even before he'd gone over the cattle guard. Hell on tires, but he didn't care.

No flashing lights showed ahead, and he thought to turn off his siren so he didn't frighten Savannah's mother up at the house. Although… where the hell was everyone else who worked on the ranch? His SUV slid to a stop right in front of the wide-open doors leading into the huge barn. Logan leaped out, unholstered his sidearm and ran inside.

He saw a small ball of human being right away. She lay terrifyingly still. Anguish squeezed his chest in a vise. Savannah wasn't dead. She couldn't be. She'd called him. Horses thrust their heads over the stall doors, and he heard more clomping, hard kicks on wood partitions and shrill neighs. The attack had stirred up the inhabitants of the barn.

Where were the damn dogs? But he knew: with the ranch workers, wherever *they* were.

What little he could see of her face was battered. Lying on her side, knees drawn up toward her chest, she had to be trying to hug herself with her arms. No, arm. One lay awkwardly.

Swearing, he reached her, holstered his weapon and fell to his own knees. She moved, just a little, and moaned.

Thank God.

"Savannah." He couldn't *not* touch her, smoothing hair from her forehead with his fingertips. "Who did this?"

Squinting up at him, she mumbled, "Man. Mask."

"Did you hear a vehicle?"

"Nah. Just…" She struggled to swallow. "Here. Gone."

Her lips were swollen and split. Damn it, damn it, damn it.

"The lights may bring your mother out," Logan warned.

"Don't want Molly—"

"To see you? No. I'll head them off, but first, let me take a look at you."

He thought her shoulder might be dislocated rather than her arm being broken. He hoped so. Her pupils were equal and reactive—what he could see of them with the one eye swollen.

"Think…ribs," she managed to say.

Yeah, given the way she had apparently unconsciously tried to protect them, he agreed that was a likelihood. His gentle, exploring hand determined that she'd been beaten to the point where he wondered if she might have lost consciousness. She didn't seem to know—but her assailant had stopped well short of killing her. Or landing her in the hospital for a lengthy stay. Logan's guess was that she'd mostly suffered bruises, the dislocation or broken arm, and cracked or possibly broken ribs. These bastards needed her to be able to comply with their demands.

He wanted to kill somebody.

Tipping his head, he said, "Here comes the ambulance. I'm not going far, but I'll stop your mother and Molly from coming in."

She gave an infinitesimal nod, those haunting eyes fixed on his face. It was all he could do to make himself leave her side.

Savannah vaguely recognized one of the two EMTs. They'd gone to school together, she thought. Both seemed efficient. They placed something around her neck to stabilize it and shifted her carefully onto a backboard before "packaging her." Or so she heard the man say.

Logan walked beside her out to the ambulance, his gaze never leaving her face, his hand resting close enough to her side to brush her own hand.

"I'll follow you to the hospital as soon as I can," he murmured.

Strapped down as she was, Savannah couldn't even nod.

Naturally, she lost sight of him as soon as they

slid her into the back of the ambulance, but when she closed her eyes, she kept seeing his face. It was as if he'd aged a decade or more, creases in his cheeks and forehead looking as if they'd never smooth out again.

Worry, simmering anger, tenderness and more were all betrayed by the darkness in his gray eyes and those careworn lines. Drifting, she reminded herself that it didn't matter how sexy, even handsome he was. *Can't trust him*, she thought fuzzily. Except…he was right. He'd come running every time she needed him.

A phone rang, and she realized it was hers, but the EMT—what was her name? Something starting with an *N*—shook her head sternly at Savannah and deftly plucked the phone out of her pocket, setting it somewhere out of reach.

"How do you feel?" Nellie—no, Naomi, that was it—asked.

"Bet…" Savannah licked her lips. "…you can… guess."

Naomi smiled. "Just hold on. Once we get X-rays and maybe a CAT scan out of the way, we'll be able to give you pain relief."

How long would *that* take? Savannah wanted to whimper, but held on. She hurt, but no worse than she had the time she'd ridden a bucking bronco in a futile attempt to impress Jared and, even more, Logan. If she'd survived that, she'd survive this. Mom and Dad had been so mad.

She thought she'd been twelve, smugly certain she could ride any horse, however it twisted and spun and bucked.

Her brother had knelt at her side while Logan ran for help. "Didn't make it eight seconds," Jared had informed her. "Where were your brains?"

Good question. What she remembered was that as she'd lain there on the ground waiting for her father to come, or for him to get an ambulance out there, whichever came first, she hadn't been looking at Jared's face. Oh, no. Just like today, she'd watched Logan for as long as she could see him.

In those days, she hadn't analyzed why he drew her when no other boy in their town did, but now she thought someone must have cast a spell on her. One that hadn't dissipated despite the intervening years.

The sad thing was, *he'd* never gotten over disliking her. And yet his touch a few minutes ago had been so gentle, his rage on her behalf strangely comforting.

As she was wheeled into the hospital, she had to close her eyes against the bright lights. She was dizzy, everything swaying around her.

Her mother showed up first, just after Savannah had been brought back to her cubicle from getting X-rays—shoulder, rib cage, back and right hip, which had begun to throb. Maybe everywhere. Her head. She seemed to remember that.

Which made sense when the throbbing seemed to get worse rather than better.

Her feet felt fine, she thought.

"Savannah!" Mom cried, snatching her daughter's hand. "I've been petrified since I saw the flashing lights and then Logan told us what happened. Your dad—"

"Where... Molly?"

"I left her with Logan's dad and his housekeeper. It was going to take your dad too long to get back to the house. Molly wanted to come with me, but I wasn't sure that would be a good idea."

"No," Savannah said definitely.

"Has the doctor told you yet what—"

The curtain rattled and the doctor, who didn't appear any older than Savannah, walked in. His eyebrows rose. "Mrs. Baird?"

"Yes."

"Well, the news from the X-rays is mostly encouraging." He focused on Savannah. "We think you have a cracked rib or two, and you'll want to keep your rib cage wrapped tightly for comfort, but there are no obvious breaks. Your shoulder is dislocated, as Sheriff Quade suspected. We'll be dealing with that immediately, and you should feel a lot better when we've popped the ball of your humerus—" he lightly touched her upper arm "—back into the joint where it belongs. The relief will be almost immediate."

That was where the blazing coal of pain centered. She had to grit her teeth to swallow the scream at the contact.

"When—"

"I have someone on the way to help me," he assured her. "To finish the catalog, your hip is bruised, your cheekbone cracked, but there's not a lot we can do for that, and you'll find the swelling goes down reasonably quickly. Ice will help with that. Lots of ice. Ah, you have one broken finger—I'm guessing you know which one."

With everything hurting, she hadn't thought, oh, my finger is broken, but now that he'd mentioned it, he was right. She could feel it. It was the small finger on her right side.

"As you may know, we'll bind it to the next finger, which will serve as a sort of splint. It's annoying, but shouldn't keep you from using your hands in most ways."

Reining a horse? She thought she could adapt, although at this exact moment, the idea of heaving herself onto a horse's back seemed as unlikely as her setting out to climb any of the Cascade volcanoes for a fun outing.

Start with Mount Hood, she told herself frivolously.

Another man slipped into the cubicle, they politely asked Savannah's mother to wait outside, and they deftly popped the joint back into place. The doctor hadn't mentioned how much *that* would hurt, despite the pain relief they were already giving her through her IV—but he was right that the stab of agony in her shoulder subsided so quickly afterward, she sighed and sank back into her pillows.

Okay. I'll survive.

As fuzzy as her head was, though, she couldn't forget what the man had said: *This is your last chance to give us what we need. Next time, we won't hold back. Be smart. We can get you anytime, anywhere.*

Part of the memory was the way his mouth had curved. He'd savored both the process of brutally intimidating her *and* issuing the verbal threat.

Her eyes stung, and she was afraid she was crying, something she *hated* doing.

Jared, how could you do this to us? she begged.

THERE WERE SO many reasons to be furious, Logan had trouble focusing on just one.

No, not true: the shadows cast by the past and the mixed feelings that had kept him from 100 percent supporting and believing in Savannah came out on top.

When he was finally able to sit at her bedside and watch her sleep, he acknowledged another reason for his rage: the fact that she'd been beaten by an expert who knew how to precisely calibrate the strength of his blows and kicks. Enough to make his point, to ensure she suffered, but not enough to cripple her. Oh, no, by tomorrow she'd be able to jump right on their demands, whatever they were. The *care* taken almost made the vicious assault worse. The guy was doing his job, that's all.

Logan had no intention of leaving her side from here on out, no matter what she had to say about that. He'd hire a husky ranch hand to help his father from here on out, and he'd do as much of his work for the sheriff's department as he possibly could remotely. The county council wouldn't like that, but to hell with them.

He'd sent her mother home, gently suggesting that Molly needed her, and taken what calls he needed to by stepping out into the hall. The one call *he* made was to Detective Trenowski in San Francisco, who sounded as appalled as Logan felt.

Trenowski was also openly frustrated. "I'm not getting anywhere with figuring out who Jared might have been working with in law enforcement, if anyone. The DEA is giving me the runaround, and the local FBI office claims they've never heard of him, although the agent I spoke with sounded bored answering my questions. I couldn't tell if he even looked up the name."

Logan growled.

The detective gave a short laugh that held zero humor. "Got to tell you, the Feds always rub me the wrong way. They seem to go out of their way *not* to be cooperative."

"I know what you're talking about. I've met

a couple of exceptions," Logan said, "but that's what they are."

During their first conversation, he'd shared his history with Trenowski, which had erased the initial wary barricade. Big-city cops didn't fully respect sheriffs and officers in rural counties. Logan understood that. His deputies didn't have the same level of training, equipment and competence as their urban counterparts. Some of his focus since he'd arrived had, in fact, been training, building morale—and firing the one deputy who'd been on the job for ten years and resented the implication that he was better at swaggering than he was at actually protecting local citizens.

Trenowski asked, "You think about packing her and the girl off to someplace they might be safer?"

"And where would that be? Do you have a safe house to offer? Manpower to guard it?"

Silence.

"They traced her here with remarkable speed. And, yes, it was her brother's hometown, so that made sense up to a point. But in these parts, people keep an eye out for each other. They notice strangers. We're off the beaten path enough not to get tourists. There's not so much as a dude ranch in the county. So how did these men— or maybe it's only one man—watch the ranch *completely undetected* for what has to have been a week or more now?" He hoped the detective didn't hear him grinding his teeth. "I've stopped in at all the neighbors to ask whether they've seen an unfamiliar vehicle tucked into a turn-out somewhere nearby. Do they have an unused outbuilding where someone could have been hiding? The answers are no. This guy has to have been sneaking around on foot, or conceivably on horseback—"

"Muscle for a drug trafficking outfit?" the detective said incredulously. "On a *horse*?" Trenowski sounded as if he'd never seen the animal in real life before.

"Hard to picture, but he's been invisible so far unless he wants to be seen. Savannah says he wore faded jeans, cowboy boots and a sheep-skin-lined coat that would allow him to blend in around here. People might see him and assume he's a new hire at one of the couple dozen ranches, large and small, in this county. Pay isn't great for ranch hands, they're frequently let go over the winter, so they do come and go."

"That makes sense," Trenowski said thoughtfully. "Any chance he has taken a job close by? That would give him access to a mount."

"I've asked about that, too. No one nearby has taken on anybody new in the recent past. If they had, they'd have noticed his strange disappearances. Otherwise, how's he getting out here? Where is he staying? The hands at the Circle B would have said if they'd seen anyone unfamiliar hanging around."

"Could they have found a local willing to do their dirty work?"

"How? Not the kind of thing you can advertise for in the *County Reporter*. Besides, this beating was done by a professional who knew exactly how far to go. I'd swear to it."

There was a pause. "You have time to ride around in case he's camping out nearby?"

"I'll do my best to get other people to do that. Me, I'm going to stick with her and the girl as close to around-the-clock as I can. I can do a lot on the phone. I'm calling every dump of a motel, resort and bed-and-breakfast within a couple of counties, for example. My bigger worry is that he's squatting in a falling-down barn or at one of the ranch properties that's been long-vacant and for sale. Even if he's found a house, there'd be no utilities. If he started a fire in a fireplace, someone might see the smoke. It's getting cold here, so if he is roughing it, he's got to be miserable."

"We can hope."

Logan grunted his agreement, although he wanted far worse for the man who'd slammed some kind of truncheon into Savannah and kicked her hard enough to crack ribs. If he came face-to-face with this bastard, he'd have a hard time holding on to the dispassion required to make a clean arrest.

The two men let it go at that. Logan returned to Savannah's room to find her awake if glassy-eyed, and looking nervously around. Her gaze latched right on to him when he appeared around the curtain.

"Hey, sunshine," he said, finding a smile somewhere as he also took his seat and reached automatically for her hand. "I was just making a call right outside your room."

"Molly's...favorite...song." Her face made some gyrations he thought were intended to be a scowl. "Don't...have to...stay."

"I do." Seeing her trying to work up a protest, he added, "Live with it."

"Bossy."

"Yeah." He outright grinned, even though he didn't feel much amusement. "So I've been told."

"Sister."

"Yep."

"Can't I go home?"

Logan was getting good at understanding her slurry words. "Doctor is keeping you overnight. They want to watch you because you suffered a concussion. They don't like giving you pain meds on top of that, but it's kind of unavoidable."

Savannah made a face he thought was cute, despite the distortion of her features. "That's why... head hurts."

"Yep." He showed her how to use the button to boost her load of those pain meds, even though he was sure the nurse had done the same. Then he said, "Sleep as much as you can, sweetheart. I'd promise you'll feel better tomorrow, except—"

Sweetheart? Had he really let that slip out?

Yeah. Might be good if she hadn't noticed.

But her eyes were suddenly unexpectedly clear, and that might be color in her cheeks. She didn't comment, though, only said, "I'd know you were lying."

Lying? Oh, about tomorrow.

"Given what you do for a living, I suppose you've been hurt a few times."

She gave the tiniest nod. "Bucking bronco."

"I'd almost forgotten. You scared the living daylights out of me. Jared, too." He grimaced. "Your dad blamed us even though you didn't tell us what you intended to do."

"Jared," she mumbled. "He got in trouble. Not me. Dad...wouldn't believe me."

Logan didn't feel a trace of doubt. She'd defended her brother, and her father had smacked Jared anyway. Jared had only shrugged the next day and said, "You know Dad. Savannah tried."

How often had Jared said something similar? Logan wondered. Why had he been so sure Jared had lied, that pretty, perfect Savannah had been smirking in the background while her brother was unfairly accused and punished?

Had he been scared to feel so much for a girl?

Logan wished he knew.

Chapter Ten

Savannah cast an uneasy glance at the spot in the barn aisle where she'd been pummeled. Somebody must have shoveled up any bloody shavings. Inhaling the sharp scent of the fresh wood chips that had been raked smooth, she should be happy stroking Brownie's neck after giving her a couple of lumps of sugar.

Logan, who'd just tossed her saddle effortlessly atop Akil, the Arabian gelding, glanced over his shoulder at her. Amusement glinted in his eyes. "You planning to take a swing at me?"

"No! But I hate this!" Mad at herself the minute the words burst out, Savannah made a face and then immediately regretted doing so because it *hurt*. "I'm sorry! I don't like feeling helpless, but... I like even less being a whiner."

"You're entitled," he said with a shrug. "You must ache from head to toe." He slapped Akil's belly before yanking tight the girth strap. "I still think this is too soon for you to ride."

"My toes are fine, thank you. And you know

I'll be better off if I get moving." Her doctor had discouraged her from raising her arm high enough to saddle a horse, however, even assuming she'd thought she could handle the weight combined with the upward swing. She couldn't even slip Akil's bridle on in case he tossed his head at the wrong moment and her arm was pulled too high.

Since she'd acquired a 24/7—or pretty close to it—bodyguard, though, it was just as well she could put him to work. Even better that he knew his way around horses.

She *hadn't* told him that part of her insistence on this outing had to do with being stuck with him in the cabin, which seemed to have shrunk now that he'd moved in with her and Molly. It wasn't just because he was a big man who took up more space than he should. No, her problem was that an accidental brush of shoulders passing in the hall, hands touching as they both reached for something, even the *sight* of him, made her body hum, whether she liked it or not. Rather than spend most of the day trapped alone with him in the cabin while Molly was entertained by her grandma, Savannah had grasped for any excuse to escape.

He'd given her a thoughtful look, his objections mild. Maybe he wanted a change in scenery, too, or just crisp, cold air to clear his head.

She waited while Logan saddled a second

mount, a quarter horse gelding belonging to her father, and a few minutes later they rode out of the barn. After he leaned to the side to open a gate and then close it behind them both, they trotted into the empty pasture. Almost a mile out, she could see small clumps of cattle grazing the winter-brown wild bunchgrasses in the next pasture. Most of Dad's herd had been turned loose on federal land in the late summer and fall, giving the grass closer in a chance to rebound. By February, the pasture closest to the barn where she and Logan now rode would be full of pregnant cows to ensure none gave birth out in distant reaches of the ranch.

The land rose gradually, clusters of juniper growing where enough elevation was gained. If she squinted, she could make out a basalt rimrock, betraying how recently volcanic activity had formed this landscape even as it looked like the remnant of a medieval castle wall. No, she and Logan wouldn't be going anywhere near it today. Trail rides were out; Logan claimed not to worry about a sniper, but still made decisions based on keeping her a good distance from any possible cover.

Savannah had pointed out that her caller didn't want her dead, he wanted her treasure hunting for his benefit, but Logan remained adamant once he made a decision.

She had to remind herself every couple of

hours, silently, of course, that he was apparently willing to lay his life on the line. For her.

The horses' hooves crunched on the morning frost that still lingered. Just being out under the cold blue sky, sharp air in her lungs, was exhilarating. It smelled different here than it had in the red rock country in New Mexico where she'd last worked, or the couple of ranches in western Oregon, for that matter. It had to have something to do with the volcanic soil, along with the ubiquitous sagebrush, so aromatic when the needles were crushed. Junipers, too, and even the more noxious-smelling rabbitbrush that was hard to eradicate.

The relaxation that allowed her to move as one with the horse was definitely compromised, she realized with annoyance. Her hip wasn't happy, and instinct had her holding herself stiffly because of the ever-present pain from her rib cage. Otherwise...she wasn't any worse off than she would have been lounging on her new sofa in front of the TV.

Logan reined in his mount, tipped back his Stetson as his eyes met hers and asked, "How do you feel?"

"Not too bad," she decided. "I'm not quite up to working any of the horses, thanks to the cracked ribs, but I usually heal fast."

His dark eyebrow expressed his skepticism, and she grinned back.

"I stink at sitting around."

"I've noticed." His voice grew rougher. "Any new ideas?"

She didn't have to ask what he was talking about. Two nights ago, her first after being released from the hospital, he had joined her in re-examining everything that Jared had sent with his daughter. They could dismiss some of the toys quickly: all they'd done with the hard plastic doll was give it a good shake to be sure Jared hadn't pulled off a leg or the head or something to insert a thumb drive into the body, for example. They'd gone so far as to steal Molly's beloved and battered stuffed bunny out from under her arm after she was sound asleep so they could more thoroughly disembowel it than Savannah had the first time around. It had taken her quite a while to stuff the poor thing again and stitch up the seams, especially given her so-so sewing skills.

Yesterday, Logan had run numbers from the outgoing and incoming lists of callers on Jared's phone. They all traced to San Francisco businesses. He'd been particularly fond of one pizza parlor. Other than that, Logan had turned up nothing of value there, and he thought Jared might have just thrown his phone in with his other things, knowing he had a burner on him.

No surprise, Molly had been terrified from the minute she saw Savannah's swollen, bruised face. Really, she must have been from the moment she heard that Savannah had been injured and taken to the hospital. She understood that Logan hadn't moved in with them and slept on their couch as a fun sleepover, but rather to keep her auntie Vannah safe from a bad man. Naturally, her nightmares came more frequently again. She still didn't remember details or couldn't adequately articulate what she saw. Each time Savannah had gotten up to go to her, she'd been aware of Logan standing in the hall watching.

Guarding them. Worrying about them.

The two nights since she'd come home had left all three of them tired, and Savannah's tension stretched like a rubber band being pulled until it must be close to snapping.

Now she admitted, "A new idea? Not a one. You?"

"You're *sure* you haven't forgotten something that came with her?" His frustration was understandable.

"I haven't thrown a single thing away, even though some of her clothes are ready for the ragbag. Well, and her shoes, too." The sneakers Molly was rarely willing to put on these days instead of her prized cowboy boots.

"Jared was too smart for his own good," she said, before closing her eyes. More quietly, she added, "Or for *our* good."

Logan watched her with keener perception than felt comfortable. "It's got to be the damn phone," he growled after a moment. "I wish I was better with technology. I think the time has come to bring someone else in on this."

She couldn't help teasing, "What, you never solved investigations by unburying a cleverly hidden clue on someone's laptop or phone?"

Logan gave her a dark look, although his mouth twitched. "Gangs in Portland weren't that sophisticated, and women in domestic disputes rarely pause to type a confession and hide it in the cloud before shooting their husbands."

"Or vice versa?"

"Yeah," he agreed. "Goes both ways. Same-sex relationships aren't immune from violence, either. And armed robbers? Not given to hiding their bank account numbers on the cloud. Or, let's see, my last investigation—" He slammed to a stop.

"Your last case?"

He said reluctantly, "An attack on a homeless man."

She had a bad feeling that it hadn't just been an attack, it had been a homicide, but she wouldn't push.

"That…sounds like a stressful job." She now knew that Logan had mainly worked homicides in Portland. No wonder he'd perfected an appearance of calm and control she couldn't match.

Whatever turmoil existed under the surface, Logan's body moved in the saddle with the ease she'd always taken for granted. His hand stayed light on the reins as he controlled his horse with his legs. He looked as if he belonged on horseback, instead of having spent close to half his life in college and then a big city.

At the moment, he'd turned his head away, either to avoid her gaze or because he felt the need to search for any visible danger. Either way, she assumed he was closing the subject.

Yet finally he said, "The job can be tough. With practice, you get so you just tuck the things you see away so they don't haunt you."

"But they'll keep piling up over time."

He flickered a glance at her. "Then you burn out and find another job."

What could she do but nod? They weren't best friends, they especially weren't…whatever she'd been thinking. Logan was doing his current job, and probably on top of that felt an obligation to defend Jared's sister and child. Why she wanted to pry open his psyche, Savannah didn't know.

Lie, lie, lie.

She eased Akil into a lope. Only a stride later, Logan's mount pulled up right beside the Arabian. Making a gradual semicircle would lead them back to the ranch buildings.

They had ridden in silence for a good ten minutes before her phone rang.

SAVANNAH BROUGHT THE gelding to a stop abrupt enough to jolt her painful torso. As she groped in her pocket for her phone, Logan pulled his mount in almost as fast, eyes sharp on her face.

Her thoughts were jumbled, her fingers cold enough to be clumsy. She should have worn gloves.

Pulling out the phone, she thought, *Please don't let it be* them. *Not yet. It could just be Mom. It could...*

The number was unfamiliar, awakening dread. She held it out so Logan could see the screen, then took a deep breath and answered.

"Ms. Baird?" a man said. Not the *same* man, but she wasn't reassured.

Gaze latching on to Logan's, she put the call on speaker. "Yes."

"Why the hell haven't you been in touch with me?" he demanded, before falling abruptly silent. "You have my call on speaker. Who else is listening?" he asked, sounding suspicious.

She jumped on his rudeness before she thought better of it. "What business is that of yours? You haven't even done me the courtesy of identifying yourself."

Logan winced.

Oh, God...even if this wasn't *him*, it might be one of his confederates. She had to be conciliatory for now, try to buy time.

"Your brother swore you were reliable," her caller snapped. "That I could depend on you to get in touch if anything went wrong."

Savannah couldn't remember the last time she'd blinked. All she saw was Logan, who effortlessly controlled his horse. *He* didn't look away from her, either.

"You still haven't told me who you are." Her voice was a husk of its usual self.

Still sounding annoyed, the caller said, "Cormac Donaldson. I'm an agent with the Drug Enforcement Administration."

The initial rush of relief didn't last. What if he was lying?

"Did you speak to a San Francisco PD detective?" she asked.

"No. I've been waiting to hear from Jared, and when he didn't surface, I did the research to find out he was dead."

"That's…kind of an awful thing to say, you know."

"Awful? What do you mean?"

"*Surfaced?* After his body was found in the bay?"

There was a pause before he said stiffly, "That was tactless. My apologies." He waited, but when she didn't say anything, he continued. "I did note the detective of record." Paper rustled. "An Alan Trenowski."

That might have been reassuring if she hadn't been certain the killers knew who was investigating the death, too.

Logan mouthed something. She caught only the gist, but nodded.

"I'm not going to answer your questions until I verify your identity."

He muttered something she suspected was uncomplimentary, but still sounding stiff, he said, "That's fair enough."

"Have you…dealt with Jared before?"

"He didn't tell you?"

"No. I had an impression…but I was never sure."

"Your brother was a confidential informant. A really valuable one. We hoped the newest information would allow us to bring down the entire organization, or as close as we ever come."

She heard weariness in the last thing he'd said. She'd read enough to know that some drug trafficking organizations operated internationally and certainly in many states. They had as many limbs as an octopus. Jared's supposed information had to be limited, didn't it?

Logan leaned forward and said, "Agent Donaldson, this is Sheriff Logan Quade. I'm sticking close to Ms. Baird for now because of threats."

"They've found her?" The alarm seemed genuine.

"Yes. Can you give us a few hours and then call back?"

"As long as you understand that they may be

clearing out warehouses and changing shipping dates even now. Sooner is better than later."

"Our trust is a little shaky right now."

"I can understand that. I'll call again from this number."

No goodbye, which didn't surprise Savannah at all.

She shoved her phone in her pocket and announced, "I didn't like him."

Logan gave a choked laugh.

ONCE THEY WERE back at the cabin, Logan sat down at the kitchen table, opened his laptop in front of him and started making phone calls in between pursuing new information online. Savannah poured two cups of coffee and then plunked down across the table from him presumably to remain within earshot, although she got bored enough to play a game on her phone—or pretend she was.

It took a while before Logan reached an agent in the Seattle division of the DEA he'd known from a task force they had both served on. At the time, his impression had been mostly positive. Ray Sheppard wasn't all ego, the way Trenowski had described too many Feds. Logan thought it was a long shot that the guy would remember him, but kept his fingers crossed.

When the agent finally came on the line, he

said immediately, "Logan Quade? Portland Police Bureau?"

"That's me," Logan agreed. He described his changed circumstances before segueing into the mess Jared had dumped on his sister, saying, "She's received several threats and there have been two incidents, including a vicious beating. Apparently Jared hid information they are determined to keep her from passing on to investigators. The reason I'm calling now is that we just heard from a man who identified himself as a DEA agent named Cormac Donaldson. He seemed to think Ms. Baird would know who he was, but her brother never mentioned the name. I presume the guy is with the San Francisco division, since Jared lived in the California Bay Area and was murdered there, but I can't be sure. We need to verify his identity before we dare talk openly to him."

"Back a few years, I knew a Donaldson when we were both assigned to the DC office. Huh. Let me check." The silence had to have lasted five minutes before he came back on the line. "Yeah, Cormac is based in San Francisco now. Why don't I call him, make sure it's really him you talked to, then call you back?"

"I'd be grateful," Logan said. When he set down his phone, he cocked an eyebrow at Savannah. "Did you hear that?"

"Most of it." Anxiety darkened her eyes. "If only Jared *had* told me about this agent."

And about the load of trouble that would be dumped on her head, Logan couldn't help thinking. It was great Jared had turned his life around and was trying to atone—Logan thought that was the word Savannah had used. He'd obviously been scared enough to try to ensure his daughter's safety, too. All good, except he'd messed up, big-time, by being so closemouthed. If Logan had been able to come face-to-face with his old friend right now, he might have planted a fist in his face.

"Something I've been wanting to talk to you about," Logan said slowly. Maybe this was lousy timing, but he thought distraction would benefit Savannah. And…he needed to know where he was going with her. Whether any kind of do-over was possible. Staying in close quarters with her had ratcheted up his hunger for her, and more. She was amazing with Molly. He felt especially bad that he'd doubted how committed she was to the little girl.

"What's that?" Savannah asked in obvious puzzlement.

With an effort, he kept his hand on the table relaxed. His other hand, resting on his thigh and hidden beneath the table, balled into a fist. "You and me," he said. "I'd really like to know if you'll ever trust me."

Her expression altered by slow degrees. The

distraction had worked that well. Tiny creases formed between the arch of her eyebrows, and her eyes sharpened on his face.

"I'm…grateful for what you're doing now. I trust you to do whatever you can to protect me. Molly, too. Of course I do. Are you afraid I'll go raring off in some direction without consulting you?"

"No. You're too smart to do that." He hesitated. "My question was…more personal. We have a history."

He wasn't surprised when her eyes narrowed. "You could say that."

Logan made himself go on. "I had something of an epiphany while I was trying to sleep the other night." He'd had long wakeful periods, in part because her sofa was too short for a man his height. He wasn't about to tell her that, though.

"An epiphany?" She looked wary, as if she wasn't sure she wanted to hear what he had to say.

"I really liked you when you were a kid." He smiled crookedly. "Trailing after Jared and me, annoyingly persistent but also gutsy and funny."

Surprise showed on Savannah's face, as if after everything that came after, she'd forgotten the way her brother and Logan teased her, boosted her up to a tree fort she couldn't have reached on her own, taught her how to throw a ball like a boy instead of a girl. If he hadn't been so nervous, he would have smiled at how furious she'd been at that description. She'd declared that girls could do anything boys could, and did her best to prove it, over and over again.

Years' worth of those kind of memories shaped how he knew the woman sitting across from him. Given that, how had he ever come to doubt her? Yeah, that question had been part of his epiphany.

"As your father started to come down on Jared harder and harder," Logan went on, "and I could see how much it hurt him, I started to blame you. I guess you know that."

"You think?"

Looking into the past, he said, "Jared did complain sometimes. He couldn't do anything right, you couldn't do anything wrong. I started to get this picture in my head at the same time you were…maturing physically. I could see you were going to be beautiful." Pause. "Already were."

"Beautiful?" She barely breathed the word. "When I was twelve? Thirteen?"

He cleared his throat. "Both. And fourteen and fifteen. Especially those last couple of years before I graduated."

She gaped. "You thought…"

"I did. The trouble is, I had to stay loyal to Jared. I convinced myself that, sure, I noticed the way you walked, your smile, your grace, your voice. Hearing you talk is like listening to music, you know."

She still looked stunned.

He cleared his throat. "None of that meant I was really attracted to you, though. That if you hadn't been Jared's sister—"

She pushed her chair back, the legs scraping on the wood floor. "You hated me!"

Holding himself rigidly, he didn't move. "It was…self-defense. I thought Jared was dead, you know. I even wondered sometimes if he and your father really got into it, and Jared was buried somewhere here on ranch land."

A quiver ran over her. Had she wondered the same?

"Him just disappearing…haunted me. Part of me had come to believe that if you didn't exist, your father would have loved Jared. You were… a mirror that distorted your dad's view. It had to be your fault. You know the deep spiral he went into. Watching him was so hard. I thought I was helping him when I set limits, but I think all I did was hurt him. I should have been there for him. Solid. I felt guilty enough about that."

How long since she'd blinked? "Jared must have thought that way about me," she said, so softly he just heard her. "How could he not hate me?"

"I thought he did." This was a hard admission. A hurtful one. "But now when I remember the way he'd talk about you, I know that wasn't ever true. Your dad had seriously eroded his self-esteem, you know. Even so, he talked as much about the way you tried to stand between him and your dad as he did about how you were just so perfect, he couldn't measure up."

Savannah's lips trembled, and she looked down at the table. After a moment, she swallowed hard enough, Logan wondered if she wasn't fighting tears.

He hated feeling vulnerable, but he owed her. He pushed himself to get this said. "I couldn't let myself betray my best friend in the world, so I refused to admit even to myself that I'd have been hot for you otherwise." That maybe he'd even been in love with her, as much as a boy that age could be.

Her head came up, and they stared at each other.

"Jared wasn't the only one you hurt," she said at last, in a voice that shook. "You hurt *me*. I had a crush on you from when I was, I don't know, a girl. Not very old at all. You were the first boy I thought I loved. When I reached an age where that really meant something, you'd become cruel to me."

He hated the expression on her fine-boned face, the darkness in her beautiful eyes. Beneath the table, his fingernails drove into the palm of his hand. He might even have drawn blood.

"Then Jared was gone, and you pretended I didn't exist." Her voice was rising, sharpening like a blade she'd been honing. "If you couldn't get away with pretending not to see me at all, you sneered like I was a pile of steaming, stinking manure you'd just stepped in and had to wipe off your boot. I had tried so hard to protect Jared from Dad, and you—" She shook her head. "I don't even know what you're asking, but—"

Logan cut her off before she could say, *Hell, no. Never.* "I messed up because I never understood how your father could treat Jared the way he did. My view of what went on in your house was skewed. I'm trying to tell you how sorry I am, and that I was so determined to be loyal to Jared, I couldn't let anyone see how I really felt about you."

Now her eyes searched his as if she was rewinding a tape, puzzling over scenes that she'd been sure were deleted from whatever film she saw. "You *had* to have known," she whispered.

His lips twisted. "Amazing what you can bury under a shovelful of guilt."

They sat in silence for an uncomfortable length of time. Logan tried not to twitch.

She sighed at last. "I don't know what to say. No matter what, there's so much going on. I have to focus on keeping Molly safe. That you're standing up for us means a lot to me, but—I can't think about anything else."

He made himself nod. "Fair enough. There'll be plenty of time down the line—"

His phone rang.

Chapter Eleven

The call was from the front desk clerk at the sheriff's department wanting to pass on phone messages. Even as he jotted them down, Logan was aware that Savannah had jumped up and appeared to be reorganizing the canned goods cupboard. Her mother had grocery shopped for them yesterday, and either didn't know Savannah's system, or else she was shifting cans from shelf to shelf just to occupy herself. She'd certainly seized the moment to end their conversation, and he had to accept that.

When she rose on tiptoe to put some of those cans on high shelves, he had to work to keep his mouth shut. She didn't raise her left arm, and she'd probably blow up if he tried to make her sit down until he could help her.

His phone rang twice more in the next hour, each time from someone at the sheriff's department needing direction. Even if he'd felt inclined, he couldn't *not* answer those calls. The last question from a young deputy had him shaking his head in something close to disbelief. Damn. He had to hope no serious situation erupted while he was working from the Circle B ranch. Not even the couple of more experienced deputies seemed capable of making real decisions in his absence. With permission from the county council, Logan had already posted the position of assistant sheriff, but hadn't had a chance to study any applications. Maybe he should make that a priority tonight when he couldn't sleep, which was inevitable. Of course, there was a chance nobody had applied. This small county in the high desert wasn't most people's idea of paradise.

The other deputy patrolling today called to let him know that he'd driven into several abandoned ranches and seen no sign of recent occupation.

Savannah had decided to heat them some soup, and was opening cans when the next call came in. It was about damn time—two hours and three minutes. His eyes met Savannah's, and she abandoned the lunch makings and returned to the table.

He accepted the call. "Ray?"

"Sorry it took a while to track down Donaldson. I did reach him, though, and he's the guy who called you. Sounds like losing this Jared seriously upset the applecart for the agents who thought they had a wedge into a nasty organization."

Logan rubbed his forehead. "All right. I hope

he can help us find this information everyone
seems so damn sure Jared had. Would have been
nice if he'd spread some bread crumbs for his sister to follow."

Ray grunted. "If he had, his bosses might have
followed them before she had the chance."

"Yeah, but at the moment we're clueless."

"Give Donaldson a chance. He sounded a little
embarrassed. He's not usually abrasive."

Savannah definitely heard that, because she
rolled her eyes upward.

"We all have our moments," Logan said dip-
lomatically, then thanked Ray for his help before
cutting the connection.

"He's supposed to call us," she said. "I suppose
we just have to twiddle our thumbs until then."

Logan's phone rang, and he half smiled when
he saw the DEA agent's number. "Neither of you
seem to be the patient type."

This time, they were all on their best behavior. Logan described their search of everything
that Jared had left along with his daughter in that
doorway. The agent said that he'd met with Jared
a few times in the past three or so years, but that
usually Jared shared what he'd learned by electronic transfer.

"I had the feeling he was using someone else's
computer. Maybe even one at the library. In this
case, the fact that he left a phone with you is
meaningful."

"This model is only a year or two old," Savannah said, "but the number is the same one he's had since he was a teenager. Um…there was a phone left on his body, too, but Detective Trenowski implied it was something he'd picked up recently, and had almost no information in it."

Logan leaned forward to be sure he was heard. "The only name in the contacts on that phone was 'sister.' He wanted his body identified quickly, and his killer cooperated in making that happen."

Donaldson swore. "Why didn't he contact me? We could have moved fast, pulled him out. We'd talked about how to do that."

Pain made Savannah's face almost gaunt, but seeing his eyes on her, she donned a mask. "He… When I talked to him that morning, he said 'they' were suspicious. I think they must have been following him. His entire focus seemed to be on getting his daughter, Molly, to me. Molly is only four years old. I know he must have *hated* leaving her alone the way he did. He may have thought he'd shaken them very briefly, then decided to draw them away."

"Was his body found the next day?"

"No, it was almost three weeks later."

"I'm assuming you called him."

"Only once. Then I found his phone in the duffel bag and realized it had been ringing in the trunk of my rental car. I never had an address for him, or so much as the name of a friend. There was no way for me to reach him, short of hiring a PI, and I had a feeling that might just put him in more danger."

"Hell," the DEA agent said, sounding more human than he had. "Ah…what kind of phone is it?"

When she told him, he groaned theatrically.

"What?"

"You haven't read about the battles various law enforcement agencies have waged with the company?"

Logan could all but hear the guy's teeth grinding and understood.

"I remember something about that," she said, sounding puzzled, "but…this phone isn't password-protected. We don't *have* to break into it."

"Do you by rights own it now?"

"Well…he put it in the duffel bag for me to find. He must have stripped any protections to allow me to open it."

He was quiet for a minute, then asked Savannah to get her brother's phone. After discussion about Logan's identification of the numbers called from the call log, Donaldson tried to start walking her through recovering any apps or files. After a minute, she pushed it across the table to Logan.

"I use only the most common apps," she admitted, low-voiced. "I train horses. I talk, text and email. That's all."

For all he'd told her, Logan was more aware of all the capabilities of a modern smartphone than she was. He followed instructions with it, not at all surprised to find Jared had set up a single file called "Info." The attempt to open it produced a not-unexpected demand for a password.

That was where they hit a dead end. They wasted a good half hour trying variations on the passwords Savannah knew her brother had used before, ones that included Molly's name, the name of Molly's stuffed rabbit—Walter—and everything else that came to mind for either Savannah and Logan, unlikely as it was for Jared to think Logan would somehow be involved. Still, they tried the year he and Jared had played on a state championship baseball team. Jokes about the nerds in the high school computer club. Favorite horses, profanities, local landscape features.

Nothing worked.

Logan had a full-blown headache by now, and Savannah looked like she might, too. It was Donaldson who called a stop to their efforts.

"We're spinning our wheels. This password *has* to be something he thought would be meaningful to you, Savannah."

"Aren't there computer programs that can figure out passwords?"

"They're not foolproof. We can try that, except…" Donaldson hesitated. "Did Jared will all his possessions to you?"

"No. I'm named in his will only as guardian to his daughter. What money he had is for her."

"How was it worded?"

She went to get the will so she could be sure.

"In other words, he did *not* will his phone to either you or the child. There's none of the usual general language about all his possessions."

"No," she said. "I assumed that's because he didn't have anything else to leave."

"Except his phone."

"But…he clearly wanted me to have it."

"That's clear to you and to me." Tension infused the agent's voice. "The problem is, if we start messing with the phone and do break into the file, will our possession of it be deemed legal? I'll need to talk to the lawyers to find out where we stand."

"What?" she said again.

Logan spoke up. "I'll explain your issues. If worse comes to worst, we may need to take a chance. But for now, I agree with you. Jared wanted Savannah to be able to open this thing."

"Your brother would have seeded a strong hint," Donaldson agreed. "I'm betting it will come to you."

"I…have a feeling my deadline might be tight," she said, more strain in her voice than she'd like them knowing.

Logan liked the agent a little better when his response was almost gentle. "I'm guessing we'll have a few days yet. Try not to obsess about it. Odds are, the answer will float into your head when you least expect it."

Her eyes held desperation when they met Logan's, but she said, "Okay," and they agreed to talk again tomorrow, once they'd all had the chance to think some more.

With the call over, Logan shoved his chair back and held out an inviting hand. "I know you're mad at me, but will you let me hold you for a minute anyway?"

SAVANNAH STARED AT HIM, torn between outrage and yearning. Despite everything, she wanted to feel his arms around her, be able to lean on his strong body just for a few minutes. And…whatever their past, he was here now.

Somehow, she'd come to be on her feet and circling the table. "I am still mad. Just so you know."

And yet, when she reached him, he lifted her high enough to deposit her on the powerful thighs she'd ogled while they rode today, and then wrapped her in the most comforting embrace that she could remember. There must have been times when she was a child, but later, she'd never felt absolute trust in either of her parents.

I don't feel it for Logan, either. No, she didn't, but right now, she trusted him more than she did anyone else in the world, at least in his determination to protect her.

She laid her head against his wide shoulder and looped one arm around his torso. Savannah tried to empty her mind, instead soaking in the moment. His chest rose and fell in a regular, soothing rhythm. She studied the strong, tanned column of his neck and that vulnerable hollow at the base of his throat. Dark tufts of chest hair showed, too, tempting her to touch. Were they silky, or coarser than the hair on his head?

She almost smiled, remembering times they'd gone swimming at the river, Jared and Logan both tall but skinny, too, their chests more bony than brawny and completely hairless. Later, she'd seen hair first appearing on their chests and underarms, along with the unpredictable deepening of their voices that embarrassed them so.

Of course, she'd been embarrassed when her body started maturing, too, starting to wear sacky sweatshirts and leaving a T-shirt on over her bathing suit when they splashed in the cold river water. The first time she'd done that and looked down to see that the shirt was now transparent and clinging to her, she'd jumped out of the water and run to wrap herself in a towel. Jared had teased her sometimes about her not-so-womanly figure, but of course Logan had never given any indication he'd even noticed. By then, he'd cooled off toward her.

She'd been wrong, though. He *had* noticed.

And thought she was beautiful? What could be more staggering than having him say that?

Her wary self roused. He could turn on her the next time his deep-seated suspicion told him that really she was self-centered and shallow, might be capable of anything.

She'd started to stiffen when his arms tightened and he rubbed his cheek against her head. Their relationship was so complicated. How was she supposed to pick out the truth?

He spoke up. "Is it a relief to find out that Jared really was trying to do the right thing?"

She felt the vibration of his voice as much as heard it, but didn't let herself enjoy the sensation too much—or imagine how much better it would sound if she were lying with her head on his *bare* chest.

Unfortunately, his question pulled her back to the terrible tangle of events that had led them to this moment. She had to think for a minute.

"In a way," she murmured finally, "but in a way I'm also furious with him for risking his life instead of extricating himself and actually looking for happiness. You know? And Molly makes it worse. Couldn't he see how much she needed him? He said she was everything to him, but that wasn't true, or he would have made different decisions."

The warm, muscular chest lifted and fell in a long sigh. "Yeah. I've…had the same thought.

If he could walk into the kitchen right this minute, I'd be incredibly relieved, but I also might punch his lights out for what he's done to you and Molly."

She choked out a laugh. "Yes. I'd have a lot to say, but I want him to be alive."

One of his hands made circles on her back, pausing to gently knead here and there. He had to know where she hurt and where she didn't, because he was so careful. She shouldn't be doing this, letting him take care of her, but it felt so good.

"It breaks my heart, hearing that Agent Donaldson met him in person." That just popped out. "Why, *why*, didn't he ever visit? If I could have seen him just once!"

In a way, it occurred to her, Logan had even more reason to have this awful hollow feeling. He and Jared had been best friends, and yet Jared had never so much as called and said, *I'm alive. I think about you sometimes.*

Yet when Logan resumed speaking, it was his frustration that had reemerged. "If this morning I'd known we'd be contacted by the DEA agent Jared worked with, and had likely located the file everyone wants so damn badly, I would have thought we'd be able to see a way out of this mess. Instead…"

She finished the sentence for him. "We're no

closer than ever to being able to fend off these monsters."

No, they weren't, but one thing had changed, she realized. She had used the word *we* and believed in it. It was no longer only she who would do anything to protect a child who'd already been neglected, abandoned and traumatized more than enough for a lifetime.

She *did* trust Logan, at least to that extent. She couldn't really believe he'd ever turn on her again, especially now when she needed him so much. That certainty let her straighten on his lap so she could see his face when she told him what scared her the most.

"Agent Donaldson talked about 'bringing the organization down,' as if they'd be able to arrest everyone from the top down to the muscle they sent to threaten me, but that isn't possible, is it? Even if I do figure out that password, and the contents of the file really are what the DEA thinks they are, what's to say they'll forget about me?" She pressed her lips together, then finished. "Will Molly and I have any future if we don't just vanish and take new identities?"

She saw Logan's shock…and the unwelcome answers to some of her questions.

No, he didn't think any more than she did that handing over Jared's information stash to the DEA would mean she'd be forgotten by the men who were determined to keep her in fear for her life. In fact, they'd be enraged.

And yet the only way forward was to figure out that damn password.

LOGAN HAD MIXED feelings about continuing to let Molly spend a good part of her days up at the house with her grandmother. That had started as a necessity; he understood that. Savannah had to work. Right now, she wouldn't be doing that, though, and Logan felt certain the bastards pressuring Savannah hadn't forgotten Jared's small, vulnerable daughter. Kick in the kitchen door at the house, grab the kid and they'd have Savannah crawling across hot coals to please them.

Considering that he and Savannah had trouble setting aside their awareness that they were walking a tightrope over an abyss, though, he also knew that in some ways, it was healthy for Molly to have a break from the forced good humor the two of them assumed for her benefit.

He was on the phone with a deputy prosecutor discussing whether or not they'd go to trial after an arrest that had happened not long after he stepped in as sheriff when Logan heard a sharp rap on the back door. He shot to his feet and got far enough to see into the kitchen, where Savannah was letting her father in. He hadn't heard her call, "Who's there?" but had confidence she'd peeked out the window over the sink.

Gene didn't give any indication he noticed Logan lurking in the hall outside the kitchen. He hung his hat on a hook just inside the door, poured himself a cup of coffee without asking, then sat heavily on one of the chairs at the table.

After locking the door behind him, Savannah sat again, too, in front of her open laptop. She stared straight ahead, occasionally mumbling to herself, after which her fingers would fly briefly on the keyboard. He made out a word here or there. Aurora was the name of the horse she'd loved dearly as a girl and mourned as if she'd been a sister.

Good thought. Jared knew how much she'd loved that horse. Muffin had been her cat, Bramble the dog as devoted to her as she'd been to him.

Apparently none of those panned out, although he knew she was listing them anyway. Problem was, the password would undoubtedly include numbers and/or symbols, too. Putting it all together would take a miracle, he was starting to think.

Maybe she thought if she gazed into the brightly lit screen long enough, it would become a crystal globe displaying a string of letters and numbers.

God. What if the mysterious password wasn't anything familiar at all? What if Jared had used a nonsensical jumble of letters, symbols and numbers, sure he'd get a chance to pass them on to Savannah?

Logan frowned. Well, then, why hadn't he? Or could they have been jotted on a tiny slip of paper that fell, unseen, out of Molly's suitcase or the duffel, say in the hotel room that first night?

No. Just...*no*.

While he'd brooded, Gene Baird had leveled a scowl at his daughter, who waited him out.

At last, the man said, "Guess I'm lucky Logan sees fit to keep me up to date with what's going on."

She raised her eyebrows in innocent surprise. "Does it matter which one of us keeps you informed?"

"You are my daughter," he snapped.

"I'm scared," Savannah said softly. "Trying to see a way out of this trouble. I appreciate you and Mom taking us in, but the ranch didn't turn out to be the refuge I thought it would be. I've never sulked in my life. If I were mad, you'd know it."

"If I could get my hands on that son of mine— Putting you and his own child in danger."

She stared at him for a long time before giving a laugh that lacked a grain of humor. "Did you ever love Jared?"

He reared back. "What are you talking about? Of course I did. If that kid hadn't been so determined to butt heads with me—" He stopped, shrugged, apparently thinking that was all there was to say.

And maybe he was right, Logan couldn't help thinking. What good would it do now to force him to understand how he'd wronged his son? If Gene ever saw his treatment of Jared the way everyone else had, what would it do to him, a man who had to believe he loved his family?

Logan didn't have to see Savannah's face to know what she was thinking. She'd have tried before. Even Jared admitted that his mother had tried to reason with his father. If Savannah gave him a hard shake right now and tried again, Gene still wouldn't get it. He'd probably just look at her as if she was crazy.

"Um…why are you here?" she asked.

"I still say Molly would be safer sleeping upstairs at the house instead of here. But I suppose you don't agree." Still scowling, Gene shoved back his chair, rose to his feet and stomped to the sink, where he dumped out his coffee.

"Logan is here, on guard and armed."

"I am, too."

"I…need to have her close." Savannah spoke so quietly, Logan just made out what she'd said.

Her father grumbled and growled some more, but did pause to lay a hand on her shoulder before he let himself out the back. Logan couldn't help noticing how gnarled that hand had become.

Her father out the door, Savannah pushed her

laptop away and bent forward to clunk her fore-head on the tabletop. "You can come out of hiding."

Logan stepped forward into the kitchen. "I wasn't hiding. He should have seen me." He cocked his head. "How'd you know I was there?"

She twisted in her seat to make a face at him. "Heard the floorboard squeak."

She was more observant than he'd known. He had made a point of memorizing every place in the cabin where the plank floor complained at even a light footstep.

Pulling out the chair kitty-corner from her, he sat down. "He'd say you're the bullheaded one."

Her startled laugh made Logan smile.

"That's Dad. I truly believe he loves me, but sometimes it's hard to convince myself. He's not exactly generous with words."

Logan remembered things differently. "He used to praise you all the time."

Quiet for a minute, she met his eyes. "I'm not so sure that's what he was doing. Especially what you heard. If you were there, so was Jared. I think Dad was more aiming barbs at Jared than he was patting me on the back."

Having something so basic flipped on end took Logan aback, even though it shouldn't. How much that he'd been so sure he knew hadn't been anything approaching the way he'd seen it? Increasingly, he felt as if he'd been spun in a dryer until he didn't know up from down.

"I...can see that," he said slowly. "Is he softer with your mother?"

"In all those tender moments? No. His idea of a compliment is an occasional grunted 'Good dinner' before he heads for the living room and his remote control. Was your father any better with your mother?"

"Yeah. He'd be embarrassed, but every so often Mary or I'd catch them cuddling. Or worse. He'd turn red and glare at us."

A smile trembled on Savannah's lips. "That's sweet."

Logan abruptly stood and tugged her to her feet. "Went like this," he said in a rough voice and bent his head. His lips inches from hers, he made himself go still and wait to see if she'd refuse him.

Chapter Twelve

Dream come true, Savannah thought dizzily. That he was waiting so patiently for her response broke her determination to keep hugging her hurt feelings to herself. Really, she'd spent half her life imagining that someday this would happen. Logan Quade would actually want to kiss her.

Unable to resist, she lifted her hand to his shoulder, pushed herself up on tiptoe and pressed her lips to his. With one arm dangling uselessly, this felt clumsy, except he took charge so fast, she had no chance to feel embarrassed.

They went from the first gentle brush of lips to an open-mouthed, passionate kiss in what seemed like seconds. He tasted like coffee and man, or maybe it was just him. He stroked her tongue with his, and she returned the favor. What had been some distance between them evaporated, with her having come to be plastered against that hard, strong body. One of his big hands kneaded her butt, lifting, while the fingers of his other hand slid into her hair and cradled the back of her head so he could angle it to please him.

The stubble on his cheeks and jaw scraped her softer skin, but she didn't care. Savannah's knees wanted to buckle, but more than anything she needed to be as close to him as she could humanly get. His hips rocked, and she rubbed against him. Nothing had ever felt so good. She moaned when his mouth left hers to skim down her throat. Her head fell back, and she reached with her injured arm to anchor herself even more tightly against him.

The stab of pain broke her out of the moment, and she went still. Stiffened. Her ribs hurt, too, but that hadn't softened her from wrapping one of her legs around his. An alarm blared. What was she *doing*? This was as far from a wish-fulfillment kiss as it could get. Would she even have remembered if Molly had been home?

He nipped her, just hard enough to sting, but he had also gone completely still. Then he carefully set her back on her feet, smoothed hair from her forehead with a hand that had a tremor and finally kissed her lips again lightly.

"That…went a little further than I intended," he said, low and scratchy.

"No. It's…okay." Startled by the heat in eyes that were often icy, she took a step back. "I'm pretty sure *I* kissed *you*." Already blushing, she made the mistake of lowering her gaze to find herself staring at the thick ridge beneath his jeans.

Heat flooding her face, she jerked her gaze back up.

One side of Logan's mouth lifted. "I think you did, too. Thank you for that."

"I didn't expect—" She hesitated. Oh, why couldn't she simply have said, *Not ready for anything that intense, guy,* and at least pretended to be more experienced than she was?

He arched an eyebrow in that way he had. "What did you expect?"

She just about had to answer. "I suppose… whatever I imagined kissing you would be like when I was a teenager." She managed a shrug. "Since at that point I'd never been kissed, my imagination was pretty tame."

"I had the impression once you were in high school that guys were hot for you."

"As a freshman?" She wrinkled her nose. "Mom and Dad would have had a fit. I didn't really date until after you were gone."

Not that she'd ever raised the subject with her parents, not when the only boy she wanted was Logan Quade, who at his kindest pretended she didn't exist.

This pain was sharper than the one in her shoulder, even if he had apologized and claimed a lot more had gone on in his head than she could have dreamed. He'd still wounded her. He couldn't take that back.

No, her body had begun a meltdown, but her trust only went so far, especially after he'd doubted the danger to her and Molly.

"Do I even want to know what you're thinking?" he asked.

"Nothing that would surprise you. I keep tripping over the past. It's hard not to."

He lifted a hand to squeeze the back of his neck. "Yeah," he admitted gruffly. "We've both come home, and it's changed at the same time as it hasn't."

"I haven't said so, but I feel bad about your father." A detour in topic seemed safer. "I mean, you're here in Sage Creek because he needs you, and instead you're hanging around here."

He grimaced. "Mind if I pour myself a cup of coffee?"

"Oh. No. Of course not. I wouldn't mind—"

He poured two cups full and brought them to the table, where they both sat down and looked at each other. He'd deliberately, she assumed, chosen the chair her father had sat in earlier rather than the one closer to her.

Logan sighed. "Dad insists he doesn't need me, you know. We were butting heads two or three times a day. He's probably thrilled to be able to order around the extra ranch hand I hired instead of sucking it up and admitting he did need me to handle things he can't anymore."

"I'm sorry." She reached out tentatively, then started to pull her hand back. Moving with startling speed, he captured it with his. She'd been determined to open distance, and now they were holding hands, their fingers twined together. It felt so good. Too good.

She was in such trouble, now on a new front.

"Something I need to say," he told her gruffly. "I'm really glad I came home when I did. If I hadn't, I wouldn't have been here when *you* needed me. If I'd found out later—" He swallowed hard, but didn't finish.

As if he'd been pining for her? She didn't think so. Why on earth was she holding hands with him? When she tugged, he let her go without resistance.

Chin up, she said, "You're glad to be here for Jared's daughter. I'll bet you hadn't given *me* a thought in years."

"You'd be wrong." The expression on his face was odd. "No, I guess I didn't often, but I knew you the minute I saw you in the pharmacy that day, and I was mostly looking at your back."

"But you saw Molly."

"It was you who stopped me in my tracks. I knew you—and then I saw Molly and thought…"

"That she was mine."

"Yeah," he agreed, an indefinable note in his voice.

"Well." It would be childish to keep arguing. *You didn't know me. Yes, I did. No, you didn't.* "It doesn't really matter, does it?"

This time, he kept his mouth shut, forcing her to realize she *wanted* to keep arguing. It was a way of releasing this otherwise unrelenting tension.

Her gaze dropped to his hand, still lying on the table, and the powerful, tanned forearm exposed below his rolled-up shirtsleeve. Even given the sprinkling of dark hair, veins and tendons stood out. A few hairs curled on the backs of his fingers. Her hand tingled at the sensory memory of his calluses. She remembered how he'd gripped her while she all but tried to climb him.

How long since she'd blinked? Could he guess what she was thinking? Sex would be one way to release a whole lot of tension—

She jumped up. "I'm going up to the house to spend time with Molly." If she could just get a break from him for a few minutes…

"I'll walk you."

Of course he would. Savannah closed her eyes, breathed in, breathed out and managed a nod.

THE NEXT MORNING, they took Molly along for their ride and succeeded in making two loops of the large pasture. In the barn, Logan suggested Molly ride in front of Savannah.

"Can I?" the little girl begged.

She obviously hadn't known the "suggestion" was a thinly disguised order. Not that Savannah intended to argue. If something happened, Logan could deal with it better than she could. The one thing she did really well was ride. She could get herself and Molly back to the barn with incredible speed. That was what quarter horses were known for—lightning-fast acceleration and unmatched speed over the first quarter mile. Today she rode one of her father's, a mare who showed promise for barrel racing.

They started at an amble, and Savannah was pleased to discover her body moved more naturally than it had yesterday. Logan chatted with Molly, which she thought was really nice of him until she tuned in to one of his questions.

"What did your daddy tell you about your aunt?"

Wait. What?

Molly screwed up her face in thought. "He said she was pretty. And he could have listened for *hours* when she sang."

"You're lucky because she sings to *you*."

Molly offered him a glowing smile. "Uh-huh!"

"What else?"

This wasn't conversation—it was an interrogation. But she didn't intervene because he was right to get Molly to open up. What if Jared had counted on his daughter passing on some tidbit that would make the password appear in Savannah's mind, lit in neon?

Molly thought about Logan's question. "Daddy said she could ride horses better than *him*, even." Her expression betrayed doubt, even if she'd never seen Jared on a horse.

"That's probably true," Logan said, looking amused, "but your dad was a good rider, too. Did he talk about the rodeos we competed in?"

Sounding uncertain, she said, "He talked about roping calves."

As if she had no clue what her dad had been talking about.

"This summer we'll go to some rodeos," Savannah suggested. "They're fun to watch. There's calf roping, bucking broncos and bulls, and barrel racing."

"Like you do with Akil." Molly appeared delighted.

"Right."

"That's what I want to do when I get bigger," she declared.

Logan and Savannah exchanged a smile, not complicated as so much of their relationship was, and they moved straight into a lope instead of trotting. Every so often they slowed to a walk, and he encouraged Molly to chat some more. She clearly *liked* Logan—and why wouldn't she? Savannah smiled encouragement as if she wasn't irrationally irritated.

Unfortunately, Molly didn't say a word that rang any bells for Auntie Vannah. She veered into talking about how Grandma let her paint. Did Logan know she had her own easel in Grandma and Granddad's kitchen? And she'd rolled out piecrusts yesterday, and today Grandma said they'd make cinnamon rolls.

She *loved* cinnamon rolls.

Logan grinned at her. "Who doesn't? Do we get any of them?"

Molly giggled, knowing full well that Logan had scarfed down plenty of yesterday's oatmeal-raisin cookies.

After the ride, Savannah and Logan ate lunch with Molly and Grandma—Granddad was off doing unspecified chores—before leaving them to their afternoon activities.

"Neither of our phones have rung this morning," Savannah said into the silence as they walked the distance to the cabin.

Logan raised his eyebrows in that expressive way he had. "You complaining?"

"No! Just—" She choked off the rest.

He took her hand and gently squeezed. He didn't have to say, *I get it*.

His phone did ring that afternoon. He'd been trying to work on scheduling on his laptop, but spent most of the afternoon talking instead. Sa-

vannah watched in fascination as the expressions
of exasperation, impatience and incredulity appeared on his face even as his voice remained
professional, even soothing.

Her frustration climbed. She was running
out of ideas. What had meant enough to her and
Jared—or just to her—that he would assume
she'd be able to guess his password? The inside
of her head was starting to feel like an old-fash-
ioned pinball machine, the ball bouncing around
unpredictably. *Whack!* There it went, until it connected with another wall or paddle and sped in
another direction.

It would help if she could turn her thoughts to
something else, the way Logan was doing, but
what? Yes, she had a schedule on her laptop of
when she'd work with which horse, and notes
about progress, behavioral issues, minor injuries
should they arise. Those notes made it easy to
keep her outside clients up to date. Unfortunately,
right now she had nothing to add to either her
schedule or notes. How could she, being unsure
of when she could resume riding beyond plod-
ding around the pasture?

Tomorrow. She let out a sigh, soundless so
that she didn't catch Logan's attention. Maybe
the day after. She could start with getting the cutting horses back in the ring. She hardly had to
do a thing except send signals to them that took
little but a twitch of her finger or slight pressure

with one knee or the other. Thank goodness that thug had beat on her left arm and shoulder instead of the right!

A silver lining.

"What are you thinking?"

Startled by Logan's question, she gave the one-shoulder shrug that was coming more naturally. "Training. Which horses I should work with first."

"That's not it."

She frowned at him. "If you must know, I was thinking what a blessing it is that my left shoulder was injured, not my right. And that brought a fleeting memory of how it happened."

He growled, "I can't believe we haven't been able to put our hands on that creep." Except he used a much worse word. "Where the hell is he?"

She would have given a great deal to know. Jared's "employer" knew too well where she was and what she was doing. It had gotten so that even guarded by Logan, she had the crawling sensation of being watched whenever they stepped out the door. He hadn't argued at her keeping blinds and curtains drawn when they were inside. Mom didn't, and the bright interior of the kitchen and dining room made her want to hide under the table. She wasn't alone, either—she'd noticed Logan's gaze flickering from one window to the next, barely pausing on the face of whoever was talking.

He couldn't be sleeping any better than she was. Savannah never got up with Molly that she didn't see that shadow in the hall and know he'd probably opened his eyes at the first whimper, if he'd managed to close them in the first place.

The last thing he did every night was walk the perimeter. He invariably waited until Molly was asleep, at which point he quit hiding the handgun he carried all the time these days. Some nights when Savannah was sitting on Molly's bed reading stories or singing softly to her, Logan hovered in the hall. Other times, he stepped in and sat at the foot of the bed, listening.

Last night had been a first. After story time, Savannah had hugged Molly, kissed the top of her head and tucked the covers around her. She'd barely risen when the little girl said, "Can Logan hug me, too?"

Savannah didn't think she'd ever forget the expression she saw on his hard face. He hid it quickly, as he did most vulnerability, and stepped to the side of the bed.

"Of course I can. Now, whether I *will*..."

In complete faith that she was being teased, not doubting him for a second, she giggled and pulled her arms from beneath the covers to hold them up. Logan gave her a squeeze, kissed her forehead and then gently tucked her in again.

Heart aching, Savannah backed into the hall. A moment later, Logan followed her, turning out the overhead light and pulling the door toward him, leaving it cracked the requisite six inches. Of course, he'd noticed how she left it every night.

Both quietly retreated to the kitchen. Savannah couldn't remember the last time she'd so much as sat down in the living room. The only time she turned on the TV was for Molly.

Again, she stayed opposite Logan. "Thank you," she said.

He looked surprised. "For what?"

"Well... Molly."

His mouth thinned. "She's a sweetheart. Even if it weren't for her connection to you and Jared, she'd have made her way into my heart." He said the last word belligerently. "Okay?"

Savannah pressed her lips together and nodded. Looking down at the tabletop, she said, "I'm just so scared for her. For me, too, but if she loses me—"

"I won't let that happen."

His absolute confidence allowed her to lift her eyes to meet his. What she saw there...scared her in a different way. What would it do to him if she were killed under what he considered his watch? He was only one man.

Nobody wants to kill me, she reminded herself. Not yet.

She shot to her feet. "I think I'll go to bed."

"That's a good idea," he said huskily. "We're

all getting tired. I think I'll stay up a little longer, though."

Her head bobbed, and she fled, even knowing that she wasn't truly escaping the tension between them. Oh, no—it was hardest to ignore at night. That intense awareness of him looking on when she comforted Molly or lay down beside her while she fell back asleep after a nightmare. The times when Savannah needed the bathroom, and couldn't resist one glimpse into the dark living room. The night-light she'd plugged into the hall for Molly's sake was enough to allow her to see the man sprawled on the sofa. Usually, his bare feet were propped on the arm of the couch.

And then there were the times he got up and prowled the house, silent but for an occasional squeak of a floorboard or rattle of a blind when he peered out. Or the way he blocked the faint glow of the night-light when he paused outside Savannah's bedroom and she knew he was looking in.

Waiting. Just as she was doing, however much she denied it to herself.

Chapter Thirteen

The call came the next morning. Logan, Agent Donaldson and Savannah had discussed what she needed to do: buy time.

She and Logan had already walked Molly up to Grandma and Granddad's house, thank God; Logan didn't want that cute kid hearing any threats. She'd been through enough. That she'd seen Savannah's battered face and knew the ranch had become an armed camp enraged Logan as it was.

Savannah's phone rang just as they let themselves into the kitchen of the cabin through the back door. He automatically locked it behind them, then raised his eyebrows at her.

Her breathing was noticeably shallow. She nodded. Yes, it was *him*.

Had he used the same phone number twice?

"Hello?" Her hand shook as she put the device on speaker and set it on the table, although her voice remained stable. Logan lifted his chair so it didn't make any noise scraping on the plank floor, then sat down.

"I've been waiting for you to call *me*," the man said.

"Oh." She managed to sound startled. Her gaze held Logan's. "You didn't say. You haven't used the same phone before. Or at least not the same number."

There was a brief silence. "Do you have what I want?"

"Yes and no—"

"Don't play games with me," he snapped, voice icy.

"I'm not! I found an unidentified file on Jared's phone. I can email you the link. The problem is, it's password-protected. Unless you know what password he would have used—"

"Your brother was stealing from us. Of course I don't know what he'd have used. But *you* do." Three words, and enough menace to raise the hairs on the back of Logan's neck.

He reached over and covered one of Savannah's hands with his. It felt chilly.

"You've scared me adequately, okay?" she said. "I'm trying so hard to figure out what Jared could possibly have assumed I'd know. I told you how many years it's been since I've seen him! We rarely talked. Thinking back to what he'd know had meaning to me isn't easy. Please." Now a tremor sounded in her voice. "I need some more time."

"I think you're playing me."

"No! I swear I'm not."

This time, the silence drew out long enough, Logan's gaze flickered to the phone. Had the connection been cut?

Savannah said more strongly, "The file may be saved on the cloud. I can't tell. If you don't give me the chance to succeed, it'll stay out there. There's always the chance someone else could stumble on it. Maybe hack into it. That's not impossible, you know. Please. Just a few more days…"

Logan wasn't given to imaginative leaps, but he'd swear the fury he felt wasn't his own.

And, indeed, when the caller spoke again, his voice had dropped a register or two and roughened. "We'll see."

Savannah snatched up the phone. "What do you mean? Are you still there? Please…"

The SOB was gone.

Her teeth chattered when she looked at Logan again. "What will they do next?"

None of the possibilities that came to mind were good.

SAVANNAH WENT INTO his arms again, dangerous as that was. She needed the closeness, the awareness of his strength, both physical and emotional. She didn't stay as long as she'd have liked, though. Her body felt like barbed wire strung too tight. If it broke, it would snap back and wrap her in vicious prongs that tore her skin. As terrified as she was, it had to be insanity that allowed her to feel anything sexual…but she did. She did. She wanted more than anything to release this tension somehow—and sex was one way.

She felt his body hardening, his heartbeat kicking up. He'd gone very still. Savannah stared at his throat, at the pulse she could see, the bare hint of stubble on his jaw. She ached.

If he turned his head far enough to seek her mouth, she might not have been able to say no. Neither of them moved as she shored up her resolve. When she scrambled off his lap again, his arms opened to let her go.

He was letting her make the decision, and she was glad. She'd hate to let herself get swept away and then have second thoughts. This was better.

Unless I die never having made love with Logan Quade, a voice in her head pointed out tartly.

She sniffed. Really? She'd be dead and not care.

Safely across the table from him again, she let herself meet his eyes. "Now what do I do?"

He let out a long exhalation, then rolled his head as if his neck had become unbearably stiff.

"The same thing you're already doing. If you keep at it—"

"I may never figure this out!" she cried. "And if I do? What? I hand it over? I'll bet Agent Donaldson would love that!"

"I'd like to think he has a plan," Logan said slowly. "It's time he shares that with us."

Agent Donaldson did answer his phone. He listened to the call Savannah had recorded, then asked, "Ms. Baird, have you made any progress at coming up with the password?"

She leaned over so her mouth was closer to Logan's phone. "Are you asking if I lied to him? I didn't. Nothing I've thought of so far has panned out."

"I'm still of a mind to hold off taking the phone from you. Our right to dig inside it could result in convictions that get thrown out."

That was the last thing she wanted, too.

"I don't know if you're aware that your brother was something of a computer wiz," he continued. "I gather he was the IT expert for this organization. But he knew you well enough, he wouldn't have made this password very complicated given that he expected you to figure it out."

"Thank you," she said dryly.

Donaldson was still an ass.

"Thank you?" His initial confusion shifted into annoyance. "That wasn't meant as an insult."

Sure.

"Let's cut to the chase," Logan interjected. "I took his closing remark to be a threat, not an agreement to give her more time. We need a plan from *you*."

"You were right, though, Ms. Baird, and he has to see it. What good are you to him if you're dead?"

"If they get to her, *your* ass will fry," Logan declared, every bit as menacing as the drug trafficker had been.

"I don't appreciate threats, Sheriff. What is it you suggest I do?"

"Put her into a safe house."

"For how long? At what expense? What if she never figures out this damn password?"

"Then she gets relocated with a new identity."

Shocked, Savannah stared at him. So much for her reawakened emotions for Logan. She appreciated him wanting to keep her alive, but apparently he was willing to wave bye-bye without a second thought.

"It's not that easy," Donaldson said stiffly.

"How long have you been working on bringing down this organization?" Logan asked. His light silver eyes held hers, but she couldn't seem to read anything he felt.

"Ah…close to two years. You must be aware how complex these kinds of investigations are."

Logan snorted. "You don't have any approved warrants?"

"Mr. Baird was going to deliver all the details I needed for that," he said. "Without, I don't have enough."

Logan swore at length, creatively.

Donaldson didn't say a word.

Feeling a burn under her skin, Savannah said, "I'm beginning to wonder why Jared risked so much when you couldn't do anything for him or his family in return."

"He wasn't doing it for the DEA," the agent said quietly. "He was cooperating with us in hopes of saving young people from becoming addicts."

Shamed, Savannah bent her head. "You're right."

"I'll try to get permission to send an agent to reinforce you, Sheriff Quade," Donaldson added. "I can do that much. If you'd prefer for Ms. Baird to come to San Francisco, I might be able to arrange for a safe house."

She gave a panicky shake of her head. Logan took in her expression and said calmly, "We'll get back to you on that." He ended the call and reached for her hands. "That's a no, I take it."

She tucked them onto her lap and knotted her fingers together. "I'm supposed to pack up, tell Molly that, gee, we're going to hide out in an apartment or house in a strange place, surrounded by strange men, but everything will be fine?" Her voice rose as she went, and she didn't care.

"I'd rather take her and do my best to disappear on our own. If that's what you want me to do—"

"Let's get one thing straight. Whatever you do, I'll be going with you." His voice was guttural. "I'm not leaving your side."

What a humiliating moment to burst into tears.

LOGAN CIRCLED THE table and had her on her feet and into his arms so fast, she probably didn't see him coming. How could she think he was tired of being her protector? Where had she gotten that idea?

Cheek pressed to her head, he held her, rocked on his feet and murmured whatever came to mind—probably useless platitudes. Still she cried. Instead of wrapping her arms around him, she gripped wads of his shirt in her hands. He expected to hear the fabric tear.

At last he said, "Enough! You'll make yourself sick."

She went still.

Feeling a wrench of…not pity, he didn't think, but he wasn't sure he wanted to identify the emotion, Logan pried her hands from his shirt, then bent and swept her up in his arms. He carried her to her bedroom, laid her down as gently as he could on the bed and stretched out beside her so that he spooned her. He slipped his arm beneath her neck to allow her to use him as a pillow.

"Relax," he murmured. "I know you're scared, and you have to get this out."

She sniffed a few times.

His smile wouldn't form given the storm whipping inside him, but he groped in a pocket and produced a red bandanna, which he handed to her.

Lying behind her, he couldn't be sure, but thought she was wiping up her tears. The sound when she blew her nose was unmistakable.

"Thank you," she mumbled.

"S'okay." Instead of her usual braid, her hair had been captured in a ponytail but was now slithering out, tickling his face. He loved her hair, thick, silky and fragrant. He'd swear that was vanilla he smelled.

Her body moved slightly with each breath. He was acutely conscious of that body, sharp shoulder blades, delicate nape, long, slender torso that curved into womanly hips.

He didn't hear anything to make him think she was still crying. With the blinds closed tightly, the light was dim despite this being midafternoon. Maybe he should pull a blanket over her... but he was reluctant to move. Some of the reasons for that weren't praiseworthy. In fact, he'd had to inch his hips back from her firm, shapely ass. She'd be rightly offended if she felt his arousal. She'd said no, and he had to accept that. What counted was keeping her and Molly safe. Later...

no, not even later. After the way he'd blown it, she had to make the move, or it wouldn't happen.

Who'd have thought that his teenage, hormone-ridden confusion going head-to-head with his determined, misguided loyalty to his best friend would have altered the course of his life so profoundly? The girl he'd wanted so much in high school was now snuggled up to him, but because she had no one else to stand beside her against the threats to her life, not because she felt anything like he did. The basic attraction was there, but the deep-down trust wasn't.

My fault.

They'd been quiet for a long time. Ten minutes? Twenty? Logan had no idea. He wasn't sleepy, too busy working out how to combat the danger to her even as, weirdly, he felt a sense of rightness and contentment just because she was here in his arms.

When she stirred, he tensed but lifted the arm he'd tucked around her waist. If she was ready to get up—

Instead, she pulled away only enough so she could roll to face him. An observant but distant part of him noted that her eyelids were still a little puffy and the bruises and swelling diminished but far from gone. Tiny hairs that had broken off curled on her temples and forehead. A desperate expression in her hazel eyes riveted him.

She searched his face, looking for something

he'd give anything to provide, then whispered, "Will you make love with me?"

SAVANNAH HADN'T EVEN known she was going to do this. It had to be a way of fighting her sense of helplessness, frustration, fear. Take control of *something*.

It was also the kind of thing she'd regret later. Baring herself to a man whose emotions were still opaque to her? Essentially, begging him to have sex with her?

The seconds drew out and he stared, unmoving. Oh, God—what was he thinking? About how he could politely refuse? That wouldn't be hard, at least; he could just pat her and say, "You're too battered for anything like that." And maybe he'd even be right, but—

"You mean that?" His voice was deep, strained.

She bobbed her head. Almost said *Please*, but thought better of it. No more begging.

"There's...not much I want more." He lifted his free hand and cupped her face, smoothing hair back, thumb pressing her lips.

She couldn't help herself: she flicked her tongue over his thumb, savoring the saltiness and how he jerked.

Moving faster than she'd known he could, he whisked her onto her back and leaned over her. As bossy as he could be, she'd have expected him to descend on her like a conqueror, plundering her mouth, claiming her. Instead, he cradled her face in both hands, the touch extraordinarily gentle in deference to her injuries. He kissed her tenderly, his mouth brushing over hers until he sucked her lower lip and grazed it with his teeth. She felt as if she were floating on air, all her aches and pains gone.

For a minute, she looked up into eyes that were as far from icy as it was possible to be. She took in the angles of his face, his thick lashes, the dark stubble on his cheeks and jaw, the faint crinkle of lines fanning out from his eyes, even the shape of his ears. She had been fascinated by Logan's face from the time she was a girl. Now she lifted a hand to stroke and really let herself feel the textures.

His lips were unexpectedly soft, and she shivered.

Something about that brought her to life. She gripped the back of his neck and pulled herself up enough to kiss *him*. And, oh, maybe it was clumsy and too hard, but she *needed* him. He took over the kiss, deepening it, their tongues tangling, she more conscious than she'd ever been in her life of the sheer size and power of the man whose weight she wanted to feel fully on her body.

He explored her throat with his mouth, tasting and nipping, even as he deftly unsnapped her shirt and spread it open. She was hardly aware of the moment he opened her front-closing bra and brushed it away from her breasts, too. But the way he stared, dark color slashing across his cheekbones—that, she noticed. He must want her, he must, or he couldn't possibly look at her like this.

He muttered, "If you had any idea how often I dreamed of seeing you like this."

At least, that was what she thought he'd said. She tore open his Western-style shirt, the snaps giving way to her determined tugs. Savannah felt a tiny moment of amusement at her recollection of the skinny, lanky boy she'd seen shirtless so many years before, but it didn't last when she could stroke and knead a muscular, tanned chest. Dark hair formed a mat that had a softer texture than she'd expected.

Somewhere in there, their mutual explorations blended together, became something more, something so powerful she was swept away as she'd never been before. They undressed each other, her one moment of clarity coming when she saw how carefully he set his gun within reach. He hadn't forgotten the threat to her, but after that, he was free to cup her breasts, to kiss them, suck them, make his teeth be felt on her nipples before returning to her mouth for more drugging kisses.

She pressed herself against him, hungry for something she'd never felt. A wish to get under his skin, to be part of him. She was intensely grateful when he rolled away for a moment and she heard him tearing a packet. For once in her life, she wouldn't have thought of that.

Then he finally moved between her thighs and she could grip him fiercely with her knees and her arms, trying to hurry him as he growled words she didn't catch but did push against her opening.

He filled her, moving slower than she wanted, but also momentarily snapping her back to herself. This was almost too much…except that wasn't true. He retreated, drove deep, and she struggled to move with him, to meet him.

Just once, she thought, *This is Logan Quade. At last.* Only her mind couldn't hold on to anything so coherent. It was all sensation, the power of his body dominating hers, claiming her.

And then she simply imploded, and felt him shudder and heard a guttural sound escape his throat only moments later.

Tears burned her eyes. Just a few, and maybe it was inevitable. She'd had so many dreams. No wonder she'd felt so much.

"Savannah," he murmured, a wealth of meaning expressed with just her name.

If only she could believe in it.

Chapter Fourteen

Logan felt Savannah's almost-immediate subtle tension that seemed as if she was trying to pull back from him without actually moving. Still holding her, he wished he could think of the right thing to say. She didn't utter a word, but began to retreat in body as well as in spirit. He had to release her.

"In a hurry, are you?" He could have kicked himself for a tone that teetered on the edge of being antagonistic, but damn it, he was both hurt and offended.

"No, I… I need to fetch Molly."

What could he do but retreat behind the mask he'd had to create as a cop? Unfortunately, the silence between them stole his euphoria and the pleasurable state of relaxation.

"Fine," he said curtly.

"Logan…"

"Get dressed."

Once she got up off the bed, she turned her

back on him as if ashamed of her nudity. She pulled on her clothes with impressive speed.

He emulated her, stamping his feet into boots at the same time she did.

"She worries if I'm late."

That might even be true, and he was being a jackass. *He* could have told her how amazing their lovemaking was, but hadn't. He didn't like wondering if she felt a sting from his withdrawal, too.

"I'm glad you put dinner on," he offered. She'd started a stew in the slow cooker that morning. "I'd rather we didn't walk back after dark."

He thought she shivered.

"No. I'm getting so I don't like the dark at all, which makes no sense given that I was attacked on a sunny morning."

"I prefer to see what's coming."

On that note, they hustled to the house, where inevitably her mother cried, "Oh, you're not staying for dinner? You know you're always welcome. Molly is turning out to be such a good cook's helper."

Logan just bet.

Savannah bent to kiss her niece. "She can help me make biscuits to go with our stew. She cuts them out and puts them on the cookie sheet for me."

"I'm real careful," the little girl assured her grandma, whose resistance melted into a smile.

"Of course you are! Oh." She focused on Savannah again. "Your dad and I are making a Costco run tomorrow. You could stock up, too, and with us all going, it will be fine—" The whites of her eyes briefly showed as she obviously didn't want to talk about risk in Molly's presence.

"I don't know." Savannah turned to him. "What do you think?"

Logan mulled over the idea. He absolutely had to put some time in at headquarters in the near future; there were conversations he needed to have face-to-face. Even if Gene and Savannah carried guns, he wasn't easy with the idea, though.

"That would give me a chance to go into work," he agreed slowly, "but I still want you to have backup. I can send a deputy out to tail you to Bend and back. If he walks you to the entrance and you call him when you're ready to come out, the trip should be safe enough."

"A deputy?" Savannah looked astonished. "Really? Can the department afford to have a deputy trailing us on a shopping expedition instead of patrolling?"

"Nonnegotiable," he said firmly.

She didn't protest any further, which made him wonder if she wasn't at least a little relieved. For all that she'd proved her marksmanship to him, accuracy at a range wasn't the same as shooting a man, and especially in the middle of an attack.

He suspected her father was a better shot with a .22 rifle, probably what he carried to protect his calves from aggressive wildlife. Gene hadn't served in the military, however, and was therefore unlikely ever to have shot at a human being, either.

That said…the young deputies Logan was trying to whip into shape hadn't, either. It wasn't just their inexperience; most cops retired after long careers without ever having to pull a weapon on the job. *Not* having to pull that weapon was their goal, unless they served on SWAT or the like.

He took Gene aside while Molly put on her boots and her grandmother fetched her coat and mittens.

"Keep a sharp eye on the mirrors tomorrow, not just the road ahead of you," Logan said. "If you can help it, don't let a vehicle sneak in between you and the deputy."

"I take Savannah and Molly's safety seriously," the older man said, his expression grim.

Good.

Back at the cabin, Logan was glad it was just him, Savannah and Molly. Dinner was excellent, the biscuits Molly helped make mouthwateringly delicious, and thanks to the chatty child, conversation even flowed comfortably.

"I wanted to ride tomorrow," she said, in a rare moment of sulkiness. "Why do we have to go shopping? Shopping is no fun."

Savannah's amused gaze fleetingly met Logan's. "Chances are good we'll do some shopping for *you*."

Molly bounced in her chair. "Are we going to look at a *pony*? Is that what we're doing?"

Savannah laughed. "No, sorry. You don't shop for a pony the way you do for...for a new doll. I've let people know I'm looking. When I hear about one that sounds like a good choice, we'll go meet it and—*maybe*—you can ride it so we can be sure it really is the right pony."

Molly's eyes narrowed. "What do you mean, *maybe*?"

Buttering a second biscuit for herself, Savannah only smiled. "I might decide to surprise you."

"Oh." Clearly, the girl wasn't sure whether she liked that idea or not.

Logan chuckled. "Your aunt has good judgment where horses are concerned, you know."

She wrinkled her nose. "So what *are* we shopping for?"

"Paper towels, toilet paper, canned goods like beans. Everything we need to bake and cook." Seeing a storm brewing, she held up a finger. "Costco does carry clothes your size, children's books and toys. We might take a look if you're patient while we load up on the everyday stuff. Deal?"

Molly slumped. "I guess."

Grinning by this time, Logan wished he could go with them. But the drive was an hour or more each way to Bend, eastern Oregon's largest city and home to the only Costco on this side of the mountains. Add in the shopping, possibly lunch there in the store and the round trip, and he should have a good four to five hours to be sheriff instead of bodyguard. If he could get out of the station soon enough, he wouldn't mind taking time to check out more of the many abandoned ranch buildings in the area. He hadn't asked his deputies to exit their vehicles, only to drive in, look for any sign of a recent visitor, then report to him. Despite his greater experience, he'd probably do the same. He'd rather plan a raid than do anything foolish.

Even as he made his own plans, he brooded about the miles of often empty highways the Bairds would have to travel. So far, though, Savannah's assailant had passed unseen. Taking on two armed adults and a law enforcement escort seemed unlikely in the extreme. There were easier ways to scare her.

The closer bedtime came, the more distant Savannah was. With a pleasant "Good night," she disappeared into her own room shortly after tucking in Molly, and definitely before he could suggest they talk or at least sneak in a kiss.

Disgruntled, uneasy, uncomfortable on the damn sofa and still less than happy about Savannah and Molly's outing tomorrow, Logan was lucky for snatches of sleep.

THE FORMALITY AND cut of Logan's dark green uniform reminded Savannah how imposing he was physically. His inscrutable expression, along with the badge pinned to his chest, made him look stern this morning. It was a little unsettling. Enough days had passed since she'd seen him in uniform that Savannah had become used to the more relaxed man in jeans and a flannel shirt indoors, fleece-lined coat outdoors.

"Walk me out," he commanded when it came time for him to go. He did sweep Molly up, swing her in a circle as she shrieked and laughed, hug her and set her down gently before raising his dark brows at Savannah.

She should be bristling at the spoken and unspoken command, but didn't because…she wished he wasn't going, even if she'd see him again in a few hours.

"Finish getting dressed," she told Molly. "We need to be ready when Grandma and Granddad get here." She grabbed a jacket hanging by the door before she went outside with Logan.

"Ah," he said. "Deputy Krupski is here. Good."

She followed his gaze to see the white SUV marked by a green stripe and the insignia of the sheriff's department and topped with a rack of lights. It was just turning onto the ranch road.

She walked with Logan the short distance to his personal SUV. It beeped and he opened the door.

"Stay sharp," he said. "I don't know how observant your father is."

"This is supposed to be a safe outing. You gave your permission for it." So easily, her pulse took a jump.

He rolled his shoulders in a tell she'd begun to recognize. "I'm sure it'll be fine." His voice became gruffer. "I'll be glad when you're home again, that's all."

"I will be, too," she admitted. "I want all of this to be over."

"Yeah." He gazed down at her for a minute, bent his head and kissed her lightly. "Call me when you get back."

Lips tingling, she bobbed her head. "Yes, sir. Immediately, sir."

He grinned, sending her pulse stampeding for an entirely different reason, then swung up behind the wheel. She stepped back; he closed the door and drove away.

She watched long enough to see him brake and roll down a window to exchange a few words with the deputy before continuing toward the main road.

Savannah stayed to greet Deputy Krupski, round-faced and absurdly young-looking, tell him when they planned to leave and offer to refill his insulated coffee mug before going back inside herself to finish getting ready.

A few minutes later, Dad gave a tap on the

horn when he stopped outside the cabin. She and Molly came out to be swarmed by four dogs who'd come running at the sound of the horn and threatened to knock Molly over as they twirled around her and Savannah, tails whipping.

Molly was giggling when they climbed in the back of her grandfather's extended-cab pickup. Thank goodness the heater was already doing its magic.

Savannah's mom beamed at them, twisting to watch as Savannah put the booster seat in place, waited for Molly to scramble into it and for Savannah to buckle her in before doing the same for herself.

Starting down the driveway, her father checked out the rearview mirror, where he could see their escort vehicle. "This is overkill," he muttered. "Don't know what Joplin will have to say about this once he hears."

Roger Joplin chaired the county council, which made him Logan's boss. She'd heard Logan talking to him several times.

"Mr. Joplin thinks a lot of you, Dad," she said mildly. "You know he'll want to support you and your family any way he can."

Her father made a few grumbly sounds, then subsided. Savannah suspected that Dad's pride had been hurt because Logan didn't think he alone could protect his family.

Mom threw out a couple of remarks, but it was

hard to hear from the back seat and they soon gave up. Savannah hadn't slept very well last night—not hard to figure out why—and found her eyelids growing heavy. She shook herself, remembering what Logan had said.

Stay sharp.

That was easier said than done from the back seat. None of the mirrors offered her the kind of view she needed to see traffic ahead or behind, and it was awkward turning her whole upper body to allow her to see out the back window, partially blocked by an empty gun rack.

Mom cast a smile over her shoulder at the sight of Molly, whose gradual sideways slump had ended with her sound asleep, her cheek planted on the door. Savannah smiled, too, but reminded herself, *Stay sharp.*

She touched the butt of her sidearm, tucked beneath her armpit, in a kind of reassurance. The seat belt crossed over it, which would make drawing slow unless she released her belt first. *Okay,* she thought, *then that's what I'll do.*

She knew when her father turned from the country road onto one of the many minor highways that connected Oregonians in these remote parts to each other. As he accelerated, the tires hummed on the road surface. She really wanted to nod off but wouldn't let herself. Probably half an hour later, she was hanging in there enough to notice a sign that said Entering Crook County.

They were at last halfway, then. This was empty countryside, the only indication of human habitation a few minor roads turning off, one gravel and a handful of what were obviously private drives to ranches or farms.

After stopping at a blinking red light, Dad took a shortcut, yet another two-lane road posted fifty miles per hour that Savannah knew would shortly meet up with Highway 26. Strange that she hadn't seen any traffic yet, Savannah mused. Or maybe not. Once they got on 26, there would be plenty of other travelers. And they *had* gotten an early start.

Needing reassurance, she craned her neck again to look back—to see only empty highway. Alarm flared. Maybe the deputy had just dropped back a little, but… Had he not made the last turn with them? Wasn't Dad paying any attention?

She leaned forward. "Dad! We've lost Deputy Krupski."

"What?" He looked into the rearview mirror. "Where the hell did he go?" His foot must have lifted from the gas pedal, because they began to slow.

Heart thundering, fumbling for her phone, she said, "I don't know, but I think we should turn around. We shouldn't go on without him."

"No. Okay." Astonishing that he'd taken Logan so seriously. The pickup drifted toward the shoulder. Only... A black SUV was coming fast toward them from the opposite direction. Too fast.

"Dad, hurry!" she cried.

"I don't want to put us in a ditch!"

Panic changed Mom's face to someone Savannah hardly recognized. Her father swore, and she looked over her shoulder to see that a second vehicle was closing in on them.

Please let it be chance. She didn't believe it. This was a classic pincer movement.

Molly woke up with a start. "Auntie Vannah?"

Savannah pushed aside the seat belt so she could pull her handgun and flick off the safety. Her hands shook, she saw as if from a distance. That wasn't good.

They'd reached a near stop and her father cranked the wheel to make a U-turn, but by that time the black SUV had swung sharply across both lanes and slammed to a halt blocking the highway going forward. The sedan that had approached from the rear did the same behind them.

"What do I do?" her father yelled.

"Keep going! You're bigger than that car. Slam into it and push it out of the way if you have to!"

She was thrown back against the seat as he stepped hard on the gas again, but two gunshots sounded and the pickup jerked. To her shock, a hole appeared in the side window.

"Dad!" she screamed.

He was yelling, "Get down, get down," and

still trying to drive, but more gunshots had to be taking out tires—they rocked now, and she could tell they were riding on rims—and she couldn't see well enough to take a shot of her own until they came to an abrupt halt.

A masked man appeared by Savannah's window. She tried to fire, but her arm wouldn't lift. She'd lost sensation, which meant she had to have been shot. He blasted a hole in the glass, then used the butt of his gun to smash it until he could reach in to open the door. Her gun…it must have fallen from her hand.

Mom was struggling with her seat belt and both screaming and crying. Dad—he'd slumped forward. Another masked man finished smashing the glass and swung the butt of his gun at Dad's head. Savannah realized Molly was screaming and so was she, but they were dragging her out, throwing her on the pavement.

"Molly!"

A hard kick felt as if it was caving in Savannah's already painful rib cage. She curled into a ball, even as another man hauled Molly out right over Savannah.

Molly kicked and flailed and sounded like a steam engine, but she was too small to be effective. A backhanded blow rocked Savannah's head. That was her last sight of Molly. Somehow, Savannah pushed herself to her feet, where she stood unsteadily. Which direction had they carried Molly? Only one man was throwing himself into the sedan, so probably the SUV.

But...what if he'd closed Molly in the trunk first? Desperate, she scrambled back to the open door and spotted her gun lying on the floorboard. She flung herself back out and propped up her good hand with her injured one to lift the weapon and pull the trigger.

Glass in the back window of the sedan crumbled. She didn't dare hit the trunk, in case. Tires.

Crack, crack, crack.

The car lurched, then spun out and hurtled off the road. Savannah didn't care if she'd killed the driver. Whirling the other direction, she almost tripped over her father, stumbled and kept her gun level.

The SUV was receding. She ran after it, shooting, shooting, until she had no more bullets. She kept running down the middle of the highway, breath burning in her lungs and throat, face wet, until she couldn't see the SUV anymore. She slowed, swayed on her feet...and collapsed onto her knees on the pavement.

GIVEN THE SPEED he was traveling, Logan hoped like hell he didn't encounter any other traffic and that no whitetail deer or pronghorn decided to bound across the highway in front of him. He'd thought he was scared the last time Savannah was attacked, but that had been nothing.

All he knew was that she'd been hurt, Molly was missing and someone else was injured, presumably on top of Deputy Krupski's life-threatening injury.

Apparently, Krupski had been shot and gone off the road. The first call had come in when a passing motorist saw his vehicle half-buried in a mess of sagebrush and stopped to investigate. Logan had passed that mess a minute ago; flashing lights everywhere, including those on an ambulance. Presumably the other car stopped on the shoulder belonged to the Good Samaritan. Under any other circumstances, he'd have braked long enough to check on his deputy. The thought hadn't even crossed his mind. Thank God the Crook County sheriff's department had called Logan's department immediately. Unfortunately, Krupski had suffered a head shot. Unconscious, he hadn't been able to tell anyone what had happened.

But Logan had known instantly. The deputy had been ambushed before making the turn onto the highway that Logan saw right ahead. Perfect timing; it would have taken Gene and Savannah a few minutes to notice his absence.

Had these bastards *known* where the Baird family was going this morning? Could they somehow have gotten into the cabin or the main house and hidden an electronic ear? Or had they just been waiting, assuming Savannah and Molly would go out eventually? It wouldn't have taken long to guess where they were headed. There wasn't a lot between Sage Creek and Bend, central Oregon's largest city. If you'd spread out your troops, it wouldn't be hard to set up a two-pronged ambush.

Logan berated himself for not guessing that they would have increased the manpower locally.

Ignoring the flashing red light, he burned rubber making the turn and zeroed in on the multiple emergency lights ahead. He didn't slow until he was nearly upon them. To his right, an unfamiliar car had gone off the road, bullet holes in the rear window and the windshield. A backboard was being maneuvered up the incline to the ambulance waiting on the road verge. Neck collar.

They'd better not be transporting this scum before Savannah and her family had been taken care of.

Another hundred yards, and he ran right over some flares before slamming to a stop as close to Gene Baird's pickup truck as he could get. Yet another ambulance was screaming away.

What if Savannah was in that ambulance, out of his reach? If that was so, Logan didn't know if he could stay at the scene and figure out what, where and who with even a grain of dispassion. All he'd want was to go after her.

He jumped out and ran toward the pickup, which sat on three flat tires. Metal dented, glass glinting on the pavement, bullet holes in the windshield, side windows smashed out.

There was one still figure in the midst of the activity. Savannah, sitting on her butt on the pavement, seemingly oblivious to the medic crouched beside her, wrapping her arm in white gauze.

And yet somehow his footsteps penetrated her shock. Her head turned, and she didn't so much as blink as he walked straight to her.

Chapter Fifteen

She hadn't even realized how desperately she hoped that Logan would come. But once she saw him, she knew she'd held no doubt. She'd been waiting, that's all.

His savage expression was what she needed to see. He flickered a look at the bulky bandage on her arm, then transferred it to the medic.

"Her injury?"

"Gunshot wound," the woman said. "A severe blow to her rib cage. She needs to go to the hospital, but she is declining to do so."

His pale eyes met hers again. "Savannah?"

"It can wait. I couldn't leave until...until..." Her voice hitched and kept hitching, and she didn't care that the salty tears now running down her scraped cheeks burned. She didn't so much as bother to lift a hand to wipe them away.

Logan looked even angrier. His hands tightened into fists at his sides. He would hate feeling helpless, and she knew his first instinct would be to blame himself for letting them go without him.

Savannah was glad he didn't take her in his arms, as she suspected he wanted to do. She'd fall apart, and she couldn't afford that yet. She had to tell him what had happened, make sure he mounted a hunt for the little girl Savannah loved so much.

"They took Molly." That was the hardest thing to say, even if he must already know. She couldn't look away from him. As far as she was concerned, no one else was here. "I couldn't stop them. I couldn't do anything. I thought I was prepared, but I was useless! Please, please. Find her, Logan."

"I'll do my damnedest. Trust me."

"I do," she whispered. "I'm so scared."

The medic shrugged, packed away her supplies and walked away.

"You must hurt," Logan said. "You should go to the hospital."

"No." She shook her head. "No. It doesn't matter. Molly matters."

"Okay." He coaxed her to stand so that he could lift her onto the tailgate of her dad's pickup. Then he leaned a hip beside her. Crook County deputies were watching him, but must know who he was and were deferring to him for the moment.

"Tell me what happened," he said. "Looks like you got about halfway to Bend."

"Did we?" She turned her head and scanned their surroundings, high mountain desert that could have been almost anywhere in this part of the state. Then her gaze latched back on to his. "We hadn't seen any other traffic in a while. I kept turning to look out the back, and I suddenly realized the deputy wasn't there." Oh, dear Lord—she'd forgotten about Deputy Krupski. "Do you know where he is? *How* he is?" If he'd had something like a flat tire, he'd have called her.

Logan said grimly, "He was shot and went off the road. Somebody saw his vehicle and called in what was assumed to be an accident. That's what started this response."

"He's dead?" She wished she could feel numb.

"No. He's on his way to the hospital. Unconscious, but I don't know any details yet."

Her teeth chattered, although talking seemed to help. She related events as she'd experienced them. It must sound jerky. From Logan's expression, nothing she said surprised him. Big SUV blocked the narrow highway, car raced up to prevent her father from completing a U-turn, and bullets started to fly.

His jaw muscles knotted. "Sounds smoothly enough executed, I'd say it isn't the first time these men have done it. You couldn't be expected to react fast enough to stop them." He shook his head. "I didn't foresee anything this sophisticated. They have to be getting desperate. Whatever Jared had on them must be dynamite."

"But...they didn't even call again."

"They wanted something to hold over you."

Something. An already traumatized child. Savannah hated at that moment as she'd never imagined she could. But she dragged herself back to her narration.

"Dad…" Beginning to stumble over words, she was winding down. "They threw him down. Slammed the butt of a pistol against his head. He's…unconscious, too."

"Your mother?" Logan asked gently.

"I think…she's mostly all right. Terrified. She went in the ambulance with Dad."

"That's best for both of them."

She couldn't decide if he wished she'd gone as well, but was sure he understood why she'd refused.

"One of them stepped right over the top of me and yanked Molly out of the truck. I couldn't see which direction they went." She sounded piteous to her own ears. "I… I thought they might have shut her in the trunk of the car."

Thought wrong. She wouldn't forgive herself for that.

"Ah. Then it was you who shot out the tires and sent him flying off the road."

"Did…did he get away?"

"No. He didn't take the time to fasten his seat belt. Flew through the windshield, which already had some bullet holes. I'd give a lot for a few minutes with him, but he's not looking good. I doubt I'll have the chance."

"You mean... I may have killed him." Shouldn't she feel more shocked?

"Are you sorry?" he asked.

After a moment, she shook her head. She wasn't feeling so good. In fact... She barely made it to the ditch and dropped to her hands and knees before she started to heave.

Logan crouched beside her and rubbed her back, giving her the gift of silence. He produced some crumpled tissues from his pocket when she finally pushed herself up. Still quiet, he waited as she wiped her mouth.

Then he said, "You need to go to the hospital. Nausea suggests you have a concussion again. That's bad so close after the last one." When she opened her mouth, he shook his head. "No. If you can answer a couple more questions, I need you to go get checked out."

As it turned out, she couldn't provide any useful information. Oh, how she hated to admit that she hadn't been observant enough. No, she hadn't seen a license plate on the SUV; her best view of it was from the side after it had swung around to block the highway. No, she wasn't sure of a model, except that it was big. Something in the size range of a Tahoe was the best she could do, even knowing how many models there were now. She couldn't come up with any identifying characteristics on the two men she'd seen best, either. Both had worn black knit ski masks. The one who shot out her window had brown eyes, she thought. Both were Caucasian. She'd tried shooting after the SUV when it took off, but didn't believe she'd hit it. She thought there'd been two men in it, but there could have been a third.

"If I'd shot out those tires first—"

Logan kept his gaze steady on her. "The guy in the sedan would have taken you out, or the others would have come back. You were outgunned from the beginning." Undoubtedly seeing her misery, he told her, "Crook County got out a BOLO pretty quickly. To neighboring counties, too. We can hope a black SUV catches someone's eye." He paused. "It looks like your father got off a couple of shots. If we're lucky, that SUV has a suspicious dent or two, or a nice round hole through one of the windows."

"I…didn't know he had a chance."

"Too much going on." He hugged her, and she realized he must have caught the eye of the medic, because there she was. "I'll get to the hospital as soon as I can. You'll be able to check on your parents once you're there."

She managed a small nod. He could do his job better once she was out of the way.

"You have your phone?"

"Yes."

"Find her," she begged, even knowing how hopeless this was. "Please."

"Nothing is more important than bringing Molly home," he murmured and kissed her forehead.

She let herself be steered away.

THE DEVIL OF it was, there was damn little Logan could do. He was out of his jurisdiction. He'd have called in extra deputies to join the hunt for the SUV, except when last seen it had been speeding west, toward the Deschutes County line. Deputies there were watching for it, but he thought these men were too experienced to do anything so predictable. No, they'd turn off on minor roads, circle back toward Sage Creek or head north or south. God knew.

Savannah must know as well as he did what would happen next. Her phone would ring. Her caller had upped the stakes—and she still couldn't trade what they would want for Molly Baird. Logan suspected they wouldn't return the little girl anyway; she might have seen faces, heard things she shouldn't, and her continuing captivity could be used to control Savannah indefinitely.

Unless they had her cabin bugged, in which case they already knew she was cooperating with the DEA.

Speaking of...

He called first Cormac Donaldson, then Trenowski. Both sounded as angry as he felt, even given that neither had ever met Savannah or Molly.

The DEA agent used some creative obscenities to express how much he wanted to bring the organization down.

Logan only said, in a voice he hardly recognized, "Yes."

He checked in with his own department, made sure anyone and everyone knew he could be reached at St. Charles Hospital in Prineville, and activated lights and siren to speed his way.

Neither Savannah nor either of her parents were in the ER waiting room. When he asked, he was allowed back to a cubicle where he found Savannah lying on a narrow bed, looking wan.

He hated to see the momentary hope on her face. He had to shake his head. "I don't know anything. I'd like to be able to talk to your dad."

"I haven't heard a word about him yet. Can you find out what's happening?"

He could and did, returning to report that her father had regained consciousness shortly after arrival at the hospital, and was currently undergoing an MRI that would tell the doctors more.

"Your mom should be here in a minute," he added. "Tell me what the doctor says about you."

Surprisingly, they didn't believe she had suffered a concussion. "I guess stress was enough to make me puke," she said wryly. "Imagine that." The wound on her upper arm had been thoroughly cleaned and bandaged anew, with the recommendation that she consider seeing a plastic surgeon in the near future. "Because I could hardly use my arm right after I was shot, there may be damage to nerves and muscles."

X-rays didn't conclusively show any broken ribs, either. The doctor thought that the fact she'd already had her rib cage wrapped had protected her from further damage, just not from pain.

They held hands, fingers entwined, while they waited for her mother. Savannah kept watching him, her emotions naked. Whatever wall she'd temporarily built after their lovemaking had fallen. Logan had the uneasy feeling she could see everything he felt, too, which was uncomfortable.

Maybe baring himself emotionally was necessary, though. Slammed by so much these past weeks, he had to realize he'd never really opened up to a woman before, never wanted to. All that had been hurt was his pride when Laura declined to consider moving across the state with him. Already, he could hardly picture her face, so shallow had been his feelings for her. Maybe she'd known that.

Savannah's mother finally slipped into the cubicle, only shaking her head when asked about Gene. Logan had to step back from Savannah to let her and her mother fall into a long embrace.

Savannah closed her eyes, a few tears leaking as her mother sobbed her fear and anguish.

"Molly must be so scared," she cried. "We have to find her. We have to!"

"We will." Savannah opened her eyes, and it was as if she'd reestablished a direct connection with him. "Logan will," she said, before her face contorted.

He put his arms around both women.

Finally, her mother mopped up and decided Gene would be back from the MRI. Her face was red, her eyes swollen, and she moved as if she'd aged a couple of decades today. Maybe she had, in every meaningful way.

He wet a couple of paper towels with cold water and gave them to Savannah to lay over her face. Then he took her hand again.

His phone rang once, and he stepped out to take the call from his own department. A passing nurse looked disapproving, but didn't say anything. He was able a minute later to return and tell Savannah that doctors had hope for Krupski.

"The bullet ricocheted off his cranium. They've drilled a hole to release some of the internal pressure. They're calling it a coma now and he's still in critical condition. Most people in his state do recover, though." He swore softly. "He's a kid."

Savannah's hand tightened on his. "Would it be any worse if it was an older deputy?"

He rubbed his free hand over his face. "No. I

don't know. It's so damn unlikely for anyone in law enforcement in a small town or rural county to ever get shot. His parents—" He broke off. They'd been so proud. Now they'd be sitting outside Intensive Care at the hospital in Bend, where their son had been transported because of the severity of his condition.

He should call them…but anguish he'd never imagined feeling for a child who wasn't his kept pulling him back to Molly. He saw the joy and trust on her face as he'd swung her in a circle before he left that morning. It shouldn't have been able to happen so quickly, but he loved that little girl as much as he knew Savannah did. Molly was entirely lovable. He kept being hit by the fact that she was Jared's daughter, too, as well as Savannah's niece.

A phone rang, and he realized right away it wasn't his. Savannah pulled out hers, looked at the displayed number, then at him.

"Ms. BAIRD. I think we have something of yours."

Pushing aside the grief to allow room for rage, she said, "Not *something*. A little girl who has already had too many bad things happen to her in her life."

"I should have said, something valuable." The cold voice hardened. "I've run out of patience, Ms. Baird. You've had plenty of chances to do

what I asked. I hope you're a little more moti-
vated now."

"You do know that your men badly injured my
father and may have killed a cop. Considering we
have capital punishment in this state, that seems
really stupid."

"Ah, but who will catch my men? Your local
law enforcement hasn't been a great deal of help
so far, have they?"

"I'm in the hospital, too. Did your hired guns
tell you that? One of them shot me. A few inches
different, I wouldn't have been around to help you
with your problem."

"Perhaps without *you* in the picture, it wouldn't
have been a problem anymore. Now, when are
you going to give me what I need?"

"We can… We'll have to set up a meeting."

"You've figured out your brother's password."

Savannah met Logan's eyes and lied with remarkable steadiness. "Yes."

"Tell me."

"No. I'll give you the phone with the password
when I have Molly back, unharmed."

Logan nodded his approval.

At least she'd provoked a moment of silence.

"When will you be released from the hospital?" he asked.

"I…don't know yet. Probably by tomorrow
morning. And in case you had visions of stopping by my room, I don't know the password by

heart. I wrote it down and hid it. All I had with me today was a shopping list."

"You really shouldn't antagonize me, you know. That cute little girl's life is in my hands. And let me say, if I get even a hint that you've shared information from that file with authorities, she's dead. Do you understand me?"

"Yes!"

"Don't let your lover spend the night. We'll be watching."

Her mouth opened and closed.

Then came a curt "I'll call you at noon tomorrow with a meeting place. If you're not alone, you know what will happen."

"Wait!" she cried, but he'd cut her off.

Logan muffled her scream against his chest, his arms locked around her.

Chapter Sixteen

It never took long for a woman as gutsy as Savannah to collect herself. Once she had, she said, "What are we going to do?"

"Set up a trap," he answered grimly.

"But...you heard what he said!"

"I did. We'll have to give the appearance that you're alone. That will take some planning. No matter what, we'll need to have enough manpower in Sage Creek, ready to go in an instant. And by God, it's time Donaldson comes up with more than talk."

Donaldson did. He had a team ready and eager to go. When Logan told him about the specific threat to Molly if the traffickers caught even a whiff of rumors that a move was being made on them, the agent was able to reassure him. He'd set up a fake investigation to explain why agents were being sent to Oregon. They'd fly to Portland immediately, then drive through the night if necessary to be available in the morning. They discussed where they could wait so as not to draw any attention at all, assuming Savannah's watcher was still loitering.

Not liking to rely entirely on anyone else, Logan called a couple of his most capable deputies to be ready as well.

He'd no sooner gotten off the phone than a nurse let him know that he could see Savannah's father.

Not surprisingly, Gene couldn't produce a breakthrough piece of information. He had no idea of a license plate. The man who'd grabbed him was dark-haired; he'd seen the hair on his forearms.

"A big bruiser," he mumbled past swollen lips. He'd lost a couple of teeth, which didn't help his speech, either. "Near my height, but broader than me. I grabbed for his mask, but he had me on the ground too fast."

"What did he wear?"

"Shiny black cowboy boots. Saw those."

Logan winced. Baird and Savannah had both been kicked. That seemed to be a favorite punishment handed out by the trafficker's enforcers, especially effective with pointed-toe cowboy boots.

"Luck they didn't hurt Susan." The shame in Gene's eyes echoed Logan's knowledge that he'd failed Savannah and Molly. "I should have reacted quicker."

Despite Logan's old anger at this man, he laid a hand on his shoulder. "You're not a special ops soldier. It takes intensive training to be ready for something this out of the ordinary. If anyone is to blame, it's me for okaying this expedition."

Gene grimaced. "Craziness."

"It was."

Logan was incredibly glad to be able to take Savannah back to the ranch. Doctors wanted to monitor her father for the night because of his head injury, and despite his gruff insistence Savannah's mother go home, she dug in her heels and stayed with him.

Logan couldn't take her to his dad's place. He didn't want to endanger his father, and anyway, Savannah was in no state to have an obligatory conversation with his father and Mrs. Sanders. Logan hoped the Circle B ranch wasn't being watched at this point; he'd rather these scumbags not know that, contrary to what she'd suggested, she wasn't actually being held another night at the hospital. He frowned. What if they went to a motel?

Once he'd lifted her into his truck and gotten behind the wheel himself, he asked what she would prefer.

He had the feeling her thoughts were turning slowly, but finally she said, "Home. I mean, the cabin. If you don't mind."

"Of course I don't."

He worried during the hour-long drive, stealing frequent glances at her. She'd crawled deep inside herself. The couple of times he tried to initiate conversation, she would turn her head, look vaguely surprised to see him and say, "What?"

These scum suckers had already made their point in a powerful way. Despite knowing how unlikely it was that he and she would be attacked, Logan stayed hyperalert watching for other vehicles, paying special attention as they got closer to home.

He parked as close to the back door of the cabin as he could get, helped Savannah out and hustled her in. He sat her down at the kitchen table and then cleared the remaining rooms. Finally, he mounted a search of any obscure place a bug could have been concealed but found nothing. As far as he could tell, Savannah didn't even notice what he was doing. She sat where he'd left her, staring straight ahead, eyes unfocused.

"Are you hungry?" he asked.

Her gaze wandered slowly his way. Her forehead crinkled slightly; predictably, she shook her head.

To hell with it. He was starved, and needed fuel to do his best thinking and prepare for action.

He was glad to find a lasagna he knew she'd made in the freezer, since cooking wasn't one of his best skills. He stuck it in the microwave to defrost and then heat, cut up broccoli and put it on to cook, and even found some French bread, which he buttered. No garlic salt to be found in her spice cupboard, but he did come across garlic cloves and crushed one so he could spread it over the bread.

His phone rang several times with updates, none important enough at the moment to intrude on her fear and grief. Deputy Krupski seemed to be getting more responsive, thank God; eyelids moving, fingers twitching, that kind of thing. He called Savannah's mother, who said Gene hurt and was mad. She didn't have to say that he was scared, too. His truck had been towed to an auto body shop in Sage Creek. It would need some significant work. The same shop did the work on sheriff's department vehicles, so they had that car, too, by this time.

A sergeant with the Crook County sheriff's department reported that the driver of the crashed sedan had died. The car was a rental. They'd pulled some fingerprints that matched those of the dead man and had a name for him.

Jimmy Barraza had used a fake driver's license to rent the car. However, his fingerprints were in the system. He was a San Francisco resident who'd served several stretches in state penitentiaries for violent crimes. Calls to the San Francisco PD suggested that while rumor linked him to a drug trafficking organization with ties to a Mexican cartel, proof was scant. He hadn't been arrested or charged with any crime in the past eighteen months.

"We think a couple of bullets we removed from the interior of Mr. Baird's pickup will match up with the Colt Barraza carried," the sergeant added. "Nice if we could have charged him, but—"

Burying him was easier all around, Logan thought.

THE AFTERNOON AND evening felt interminable. Logan suggested Savannah lie down, but how could she sleep? Waking nightmares flickered through her head like poor-quality film.

She relived the minutes from when she'd noticed they'd lost their escort until she'd collapsed screaming on the roadway. Over and over, her last glimpse of Molly being pulled out of the pickup, right over her, played. The terror, the instant their eyes met, Molly not understanding why her auntie Vannah didn't *stop* that man. Daddy said she could *trust* her aunt.

The very young brother she'd loved kept coming to her, and sometimes she felt only grief, other times rage because this was *his* fault—except it wasn't all, she knew that—and ending in guilt, because he had trusted her to protect his "everything." Worse, because she loved Molly for her own sake, loved her as if she was her own.

Savannah was dimly aware of Logan on the phone, restlessly pacing the kitchen, slitting the blinds to peer out—and watching her. She did let him persuade her to eat some dinner. She wasn't hungry, but he was right; she needed to be ready tomorrow for whatever came. Aware, *smart*, not the zombie she felt right now.

A couple of times, she shut herself in the bathroom when she absolutely had to cry. Not that she was fooling him. It was hard to hide puffy, bloodshot eyes. She didn't even know why she had tried, except she didn't want him to feel worse than he already did.

She worked up some resentment because, while he felt he'd failed her and Molly, he was still able to plot, to weave the strands surrounding him into something meaningful. He talked with fellow cops from several jurisdictions, hospital personnel, the DEA agent who was zealous enough to be on his way to Sage Creek, Oregon, along with his fellow agents.

Logan pulled up USGS maps of the county on his laptop, comparing them with paper maps he brought in from his department SUV. Savannah did rouse herself enough to ask how he could possibly think he'd be able to predict where these monsters would choose to set up an exchange.

Face heavily lined, he said, "I can't, of course, but I'm eliminating possibilities and trying to see through their eyes. How much have they actually driven around the area? Is their hideout also a logical place to meet you? They have to know you'll do your best not to be alone, despite their demand. Fortunately, I doubt they'll expect federal agents, but they know I'm the sheriff and will try to corner them if I can."

That alarmed her. "Will you? If they have Molly?"

He shook his head. "Not until the trade is made." He hesitated. "If it's made. I expect they'll bring her, but what if they want to keep a hold on you?"

"Why?" she cried. After a moment, her shoulders sagged. "Because they think I might keep a copy of the file so I can pass it on to somebody like the DEA." She had to say this aloud, however horrible it was. "They don't really plan to give her back to me at all, do they?"

Expression compassionate, he was still honest. "No. I don't think they do." Then he shook his head wearily. "They're going to assume we'll try to set them up. That…introduces danger."

"Maybe…maybe we shouldn't. What if I really did go without anyone—"

He took one of her hands in a warm clasp. "They have zero ethics, Savannah. No sense of morality. They don't care that Molly is a scared kid, or that you're her terrified mom." When she opened her mouth, he said, "Aren't you?"

Her eyes got watery again. He apologized, and she jumped up to retreat to the bathroom again. Except this time she felt compelled to bypass it and go to Molly's bedroom. Pink and purple, unicorns and night-light, a lamp with a base of a rearing china horse that Savannah had forgotten all about but that Mom had retrieved from the house.

Hugging herself, she turned slowly in place. They'd probably gotten carried away with the toys and games. Stuffed animals especially; Molly loved them, although it was the rabbit with worn fur and a tattered ear she'd loved most. Savannah wished suddenly that Molly had taken it with her this morning. Maybe she could have held on to it. Maybe *they* would have let the kid keep it, if it would keep her quiet.

Or…maybe it would have been lost forever.

Just so Molly wasn't.

Savannah sat down on the edge of the bed, picked up Rabbit, studying him and finally pressing her cheek to his furry stomach. He smelled a little peculiar, but she imagined some of that was Molly.

She heard the high, sweet voice.

Will you sing "Sunshine" to me?

Her voice wanted to crack, but she began to sing, "You are my sunshine, my only sunshine." By the time she reached the part where she was begging for her sunshine not to be taken away, her nose was so clogged that she could hardly breathe. How terribly fitting the lyrics had turned out to be! If she never saw Molly again, Savannah knew she'd never listen to this song again, much less sing it.

How strange that Jared had remembered it as her favorite.

As if she'd been hit by a Taser, she quit singing midphrase. Wait. Why hadn't it occurred to her that *this* was the one oddity Molly had shared? The only thing that resembled a message for her? A song she had had to learn off the internet? He'd been there when she was growing up. He'd have *known* their mother either didn't know it or didn't like it for some reason.

He'd all but *made* Savannah learn the lyrics.

Stunned, she felt her chest swelling with hope. This had to be it. It *had* to be.

She set Rabbit on the pillow, jumped to her feet and called, "Logan! Logan!"

SHE'D ABOUT STOPPED Logan's heart. The way the day had gone, he expected a cherry bomb had exploded through the window, at the very least.

Her face was wet with tears, but her entire expression had changed. Standing by Molly's bed, the worn stuffed rabbit lying askew on the pillow, Savannah fairly vibrated with new energy.

She rushed to explain and said, "I think 'You Are My Sunshine' *has* to be at the heart of that password. It's the first thing that makes sense."

She was right. He was careful not to say, *Being*

*able to access the file may not help us bring Molly
home.* Savannah had to know that.

They went back to the kitchen to try to figure
this out. Savannah detoured on the way to grab
a printout of the lyrics for a song that had orig-
inally been embraced as country music. Once
they'd sat down at the table, he skimmed over
the lyrics and was horrified. The damn song was
heartbreaking. It wasn't a reassuring love song;
it was about heartbreak. Hadn't Jared *noticed*?
Or was his choice influenced by his own sense
of impending tragedy?

Logan looked up. "You don't sing the whole
thing to Molly, do you?"

"Heavens no! It's beautiful, but awfully sad."

They finally got out a notebook and wrote numerous alternatives. *YouAreMy. MySunshine.* On
and on. Logan eyed the line about how the lost
love would someday regret leaving the singer. At
the moment, that sounded like a threat.

They moved on to possible numbers. Molly's
birthday seemed most logical, so they played
with that. Symbols? How were they supposed
to know?

Except Savannah said suddenly, "An exclamation point. I was way too fond of them when I was
a kid. Even my teachers had to constantly replace
them with periods and write me notes in the mar-
gin about how overuse weakened the punch. Jared
gave me a hard time about being so sunny—" she

faltered there "—that everything had to be *great*!" She was obviously mimicking her brother with the last part, each word bouncing high.

"I remember that." He stretched with both arms over his head while he thought about it. "I don't think this is about Molly at all. It's about *you*. He may have been using this password before Molly even came to live with him. Clearly, he's always had you in mind as his backup."

Savannah stared at him, seeming stunned. "Me?"

"He constantly used the word *sunny* when he talked about you. I'd…forgotten." Even his memories had been filtered through his biases. He wanted to give himself a kick in the rear. "Jared knew sometimes you were pretending, but he said you did it well. So let's try parts of *your* birthday." Logan paused. "He loved you."

Savannah swallowed and nodded.

Back to symbols. She pulled up texting on her phone to stare at the options. "What about 'at'?"

He jotted down his version of @.

"The symbol for *number*. He and I constantly played tic-tac-toe, especially on trips when we were crazy bored in the back seat. Naturally, I never had a chance after he figured out how to inevitably win, and it took me ages to realize that if he'd ever let me go first, *I* could have won. We'd end up squabbling, and Dad would yell at us, but—"

went down on their list.

Thank God Jared hadn't set the log-in—or,

even worse, the file itself—to self-destruct when someone made too many attempts at passwords. Logan lost track of the number of alternatives they tried, and that was just today's effort. Then she typed in just the day and month of her birthday, followed by #, MySunshine and an exclamation mark.

And they found themselves looking at a letter.

Vannah,
I hope the worst hasn't happened and you're reading this. If it has—God, I'm so sorry. I guess you've figured out that I'm doing everything I can to bring down the entire drug trafficking organization that got their talons into me when I was at my weakest. Give this file to DEA Agent Cormac Donaldson.

Jared used the #, followed by a phone number Logan already knew.

I know how hard you tried to protect me from Dad. I wish I'd been mature enough to let his abuse roll off my back. I could have had a different life. But I didn't, and I can't regret Molly. My love to you both. Always.
Jared

Logan's first thought was that Jared had provided the permission the DEA needed to use this document.

Savannah leaked a few more tears, they flipped through some of the multiple pages that followed, and she said finally, "Should we call Donaldson?"

Logan didn't hesitate long. "No. He can wait. I don't one hundred percent trust that he wouldn't get excited and push for a warrant, assuming it could be kept quiet. His priority and ours aren't the same."

They copied the file to Logan's laptop and to Savannah's, too, then closed it on the phone.

"You're a genius," he told her, and she gave a watery laugh.

"Hardly, but no matter what, I'm glad we did figure this out. Except for getting Molly back and loving her, this is the last thing I can do for Jared."

"Yeah," Logan agreed gruffly. "Now we'd better try to get some rest. Do you think you can sleep?"

Exhaustion and strain making her look fragile, Savannah said, "No, but I'll try. Only…will you lie down with me? I mean, not to—"

"I know what you mean." He managed a crooked smile.

"I shouldn't ask, since you can't stay."

That was part of the plan. She had to appear to be compliant. She also knew that two deputies, six DEA agents and Logan would by morning be spread out across the county so that at least a couple of them should ideally be close once she was told where to go.

That, of course, was assuming Logan was able to overhear the instructions the way they'd planned.

"You don't know how much I'm going to hate leaving. Right now... I need to hold you."

As usual, he made a perimeter walk outside before checking all the locks and turning out lights. Then he went to Savannah's room. She'd removed her boots and jeans, but hadn't bothered taking off her T-shirt and, he presumed, her bra and panties. Logan followed her example, leaving his boots beside the bed where he could put them on quickly and tossing his jeans over a chair. Then he climbed under the covers, stretched out and gathered the woman he loved into his arms.

He felt her letting go of some of her tension. Tonight, that was enough.

She set out in the aging pickup truck at 12:05 on the nose. Ranch hands may have known what was happening. She didn't know, only that they watched her as she started down the driveway, their expressions grim. They probably assumed she was on her way to see her dad in the hospital.

Savannah would have been scared spitless, except she clung to her hatred for these monsters as if it was a supercharged heating pad that kept her from the creeping cold she'd battled since

Logan had slipped out of bed in the middle of the night and left.

She'd dozed off and on until then, but the moment she'd felt him lift his head to look at his phone or the clock, she'd lost any ability to sleep.

He brushed her nape with his lips—she couldn't think what else that sensation could be—and then murmured, "If I had any choice, I'd have stayed with you as long as you needed me. I hope you know that."

She'd heard her own croaked "I… I do."

"Good. Remember, I won't be far."

She thought she'd nodded. Then he slipped out of bed. A few rustles and a faint squeak of the floorboard told her he was getting dressed, and not a minute later the back door closed.

Now, following the directions the cold voice had given her, she held on to Logan's promise.

I won't be far.

How he'd accomplish that, she had no idea, except that, using Jared's phone, she had the line to him open and her own phone on speaker. She could only hope he heard enough snatches of the directions she'd been given through her phone.

Unfortunately, the man hadn't been stupid enough to give her a final destination. She could only drive, trust in Logan and make the silent vow to do anything to save Molly.

Chapter Seventeen

The two phones might have started lying next to each other on the passenger seat in Savannah's ancient pickup, but once she started driving, Logan suspected they'd slid apart. The creep giving the directions was both angry and incredulous when she told him she didn't have Bluetooth. Ticked that the phone was on speaker, he remained suspicious but evidently resigned himself when she snapped, "I can't clutch a phone in my hand and drive safely, especially when I'm already rattled!"

Logan had no trouble hearing that. The rejoinder was a little muffled.

"If you have someone else in the vehicle with you, this meeting is canceled."

"I don't! I'm telling you the truth."

Clearly, they weren't able to use GPS to locate Jared's phone. He'd probably had multiples, and they'd never known this one existed.

Logan was doing some serious sweating. He'd had to make choices, knowing how flawed they could be. But he didn't have an army to disperse on this battlefield. What he did have was fewer than ten men—and superior knowledge of this county. Some of that was courtesy of his childhood, but once he'd accepted the job of sheriff, he'd driven as close to every inch of his new territory as he could come. He knew which ranches were for sale, some still under operation, others long deserted. He knew the dead-end roads where teenagers parked, the falling-down barns where those same teenagers held keggers. He'd also had an epiphany yesterday as he studied the maps.

On a road map, the county was laid out like a spider's web, with the town of Sage Creek being the spider at the center of it. The main highway—if you could call it that—crossing the county went right through town, the speed limit dropping to twenty-five miles per hour. Otherwise, most roads of any significance radiated outward. His conclusion was a gamble, but he also thought it would prove to be right: the guys who'd terrorized Savannah, who'd been able to appear like wraiths in the night on her father's ranch, hadn't been driving from some distant part of the county. As strangers in a place where everyone knew everyone else, they wouldn't have wanted to be seen passing back and forth through town every time they went out to the

Circle B to keep watch—or beat the hell out of a woman.

Logan concluded their hideout had to be in the same quadrant of the county as his own dad's ranch *and* the Circle B. Theoretically, his few patrolling deputies had been looking for likely places for out-of-towners to squat temporarily, but there were a lot of them. Ranching as a family-run business was failing, and not only locally. Corporate-owned ranches were taking over, but not a one of them was situated in this notoriously dry part of eastern Oregon. His dad and the Bairds had hung on, along with half a dozen other ranches in the county, but most had gone under or were now only a hobby or a sideline to people who held other jobs.

On the map, he'd long since pinpointed half a dozen possible hideouts within four or five miles of the Baird ranch and had them checked out by deputies, although now he wished he'd done it himself. He added half a dozen other locations where passing traffic wouldn't be able to see today's meeting. He'd spread a couple of his too-few troops farther away…but damn, he hoped he was right.

He was waiting at a spot that seemed a good possibility—one of the closest to the Baird ranch—but he was also ready to hustle and move if he proved to be wrong.

Right now, he sat tensely, knowing she must be approaching the stop sign where one of the big decisions would be made.

Her voice came through the speaker. "Which way do I turn?"

"Left."

Logan breathed a prayerful thanks. Right would have taken her toward town, straight ahead into some mighty bleak country without a lot of habitation. Left had plenty of turnoffs that would put a man within riding or hiking distance of the ranch.

Silencing his own phone very momentarily, he used his radio to inform everyone else waiting. A couple of them—a deputy and a Fed—would be leaping into their vehicles to speed this way.

He had a good idea when she drove past his preferred location where he waited. A moment later, the voice said, "Left on the next dirt road."

"The one with a falling-down sign that says Horseback Riding?" she asked, voice clear.

The scum whose voice Logan had grown to hate answered with a clipped "Yes."

Logan murmured into his radio, then grabbed his phone. Wearing his flexible tactical boots rather than the cowboy boots that let him fit in locally, he set out cross-country at a hard run. Fumbling as he went, he poked in an earbud so he could hear any additional directions to Savannah, then unholstered his weapon and raised it into firing position in case he encountered a surprise.

SAVANNAH HAD PAID more attention yesterday than she'd realized to Logan's calculations with the maps. He'd left one of the maps he'd marked up for her to take today, with *X*s telling her where surveillance would be set up.

This was one of those places. The moment she made the turn, she crumpled the map in her hand and, bending, stuffed it under the seat.

A family had lived here until Savannah was ten or so; a couple of kids had ridden her school bus. But they moved away, and Dad had said there'd never been an offer on the ranch, not even a low-ball one. She drove as slowly as she could without occasioning suspicion, her heart drumming harder and harder as she watched for any sign of life. The ground wasn't frozen today, and dust rose behind her, announcing her arrival. Had whoever was watching her been staying here? A deputy must have driven in here sometime, but had he gotten out of his vehicle to walk around the derelict ranch buildings? Would he have been gunned down if he had?

Had they watched him come and go, and now felt safe here because they'd been undetected?

This land was slightly higher than her father's

ranch, and lacking a stream, if she remembered right. With no cattle grazing, what had once been pasture was growing up in the junipers that ranchers, and even the state, often tried to eradicate. Scruffy trees, they made it hard to see ahead.

"There's a gate on your right," the man said abruptly. "Turn into it."

She wouldn't be going as far as the house or barn, then. Bile rose until she could taste it. If there was a cop here somewhere, he or she would be somewhere near the ranch proper, but she had no choice but to follow directions.

Gate was a generous word for a rusting barbed wire section that had been strung to a post not set in the ground so that it could be pulled aside. She bumped slowly over hard, uneven ground. The shock absorbers in this pickup had needed replacement at least a decade ago, and now each jolt felt like it was giving her whiplash. Oh, God—what if this led back out to the paved road, after which she'd be directed somewhere else altogether?

But then she saw a glint of metal ahead. She shifted her foot to the brake. An all-too-familiar large black SUV backed up to a tumbledown shed with a juniper growing right up through the roof. There was a second vehicle here, too, parked facing her. A nice shiny pickup truck. Another rental?

A part of her was astonished that she could still think at all.

"Stop," said the hard voice. "Get out of your truck."

Please don't let me be alone here, she begged, before turning off the engine and touching her side to be sure she had her own gun. Would she dare fire if they'd really brought Molly? She took a couple of measured breaths. Then, leaving her own phone on the seat, she picked up Jared's, opened her door and stepped out. She didn't move beyond that, though, using the open door as a shield the way cops on TV shows always seemed to do.

A man walked toward her, halting about halfway between the SUV and her pickup truck. Medium height, not lean, he clearly wasn't the muscle here. He had long dark hair smoothly pulled back from a terribly ordinary-looking face. She was still studying it when he lifted a gun she hadn't noticed and fired twice. Instinctively, she crouched as her pickup jerked. Tires. He'd shot out her front tires. Savannah had to force herself to rise to her feet again.

"Just in case you had any ideas," the man said coolly.

It was *him*. She knew that voice from his first call. Hate came to her rescue, steadying her hands.

"Do you have the phone?" *he* asked.

LOGAN WAS CAREFUL not to accidentally brush against the bristly branches of any of the junipers and therefore betray his approach. His lungs burned and, winter or not, sweat stung his eyes by the time he was able to hear a voice. .

"Stop. Get out of your truck."

His blood ran cold. He didn't slow down, but stayed low as he wove between trees, sagebrush, rabbitbrush and a few outcrops of volcanic rock.

Savannah apparently turned off her engine. Her door had a distinctive squeal as it opened.

Close now, Logan scanned for movement. Yeah, there was someone beside the SUV, the first vehicle he could see clearly. Two men—no, three, one standing beside a pickup that from his vantage had hidden behind the SUV. This guy held a rifle loosely in his arms.

Crack. Crack.

Terror ran through Logan like an electric shock. If that bastard had just shot Savannah, he was dead.

He ordered himself not to let panic drive him into acting prematurely. Taking each step with care now, Logan eased himself behind cover where he could finally see her rusting truck and crouched low. She stood behind the open driver-side door. So who'd shot, and why— Flat tire. They'd shot out at least one of her tires.

A federal agent had been positioned at the barn. Logan hoped he'd ever set foot outside a city and knew how to approach without crashing through the high-desert vegetation. If he'd been listening to his radio, he should already be here, set up in a position that would allow him to intervene. Cormac Donaldson himself should be approaching from the next abandoned ranch to the north. He'd have had a longer run than Logan's. Logan hoped neither man was trigger-happy.

"Do you have the phone?" the man standing in the open demanded.

"Yes." Savannah lifted it so he could see it.

"Bring it here. Let me see the file."

She didn't give away any of the fear she must feel. She typed what he presumed was the password into it, then walked forward but stopped a few feet short of the bastard. "Where's Molly?"

He jerked his head toward the SUV.

"I can't see her."

He raised his voice. "Let her see the kid."

A back door of the SUV opened, and a man lifted a little blond-haired girl high.

"Molly!" Savannah called, but man and child vanished back inside the vehicle. If Molly had cried out or screamed, Logan hadn't heard her. Would they have her mouth taped?

"Show me," the man said.

"Look but don't touch." She held the phone up so he could see what Logan knew was one of the first pages of the document, detailing shipping dates and locations, rather than the letter.

The man grabbed for the phone.

She snatched it away and backed up a few steps.

"I've closed it. You can't see it again without the password."

"Open it and give it to me," he snarled. "You're outgunned here."

She stared her defiance at him. "Bring Molly to me first. Show me you're a man of your word."

She didn't believe that was even a remote possibility any more than Logan did, but she was pretending for all she was worth. Damn, he was proud of her.

"Bring the kid out," the guy called, baring his teeth.

Again, the SUV door opened, and the same man emerged with Molly in his arms. She wasn't struggling; if Logan had to guess, she'd been doped up. He hadn't thought he could get any angrier, but he'd been wrong.

The guy carrying the little girl approached to within a few feet from Savannah and the SOB calling the shots.

"Password."

"I'll give it to you once you hand my niece over."

"You think I'm stupid?"

She thrust out her chin. "Do you think *I* am?"

Logan held his Sig steady, ready for the moment this scum made the slightest threatening movement.

"Take her back," he snapped, half over his shoulder.

Savannah drew her arm back as if to throw the phone, but the bastard was on her, gripping her wrist until Jared's phone fell from her hand and he forced her to his knees.

"Molly!" she screamed.

Bullets started flying.

IT WAS THE kind of battlefield Logan most feared, the kind where the good guys didn't know where one another were, and the bad guys felt free to fire at will.

He didn't waste any time, taking down the SOB whose brutal grip held Savannah in place and who had just pulled a handgun. He dropped hard, taking her down with him. Unwittingly protecting her with his body, Logan thought with fierce satisfaction.

He tried to wedge himself behind an insubstantial juniper as he took aim and fired again. He'd worn his vest, but was excruciatingly conscious of how much of his flesh it didn't cover.

At least two men were shooting at him, but were either unable to see him clearly or lousy at hitting their targets. Bullets buzzed by.

Guns barked everywhere, and he saw the man holding the rifle drop, too. Not his own shot, so either Donaldson or the other agent were here, too. Or both. Death by friendly fire had become a real possibility.

The engine in the SUV roared to life. He had to get to Molly. As he bent low and ran full out, Logan was horrified to see Savannah crawl, then propel herself to her feet to run the same direction he was. Thank God she wore a Kevlar vest, too, since bullets flew from every direction. He saw her fall. Before his heart stopped, she rolled and scrambled to get up again.

She was too far away and directly in the path of the SUV if it leaped forward.

A hand reached to pull closed the back door. Logan refused to let them accelerate out of this clearing with Molly in there. They wouldn't get far...but would she survive?

Out of the corner of his eye, he saw someone scoop up the phone and then race in the same direction he was. Donaldson appeared and rammed the fool, crashing them both down hard onto the ground. Grunts were followed by curses and thrashing.

Logan wrenched open the back door that hadn't quite latched. The SUV started forward and he had to take a couple of running strides before he could leap in. He saw enough to know there was a driver and a second man in the back seat rearing over the little girl who was curled in an impossibly tight ball. Logan wanted to pull the trigger, but as the SUV lurched over a bump—or a body—he knew he didn't dare. Instead, he flung himself over her.

The pain searing his shoulder came a fraction of a second before the explosive sound of the gun firing rang in his ears. His vision sparked with black, but while he could still move, he made sure he had entirely buried Jared's little girl beneath him.

TERRIFIED BEYOND MEASURE, Savannah dived out of the way of the black SUV, skidding across the ground and ending with a pungent smell of sagebrush as it scratched her face. Whimpering, she backed up…and realized the SUV had shuddered to a stop. Raising her head, she saw that bullet holes peppered the windows.

Two men were advancing on the vehicle, handguns held out in stiff arms. Both had a thickness to their chests that told her they wore Kevlar vests, and the one she could see best had a T-shirt that said POLICE in big letters across the back. Blood ran down the other man's face.

She was undoubtedly crying; why else was her vision so fuzzy and the scratches on her cheeks on fire? The best she could do for a moment was crawl forward, but then somehow she wobbled back to her feet and ran the last few steps toward the half-open back door that first Molly, then Logan, had disappeared through.

"Better let us check first," one of the two unfamiliar men called. He had just kicked a gun away from a prone body.

The second one was crouching to check for a pulse on another.

She ignored them, terrified of what she'd find inside…and rounded the open door. More dead bodies— No, no! The slack face she could see was that of a stranger, but the man sprawled face-down across the seat was Logan. His gun had dropped to the floorboards, and a copious quantity of blood ran down his arm to drip from his fingertips.

"Please. No." That was her. Whispering, or was she screaming? She had no idea. Logan couldn't be dead. He couldn't. And where was Molly? Had one of them gotten away with her? How *could* that have happened?

Logan's body moved oddly.

"Molly?" Savannah whispered.

A small hand worked its way out from beneath him.

"Molly." She stretched forward over Logan.

More squirming. Finally, the smallest voice. "Auntie Vannah?"

"Molly. Oh, God. You're all right. I love you."

She loved this man, too. One she had feared to trust, but who had been willing to die to protect the child she thought they both loved. Her hand shook as she reached out to touch her fingers to his neck…and felt his pulse.

She screamed for help.

Epilogue

At least this time when Logan woke up, he felt confident he really was alive. The first few times, he hadn't been at all sure. He remembered vaguely thinking, *I should hurt more than I do.*

This time, he did hurt. One hell of a lot. *They must have given me an internal pain reliever during surgery that's worn off,* he decided.

Just to be sure, he squeezed his right hand into a fist. Not easy, but it happened. Alive.

He pried his eyelids open, blinked blearily up at an unfamiliar ceiling, then turned his head on the pillow. Curtains surrounded the bed. Hospital. All that mattered was the woman sitting beside his narrow bed, watching him anxiously.

Savannah. She'd been there one other time, but he'd been sure he had dreamed her.

He croaked her name. Man, she was beautiful.

She smiled. "You sound like you need a drink."

He mouthed the word *Yes.*

She pushed a button that raised the head of the bed, then held a glass of water so that he could get the straw in his mouth and suck down half the contents before turning his face away to indicate he'd had enough. She set the glass down on a tray table to one side.

"You're here," he said, not so intelligently.

"Of course I am. Your dad has been here off and on, too, but it's evening and I sent him home. He looked...shaky."

"Wouldn't have told you that."

She wrinkled her nose. "Of course not."

Savannah had pulled a chair up to the left side of the bed. That arm worked as advertised, and he was able to hold out his hand. To his relief, she placed hers in it. "Chilly," he said.

"It's cold in here."

Was it?

"Tell me what I missed. Molly?"

"Is fine." Her throat worked. "Better than I expected. I think they kept her mostly knocked out. She...doesn't seem to remember a lot, except she's back to being clingy."

"Don't blame her." *He* wanted to cling to Savannah, too.

"No."

"Where is she?"

"Home with Grandma and Granddad. Dad's feeling much better, but not looking forward to getting dental implants. I told him he looks like a kindergartner missing his front teeth, and he glared at me."

Logan's mouth pulled into a smile.

"You're the only one of us who was badly hurt. Donaldson was grazed by a bullet—it left a bloody furrow on his head. The other agent is unscathed."

"Bad guys?"

"Dead or, well, not in jail yet. Actually, two are dead, including the one that went down on top of me. Three are currently still hospitalized, but they'll be locked up as soon as possible."

"They'll fill up our jail."

"Yes. Donaldson didn't sound impressed by your facilities."

He gave a bark of laughter that he instantly regretted. Savannah guided his hand to the button that provided pain relief.

"He's thrilled by the information Jared had gathered, though. It includes physical sites they can search, lots of names, and pages of data on how they laundered their proceeds. He already has a team of lawyers preparing new warrants, and agents serving the warrants they already had almost ready to go."

"Jared did what he set out to do."

"He…he did. Even Dad…" Savannah tried unsuccessfully to smile, but he understood the magnitude of what she felt.

"Your father damn well should," Logan said gruffly.

For a moment there was silence. Savannah broke it, voice thick. "You saved Molly's life."

"I'd have prioritized saving any child," he told her, hoping that wasn't too much honesty. "But Molly...of course I did. She's... Jared's, yours. I love her, too."

Savannah sniffed a few times and snatched a tissue from the box on his table to wipe her eyes and cheeks.

"Thank you."

He shook his head. "Don't need thanks."

She seemed to be looking deep inside him, an unnerving experience. "What do you need?"

This was probably too soon, but... "You," he said simply. "I've fallen hard for you. I know you have plenty of reason not to believe me, but... I hope you'll give me a chance."

"You just risked everything for Molly. How can I ever doubt you again?"

"Not the same thing."

"No." Her smile shook. "I... I love you. I think I always have, or you couldn't have hurt me as much as you did."

He winced. "When I was a teenager, or recently?"

"Both."

His hand tightened on hers. "Never again," he swore, huskily.

She let out a shaky near-sob and stood so she could bend over to kiss him. There and gone, but he probably had lousy breath anyway. He could only imagine how ragged he must look.

"I like my job here," he told her. This would matter to her, and he'd wanted to be sure how he felt about a life spent in his hometown in case he and she ever got to this point. "I'll have to win an election next time around, but—"

"Of course you will. Oh, Logan. You know how I feel working with horses."

"Magic with them. Would never ask you to give it up."

"You're fading on me."

"No." But she was right. "Love you," he managed.

Maybe if he just closed his eyes for a minute…

Savannah loves me. Trusts me. We're all okay. Really believing that all good things could happen, he fell asleep.

* * * * *

INTRIGUE

Seek thrills. Solve crimes. Justice served.

Available Next Month

A Place To Hide Debra Webb
Swiftwater Enemies Danica Winters

....

K-9 Detection Nichole Severn
The Perfect Witness Katie Mettner

....

Wetlands Investigation Carla Cassidy
Murder In The Blue Ridge Mountains R. Barri Flowers

Larger Print

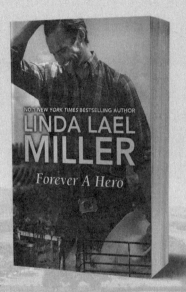

Subscribe and fall in love with a Mills & Boon series today!

You'll be among the first to read stories delivered to your door monthly and enjoy great savings.

WE SIMPLY LOVE ROMANCE